Zenegades

ZENEGADES

JOE WIRTH

WIRTHWHILE WRITING, LTD.

To request permissions or for media inquiries, contact the publisher at info@wirthwhilewriting.com

ISBN: 979-8-218-25106-2

Edited by Joe Pierson
Cover photos by Sergey Pesterev, Tus Van Leur, William Olivieri, Jakob Owens @ UNPSLASH
Cover Layout and Interior Design by Stewart A. Williams

Lyrical excerpts from "She's A Rainbow" by Rolling Stones and "He's Gone" by Grateful Dead. Reprinted by permission.

Printed by Amazon Kindle Direct Publishing in the USA.

Wirthwhile Writing, ltd.
PO Box 8582
Breckenridge, CO 80424

www.wirthwhilewriting.com

For John and Salvador, because this book merely amounts to a small fraction of what you've both taught me about living life to the fullest.

I

broad, overarching review of life transports us through every decision, every fork in the road, every triumph, every downfall, and every mundane minutia within milliseconds, and without us even realizing. Each day provides an opportunity for doors to open and close, but are these doors opening when we wake up, or when our heads make contact with our pillows? Within that very first glimpse of waking life on any given morning, that moment in which your mind and body transcend from one edge of the Unified Field to the other, hinges creak, for better or worse. Some psychiatrists would say it's a sign of depression when an individual wakes up and almost instantly thinks about the past and everything they've done to get them to the very point they're at, but would it be depressing if in that moment you had little to no regret? Some psychiatrists would say *possibly not*, but any decent psychiatrist would know beyond any otherworldly doubt that each and every one of us stores specific memories within the crevasses of our psyches, whether we like to open those doors or not ...

For an individual as flamboyant with their thoughts as James Byrd, this moment of self-consciousness was a regular occurrence during the first few seconds of each day. Although it was generally effortless to overlook those milliseconds of retrospective evaluation, his past had become so ingrained to the point that it would irrelevantly commingle with his present, serene circumstances. Nevertheless, his wits would regain their momentum within seconds as he woke up each morning on top of open grass in a sleeping bag. However, before these microcosmic self-interpretations would cease to exist yet again, he couldn't help but think about different lives within his own distant memories and what should've been if he just could have, maybe, who knows, there was always the possibility, but *fuck it*. The sun had risen once more, he was still here, and he was even hungrier than yesterday.

On June days when the sun rose earlier and lasted into the evenings forever, he knew he'd have plenty of time to kill before checking in again to see what exciting things may happen on the other side of the Unified Field. The likelihood of an afternoon nap underneath a creekside tree always seemed appealing, so maybe he wouldn't have to wait too long for another hidden journey toward unpredictable silence. There was no denying that today would feature a balmy Utah morning as compared to later in the summer, but like every summer day in Utah, the need for shade and cold water was much more than a vagabond luxury. But first things were always first, especially when they included an increasingly warm bag of fruit in a motorcycle pannier.

It was a Saturday, so he knew the likelihood of city folks from Salt Lake City coming through this part of the high desert wilderness for some good ole recreation in God's country was more than probable. The dilemma of deciding whether to beat the crowd or stay put for the day was what he was thinking as he sat down by his extinguished campfire and manually reignited a flame within thirty seconds via a wooden hand drill. He blew on the dry grass before placing it under a few tiny sticks, which caught instantly. He chomped down on a crisp red apple and swished it with the fluid contents of his canteen, and he munched on stale granola as he tended to his friend that now required more skinny sticks. He monitored the fire as it continued to grow, and he realized how that day would be a *no shirt, no shits given* kind of occasion.

He looked around his campsite and nodded at how well he'd maintained it, especially considering the fact that he'd slept directly on the dirt for nearly a week now. This was always his favorite campground within the canyon, because it was somewhat easy to get to on his motorcycle. This spot was also coveted due to the copious amount of shade underneath a rare cottonwood grove, which enjoyed its circadian rhythm next to a brook that peacefully gurgled every nearby sentient being to sleep each night. Another perk to this site was that it was five miles down a dirt road to a trailhead that led to cascading rapids, waterfalls, and eventually hot spring pools. Not too many people knew about this canyon because it was Bureau of Land Management wilderness, but the people who did know about it continuously came back for the natural springs. He knew these REI aficionados would be arriving momentarily, and that the isolation he'd enjoyed over the past few days wouldn't last much longer. As straightforward as this ensuing reality was, the fear of a disorderly family plopping their pickup truck and tents right next to him created a sense of urgency to get *something* done that morning before the day-trippers showed up.

Stress management was something Byrd at least thought he'd come to know throughout his brief twenty-three years on Earth, partly because he'd come to know how the hinges that creaked within him on a daily basis were abnormally loud. He'd try to consider his personal stresses as any other cyclical pattern that he experienced, and he now considered that he'd gotten past the more introspective portion of his morning. This meant it was time to walk toward the trees by the creek to treat himself to guitar for the next few hours. He placed a shabby, brown, full-brim hat on his head and scratched his shoulders and torso as he meandered about sixty yards toward the canyon's shadiest area, and as he gazed at his guitar case resting against a tree trunk, he heard an all-too-familiar Utah sound: *rattling.*

A jolt of adrenaline coiled through his belly and woke him up faster than any cup of cowboy coffee ever got him going. His pupils contracted on the source of the sound. Not one, not two, but three rattlesnakes rested in the early morning rays between him and his most-prized possession. He was used to seeing snakes in the canyon, but these were the first rattlers that had come within close proximity of his sleeping bag. They were now rattling at him more persistently, and the three snakes remained entangled with each other as they fashioned themselves into an obscure, Medusa-like creature. He swallowed every last bit of saliva in his parched mouth, and every memory began to internally resurface as if the encounter was intuitively guided. *Why did I leave it by the creek? Sleeping on the ground is getting too risky.*

A series of deep breaths, the hairs on his neck standing fully up, and the creepy rattling of the threatened snakes made the next minute seem like five. As he stepped toward the snakes, he heard another all-too-familiar sound for that Utah canyon: *MURROOOOOOOOOO.*

He looked to his right and saw a small herd of about a dozen free-range cattle approaching the campsite. The adult females scratched their hooves on the dirt as their calves made plaintive cries of distress, and it became clear to Byrd that the Mojave rattlers were also in the herd's path. The calves circled back behind their mothers as their high-pitched bleats and bawls echoed throughout the nearby vicinity. The mothers then formed a line and began approaching the snakes as their eyes glared with stranger danger. They bellowed out war cries as they stomped their hooves, causing the snakes to uncoil and scurry into the cottonwoods.

Byrd remained motionless as the cows continued their march along the valley floor, and only a few seconds went by before the calves became distressed again by his presence. The agitated mothers turned toward him and made their feelings known, and *recognition* was the only word that came to his mind as he inhaled deeply and dissected the situation further. He considered saying something like *easy there* or *one love cows*, but the calves stopped screaming and the herd began refocusing on their collective stride. He knew to never get too close to an angry momma, so he circled back to his sleeping bag and glanced on as the herd returned to their morning routine of walking in the direction of the canyon's mouth.

Grasping the neck of his acoustic guitar felt better that morning as compared to most others, and he laughed, knowing he'd have a funny story to tell his work buddies the next time he clocked in. This particular notion of telling a story strung up the inspiration to write it down, so he walked back to his barely operable Honda and whipped out a notebook and pen. He strummed random riffs and thought about the choice and placement of words for over two hours, and he considered how things like *snakes in your path* and *a mother's protection* could be relatable on a broader level. He never considered himself to be great at writing lyrics, but he still did it for fun and considered himself a songwriter of meaningless potential. To Byrd, music was a launching pad that took him far away from the thoughts he'd rather forget and closer to the thoughts he not only wanted to express, but felt like he needed to. This proclivity toward pure, poetic expression inevitably reached a full circle around his own repressed thoughts, and the therapeutic sensation of playing his own songs was what made every lonely wilderness jaunt worthwhile.

After a few hours of fine-tuning his latest composition, he decided to switch it up and play some of his favorite classics. He sang songs like Steve Miller Band's "Take the Money and Run" and Stealers Wheel's "Stuck in the Middle With You" while picturing an imaginary audience that he'd just told his goofy snake-cow battle story to. When he finished the Stealers Wheel hit, he heard a distant clapping from behind him. He turned around from the log he was sitting on and saw an older couple on a trail about a hundred feet away, who were approaching him with friendly smiles and waves.

"That sounded *just right!*" the woman called out as she quietly clapped her hands together. They looked like they were in their early sixties, and they both grinned at Byrd as if he were a rare desert animal that they luckily encountered.

"Good morning! I didn't know I had an audience," Byrd responded with a smile as he stood up and placed the guitar down. "Just to let you guys know, there's a path that goes along the creek, but I saw three snakes earlier this morning. You should be fine, the cows scared them into the brush, but just be careful of Mojave rattlers as you get deeper into the canyon."

He noticed how both of their pearly white smiles dropped.

"Oh, my goodness, *three* snakes! That's absolutely *terrifying!*" the woman replied. "How did the cows scare 'em off?"

"They were protecting their calves. It goes to show you can't underestimate a mother's sense of security."

"Ain't that the truth!" the woman agreed. "We got a few of our own, and now they got a few of their own. I'd jump in front of a snake to save my grandbabies in a skinny minute! You wanna see pictures?"

The next few minutes consisted of Byrd learning all about the couple's family as they scrolled through a digital album on a cell phone, and they also explained how they lived about an hour's drive north along the southern edge of the Salt Lake Valley. They didn't ask any questions about why he was camping alone, and Byrd sensed they were too embarrassed to probe his outdoor lifestyle when he explained how he didn't have any family photos of his own to share.

"Well, you got some real pipes on you, son. You should go try out for *American Idol* or one of them singin' shows!" the man joked as they said their goodbyes and continued along their way.

Byrd walked over to his bike and got out a wristwatch that read 11:06, which seemed a bit early for hikers to be over five miles into the canyon. It was proof that it was yet another Saturday, and he knew his solitude had officially been compromised as he watched a caravan of pickup trucks barrel down the dirt road. The morning had been productive, considering the snakes and cattle, the half-written song, and a conversation with real humans, but seeing the couple so clearly accustomed to each other made him think about women. Any thoughts of loneliness were amplified out in the canyon, so without further procrastination, he slipped his clothes off and walked to the creek with a tiny towel wrapped around his waist and camping suds in hand. The stretch of the creek right by his site was the perfect depth for lounging, about two and a half feet, so it was comfortable for him to sit and keep his upper torso and head dry. The water was chilly, but the sun had warmed it up for a few hours and gave it a refreshing feeling that would last for the rest of the day. He dunked his head in, got out the suds, and reluctantly lathered himself up. He didn't like putting the suds into the creek, but he didn't have much of a choice if he wanted to maintain any kind of personal hygiene. It was his first time using soap that week.

After drip-drying on a rock for a few minutes, he toweled himself off and started preparing a presentable outfit. He only had a few clothing options, and all of them were dirty. Although he'd rinsed his five pairs of underwear in the creek that previous Wednesday, even those were beginning to develop a unique stench. All three of his shirts were in need of washing, as well as his two pairs of convertible pants. He figured he'd rinse his clothes in the creek and let them dry in the sun like he usually did, but when he recognized his dwindling food supply, he made the executive decision to pack everything up and head to the nearest town for a laundry load, a food run, and a chance to catch up with the outside world at the Surf Zone Internet Café.

"It's okay for Saturdays to suck sometimes," he thought out loud.

Within minutes, he had all his clothes, camping supplies, and guitar case packed up in panniers and other storage compartments along the sides of his rickety motorcycle. He took a long glance at the empty campground and was sure it would later be occupied by weekend warriors, and then he cranked the bike into gear and rode off. Dark-red walls over two hundred feet high encircled him on both sides as he wound down a bumpy road that wasn't the safest for an old Honda. After twenty minutes of maneuvering up and over rocks, the dirt turned to pavement, and he made his way onto a state highway that connected the high desert to the southern reaches of the Wasatch Mountains. The sky was more than wide open on this road; it was all-encompassing. And the further and faster he rode, the larger his smile grew.

When he arrived at the desert town that he frequented for supplies over thirty minutes later, there were quite a few errands he wanted to complete. But the first and foremost thing on the to-do list was to fill up on fuel and drink an ice-cold Coca-Cola. There was something about drinking a Coke when he hadn't had anything like it in a while, and he felt a nostalgic sugar rush as he sipped from the red aluminum can. He heard a loud rumbling sound as a large semi barreled past the gas station with cattle in tow, which reminded him of the morning's obscure encounter, as well as the fact that he hadn't spoken to his mother in quite a long time. It wasn't as though she kept tabs on him, but she knew about his lifestyle and often expressed her worries.

He adjusted the bike's storage compartments at the gas pump, threw out the Coke, and looked across an open valley facing the Wasatch peaks. He then recited a stress-relief mantra that was based off lyrics from one of his all-time favorite musicians, Bob Weir. "Ease up, Byrd... Ease up and fly away *slooowly*," he whispered as he watched cars pass by on the desert highway.

His heart began beating the slightest bit slower, so it was time for Surf Zone. After a five-minute ride, he parked outside a tacky internet café that was connected to a convenience store. Its stucco exterior was slightly damaged with cracks going up the front wall, and a massive cartoon sticker of a surfer with long blond hair in the middle of a breaking wave and a laptop in one hand decorated the large window. This sticker was partly why he kept coming back to get online, and when he walked inside with his biking helmet still on, the owner instantly shot up from a bored stupor.

"Good to see you again, Byrd! It's been a little while. How's work going?"

"Good to see you too, Billy," Byrd responded as he sat down at a computer. "All right I suppose, I'll find out more now. I was off this past week, back on next."

Besides the hiking couple that he came across earlier that day, Billy was the only person he'd spoken to in over six days. As he opened his email account, he was primed and ready to start reaching out to his mom, coworkers, and old friends. So when he scanned his inbox and noticed a message from a friend, Thayer Feldman, a reassuring feeling rushed through him that someone was interested in talking to him. The email read:

Hey Byrd!

Long time no see! I hope all is well out there in the desert. I recently moved back in with my folks after my lease up north ended in May, so alas, I'm back in the confines of my childhood home and am once again bored to be here.

Let me know if you want to make a trip out here once the weather starts to turn, and I might try to see if I could come out there some-how. The wilderness sounds nice right now as compared to these smoggy cities, but I don't mean to come off as if I'm miffed or anything. I'm honestly fine, just a little stressed that I can't find any work... It's crazy to think college is over. It seems like just yesterday we were prancing around Tamalpais without a care in the world and you were talking like Yoda for hours :-)

Oh well, absurd the world is, right? It would be great to hear from you and know more about all those adventures you're having. Say hey to the punks for me!

Miss you,

Thayer

2

Very few cities draw people into their limits like Los Angeles, a megacity completely full of transplants no matter how far your Cali roots grow. This unique type of inundation is partly because very few cities draw in people who have close to, if not the exact same dreams. The archetypal LA storyline is personified in the slews of ambitious artists and fame-thirsty wannabes who flock out west toward the allure of a microcosmic yet somehow limitless pipe dream that they'll be *found* in La-La Land. Finding yourself in a city like Los Angeles offers crashing wave after crashing wave, just like the swells off Venice Beach each winter. But out beyond the shorebreak of congested freeway traffic jams, smog-ridden skylines, conceited superiors, unanswered emails, uncertainties of getting the next gig, next month's rent, and every doubt imaginable, there's relief. It's a type of relief that begs for attention and can appreciate the blending of dull Mondays into urban hiking adventures in the Santa Monicas. It's been foretold that Los Angeles is in danger of an imminent disaster through the likes of a high-magnitude earthquake, and socioeconomically, that imminent strike, that break that's not caught, is exactly what keeps all those quintessential transplants grinding toward the potential relief and satisfaction in confidently knowing that *you fucking made it.*

Many can't help themselves from staring up at the luxury club on top of the LA Basin's ridgeline and thinking something along the lines of: *if they're there, why not me?* The city will answer that question regardless of whether you want it to or not, and 99.99 percent of the time, it says: *just cuz*. We all know this when we stare up at the Hills, and that's one of the many ironic aspects of Los Angeles that makes it a perfect place to better find ourselves. There's enough potential out there for anyone to take hold and make the most of, but the self-absorption and blending in among the hordes of people who want exactly the same thing can be an overwhelming turnoff to the entire region. You either love LA or you hate it. You're either born into it or you come to it. You either have it or you simply don't, *just cuz* ...

Thayer Feldman wasn't only born into it and had it *just cuz*, but she also despised everything about Los Angeles and what it represented within her budding young mind. She unquestionably had a privileged perspective on show business, but she unfortunately was exposed to the city's underbelly from the time she first started realizing what the people around her were doing. She was around ten years old when she began recognizing the subtleties of how people would kiss her ass as a formality toward kissing her father's ass. Her dad, Saul Feldman, was one of the very few Baby Boomers who migrated to California to make movies and was actually able to withstand the test of time as an independent film producer. After a few successful movies, his actress wife, Isabella Consuelo, popped into his life. Their marriage subsequently led to Thayer and two younger, twin daughters, Daphne and Eva. Before either of them could check the time, they were watching *60 Minutes* as a family of five on Sunday evenings, looking out at the city's distant, shimmering lights from the Brentwood Hills. As Thayer grew into her teenage years and continued developing a strong disdain for the contrived pretenses she exhibited on a regular basis, Saul went in on a couple CGI-heavy flops. He eventually returned to investing in low-budget indie flicks on Isabella and Thayer's advice, and he began seeing potential in Thayer's natural sense to know which scripts were better than good. Thayer refused to live the normal teenage life that her parents intended, and she didn't. Instead of going out with her friends on Friday nights, she often stayed in when new scripts were floating around the house.

She wasn't a part of the popular crowd at the private, all-girls high school she attended, and Isabella started realizing around the time she was sixteen that Thayer was actually hanging out with a punk-rock crowd and barely knew the girls she went to school with. Going to a prissy, all-girls school was like a punishment to Thayer, and it only made her want to revolt even more. She did so through music, and going to shows with friends was her favorite way to release everything she tended to bottle up. Her parents didn't mind if she'd go to obscure venues in Silver Lake that they'd never heard of, just as long as she kept in touch as the evenings progressed. They rightfully thought she was going back to a more normal teenage life as she ventured out to concerts, but their general leniency made it all too easy for her to lie and stay out essentially wherever she wanted on Friday and Saturday nights. Alcohol pretty quickly came into her sphere of friends, and people liked getting drunk with Thayer because she was talented at playing piano and could hang during jam sessions with other aspiring musicians. When people would ask her how she got so good, she'd simply mention that she used to be introverted and didn't get out much.

Thayer was never the most physically attractive girl in her friend circle, and being unfairly compared to her high-status Brentwood neighbors with skinnier body types also didn't help when it came to her early sex life. After a couple years of wondering why she was the last of her friends to lose their virginity, she started to recognize how most of the punk guys she hung out with looked at her in the exact same way her parents' friends did when she was little: a friendly formality. All of the *hey, I know your dad's a producer so let's jam* looks started to build a broad connotation that everyone she knew was full of shit, which led her back home to reading scripts and playing her mom's Fazioli throughout the majority of her junior and senior years. She was still a virgin and steadily more introverted when she left LA for community college in Berkeley.

Berkeley was where Thayer became *Thay*, and it ended up being the very best place she could've ever gone to continue her personal journey as an aspiring pianist. Music was all anyone wanted to talk about in her circle of college friends, and her hip perspective blossomed as she valued a stress-free lifestyle of going to classes, playing music, going to a friend's house to play more music, and seeing live performances as much as possible. She ended up developing a reputation for herself throughout parts of Berkeley because she was always willing to sit in during jam sessions when the moment struck, and these moments struck all the time.

It was during one of these random jam sessions at her friend Meryl Martinez's house when the moment struck just right for her to be introduced to an incredibly smelly guitarist who looked like he only owned one pair of clothes and never washed them. That smelly guitarist was James Byrd, and Byrd was one of the first guys to openly tell Thayer she had *it*. She was initially grossed out by his lack of hygiene, but even back then with all his vagrant vibes, Byrd had his bright eyes set on a beauty queen who continued to haunt his waking moments years later.

That same Saturday was like any other June weekend in Los Angeles, with a marine-layer morning that turned cloudless by noon, and newly graduated Thayer had nothing better to do than sit by her parents' pool and read a chick-flick script from an unknown auteur who was eager for Saul's approval. She obviously had more important things she could've been doing, like hopelessly looking for a job that was anywhere remotely relevant to her community college music degree, but she'd recently come to realize that there was little to no use in looking for work anywhere else than through the musicians she'd already met. That was one reason why she sent an email to Byrd a handful of days earlier, because she knew that he knew how it felt to be nervously unemployed (and even nervous about where to find his next meal). She couldn't relate with Byrd to quite the same degree as she lounged in the cozy comforts of the Brentwood Hills, but she was confident that she could turn to his advice, since he always seemed to have something bright to say.

The unknown filmmaker's story had her captivated with a desperate woman on the verge of a breakdown after finding out her husband no longer loved her, but the script had to be put down immediately when her phone vibrated and she saw that Byrd had finally responded. She adjusted her posture in her cushioned lounge chair and tapped in her phone's PIN, which took her to an email app. There it was, her highly anticipated message from James Byrd, which read:

Hey Thay,

Great to hear from you too, and I'm sure your house is a little more comfy than the patch of grass I've been sleeping on lately. I'm not sure just how "adventurous" I've been lately, but I did come across some rattlesnakes today in an area I didn't expect them to be. A cattle herd ended up chasing them off, so I guess that was kind of adventurous to see!

I remember that Yoda hike in Tamalpais. You told me about how much you thought you'd changed since high school, so if you've changed so much, then hasn't home changed too? I got the same "what happened to the time" feeling when I got my certification, but you should embrace being home and seeing old friends and family. I know I miss my friends and family a lot right now. It's hard to not be lonely out here sometimes, so please come visit, and feel free to bring friends!

The wilderness out here is nice, you'd like it. I hope you're still rocking that portable keyboard like old times, although I'm sure you are. Like I told you a while ago, you're by far the best pianist I've ever met. If you're having trouble finding work right now, then just know it'll work out for you when the time is right.

So, how are you possibly bored in a city as big as La-La Land? I'm bored, but I'm in the middle of nowhere right now! Get out there, see a show, and then email me back to let me know all about it. You I miss.

One Love,

JB

Thayer stared trancelike at tiny fragments of sunlight bouncing and undulating off the surface of the pool. She visualized the same sunlight somewhere far off in the Utah desert, and thought, *What am I doing right now? I guess it could be worse.* Her beautiful backyard suddenly started to feel confining and quite literally began representing a box of land that was her comfort zone. *Byrd is 100 percent right,* she thought as she marked her page in the script, stood up, took a deep breath, rolled her leisure apparel off, and dove into the pool. She glanced around under water, seeing the exact same sun rays, but from the opposite, more thrilling perspective.

She began breaststroking as if she wanted to reach the end of the pool to win a big race. The end of the pool arrived within a few seconds, which led to an abrupt nosedive toward the bottom of the deep end. She moved her legs together and kicked in unison like a mermaid, because that motion simply felt right, given that she was completely naked. She laughed at herself when she was about ten feet under the surface, and it was the most visible laugh of her life. Never before had she noticed the physicality of laughing sounds, or at least she'd never exhaled quite so many air bubbles during an underwater chuckle. She glanced at her body sparkling in the diffused light, and a tiny surge of sexiness rolled from her throat down to her stomach.

Just as she'd gotten out of the pool and was covering herself with a towel, she got a call from one of her high school classmates, Madison Abernathy. They had kept in touch over the years, but Madison always lived in Los Angeles, didn't go to college in order to try out modeling, worked at Hugo Boss, and ultimately was drifting in a much different path than Thayer. Madison wasn't gravitating in the direction of all people and dogs with dreads, she wasn't listening to alternative bands that had no chance at the Billboard charts, and she certainly thought she looked sexy on a more consistent basis instead of solely when pretending to be a mermaid. It had been over a year since the two of them had last spoken to each other, but neither of them was keeping track.

"Hello," Thayer said as water dripped down her face, forcing her to wipe it up with the towel.

"You're in LA and didn't tell me!" Madison responded. "What are you up to right now, Thay? I miss you!"

"I'm just sitting by my parents' pool. I'm living with them now. I just got back from Berkeley a couple weeks ago. I —"

"That pool is so fun. That's amazing, Thay, congrats on graduating!" Madison interrupted. "I'm with my boyfriend, who I actually live with now. I honestly don't know what I was thinking by moving in with him, *kidding*! But yeah, his name is J. P., and he manages a sweet bar downtown in the Arts District near Little Tokyo. I just wanted to say hey because I'm *actually* up in Brentwood and was thinking about you."

Thayer didn't know what to say, but she laughed to herself when she thought of mockingly responding something like, *I was actually just thinking of you too!*

"I saw on Eva's Instagram that you were back. She's so cute now! She said you guys were planning a sister hike in Malibu the other day, but the plans fell through or something like that. Hate how that happens, but that's LA. A big bunch of flakes," she continued rambling on. "She flaked on you, I think. Right?"

"She sure did. I ain't no flake," Thayer responded, sarcastically callous.

A pause ensued for a few seconds, which was just long enough to make things awkward.

"I ain't no flake either! We're both not doing shit right now near each other, so let's hang out, and you can meet my new boy toy," Madison finally spurted out.

"Okay. You know where I'm at, *queen*. See ya soon," Thayer finalized as Madison laughed loudly while ending the call.

Thayer realized she was soaking wet and still only wearing a towel, so she ran up to her room and dug through her dresser until she came across a black Rolling Stones shirt with the iconic giant tongue logo. She searched for pants, which was an easy call when considering the fact that she'd soon be hanging out with Madison: Lululemon all-black, hot-fit yoga pants. With her new outfit on and her hair now thoroughly examined in the bedroom mirror, she ran back down to the backyard and assumed her previous position of reading the movie script on the lounge chair. She couldn't focus at all on the text and pretty much flipped through the script while pretending like she was reanalyzing the previous scenes she'd already read. About a minute of reanalyzing went by until Madison and J. P. walked through the wooden side gate. Thayer methodically turned around like any highly concentrated individual would while analyzing a screenplay scene they'd already read, and she smiled slightly, as not to seem surprised, yet comfortably pleased, by their arrival.

"We're here, Feldman Fam!" rang out throughout the yard, stirring nearby birds off their sycamore perches.

Over an hour passed by of Madison ranting on and on about her modeling career, her newfound fashion industry connections at Hugo Boss, and how she had such an illustrious plan to continue living such an illustrious life while working with such talented—and illustrious—people. She also managed to bring up how she and J. P. met at his Little Tokyo bar, and J. P. succinctly acknowledged his tiny portions of their *how we met* story in between sporadic text messages, emails, social media swiping, and the occasional acknowledgment of the Feldmans' fancy back yard. As long as it had been since Thayer spent any in-person time with Madison, she couldn't help but think that her pretentiousness hadn't changed at all since high school. She began zoning out during Madison's continuous ranting while reflecting on how the overall effect of four years in Berkeley had saved her from the LA lifestyle she so defiantly sought to escape as a teenager.

As the conversation progressed, Madison couldn't pass up the chance at a photo shoot by the pool. With a self-preserving sigh, J. P.

obliged as always to be the iPhone photographer, and the shoot began with duo shots of Madison and Thayer sitting next to the pool with the sunlight hitting them entirely too directly. Thayer instantly regretted her decision to wear the Rolling Stones tee when she compared her clothes to Madison's head-to-toe BOSS ensemble. *At least these yoga pants make my legs look cute,* she thought.

Madison walked over to J. P. after a few pictures were taken and examined every detail of the images, and she judged each picture with her own binary system of one-word classifications: *cute* and *ugly*. She decreed that she and Thayer got one cute and five ugly, which meant they needed to spice things up a bit to make their shoot worthy of a social media post. She asked Thayer if she had a swimsuit on underneath her "rock 'n' roll shirt," and Thayer admitted she was wearing a sports bra that kind of looked like a swim top. Madison pulled off her sundress, revealing the bikini she was wearing, and without saying anything, Thayer pulled her Rolling Stones shirt over her head as well. Thayer's eyes darted in every direction except toward the camera, but Madison's determination to get the *perfect picture* was gaudy to the point that embracing the amateur modeling absurdity became easier. As Madison's ideas manifested themselves into self-absorbed poses, Thayer's smiles blurred the lines between sarcasm and sincerity.

J. P. repeatedly sighed and glanced down at his phone before he upped his efforts as the photographer in a blatant attempt to speed up Madison's self-validation. He did so by recommending that the girls look at each other like the long-lost friends they never were. Madison squealed at the idea, and Thayer was essentially on the same page as J. P., so they followed his histrionic instructions until Madison finally said *that's the one.*

Madison then proceeded to usher J. P. around the Feldmans' back yard while directing more solo bikini shots, which featured her lying on the perfectly manicured grass next to a perfectly innocent plastic figurine of a young girl holding a sunflower, and then dozens more pictures in and around the pool. Madison didn't submerge into the water, but she did utilize a large swan float by wrapping her legs around it in the most Coachella Spring Break style possible. She embraced every minute of the camera's attention, and she didn't take a moment to realize that Thayer had been alone in the kitchen preparing a plate of crackers and cheese for going on ten minutes.

Thayer, being the generous host she was raised to be, brought the charcuterie delights to J. P. and Madison, who ravenously munched on the snacks and requested anything alcoholic to quench their thirst. Thayer ran back into the house and made the executive decision to collect one of Isabella's bottles of Louis Latour and three wine glasses, which she then retrieved to her guests at a light jog. Her recently dried, stringy hair bounced up and down like a chocolate labradoodle playing fetch as she returned to the lounge chairs, and both Madison and J. P. were impressed by her acclaimed white wine choice. She chose not to admit it was merely the first bottle she saw, so she nodded as if to insinuate she drank wine all the time. After about fifteen more minutes of lounging, J. P. looked up from his phone and said, "My boy Pierre invited us to come to his place in Malibu."

Madison gasped, and Thayer subconsciously sipped her wine more forcefully as they awaited more details from J. P., who sat in his lounge chair while furiously typing on his touchscreen.

"You wanna come with?" he finally asked Thayer, which came off as more rhetorical than an actual request.

"*Of course*, she's coming with!" Madison barged in. "You're going to *die*, Thay. This beach house is the *tits*!" she continued, now looking to J. P. "We have to bring *something*, Jay. We can *not* just show up empty-handed. What should we bring? Beer? No, they'll have plenty. Vodka? Would you guys want some? Wine? I *love* this wine. We have to drink more!"

"I could bring another bottle of this. It's my mom's, but *fuck it*. They're at my sister's soccer tournament in Bakersfield all weekend," Thayer said coolly, while having an intuitive inclination they already knew that.

"You *fucking rock*, Thay," Madison responded. "What about us, babe?" she said, trying to pull J. P.'s attention away from his phone by touching him on the arm.

"I got us covered already," he said, without looking up from his screen.

The trio still hadn't arrived at Pierre's house over an hour later, and the inevitable boredom and subsequent frustration of being stuck in a Saturday afternoon traffic jam on the PCH started to sink in. Deeper they crept at a snail's pace as the internalized state of J. P.'s thoughts got closer to a temper tantrum while he dealt with a clusterfuck of cars. Madison and Thayer chatted in the backseat of his BMW convertible, which made J. P. flare his nostrils and exhale derisively at his chauffeur-like highway appearance. And as for Thayer, she wasn't even hot in his eyes. She wasn't even going to know anyone at Pierre's house, and he sure as hell wasn't going to put much effort into introducing her around. He began to worry that Pierre and his friends would think differently of him when he brought a single girl to the party who looked like *that*.

He peered at Thayer through his driver's-side mirror and noticed how she was looking out at the ocean as Madison gabbed on and on about the pop stars they were currently listening to at an obnoxiously loud volume for standstill traffic. As they continued to crawl down the highway, J. P. thought to himself how every song they'd listened to from the time they'd left Thayer's house radiated complete garbage, *no, worse, nuclear radiation*, from Madison's phone. He considered the notion that listening to Madison's music was potentially cancerous, and that was when he cracked his first smile of the day.

"This music sucks," he said in a deft monotone.

Madison stopped mid-sentence, paused, and then laughed off J. P.'s insult. She smiled and patted her boyfriend, *her king*, on the shoulder, almost like a dog, *her dog*.

"Babe, they were nominated for a Grammy. I think you'd like it if you gave it a chance," she said in a way that implied there was no way she was making the effort to move her thumb three inches to change the song.

"I agree," Thayer said as she turned back from the crashing waves.

"See, even *Thay* thinks you'll like it, babe," Madison pronounced, confirming her place with the upper DJ hand.

"No, I agree that this music sucks," Thayer said, causing Madison's eyes to flutter involuntarily.

Madison tried hard not to scoff and resorted to her fake giggle, but J. P.'s billowing laugh was truly genuine as he couldn't stop himself from slamming the brakes. As he looked back at Thayer in the driver's-side mirror, he saw her slyly smiling behind her sunglasses. In an instant, all his piggish, preconceived notions about her began to vanish. He thought to himself that Pierre was actually going to like her, and he even considered the idea that Thayer could maybe one day be hot if she tried a little harder like all the other girls. But that was exactly *it*. In the middle of a Malibu traffic maze, J. P.'s myopic mind came to the realization that Thayer didn't seem to be even close to anything like all the other girls he and his friends usually hung out with, because she wasn't trying so damn hard to fit in.

"Hell yeah, Thay!" J. P. said, holding his fist out toward her in the back seat, which Thayer dapped with hers. "How about I play a song just for you?" he asked, while making direct eye contact with her in the driver's-side mirror.

"I'm down," Thayer approved as J. P. began fiddling with a screen to switch the Bluetooth settings. "I'm also down to get some food too. I'm starting to get hungry," she acknowledged as they drove past a chain of seafood restaurants near the entrance to Topanga Canyon.

J. P. nodded as if he'd been expecting Thayer to say something like that. Waiting at a seafood restaurant for lunch was not happening, so when J. P. put on "Sympathy for the Devil," he also reached into the center console and pulled out a clear, glass vial that contained what Thayer recognized as cocaine. He popped the cork cap and tapped the powder onto his thumbnail, which he had tightly cupped against the soft tissue of his left index finger's second knuckle. Nonchalantly yet blatantly knowing how visible he was in the convertible, he reached his left thumb up toward his left nostril and snorted the bump with one deep inhalation. Without saying anything, he passed the vial back to Madison, who tucked it out of sight near her left hip.

Thayer had seen cocaine a good amount while in high school and college but was never one to indulge in it herself. Her adverse reaction to coke was primarily due to the drug's own stereotype of being popular among spoiled rich kids, which exacerbated the guilt she strived to disassociate from. She continued watching Madison get herself prepared to do a bump, not just in a car, a convertible, in almost standstill traffic. *That's just asking to get in trouble*, she thought.

"It'll help ease your appetite," Madison said as she rubbed her fingers across her nose to ensure she didn't leave anything hanging. "I was kinda hungry too, and I swear I won't be hungry at least for a couple hours now. *Holy shit*, this is really good, babe!" she said as she unbuckled and pecked J. P. with a kiss. Her king had once again come through, and now the dawg party was just getting started. Mick Jagger's yelps were getting louder as the first line, *please allow me to introduce myself*, approached.

"Do you wanna try it?" Madison asked as she placed her hands on Thayer's and showed her how to use her thumbnail as a tiny spoon.

Sure. The powder softly poured onto her thumb, and she looked around to see if anyone in traffic could see them, but the car was starting to move again, and there was now no one there with them except the Stones. Without hesitating, she brought the coke up to her right nostril and sucked it up much longer than necessary. *What would Keith Richards have done?*

She instantly felt a gaslike bitterness travel through her nasal tract and down her throat, and she realized how she was no longer hungry a few minutes later. Her throat became parched and she felt the craving for a cigarette, which Madison provided right on cue. By the time their cigs were out, they'd arrived at Pierre's house, which looked more like a resort with its metal gate at the entrance to the beachfront estate. A text or two later and the gate opened, which led them down a long driveway that ended with an assortment of sports cars parked close together. *There must be thirty cars here,* Thayer thought. *Has no one here heard about Uber?*

It didn't take long for Thayer to recognize the same crowd of people she tried to avoid during high school. She didn't actually recognize anyone, but they simply were that same type of white-sneaker-wearing people she kept in the back corners of her mind. All the pastel shorts and tight tees on the guys, the nearly identical dresses on the girls, the skimpy thong bikinis, the chiseled abs, and the sparkling smiles insinuated everyone was there at the fancy party *just cuz*. Madison and J. P. were her sole companions, and subsequently her codependency for acceptance. So she went wherever Madison wanted to go, and as Madison made the rounds of introducing her to one rich guy after another, the sweat on her palms began to slowly accumulate.

"You wanna do a line?" J. P. asked as he handed over a glass of her mother's Louis Latour. She was initially surprised by the fact that he acknowledged her, and she weighed out how the coke could be the source of or solution to her social anxiety. She delicately nodded and followed J. P., Madison and Pierre to another, less populated room.

This other room was a library full of books that belonged to Pierre's parents, who were cycling somewhere in France. The room's soft bamboo flooring and shelves gave off a quaint bungalow ambience, but the large windows overlooking the ocean from atop a 150-foot cliff screamed out *Malibu*. They sat down on leather couches in the middle of the room that surrounded a large glass coffee table. Madison poured nearly the entire vial of powder onto the glass, and J. P. started flattening it down with a credit card. As he prepared four lines, Thayer sipped her mother's white wine and looked around the room. She wasn't listening to whatever they were discussing, because she was too busy staring at the piano by the windows. She gawked at the majestic masterpiece of an instrument as she recognized it as one of the most beautiful pianos she'd ever seen. Pierre noticed Thayer, which caused Madison to notice as well.

"You should *totally* play, Thay!" she exclaimed, jolting her back into the party scene. "She's *amazing*. She went to music school up north in Berkeley," she told Pierre in a vicarious attempt to impress him, while unknowingly mistaking the Bay Area for Boston's acclaimed Berklee College of Music.

J. P. allotted four lines on the table and took his with the help of a hundred-dollar bill that he then passed to Madison, who voraciously did hers and complained about her nose before passing the bill to Pierre.

"I like that shirt you're wearing," Pierre said to Thayer as he bent down toward the glass table and did his line.

"Thanks," Thayer responded as she grabbed the bill out of his hands and eyed down the last remaining line.

She bent down and stuffed the bill up her nose a little too far, and she shuffled herself around the table for a moment while trying to get comfortable in an uncomfortable position. A moment passed and she looked up at Pierre, who was getting a kick out of her struggle for the right stance. That's when Thayer said *fuck it* and got on her knees and leaned straight in for the line. It was much different than the thumb bump on the way there, and it technically was about twenty times more blow. The way it hit her felt like a rush of five café lattes all at once, and she liked that. She smiled as Pierre started laughing, which subsequently made J. P. and Madison laugh.

"Do you know how to play any Rolling Stones songs?" Pierre asked after the laughter started to die down. Madison prepared a few smaller lines and handed Thayer the bill, which she used for another nasal espresso shot.

"Of course I know how to play Stones songs, Pierre," she said confidently as she walked over to the piano. "I wouldn't be wearing this shirt if I didn't."

"*Yas*, Thay, *slay!*" Madison called out from the couch as they continued to hunch over the glass table.

She approached the piano and ran her hands across the tops of the keys as to not create any sound, and she sat down on the bench. She flirtatiously stroked the keys with her fingertips, excited by the extenuated tingling it created.

"You guys wanna hear some *motha fuckin Rolling Stones?*" she yelled out, doing her best Mick Jagger imitation.

A few stragglers from the party had now shown up, and Thayer's eyes started darting around the library at her growing audience. She stretched out her back, her arms, her neck, her hands and her tongue as she breathed in deeply before playing the opening notes to "She's a Rainbow."

When the moment came to sing the lyrics, she didn't shy back. "She comes in colors everywhere, she combs her hair, she's like a rainbow!"

3

The sun's rays are a reliable promise with each new morning, but no one seems to recognize the different *ways* of sunrays. Each speckle of sunlight upon each speckle of earth is unique, and yet daylight is the most modest natural phenomenon on the planet. We used to worship the sun for all its power and glory, and some even thought the sun was God. That was a long time ago, but how exactly do we venerate the sun today? How much vitamin D do we need to maintain our health? *How much longer can I maintain this lifestyle before going crazy?*

These were some of the thoughts running through Byrd's mind as he sipped on a cold, aluminum can of Coke while taking in some desert sunlight outside a gas station in the middle of Utah. It was still early in the day, at least for drinking soda, and he stared off into nothingness as he concentrated on the flat horizon's ceaseless blur. He was procrastinating, and this particular procrastination featured a second-guessing of what exactly he was doing so far away from home. He understood how these types of toxic thoughts could often consume his asceticism, and he knew how his life as a desert-dwelling hermit was inevitably coming to a close. *But where to next?*

His anxiety had a knack for building itself up in fluctuating ways, and for Byrd, one of his best ways of handling it was drinking Coke. The caramel-colored sugars swished around his teeth as the morning's temperature increased with each passing minute. He took one of his only shirts off to extend its newly laundered aroma before resuming his laid-back posture against a picnic table, which was now his sun-drenched refuge away from any real-world obligations.

A few more minutes passed by as he embraced tiny droplets of sweat around his ears and down his back, and the only thing that took him out of his slumber was the only thing that could: loud music. He opened his eyes to see where the music was coming from and noticed two young women parking a white Astro van with Colorado plates near the station's pumps. The windows were down, and Byrd sat up from his reclined position to listen and get a better look. The driver looked to be in her early twenties, with dirty-blonde hair extending well beyond her shoulders, and she was singing a folk song Byrd didn't recognize. They both got out to stretch, fill up the van's tank, and clean the windows with the available squeegees.

Byrd continued to glance over at them from about a hundred feet away as the passenger walked toward the restroom and the blonde driver moved about the van. He couldn't help himself from recognizing just how beautiful her tanned figure was. Her running shorts were as mesmerizing as the blurry horizon as she reached across the windshield, and an involuntarily increase in his heart rate continued to beat faster and faster. He realized how his hormonal instincts were beginning to progress a bit too fast, so he closed his eyes and took a series of deep breaths in an attempt to stray his mind far away from the attractive stranger. When he eventually looked back up, she was walking straight at him.

"Hey, sorry to wake you! You just look like you know this area, and we kinda need a little help cuz my phone's GPS isn't working. You know how far the hot springs trail is from here?" she asked.

He had to gather himself for a moment before speaking, even though he knew the information she needed. "You're about thirty minutes away from the left turn into the canyon that'll take you to the hot springs trailhead," he replied. "You'll see some big cliffs and a BLM wilderness sign on the side of the road right after the turn. I was just camping out there this past week; it's a really beautiful spot. The pools feel great right now, especially at night. I'm sure you'll enjoy it."

"Awesome, thanks so much. I'm glad I asked! I'm really pumped to get out there. I just didn't realize that I'd have no service on these roads, so I can't plug in the coordinates. Is that your bike?" she asked, glancing at the beat-up Honda with a guitar case and panniers strapped to it. Byrd nodded. "So, is that all your camping gear?" she asked facetiously.

He went over his lifestyle in about a minute and could see how she was becoming more interested by her growing smile, which didn't help alleviate the rapid thumping in his chest.

"So, you're like a *real* wilderness guy? That's too cool. I'm Jane, by the way," she said with a gentle smile as she extended her hand.

"Nice to meet you, Jane. I'm James," he responded, while trying not to show how shook he was by shaking her hand.

They continued talking for a few minutes about where to camp in the canyon, how to find the best hot spring pools, and where to avoid rattlesnakes. Byrd mentioned how he heard her singing, and she explained how she always sang while driving. Jane's voice sounded smooth as she spoke, and her eccentric mannerisms helped Byrd sense that he wasn't just another desert-dwelling nobody in her eyes.

"What're you doing today?" she asked, which in Byrd's mind took the cordial conversation to another level. "We're gonna be camping in the canyon, just the two of us. It could be nice to have a guide that knows the area."

His pants were practically pulsating. He sat silently for a few seconds while considering an out-of-the-blue reality shift in which he put everything aside just to hang out longer with Jane and her friend, who was emerging from the gas station with two plastic bags full of snacks.

"I wish I could, but I have to go to work soon. I'm working the next six days, but I'll be camping in the canyon this weekend."

"We're heading home tomorrow, but lemme get your number and maybe I'll text ya about some other hikes around here sometime," she said with a smile that made his heart skip a beat.

"I don't have a phone, but I can give you my email," he replied, returning her bright smile with his.

☯

About half an hour later, Byrd pulled up to a group of large ado-be buildings. A rundown, off-white school bus corroded near the complex's front entrance, which had bold, black letters along its sides reading: The Intercept. He parked next to the bus and looked at the hand-painted letters that were beginning to chip away, and he thought back to the day when he painted those words himself. Although it wasn't too long ago, he began comparing himself to the aging paint. He pictured himself as the overextenuated T of *The*, and laughed as he considered his coworkers to be the other letters.

The white bus had *The Intercept* painted on it because Byrd worked for the Intercept Program of a wilderness rehabilitation company called Fundamental Roots Therapy, which helped at-risk youth hit the reset button through temporary paradigm shifts in the middle of the Utah wilderness. The broad intention for the wilderness rehabil-itation was to assist kids in remolding perspectives about themselves and their purpose, which parents assumed would lead to positive and meaningful progressions. Most parents also assumed that the Fundamental Roots staff members had pretty good heads on their shoulders, and there was little to nothing on their website about how some guides went through the program when they were younger.

The Intercept Program's behavioral-health approach was for teens who were mentally struggling in one way or another, and Byrd's job was to take a group of a dozen kids into the desert and show them basic survival skills while guiding them to dispersed campsites. Although he was a far cry from the rest of his colleagues as a one-on-one coun-selor, he was generally good at connecting with the kids because he never patronized them and always let them speak their minds freely. There were, of course, parts of the job in which he had to be inspiring, and he was always going to lead campfire games and venting sessions while working for Fundamental Roots, but those strategies were never quite enough to actually convince any teen to make legitimate changes. That's why no matter how much weight was necessary for each trip, Byrd always had a vintage ukulele strapped to his backpack like a miniature shotgun. The ukulele, which he nicknamed Uncle Tito, was a favorite instrument of his that he cherished like the real uncle he never had. He couldn't safely strap both his guitar and ukulele to his bike, due to all the other gear he carried on a regular basis, which was why he often kept Tito safe in the Fundamental Roots headquarters when he was off duty in BLM wilderness.

He kept thinking more about the girl he met at the gas station while he turned the bike off and began detaching the panniers. Jane, *she was someone,* or at least the only someone he'd talked to in months. He'd gone long enough without getting laid to the point that simply talking with someone as pretty as Jane was encouraging, although in reality he knew the only thing he'd likely get from their conversation was another needless regret to wake up to. *Shit, I should've got her email.*

"How's she flying out there, Byrd?" yelled a gentleman by the name of Gil, short for Gilbert Monroe.

"She flew like a mother goose flies through traffic to keep her babies at the front of the arrow," Byrd responded. He didn't get the laugh he expected as Gil quickly switched into boss mode by holding out a manila envelope.

"Here's the lowdown on the group getting in tonight," Gil said, handing Byrd the envelope. "You don't need to look through it too much, but you know the drill."

"Where's Uncle Tito?"

"If I tell you where it is, you're not just gonna play songs and never learn the kids' names, *right*?"

"*Sure.*"

"It's safely stashed away on the bus."

"Can I get the keys?"

There was another pause, this one a little longer and a lot more awkward. Gil blatantly avoided eye contact with Byrd, who sensed an ensuing power trip about to blast off.

"You can have the keys *after* you look through the envelope," he replied, only making eye contact for a split second.

"Fine. I'll be in my room, *Dad.*"

Each piece of paper within the manila envelope had a picture of a teenage boy and a brief description of who they were, where they were from, and why they'd been admitted to Fundamental Roots. They came from all over America, and all of them had a unique story as to how they ended up being a part of Byrd's multiday hikes into the desert. He flipped through the headshots and names, twelve in total, and then he picked up his guitar and started playing soft riffs on top of a rock-solid mattress. He found the room he stayed in to be eerie, with its blank cement walls and floors, and the only redeeming quality of the space was a small, thumbtacked picture of a group of boys on the precipice of a scenic cliff. He remembered taking that picture, and how the late afternoon sunlight blasted through the clouds at a perfect angle and illuminated the mesa in a different way than it normally did. He looked at that memory and started drifting away into a dreamy riff, one that slightly resembled the acoustic song he heard coming from Jane's van. Jane's song put him into another spiral, which led to a couple hours of notepad scribbles about *passing by.*

The boys arrived a little after ten. Each of them had flown into Salt Lake City earlier that day, where they congregated at the airport like a flock of sheep onto The Intercept. They ate dinner together at a Mexican restaurant in the city, and later were driven a couple of hours into the depths of the desert. Everything was seeping with repetitiveness as he heard the bus arrive from outside his window, which confirmed it was time to get to work. He slipped on his mandatory uniform that looked like a park ranger's boring, beige shorts and matching SPF 80 button-up with dual chest pockets. Every time he put on his work clothes, he'd imagine to himself that the entire outfit indirectly said *I live for REI clearance sales.*

Gil and Byrd waited in front of the main building as the boys slowly walked in their direction with their scant amount of luggage. A few of them barely had anything on them, which was usually an indication that their parents forced them intervention-style to fly to Utah for therapy.

"Welcome, boys! My name is Gil, and I'm the head counselor of this Fundamental Roots Excursion Center! We're going to learn a lot about each other, and especially ourselves throughout the next week! We're very happy to have you here with us, and we know that this will be a life-changing experience for all of you! Right now, we're going to go inside and show you to your designated beds for the evening, and tomorrow morning, you'll begin your adventure with your guide right here, Mr. Jim Byrd!"

"Hi, guys. You can just call me Byrd …"

At six sharp the next morning, Gil was yelling in the boys' dormitory about showering and eating breakfast. He reminded them that this would be their last home-cooked meal for the next five days, and that they all needed to be outside with their assigned gear in an hour. Byrd could hear Gil's excessive clamor, but instead chose to crank the volume up on the only FM station he could pick up with his bedside table's digital clock.

"Okay, boys! Gather around!" Gil yelled out to the group when the clock struck seven o'clock. "I'm going to go over the ground rules, so this is *very important*! Okay, so rule number one: do what Jim tells you! Rule number two: no deserting the group, for your own good, I might add! Rule number three: no fighting or bullying! You're all going to need each other's help to survive! And last but certainly not least, rule number four: have fun and enjoy your time in beautiful Utah!"

"What if one of us gets bit by a snake or scorpion or something? What are we supposed to do then?" one of the kids asked.

"There are rattlesnakes and scorpions where we're going, so that's a good question," Byrd chimed in. "But snakes and scorpions should really be the least of your worries. Just don't get too close, and they'll leave you alone. The bigger danger will be mountain lions, bears, and coyotes that sometimes appear where we'll be camping. And this reminds me of something Gil forgot to mention, and that's that you don't wanna be like Theodore from earlier this year, who tried to convince me he got bit by a Mojave when he actually just poked two holes in his leg with a cactus thorn."

"Yes! Please do not fake any diseases or injuries!"

"How'd you know he was faking it?" another kid countered.

"He confessed when I told him the helicopter ride would cost his family over ten thousand dollars if they found out he was faking, but you should all know that you'll be just fine if you *actually* get injured. I'll have antivenom serum and an SOS device on me to call in a chopper to our exact location in case of an emergency."

"Byrd's bitchin', but this other guy's a lil bitch," another kid squeaked under his breath, causing the entire group of teenagers to giggle.

Hours of hiking passed by in the dry heat, and Byrd led the whole way while strumming simple chords on Uncle Tito. Each of them had an adequate amount of equipment and maybe enough dehydrated rations to get through the five days, but one of the most important factors of wilderness therapy through Fundamental Roots was that it was on the kids to cook, shelter, and generally survive on their own. Byrd was only there to supervise and provide guidance, and the boys started to figure that out as he continued to strum away in the front of the line while not paying any attention to what was happening behind him.

Byrd knew he didn't have to take any water breaks during this portion of the trek because they all had full bladders in their packs and were hiking to a stream where they'd sleep that evening, but the kids had no idea where he was taking them. This inevitably led to excessive whining and bickering, which was why Byrd zoned out until they arrived at their first of the week's five dispersed campgrounds. Tents were pitched in the early evening, and Byrd set his dusty sleeping pad and bag on the ground near the other tents that were predominately grouped close to one another.

Once the boys had put some food in their bellies, it was time for therapy around a fire pit. Byrd always played a lot of music by himself while living out of his motorcycle, and the young kids who were forced to camp with him were often the type of adolescents who had computer and internet addictions. This subsequently resulted in most of the Fundamental Roots students being completely desperate for entertainment, especially during the first couple of nights away from their routines. This general desperation for entertainment was one reason why Byrd considered them to be the perfect audience to test out his newest, original songs.

"All right, you boys wanna hear a song?" Byrd asked as the group seemed about done with their dehydrated meals.

A couple of boys squeaked *yeah*, and a couple of others nodded silently, but they predominantly stared indifferently while waiting for him to begin.

"Okay, here we go! I wrote this song last night and was working on the chords while we were hiking here," Byrd explained as he started strumming a beachy rhythm on Uncle Tito. He called the song "She Passed By" and bestowed it with soft lyrics that he sang out to the tired boys:

Have you ever noticed, the ways of sunrays?
Do you see me, behind those pretty black shades?
Will you stop here, and maybe stay a while?
I saw you comin', what a great big smile

Sun beatin' down, air oh so thick
You wanna talk to me, you got a bone to pick?
Sittin all alone, just wasting time
Have I waited my whole life, for you to find?

She passed by, just like desert dust
Like rays from the sun, my heart begins to rust
She passed by, I'm just another pawn
Maybe you'll come back, or are you long gone?
She passed by, yeah she passed by
I see the whole world, it's right there in your eyes

I told her where to go, too far away
Yeah she passed by, I wanted her to stay
She passed by, yeah she passed by
Into the sun, another lonely lie

We'll meet again, when you look at the stars
Reflecting on water, reflecting my scars
Till another time, I'll be waiting here
All of these days, go see this big sphere

She passed by, just like desert dust
Like rays from the sun, my heart begins to rust
She passed by, yeah she passed by
Into the sun, another lonely lie

When Byrd and the boys finished up the trek five days later, he had the next six days off. He wasn't sure what he wanted to do, but he decided to first go to Surf Zone and check his emails. He said hey to Billy and began sifting through a bit of junk mail until he noticed another message from Thayer, as well as a message from an old friend he grew up with in Delaware that he hadn't seen in a while. His buddy's name was Skylar Rose, and his message read:

Hey Byrd,

I'm driving through Utah on the 13th with a buddy on our way to California to go camping, see family and a couple shows. It would be so dope to camp with you that night! I think the general area where you are in Utah would be a good pit stop for our first day on the road, but I'm honestly not too sure where you are.

How've you been man? You still working with those kids?

Let me know where you'll be on the 13th and maybe we can meet up.

Sky

4

hree days later was the thirteenth of June, year 2012, United States of America, Utah, a remote canyon in the dead center of the state, Byrd's sleeping bag, Byrd's mind now ceaselessly moving until a sharp, magical moment occurred. The internal triumph over his mind's monkey slamming its cymbals over and over again with thought after thought after thought began to take form as his internal grind began to slow down and even came to a complete halt.

Living alone in the wilderness tended to help when it came to finally getting that damn monkey to shut up every once in a while, but at the exact same time, the sporadic seclusion of his guiding schedule made its cymbals slam even louder once they got going. *It's worse than before,* he thought. *That damn monkey ...* It started screeching again. *No ... Stupid monkey in me ... me and my monkey ... everybody's got something to hide except for me and my monkey.*

Damn, it's winning. He gave the monkey a point on a cognitive scoreboard, and he knew what he needed to do to get back at it. There was only one thing he admittedly could do to curb the effects of his Curious George at the crack of dawn. *Why always in the morning? Of all the Beatles songs, right now? Who's coming here with Sky?*

"Ease up, Byrd. Ease up and fly away *slooowly*," he whispered. "Ease up, Byrd ... Ease up and fly away *slooooowly*," he whispered even slower.

Something started mixing around upstairs, a something that

could've easily popped if it were at all tangible. He kept at the mantra for ten repetitions, but he couldn't eliminate the distinct image of a furry, beige monkey. *What's up with this damn monkey?*

"Everybody's got something to hide, except for me and my monkey," he slowly whispered. "Everybody's got something to hide, except for me and my *moonkeeeeey,*" he whispered even slower.

That was the ticket to Magic Mountain. That was the feeling that so many people before him, generations upon generations of wise men, preached about: nothingness, the empty abyss. He entered the long, dark tunnel of breath toward the light of elemental composure, and he soothed away remaining tensions with each exhaling release. *Now, I'm winning …*

Byrd's physical self rested directly on the ground while still wrapped up in a sleeping bag, and he began drifting from nothingness into dreaming. His mind settled within the slightly less familiar side of the Unified Field as he became entrenched between the thick rows of a cornfield. He went somewhere deep through the confines of lucid consciousness to a place where sentience doesn't apply, and he could tell how the rows of corn were clearly a mental mirage. If only there was a way to stay just a little longer bit longer, *but it's too late now.* The first, tiny, macroscopic ray of direct sunlight struck his face, and his eyes opened.

He was back, and he couldn't help but think about the mystery person that Sky was traveling with. He looked at his watch, which read 6:30.

Boulder, Colorado: the twenty-first-century Height-Ashbury, where misfits and privileged teenagers from all over the USA come together to marvel at natural beauty while getting high on life.

Skylar Rose sat in the driver's seat of his rundown Chevy van and stared at his phone as he dialed an O'Donnell contact, and he continually called five times without an answer. He blared the horn and looked toward a dingy, party-torn house in the middle of the Hill.

He glanced at remnants of trash on the front porch and broken roof shingles as he shook his head, realizing how O'Donnell had no place living in the frat-like environment at his age of thirty-one. He was starting to get annoyed, so he blared the horn even louder.

"Shut up out there!" yelled a random voice from inside an upstairs window of O'Donnell's neighbor's house.

Sky reached his whole body, except his legs, out the window and said, "I'm trying to wake up my friend! He's not answering his phone, my bad!"

A few seconds passed, after which a college-aged girl subtly appeared behind her window's screen.

"Are you by chance looking for O'Donnell?" she more calmly responded.

"Yeah! Do you know if he's here or not?"

"He's in there, all right. I hung out with him last night. I mean, if you like knock on his window or something, he might wake up. I don't know, though, he was a mess. Are you guys supposed to be going somewhere or something?"

"Yeah, we're going to California."

"Oh, *right on*, dude! I'm born and raised in San Luis Obispo! That's gonna be such a fun road trip!" the voice rang out from behind the screen.

"Yeah, we're going to San Francisco. I'm really stoked, but ready to get a move on."

"*Damn*, yeah, you guys need to get going if you're gonna go all the way to Cali!" the voice responded, after coughing loudly from her blatant wake 'n' bake.

"Yeah, go back to Cali and shut up! It's 6:30 in the fucking morning!" another random neighbor yelled from behind a window.

Both Sky and the first random voice started laughing obnoxiously loudly, and somehow through the rowdy laughter happening right outside his first-floor window, a besieged form of drunken consciousness revived itself within the swashbuckling, Irish-born Scotsman of no lassie's dreams: Ryan O'Donnell. Nothing could've woken O'Donnell up that morning, including his alarm clock that was set and currently ringing, his cell phone that was charged and ringing, and not even Sky's van honking a little over fifty feet away. Nothing could've brought him out of his drunken stupor, except the exact same thing that brought him into it: FOMO. He rolled himself over toward his window and barely projected enough to be heard by Sky, and subsequently everyone else on the block that was listening in on the neighborhood yelling match.

"I'll be out in a few minutes! My head feels like *a bowling ball* just fell on it!" he yelled into the street.

Sky decided to take things into his own hands, so he jumped out of the van and walked up to the window where he heard O'Donnell's voice. When he got there, he peered into the dark chasm that was O'Donnell's bedroom and noticed the smells of stale beer and moldy carpets.

"C'mon, man. You said you'd be ready to go at the crack of dawn. Are you packed up?"

O'Donnell pointed toward a backpack and large case by the bedroom door.

"Is that what I think it is?"

"Yeah, you know I gotta bring it. Now get out of my window. I ain't dressed and need to get changed, ya creepin burglar."

A few hours later, Sky and O'Donnell were passing through Glenwood Canyon on I-70. As it was O'Donnell's first time going through the majestic stretch of the Colorado River, it came across Sky's mind that O'Donnell wouldn't mind waking up again.

"Jeez, look at these cliffs!" he yelled as he realized where he was. "I have to play a sick song, pronto."

Sky looked down at his phone playing music through a tape player. "Nah, your taste in music sucks," he teasingly rejected, which he knew would hit some buttons.

"Yeah right, like *you* would know! Step aside and let a pro have at it."

Sky laughed at just how much O'Donnell was still slurring his words at 10 a.m., and he realized how to hit some more derisive buttons.

"No one even listens to the radio anymore. You're a pro in a long-forgotten, fading profession. I'm surprised they still let you on the air, considering how often you're slurring your words just like right now!"

This remark caused O'Donnell to crack a smile. "I'm still on the air because I'm a living legend gracing all you goofball Americans with my brilliance. So, fuck off and drive me to Cali, ya van bum. I don't have a license, so you're doing the whole way."

Sky liked the sound of that, not only because he thought O'Donnell was still too drunk to drive, but also because he genuinely loved driving. Cutting each sharp curve of Glenwood Canyon was like playing a video game, except even better with its real-life implications. His Chevy couldn't go much faster than eighty, but it still had a nice feel to it when he gripped the wheel a little looser and let it slide back and forth through his fingers. He knew O'Donnell didn't have a driver's license and he already was planning on driving the whole way, which was exactly why he decided to break up the trip the way he did. Just an easy, no-rush adventure to the West Coast, with a pit stop featuring a freak of nature they'd meet halfway.

Sky looked at himself in the van's side mirror as they passed the area where the Rocky Mountains meet the desert near Grand Junction. He examined his long, blond bangs flying everywhere in the wind and gave himself a look of approval that said *you got this*.

He started thinking about the possibilities of what would happen once they met up with Byrd, and he knew that the campsite being near a series of hot springs meant they wouldn't necessarily be alone. Mountain women scattered his other brain, and he began imagining the three of them in a steaming-hot pool with three girls who loved to party. They started smoking a massive joint, and Byrd was puffing it like a champ, just ready to keep things mellow. Byrd passed the joint and he took a hit while looking at a beautiful, brown-haired girl next to him. Underneath the water, he felt a foot rubbing against his and gravitating up around his ankle. They locked eyes. Without saying anything, he went in for a kiss. When they finished kissing, she exhaled smoke that looked way too cool for reality's school.

Sky kept his head in the clouds the whole way to Byrd's campsite, and they found him playing guitar underneath a cottonwood tree when they arrived. Byrd noticed them after hearing the van's blaring horn, and he lit up like a junior high student getting tipsy for the first time at a Christmas party. He stood up wearing just his brown full-brim and shorts, and he continued strumming his strings as he walked toward the driveway of his BLM home. As they got closer to where Byrd pointed to park, they both busted out laughing as they realized he was singing the Beatles hit "Drive My Car."

"You crazy son of a bitch!" Sky responded as he wrapped his arms around Byrd's shoulders for a bear hug. "You can always drive my car, Byrdie Baby!"

"What about me? You're not gonna leave me out of this bromance moment, are ya now?" O'Donnell interjected as he stepped out of the Chevy's passenger seat. "Save some for me too, Sky. I don't wanna be the only one not getting laid tonight," he continued with a wry smile.

"O'Donnell, this is Byrd," Sky said, as if O'Donnell didn't already know. "Byrd, this is Ryan O'Donnell. He's coming out with me to Frisco because ... shit, what exactly is it that you need to do out there again?"

"Well, I still wanna see all these big trees and cliffy beaches I've heard about, but I also have a big gig with a group of world-famous musicians this weekend."

"That's sweet! Where are you playing?" Byrd chirped in, genuinely interested.

"A funeral in Berkeley. Some bampot my auntie knows killed himself speeding off a road in Marin," O'Donnell said with a smile, which Byrd reciprocated with his eyebrows fully furrowed.

The three of them proceeded to relax in the creek before taking afternoon naps, and by 6:30 p.m., they'd each had a few beers and a couple shots of whiskey. The excessive pale ale hops gave Byrd persistent hiccups that he couldn't get rid of. It had been a long time since he'd even had a sip of alcohol, and even longer since he'd had alcohol-induced hiccups. But the hiccups were how he knew he was starting to feel *it*: that intuitive impulse for a weird night ahead.

By 7:30 p.m., they'd piled into the van and were driving the five miles down the dirt road to the hot springs trailhead. Sky knew he was far over the legal limit to drive, but the single-track road in Byrd Land made it feel less taboo to take another few swigs of whiskey from behind the wheel. By eight o'clock, the day's light was at its climactic moments when only the very tops of the red rock cliffs were still lit, and Byrd looked around approvingly as he noticed only one car in the parking lot.

"This will be great. There's barely anyone here! Some nights this spot gets a little blown up," he explained.

"Why does it get so blown up *around these parts*?" O'Donnell asked, failing miserably to imitate a Utah cowboy.

"Because this is *the place*," Byrd responded.

"Is that so? Well, this *must be* the place, then!" O'Donnell howled. "Hey, I'm thinking I'm gonna bring my recorder. How long are we hiking, Mr. Byrd?"

"About an hour up and an hour back," Byrd replied as he tested a headlamp.

"No shit, an hour up? Well, I'm *def* bringing the recorder then," O'Donnell confirmed to himself as he scoured through his large case as quickly as he could.

For the next half hour, Byrd and Sky were subjected to O'Donnell's slow hiking pace and consistent whiskey breaks in between failed renditions of the Talking Heads hit. After about a mile of hiking, the incessant recorder sounds began to irk Byrd, mainly because he was used to night hiking the trail in complete silence. Sky noticed Byrd begrudgingly stepping foot after foot, and how his headlamp was barely lighting the path ahead due to him staring straight down.

"*Hey*, let's harmonize Talking Heads like we used to with those Taking Back Sunday songs when we were kids!" Sky said while patting Byrd's back in an attempt to stoke him up, which led to more hiccupping. "*All right!* Take it from the top, O'Donnell, and *don't forget* to transition when the lyrics are supposed to come in!" Sky sarcastically commanded, knowing it would sound mediocre at best.

O'Donnell began playing the introduction to "This Must Be the Place," and at this point in the hike, he'd practiced enough to actually sound somewhat close to the real thing. His fingers moved swiftly atop the plastic keyholes, and he swirled the notes together with drunken imperfection. The first verse was coming up, so Byrd grabbed a water bottle and took a swig of whiskey as a tingling ran through him.

"I don't remember the words," he whispered to Sky.

"Yeah, you do, you can't lie to me. Okay, here we go. Now, shut up and let's sing," he encouraged with a wink, which made Byrd crack a smile.

And that was what they did for the rest of the hike: shut up and sang. They couldn't make it beyond the third verse without O'Donnell needing a break, but Sky and Byrd were more than satisfied with their sloshed harmonies. It was a nostalgic moment that brought both of them back to their teenage years, and for O'Donnell, thinking of the famous Scotsman David Byrne during another drunken night in a strange land far from home was nostalgic as well.

By the time they finished their singing escapade, they'd arrived at their far-off destination. It was now dark out, but the clear night's full moon illuminated the area enough to the point that headlamps were barely necessary. They stared at a twenty-foot waterfall with a cascading creek beneath it, as well as a manmade rock shelf that separated the freezing creek water from the steaming-hot pools.

"C'mon, let's go above the waterfall. That's where the best pool is," Byrd explained as they continued up the trail. "But first, let's check this out," he said as he drunkenly stumbled over to a large sandstone wall with shallow holes. He reached into one of the holes and pulled out a three-foot snake by the tail, which caused it to shake in the air between his body and outstretched arm.

"What the hell are you doing, mate?" O'Donnell yelled. "That could be venomous!"

"It's all good, none of these are poisonous. The rattlers don't come up this high in the mountains. They like it better down in the valley where we're camping," Byrd replied with an *are you actually scared* smile. "All you have to do is grab them from out of these holes, and you'll have it perfectly by the tail."

Sky watched Byrd carefully put the snake back in its cubby and whisper tokens of gratitude to it, and he then walked up to one of the holes. He took a deep breath and slid his hand into the corners of the crevice. Slowly but surely, he inched his fingers forward.

"You have to do it with one fell swoop," Byrd said from behind him. "The moment you feel her, you gotta grab her tight!" he jokingly advised as O'Donnell initiated a fist-bump.

Sky took a deep breath to slow his raging heartbeat down, and he inched his hand further until he felt the cold, slippery surface of the snake's skin. He clenched on to it as tightly as he could, and swung the snake way too aggressively toward Byrd and O'Donnell, who leapt out of the way while laughing. This snake was much larger than the one Byrd had just held, and O'Donnell could barely control himself as he filmed Sky on his phone.

"There he is, folks! Skylar Rose, the snake-wranglin' cowboy of Utah! Grab her tight, Sky! Hold on to your baby, you crazy sonuvabitch!"

A few minutes later, they arrived at a large hot spring pool just above the twenty-foot waterfall, which just so happened to be underneath a series of even larger falls that cascaded down a steep slope. Sitting in this cozy pool were two middle-aged men, both of whom had short, blond hair. O'Donnell, Sky, and Byrd quickly found out all about them, their names being Gideon and Dallen. They were a gay couple, but they were each other's first male partners at the ripe ages of fifty-three and forty-nine.

The short story of how Gideon and Dallen ended up in the hot spring that night was that they first knew each other for many years as friends, through their wives. They both grew up in a much different era of the Mormon Church when even the thought of homosexuality was against all things that Jesus and Joseph Smith stood for. Gideon and Dallen lived the first forty-five years of their lives truly believing that sex should only ever be had with a woman, and this led to each of them having marriages that lasted over twenty years. Gideon had two daughters and one son, and Dallen had three daughters. Dallen explained how one day he finally took a real look in the mirror and admitted to himself that he was gay. At that point, the entire thought of coming out and losing everything was too much to consider, so he sought help through someone he could trust outside of the church: a psychologist. Dallen told his family that he was having anxiety attacks induced by his job as a contractor, but he and his therapist pretty much only talked about the church and being in the closet. He was eventually advised to come out to a person he trusted inside the church after over a year of hiding his sexuality, and Dallen couldn't think of someone he trusted more than his friend of many years, Gideon. It didn't take much longer for their affair to develop, and they eventually decided to come out together and leave the church behind them for good. They were both very successful in their careers and decided to start living life to the fullest, which manifested itself in traveling more often and embracing their truest selves for the first time. Their newfound sexuality ended up liberating them in countless ways, and they each kept good relationships with their ex-wives and kids. They were in love with each other to the fullest degree, and they were proud to tell their story to a random group of drunk guys who didn't quite know what they'd stumbled upon.

O'Donnell's face lit up. He'd never met a Mormon before, and Gideon and Dallen shattered all his expectations. He, Sky, and Byrd admired their journey, and they drunkenly felt the need to overcompensate themselves as good allies by telling them about their connections to the gay community via friends and relatives. Gideon and Dallen loved it as they dished out compliments about them being *so cultured.*

"Oh, I have a fun idea!" Gideon said to the group a handful of minutes later, as if he'd come across a life-changing epiphany. His bright-blue eyes glistened as he keenly surveyed the boys. "Now that we've told you about our sex lives, we wanna hear what you've all been through. I'm fascinated about what young men's lives are like outside the Mormon Church, mainly because we grew up so differently than you guys. So, let's hear it. Tell us your best sex stories!"

"Yes!" O'Donnell yelled in approval. "I'll go first!"

The group became enthralled with tales of faraway lands like Glasgow, Amsterdam, Paris, and London. O'Donnell had a geographic pedigree, to say the least, but the actual details of his stories were beyond ridiculous. Sex with a rich American girl (who he was looking forward to having a reunion with in California) at a Glasgow hotel, a threesome in London, a prostitute in Paris, and a dominatrix in an Amsterdam brothel. After over fifteen minutes of O'Donnell's ramblings, it was Sky's turn to tell a sex story.

Sky's love life may have been a bit more tamed down than O'Donnell's, but only slightly in his own Americanized way. He explained how his summer job in high school was being a lifeguard at a beach along the Delaware Bay, and that young girls would approach him without him even having to step foot off his stand. He divulged how being the beach community's *hunky lifeguard* led him to more flirting than actual safety surveillance, and that his sexual encounters only escalated when he left home to attend community college in Colorado. He described Boulder girls as the most fun he'd ever met, and O'Donnell was quick to agree. After another ten minutes of hearing the details of Sky's goofiest relationships, Gideon and Dallen were glowing like Christmas at the Salt Lake Tabernacle.

"*Wow*, you guys have had some *wild* experiences!" Dallen commented. "What about you? What are your best sex stories?" he asked, motioning to Byrd.

"I really don't have much to talk about. I've only slept with one woman my entire life, and I honestly can't even remember when the last time I had sex was," he confessed.

"Oh, *c'mon*! A guy as good looking as you has to easily be getting laid at least *somewhat* memorably!" Gideon hollered. "You seriously can't remember? How long do you think it's been? Try to guess."

"I'd say a little over three years."

"What the hell? How does something like that happen to *this?*" Dallen asserted, motioning to Byrd's bearded face and making the whole group laugh.

"Our friend Mr. Byrd is a true woodsman," Sky decreed.

"Yeah, a true woodsman with an unsatisfied woody!" O'Donnell yelled as everyone in the hot spring cracked up, including Byrd.

The next thing Byrd knew, it was 6:30 in the morning as he looked at his wristwatch. He woke up to a harsh shrieking sound, followed by a deep rumbling tone that shocked him out of his drunken slumber. He reached for his canteen, which had only a tiny sip left, and looked around to find the source of the noise. It was O'Donnell, who was playing bagpipes about fifty yards away while attempting to steer a small herd of cattle away from the campsite. He was playing a rendition of "Scotland the Brave" as the cows scurried in a frenzy.

"What do you think you're *doing*, O'Donnell?" Byrd yelled, which caused O'Donnell to stop and spin around.

"These cows were about to stomp *all over* you! They were about to trample you to rubble if I didn't hear them coming and decide to scare them off. My gig is tomorrow too, so I figured I'd scare them off with the pipes to practice before we hit the road!"

Byrd looked over at Sky, who was emerging from his tent and pulling the trigger on an imaginary gun pointed toward his head. They both laughed, indirectly acknowledging how they were still drunk.

"Be sure to send me a picture of Lin when you get there," Byrd said with a big smile. "I wanna see how big he's gotten."

5

There's an involuntary response of sporadic blinking and pupil dilation as a driver looks out upon a hot summer horizon engulfed in a glistening effect that morphs all surroundings at eighty miles per hour. The sense of relaxation that the open road provides can at times feel as if there's so much more to these moments than just sitting in a seat along the way to a destination. In some ways, these moments provide a destination in and of themselves, albeit a rather ubiquitous destination that shares little resemblance to anything on this side of the Unified Field. This destination is an empty, ever-winding void that just so happens to entail portals near rural roads in the most mind-numbing centers of nowhere. It's out here, and way in *there*, that it's possible to tangibly see the real destinations we're meant for on this convoluted space rock we call home.

Sky continued to sink deeper into daydreams and drown out the sounds of classic rock playing from his van's stereo, and he also did his best to drown out the emphatic snores exuding from O'Donnell every ten seconds. He started thinking about all the people who inhabited what he saw as a wasteland off I-80 in rural Nevada. *But what exactly makes any land a waste?* Against all natural odds, human life still found its way, with town after town claiming Nevada as their unique destination. It didn't take long for these thoughts in Sky's mind of *our homes* to stretch to thoughts of how we all ended up on this luscious miracle in space within the middle of maybe God-knows-where in the cosmos. *Seriously, though,* Sky thought. *How did we make it here? Were there actually gods who helped us find this place?*

He continued considering his present place in the universe as merely what his occipital lobes would allow him to view, and how everything he could physically see was indefinitely a part of his own creation, his own work of art, and his own reality: Nevada, where the nation's government has admitted to the reality of a military base that may or may not hold the world's deepest, darkest secrets. Maybe the keys to multidimensional doors were hidden in plain sight out in the middle of nowhere, and maybe they were exactly where Sky's van just so happened to be rolling as he meandered his way in the exact opposite direction of rural tranquility. He knew what lay ahead of him: the pungent, aromatic smells of San Francisco's Chinatown and the clusterfuck that is the Bay Area. Everything about San Francisco seemed so much more exciting than anything that could ever be found within that part of Nevada, but he still didn't feel quite ready to leave. *Byrd would like it here,* he thought as the van rolled down an exit ramp.

"I could eat a pony right now!" O'Donnell burst out as he woke up. "Where in the ... Where are we? All that's here is rocks and sky, Sky."

"I'm not sure where we are, but there has to be a place to eat around here somewhere. I'll just drive this way and see if we find something. I 100 percent saw a sign for a town, I think."

Over twenty minutes passed along a rough dirt road, until they arrived in a quaint town that was nestled underneath a desolate ridgeline. Beige mounds shot up for miles, and there was a whole heck ton of identical onyx rocks as far as the occipital lobe would let one see. The town was a strip of barely functional buildings, and as they continued down Main Street, Sky noticed an old mural on a brick wall that featured Uncle Sam pointing out toward every passerby. Some of Sam's hat and beard were missing from apparent years of decay, but the sheer magnetism of his glare spoke volumes alongside the caption that read: *We're all counting on YOU.* Sky slowed down to a stop to take a better peek at the decrepit mural, and he guessed that every man and woman who'd glanced up at Uncle Sam had slowly but surely recognized his long-term deterioration for decades.

"Is *this* the American Dream I heard so much about back home?" O'Donnell sarcastically asked as they stared out the van windows.

"I'm not sure, but that's just about as *America* as it gets," Sky replied as they continued crawling down Main Street, until seeing a sign that read Odessa's Diner.

Odessa's smelled like a combination of eggs, hash browns, bacon grease, and coffee, and the packed dining area made it clear that this fine establishment wasn't only a diner, but also the place to be in town. Old black-and-white pictures depicted the original construction of Reno, and even older photographs hung on the walls showing the times when that part of Nevada truly was the Wild West. Other farming artifacts rested for posterity near the ceiling, and Sky nodded with the satisfaction of finding a bona fide destination. He imagined the patrons currently eating at Odessa's to be the next ones to go up on the walls, which meant they'd become part of something so much bigger than themselves. *Isn't that what anyone, no matter where home is, could ever want?*

Sky noticed the disheveled auburn curls of O'Donnell's hair as he watched him sip from a coffee mug, and he couldn't help but start laughing when he thought back on what had taken place the night before.

"You really had some wild stories last night," Sky said with a smirk as he took a sip from his mug. The waitress approached them and placed a massive omelet in front of Sky, as well as a stack of four pancakes, a side of grits, three over-easy eggs, and toast in front of O'Donnell. A witty smile ran across O'Donnell's face while he exchanged niceties with the waitress and watched her walk away.

"I'm surprised you wanna bring it up, considering them tales you told about being a kinky lifeguard and all. It was like reading a *Penthouse* while lounging in my living room watching *Baywatch*," he said as he cut a thick triangle out of the four stack.

"Yeah, well you're the one that put me on the spot! I didn't know what to say, so I just told the truth about some of the most ratchet nights I've had. Please, don't tell anyone about those sex stories. I don't want any girls back in Boulder thinking I'm a fiend or anything like that."

"You know I love ya, Sky. I'd never divulge your kinkiest secrets to no one. And you know I love it to bits when you tell me the Uncle Sam truth about ratchet stories like the ones last night," he said as he saluted him from across the table.

Sky laughed, and they sat in silence for a few more minutes as they finished their breakfast plates.

"You think Byrd might tell people about our stories?"

"Are you serious, mate?" O'Donnell replied with a chuckle. "That scabby Jake doesn't know what's going on outside that little universe between the desert and his ears. The tube can't even remember the last time he got laid, for Chrissake! Poor guy is probably wondering if he'll be able to switch things up and go leftie for all of his lonely nights! What is he even doing out there with no tent, just living out of bike panniers? The bloke's completely mental!"

A triumphant sensation boils through those who've driven consecutive days along endless highways as their destination approaches, almost as if ending a long drive is a way of reclaiming the open road via not being claimed by it. Out in the rolling hills of the San Joaquin Valley, there's a specific type of bliss that can only be fully appreciated by those who see what this rural area represents: the end of America's western frontier. Although the ever-increasing number of cars along those highways unmistakably signify an ensuing shitstorm of people, there are still miles upon miles of a Nevada-like emptiness that can be found within this special agricultural region. It's here that the vast Sierra Nevada Mountains skyrocket from California's eastern border with pure, granite madness to then only flatten themselves into rounded hills. These hills feature small towns dotting the highway exits, which completely contradict the rat race along the nearby coast.

Any final stretches of a long drive where the end is within grasp inherently stir up the innate resolve needed to see any accomplishment through, and as effortless as driving an automatic van from Colorado's Front Range to San Francisco technically was, it still withstood the basic requirements of an achievement for Sky. He'd set a goal of arriving to the Bay Area around the exact time of their estimated arrival. They'd begrudgingly woken up early each morning to get in enough daylight hours, they'd gotten in touch with Byrd and experienced his unique home in their own hedonistic way, they'd seen the spirit of America at Odessa's Diner, and above all else, they'd turned their quick road trip to California into an unforgettable ride.

Nevertheless, driving west through Utah and Nevada in the middle of June left Sky desperate for some kind of temperate destination along Cali's eclectic coast, and a city like San Francisco seemed like the perfect cultural melting pot to fully satiate this desperation. With its mazes of steep streets, endless cuisine, scenes of collaborative artists and breathtaking ocean landscapes, it was easy for Sky to see why San Francisco was the initial place where the gentle breeze of NorCal culture gusted itself eastward. It had always been a massive American metropolis unlike any other, and for Sky and O'Donnell, it was their home for the next few days.

They arrived in Berkeley just before sunset, which was where Sky planned to drop O'Donnell off at a friend's house. O'Donnell's Berkeley friend who was kind enough to let him crash the night before his funeral gig was Meryl Martinez, and she'd been waiting on their arrival for hours. From her vibrant outfits accompanied by her electric-blue hair to her ceaseless need to be a voice against injustices of all kinds, Meryl was all that was beautiful about Berkeley. She was the girl in the neighborhood you turned to when you thought it would be a cool idea to have a community picnic in the park, and she was the girl who couldn't walk more than fifty yards down a southside street without having a chat. She was a sweetheart who emanated good vibes wherever she went, and she was even kind enough to save Sky a parking spot right outside her house.

Meryl lived with three other girls and two guys, and they had a relatively cohesive synergy as a college town household. The fact that they each paid $1,500 in rent and grew all types of vegetables in their festive backyard did always go a long way in terms of making the whole group feel as though they needed to make the most of their living arrangement, and they did. The entire house reeked of ganja as Sky and O'Donnell met Meryl in the elaborately decorated foyer featuring long runner rugs, house plants, and a wooden bench, and it smelled more like baked weed as opposed to smoked.

"I love what you've done with the place, Meryl," O'Donnell said. "It really is a true Bohemian paradise in the heart of Berkeley."

"*Aww,* thank you, Ryan! It's so good to see you *not hammered* in Glasgow!" she replied with a wink. "So, now that you guys are here, let's go enjoy the dinner we've prepared for you. Everyone's chilling in the back yard, follow me."

Meryl ushered them to the back of the house and opened a white door that went out to a rusty staircase. The staircase led down to a lush vegetable garden that ran along the perimeter of the back yard's fence, and their open grassy area featured a long, wooden table that was already set up for a feast. A few of the housemates had already begun the festivities by drinking wine out of a glass jug, and the whole group cheered when the three of them appeared in the doorway. They'd been patiently waiting to uncover a large chafing dish containing vegetarian curry and rice, and each of Meryl's roommates politely introduced themselves as they prepared their plates and gathered around the table.

O'Donnell forgot to mention that a dinner party had been planned, and although it was something Sky typically wouldn't miss out on, he knew he couldn't stay too long. About forty-five minutes later, O'Donnell was tipsy and flirting with Meryl as they giggled in a hammock underneath the outdoor staircase. Seeing them begin to catch up with each other was Sky's cue to get going and drive across the bay to San Francisco, so he gave his cordial thanks to Meryl and her roommates while explaining how his aunt, uncle, and cousin were expecting him.

Sky's uncle, Jacob Rose, was an environmental lawyer who had worked in China for many years, and it was in Beijing where he met his American wife Leanne, who at the time was working as an English teacher. The two of them had already fallen in love with Chinese culture prior to falling in love with each other, and they eventually were married in China when Sky was a toddler. Before Jacob and Leanne returned to the United States, they adopted a Chinese boy, who they named Lin. They moved to Delaware when Lin was a newborn, and their home was less than a half hour away from where Sky and Byrd grew up. After about six years of living on the East Coast, they started missing Chinese culture and decided to make a consolation move to the middle of San Francisco's Chinatown. Jacob and Leanne were always more financially well off than the entire Rose family, so they'd fly to Delaware for holidays and all sorts of family gatherings. Because they insisted on traveling east, it was Sky's first time meandering the steep Chinatown hills as he drove his Chevy past fish markets, produce stands, and authentic Chinese bakeries.

Sky was a little more than five years older than Lin, and they quickly started to drift into polar opposites after Jacob and Leanne decided to move to California. Sky was often jealous of Lin as they grew up, because it became clearer with time that Lin was a wonder child and Sky simply wasn't quite as wonderful. When Sky was rebellious and experimenting with drugs as a teenager, Lin was getting straight As and on edge about the dangers of gateway drugs; and when Lin started getting opportunities to advance his budding career as a violinist, Sky started an entry-level position at a record store in Boulder. They didn't have too much in common, except for one very important aspect of their lives: music. They also happened to be polar opposites as musicians, even though they both started music classes at the same spot in Delaware. But Lin was only six years old when he and his parents moved to San Francisco, and growing up in the city ended up shaping Lin's insatiable interest in playing traditional Chinese songs on violin.

Tourists and locals alike would marvel at Lin's childhood talents when Leanne would let him perform on their neighborhood streets, but learning and ultimately mastering the violin was only just the beginning for Lin. By sixteen, he had become one of San Francisco's most prized teenage philharmonic virtuosos. He could play just about anything with strings, but the way Lin played violin would seamlessly transport his listeners to the classical past in a wholesome way that brought tears to even the most experienced conductor's eyes. Lin also had a knack for building up an audience too. Jacob and Leanne gave him a DSLR camera one year for Christmas when he was thirteen, and he ended up creating countless videos of symphony classics and contemporary covers that took off throughout the Web. Before Lin even began his senior year of high school, he was offered a full-ride scholarship to NYU's Steinhardt School, which was blatantly attempting to get a leg up on Julliard. It was now the middle of his last summer before college when Sky came to visit and inadvertently wreak havoc on everything his achievements had built up to.

Sky glanced down at Leanne's email instructions that told him to drive into the alleyway behind their building and click 2541 on the garage's keypad, park in a guest spot, and take the elevator to the top floor, where they'd be in unit 302. As he glanced at his TomTom GPS device, he scanned his Chinatown surroundings and noticed how the final 0.3 miles comprised the steepest hill of the entire road trip. He slowly made his way up the hill while yielding to pedestrians and braking for traffic, and he luckily recognized the extra spacing between cars to accommodate the time it took to release brakes and accelerate. *These hills are no joke,* he thought as the van barely moved at over 4,000 RPM. Sure enough, he found the garage in what he figured was one of the smelliest alleyways he'd ever been in. He noticed a few homeless guys smoking cigarettes next to a small stoop, and it was obvious that they had dinner plans with the strong stench of vegetables and meats emanating from the nearby restaurant dumpsters. He'd never witnessed a scene quite like that with people waiting for a restaurant to throw out some trash, so he got out of the van and handed each of them ten dollars before backing up and turning into the residential garage.

As he entered the garage, the entire atmosphere shifted to a chic, affluent ambience with everything being brand new, including the parked cars. He noticed his uncle's silver Jaguar sedan by the customized license plate, ROSEESQ, and he parked his crumbling van in a guest spot next to a swanky sports car. He brought one tiny backpack up the elevator, which took him to a long, skinny hallway on the building's third floor. The door at the end of the hallway to his left had #301 on it, so he proceeded to his right in the direction of the only other door that read #302.

He exchanged familial niceties with Leanne, Jacob, and Lin, who then gave him a tour of their longtime home that they knew he'd never been to. Sky perused their collection of expensive art with Chinese influences, and he scratched his head in amazement at their personalized museum. The feng shui of each room was clearly noticeable, and everything was spatially organized to absolute perfection. One décor theme that spoke out to Sky was their collection of antique instruments that hung from the walls, including an Erhu, Dizi, Pipa, Suona, and other traditional Chinese instruments that they'd collected over the years. Although these instruments weren't necessarily for playing, they acted as indirect testaments to how Jacob and Leanne were supportive of Lin's musical endeavors throughout his childhood. *God knows they had the money to support him,* Sky thought as they showed him their large balcony perched above a bustling Chinatown street.

Aunt Leanne and Uncle Jacob were as kindhearted as he'd remembered them to be, but he couldn't help but sense a strange detachment with Lin. Throughout the entire house tour, Lin remained silent and let his parents do most of the talking. Lin did ask a couple of basic questions about Boulder and answered a couple of other basic questions about his upcoming departure for New York, but Sky noticed a disconnect between Lin and just about everything else around him. He almost seemed blind as he'd blankly stare out the windows while Sky and his parents chatted with each other, and his mind-drifting idiosyncrasies reminded Sky of Byrd. So when Leanne suggested that Lin show Sky their music room, Sky took this as an opportunity to separate from the parents and actually try to be reintroduced to his prodigy cousin.

Sky recognized the music room from the many YouTube videos

Lin had put out over the past few years, but actually being in the room instead of seeing camera angles helped him notice just how grandiose of a practice area it was for a teenager. It was technically an extra bedroom or office that could've been utilized differently, but providing Lin with a getaway space was exactly what he needed to constantly practice and not disturb the entire household. There was no denying that this room was Lin's sanctuary, and the assortment of string instruments that hung on the walls gave Sky a tiny glimpse into the overall versatility of his cousin's artistry. Sky continued to see how Lin wouldn't provide the type of conversational norms that most people were accustomed to, but he was starting to see that maybe he simply wasn't much of a talker. They were both silent as Lin rummaged through a drawer in the corner of the room looking for *something*.

"Do you wanna play some music?" Sky politely asked, while also imagining that Lin didn't collaborate with just anyone who walked into his refuge.

"Do you have any pot?" Lin responded without looking up from the drawer. "I thought I had some in here, but I can't find it. I think I might've lost it earlier today."

"I didn't know you smoked pot."

"I just started a few months ago when one of my friends said it would ease the pain in my hands. I've also been rubbing CBD cream on my hands lately. No one knows, but people have kept telling me that I've sounded better since around the same time I started smoking and using the cream. We can play a little music tonight if you want to, but the thing is, I just played a lot before you got here, and my fingers are feeling sore. *So*, do you have any pot we could smoke? My parents won't smell it, I promise ..."

The next twenty minutes consisted of Sky taking the elevator down to his car, putting a plastic bag of weed and rolling papers in his pocket, taking the elevator back to the third floor, rolling a joint, and smoking with his cousin for the first time on a narrow fire escape that overlooked an alleyway. It was quite a surprise to find out that Lin liked marijuana, but it made more sense that Lin's smoking habits were oriented around helping him alleviate the pains of playing violin for several hours on a daily basis. It seemed like Lin was always thinking about how to advance his music career until he somehow *made it,* and everyone in the Rose family knew he was easily good enough to one day play in a prestigious symphony orchestra. But no one in the Rose family, except for Sky, knew that Lin *really liked* getting high. As they smoked the joint, they talked about reggae, psychedelic rock, and other stoner music, while also bringing up old memories of Delaware.

"We should go inside and take a picture for Byrd. He said he wants to see how big you've gotten."

"I don't really remember that guy," Lin responded as they stepped off the fire escape and back into the music room.

"Well, he remembers *you.* Do you have any guitars laying around here?"

"I actually don't, which is weird because I could've sworn there was one in here not too long ago. I think my buddy that I buy pot from might be borrowing it. I'll have to text him and see if he's got it, but I have a really great mandolin hanging up in the closet. Check it out and see if you think you can play it," Lin offered.

Lin didn't know that Sky had recently been teetering around with his boss's mandolin in Boulder, and when Sky looked into the closet, he saw what he deemed to be the fanciest mandolin he'd ever seen. It had intricate wooden etchings of roses all along the base and up its tiny neck, and Sky's jaw dropped as he examined it more closely. He started playing rapid, unpredictable chords, and Lin smiled as he examined Sky's swift dexterity.

"So, you know what you're doing," Lin said approvingly as he continued listening to Sky's random riffs. "Should we play a song or something?"

"Yeah, sure," Sky said, stopping on a dime. "What do you wanna play? How about some kind of stoner music cover?"

"Like what? I don't really know stoner music like you do, but I do like playing a couple Pink Floyd songs, and I also know a couple Dead songs like 'Ramble on Rose' and ... I don't know the other song's name about roses," he said with a stoned giggle.

"How about Tom Petty? 'Mary Jane's Last Dance' is about as stoner as it gets, and I know it sounds good on strings."

Within the next half hour, Lin was able to listen to the Petty song online, look up how to play it on violin, rehearse it a handful of times, and memorize it perfectly. Sky didn't need the practice as much because "Mary Jane's Last Dance" was one of the few songs he actually knew how to play on mandolin, and he'd played it on multiple occasions when the record store he worked at was empty. Once Lin felt comfortable playing the whole song, he recommended another joint. So they once again smoked outside and came back into the music room fully lit like a firework-filled night. Lin set his camera on a tripod in the corner of the room and readjusted it for the perfect focal length to accommodate him and another player.

"We should send Byrd a picture of us holding our instruments before we start playing. I'm sure he'd get a kick out of that!"

"Why would we send him a pic of us holding instruments when we can send him a video of us playing them?" Lin asked as he pressed record on the camera and gave a thumbs up. "*Hey guys,* this is my cousin, Skylar Rose. He's here in Frisco visiting from Boulder, so we're going to do something a little different tonight and play a cover that's pretty popular out in Colorado."

Sky glanced down at the camera's blinking red light, and took a sigh of relief as butterflies ran through his chest and down to his stomach. He hadn't played in front of a camera in a long time, mainly because he was self-conscious of singing in front of people he didn't know.

"You ready?" Lin whispered as he turned away from the camera and looked Sky directly in the eyes. Lin gave a brief wink that said *you got this,* and Sky's side-mirror smile revealed itself.

"Let's break it down one last time for a sweet, sweet, lovely lady by the name of Mary Jane!" Sky emphatically said into the camera. "And a one ... one ... one, two, three, four!"

And the Roses began to bloom.

T here have been countless artists who have uniquely cemented their cultural analyses within the human experience forever, and one of those infinitely famous bands is The Grateful Dead. The Dead were a group headed by the legendary Jerry Garcia, who transcended their art into something so much bigger than their unique sound. They didn't just build an enormously dedicated following of Deadheads who found peace within themselves through the music's uplifting, uninhibited spirit, because they also shaped society toward a distinct interpretation of love. Although The Dead's last studio album was released in 1989, it has been empirically proven that the music itself has a flawless ability to transition from one generation to the next and retain its magic that truly has never stopped. It's safe to say that the vast majority of Millennials and Gen Zers were just a bit too young to show real interest in the reunion bands like RatDog and The Other Ones who followed Garcia's death in 1995, but that all changed when Bob Weir and Phil Lesh teamed up again through the cover band creation of Furthur in 2009.

Two of these newfound Furthur fans, who saw it to themselves to carry on a tradition of following the band from concert to concert, were the catalysts in a destined chronology that formed a new chapter in music's history.

Catalina (Cat) Carvajal was the type of person who was always organized and tried her very best on a daily basis to retain some sort of
order among her personal responsibilities, but the main things that
held her back from achieving her daily goals were her endless strings
of what she considered *golden thoughts*. She was only nineteen when
she started following Furthur around the country, and she was quite
a bit different from most of the vendors you'd see in concert parking
lots. She barely knew what she was doing at first, yet somehow kept
her tiny business at least a little bit manageable. Her *only one way to
find out* mentality inevitably endeared her to a lot of people partying
before or after the shows, and the biggest Deadheads saw her as an
opportunity to pass on their decades of Shakedown street smarts.

Another big factor in terms of what separated Cat from some of
the other vendors who traveled with Furthur was that the amount
of money she made on a nightly basis didn't make all that much of a
difference to her. Cat hadn't experienced a negative thought in her
entire young life when it came to the amount of money she had or
would come to have, and this was mainly because she was from the
same neighborhood of Brentwood as Thayer. Her inherent privilege
did play a significant role in how she was able to afford to travel
around the country as a teenager, but anyone who met Cat could tell
right away that she was different than most other Brentwood girls.
Although she was beautiful like many of them, she had an emphatic
depth that anyone could notice within seconds of talking to her. She
was simply easy to talk to and had a ton of ambition to boot, but her
transition into a teenage hippie following Furthur would've never
been possible without Ruben.

Ruben Bazan was what a lot of prejudicial people would call a
wook, alluding to Chewbacca and the excessively hairy wookiees
of *Star Wars*. He started growing dreads when he was nine, and by
twenty-one, he'd only had a couple of trims here and there to re-
move a few pesky knots. He also grew up in LA, but pretty far from
Brentwood in Pico Rivera. But being anywhere remotely close to
the Pacific would cause Ruben to gravitate toward swimming and
surfing, no matter what time of year it was, which was essentially

the driving force in how he met Cat in a remote corner of Point Dume when they were both enjoying Christmas vacations during their junior years of high school. It was immediately apparent that Ruben was unlike all the guys Cat had grown up with, and they hit it off and had kept going steady for over two years by the time they were journeying across the country in the same directions as the Furthur buses.

There was never any denying that Cat was taking a major chance by entrusting her time to a surfer bro she met on the beach, but when she found out about Ruben's talents beyond sex and surfing, it helped her better understand that their new love could be a long-term partnership. Ruben's parents followed the Dead in the seventies, eighties and early nineties, and they sold all sorts of different shirts before eventually investing in a brick-and-mortar shop that sold psychedelic retail, bongs, pipes, and other *head* products. Ruben was just six years old when his parents opened the shop, so he also went along for the ride to many shows when he was a toddler. The Bazans were an authentic California hippie family, and their entire journey infatuated Cat.

When she found out that Ruben was the designer for many of the shirts in the store, it was like he gave her the keys to the door she didn't know was right in front of her. She made him teach her how to do perfect tie-dyes and design trippy shirts that would sell, and as Cat learned the trade, she also kept tabs on how Ruben's parents operated their modest business. Ruben's weekly position as the drummer in a surf rock garage band, which didn't actually play anywhere else but in garages, was also a major turn-on that kept Cat more than curious as they continued to get to know each other.

When it came time for Cat and Ruben to apply for college, they decided not to go with the rationale that it wouldn't be a good use of their time. This plan didn't sit too well with the Carvajal family, so Cat single-handedly consolidated a new plan that was based around the idea of her parents helping fund her future in a different way than an education. This ended up manifesting itself in a used Volkswagen van, a portable printing press, a large assortment of high-quality inks, cooking equipment, an Exxon credit card, and a humble investment in blank T-shirts of various colors. She also presented a clear-cut business model to reinvent what Ruben's parents did while following the Dead, except she'd go a bit further with social media marketing. Surprisingly, her parents were on board to see how her entrepreneurial aspirations would pan out, and within a few months, she and Ruben had created hundreds of stellar tie-dyes that would sell like hotcakes at every show's parking lot.

When their first Furthur tour ended, Ruben and Cat decided they didn't want their van life to stop. Cat ended up spending a portion of their profits on a Shiba Inu puppy, and she began utilizing her small social media following to be a spokesperson for dog products, athletic apparel, and just about any brand that liked her. Within a couple more months of living on the road together, she was essentially a model for a variety of different companies. Her newfound success as a brand ambassador caused her accounts to skyrocket in popularity, and by the beginning of 2012, she had over twenty-five thousand fans.

Ruben renovated the van while they kept warm during the coldest portions of that winter at his parents' house, and being by the beach naturally led Cat to bikini and surfing modeling. She started raking in checks that allowed them to get more upgraded equipment and supplies, and the van restoration project took Ruben just about the entire winter as he shifted his time between surfing, tie-dyeing, and taking pictures of Cat.

Her following rose beyond fifty thousand by the time they hit the road again for their second summer tour. Her newer followers quickly noticed how much of a hippie she was, which then allowed her to promote all sorts of tour products to an entirely new target audience. Whether it was psychedelic jewelry, clothing, or any type of retail, various vendors started paying Cat a significant profit percentage to sell their products at concert venues and online. So, within two years, Ruben and Cat were essentially changing the game by making plenty of cash even before they arrived at each Furthur show.

Cat's clients' products were selling extremely hot, but their tie-dye shirts were lingering longer than expected. There were also some nights when Ruben wouldn't sell any shirts at all and instead would do a hit of acid and find a random drum circle to join. Although she couldn't always keep Ruben under wraps, Cat maintained strict accounting efforts of her sales and subsequent earnings from each show. This financial organization provided her with tangible proof of dramatic sales decreases whenever Ruben skirted away, and she was never afraid to let their numbers do the talking.

On the fourteenth of June 2012, Ruben was driving the van through Arizona en route to Brentwood while Cat sat in the passenger's seat with their one-year-old dog, Nikita, in her lap. Their second tour was coming to a close as the traveling circus of hippies began descending upon LA, and at that point, there was no denying that Cat's social media clients were keeping them financially afloat. In the middle of the desert, Cat had one of her first signs of doubt in terms of what she'd been doing with her life, and for the first time in a very long time, slight slivers of regret in not going to college crept in. She always told herself that she could go back to college later in life and not need her family's finances to make it work, which seemed even more plausible now that she'd solidified herself as an influencer. They sat in silence listening to live Dead recordings while Cat furtively looked into tuition costs at several community colleges across California, and although the adventure bug still held its lasting bite on each of them, Cat was excited to be going back home to see Furthur play at the Greek Theatre on the fifteenth.

She swiped out of the community college tab on her phone and went to one of her social accounts, which reported her current following of 70,286 people from across the world. She smiled looking at the number on her screen, because reaching seventy thousand followers was a personal milestone she wanted to reach by the end of that tour. There was still plenty of room for improvement with a couple of shows left to go, so she rolled down the window and turned the focus of her phone's camera toward herself in selfie mode. As Nikita reached her nose into the rushing stream of Arizona air, Cat extended her arm into the wind and revealed her bright white smile that attracted so many people to her vending stand. She approved of a picture and edited it to perfection as she prepared to post it, and she ended up tagging only one dog brand that provided Nikita's psychedelic bandanna before creating the caption: *Can't wait to be back home in Brentwood. See you guys at The Greek Theatre tomorrow!* Thousands of people liked the picture within seconds and commented about how cute Nikita looked, and one of those thousands of people was Thayer Feldman.

Thayer wasn't doing much, just lazily starting her day by reading a screenplay in her back yard. As she glanced at Cat's selfie and looked through her profile, she started catching up with her high school friend who she hadn't seen in years. Thayer could barely believe how Cat was able to grow such a huge online following, and she couldn't help but feel a bit jealous of how serene Cat's life appeared on her screen. Thayer was also bored beyond belief with the morning she was having, so she went out on a whim and commented: *Hey Cat and Ruben! I'm in Brentwood too. Would love to see you guys!*

For Cat, seeing Thayer's comment was a much-needed sign that her childhood friends still wanted to know her beyond social media. They began to message each other privately, while also coordinating what they could do in LA together. Cat was adamant that she clearly wanted Thayer to come with them to the show at The Greek the next day, and their reunion plans were solidified when Thayer confirmed her ticket purchase. Thayer also invited them to her parents' house so they could take a road trip–cleansing swim later that afternoon, which they cordially accepted.

Cat, Ruben, and Nikita arrived at Thayer's house around 3 p.m., and Ruben almost immediately left to meet up with his buddies for an afternoon surf session along the PCH. Thayer was surprised by how much Cat was interested in exploring Brentwood, so they went to a few neighborhood shops, where Cat tried on and eventually purchased a new one-piece swimsuit. It was just after 6 p.m. and still plenty bright out when they got back to Thayer's house after doing happy hour at a sushi restaurant, so Cat decided to put on her new purchase and have Thayer be her photographer by the pool. But before Thayer could even register what was going on, they were taking selfies together while sitting on lounge chairs. It was a pretty typical pool pic, except for the disparity between Cat's perfect body in her new suit and Thayer's sunburnt complexion, wearing jeans and a T-shirt. No one was ever going to think much of that picture's blatant disparity except Thayer, but after a few minutes of reflection, she decided to post it on social media to her 167 followers.

One of Thayer's fans was Madison, who didn't take longer than fifteen minutes to arrive at the pool unannounced. Thayer held her eyes shut and tried to hide her laughter as Madison triumphantly walked into the back yard, as if her arrival indicated some kind of grand reunion between her and Cat. Cat kind of remembered Madison but didn't talk to her all that much during high school, and she also had no idea how much Madison envied her social media following and would do just about anything to get that same kind of online attention.

"O-M-G, Cat! Welcome back to the hood, *girl*! I saw Thayer's pic and thought I'd stop by and say *whassup*! How long are you in town for?" Madison rattled off.

"We're only here for the Furthur show at the Greek Theatre tomorrow night, and then we're heading up north for the tour finale."

"Oh ... what's *Furthur* like?" Madison asked.

"It's the same guys from The Grateful Dead, so they play their old songs ..."

"Wait, shut the fuck up! The *Grateful fucking Dead* is playing at The Greek tomorrow?" Madison asked rhetorically, while Cat smiled and nodded. "I'm *so* down. I'm telling J. P. to get us tickets, *for sure.*"

Thayer kept nodding her head slightly as she reassured herself it was a good thing that Madison and J. P. were coming along for the concert as they meandered down Sunset Boulevard in a rideshare that next afternoon, but she more than likely would've arranged a different ride if it weren't for the fact that Cat and Ruben needed to arrive in the parking lot several hours before the show started to claim their vending spot. Thayer promised she'd provide a hand before and after the show for whatever was needed, but arriving roughly eight hours early seemed *almost* as awkward as pregaming with Madison, J. P., and their seemingly limitless cocaine.

As they inched down Vermont Avenue in a midafternoon LA traffic jam, it came across J. P's ever slowly racing mind that they could more comfortably walk the rest of the way to the venue instead of steeping in the East Hollywood heat. Madison looked at the driver's displayed phone indicating there was a mile left on the ride, and this didn't sit too well.

Thayer cowered in the corner of the back seat as J. P. and Madison exchanged their rationale behind why exactly *this* was best. Her head began to pulsate as the debate thickened, so instead of listening, she stuck her head out the window and began people-watching in the heart of Little Armenia. She homed in on a group of homeless people meandering along the sidewalk together. *Where are they planning on going tonight?*

She tried putting herself in the shoes of a homeless woman pushing a shopping cart full of blankets, clothes, and other miscellaneous possessions. As she continued wondering what it might be like to not know what to do on a daily basis and perhaps choose to walk around unnecessarily to spend time, she began experiencing a strange connection to this random woman. It had been well over a month since she'd finished school, and she still had zero idea as to what her plans were, or even how to spend her time each day. *Unnecessary walking* just so happened to seem like an obscure, out-of-nowhere answer to what she was currently going through, and it also just so happened to be Madison's reasoning *not to walk* to the venue, due to already almost being there.

Thayer looked through her pockets, found a twenty, and got out of the car to catch up with the shopping-cart lady. J. P. immediately followed, which made Madison loudly cuss into the street.

The driver assumed he'd completed the fare, but Madison insisted that they continue the ride with her as the sole passenger. She then mockingingly yelled out the window about how she'd be waiting at the entrance for them, but neither of them was listening as Thayer initiated a conversation with the homeless woman and handed her the cash. Madison did eventually succumb to unnecessary walking about ten minutes later when Thayer and J. P. walked past her about a tenth of a mile from the parking lot, where Ruben and Cat were doing their thing at the tour's biggest marketplace.

All the LA Furthur fans loved hearing Cat's story about how she grew up in the city and turned herself into a young Deadhead entrepreneur, and Ruben was remaining as competent as ever while frothing with the dudes considering one of their custom screen-printed shirts. They were unquestionably the youngest couple who followed the band, and it was easy for them to lure people toward their van, with Cat looking great as always and simply saying something like *Hey, how's it going?*

"OMG, you guys are seriously the cutest wook couple I've ever seen in my entire life! *Wow*, look at these *shirts*! They're so *hippie-dippie*, I *love* it!" Madison yelled as they came across their setup. She and Cat started going off on a tirade of topics including clothes, concerts, and social media, which left Thayer, J. P. and Ruben staring blankly at each other.

"Let me know if you need anything. I'd be happy to help you guys sell some shirts," Thayer offered Ruben, who was now drifting off while looking in the direction of the other vendors throughout the parking lot.

"Yeah, actually ..." he responded, recognizing that Cat was busy with Madison. "One of my tour buddies sometimes lets me play his drum set before the shows, so I might need to bounce soon. Stand here behind the table and just talk to whoever's interested in the shirts. I'll be over on the other side of the lot, jamming with a few friends for a few minutes. But yeah, you got this," he encouraged before disappearing into the endless crowd of hippies.

Selling shirts in a concert parking lot was new to Thayer, so she watched Cat for a couple of minutes and quickly picked up on the typical greetings and questions that worked well with each passerby. After ten minutes, she sold one of Ruben's tie-dyes, which caused Cat to give her a congratulatory golf clap. Cat called her a *shakedown natural*, which prompted a wide smile.

All this casual companionship happening right in front of Madison bottled up the envy inside her ever-so-feeble mind. She had just taken a large bump of coke with J. P. in the back of Cat's van, and her passive-aggressiveness began to effervesce like the tiniest of hermit crab air bubbles gurgling on a beach.

"Isn't Cat just *amazing*?" Madison asked Thayer upon her return to the tie-dye table. They noticed how Cat was once again describing a product to a shopper, this time a zip-up blanket featuring colorful cartoon bears.

"Yeah, I like her a lot. I'm really happy I messaged her yesterday." Thayer replied with another wide smile.

"Me too," Madison responded as a long, awkward silence fell among the three of them, which didn't bother J. P. as he watched a Dodgers game on his phone. "It's kinda crazy how her and Ruben have been a couple for *so long*, don't ya think?" she asked innocently.

"Yeah, I guess so, but it's also pretty crazy that *anyone* can stay a couple after years of living in a van together!"

"OMG, I know! I can't believe they actually *live* in *that*," Madison teased as she scrutinized the details of the van. "She can seriously do *so* much better than *this*."

Thayer looked around to get her own understanding of what *this* was, and she instantly recognized a few psychedelic enthusiasts roaming past them with their eyes sparkling from the early effects of LSD. She saw young kids playing tag as their parents looked on while drinking beers, as well as countless groups of people in tie-dye shirts laughing, smoking weed, and meandering through the maze of merchants. Some people she saw were old with gray hair and long beards, and some were just as young as she. She realized how every age demographic was right there with them in the parking lot, and everyone was celebrating the same music.

"I don't know, I think Cat likes *this*. At least it seems like she's living the life on the internet!"

"I know, *right*? I just think she's like *perfect*, ya know? She can do anything she wants cuz she's smart, funny, good with business. She's literally like the *real deal*. But I just don't see why she stays with Ruben. I mean, he's kinda like a *total wook*. Ya know what I mean?"

Just as Thayer was failing to think of something polite to say, she heard loud music off in the distance and came to the conclusion that helping Cat wasn't worth being around Madison any longer.

"I'm gonna go see what our *total wook* friend is doing over there," she said, while motioning to the music with a smug smile. "You wanna cover for me here and help out Cat?"

"Of course! Go ahead, we've got it covered!" she said as she began clamoring out an unnecessary sales strategy with Cat, as if serendipity was coming together and the Dream Team was finally forming.

"You wanna help me get something out of the van real quick?" Thayer asked J. P., getting his attention by putting her index finger up to her right nostril.

It was more than enough said. The two of them met up with Nikita in the van and tooted a couple bumps up their honkers, after which Thayer meandered through the crowd as she walked toward the familiar sounds of "Franklin's Tower." Within a minute, she was in front of a band that looked like they jumped straight out of a 1968 Ralph Lauren magazine with all of them wearing cricket sweaters and flannel suits. Two guitarists and one bass player were hooked up to large, portable speakers and microphones as they played in front of about forty fans who were more than ready to start dancing. Their upbeat rhythm was anchored by the andante tempo set by a sweater-clad Ruben on the drums, and Thayer was more than impressed by the gig he'd casually stumbled into after his departure from the vending stand. The four of them played perfectly in sync with one another, until a few cops showed up to kill the vibes and shoo the nonpermitted crowd away after about fifteen minutes. But before the buzzkill, Thayer got her first real glimpse into the relationship between the Dead and the Deadheads. To her, it was like everyone was experiencing a Pavlovian response to rotate their hips, tap their shoes, and lose themselves in the jam.

Later that evening, all five of them were at the tippy-top of The Greek and looking down at Bob Weir and Phil Lesh like they were mini-munchkins capable of magically bending thousands of minds with each stroke of their strings. Things were starting to get weird as Furthur meandered through a ten-minute instrumental jam, and Madison started complaining about how *they never sing* and how she was *too stoned to dance*. A silent meeting of the minds between Ruben, Cat, and Thayer indicated it might be time to split, and that was the exact moment when the complex jam calmed itself and revealed the initial riff of "Franklin's Tower," to the crowd's delight. Ruben's classical conditioning caused him to immediately jump up from his seat and start dancing in a wayward circle with Cat.

"Screw these seats, let's go down to the bottom!" he yelled out as Cat agreed, and they started dancing down the steps.

Cat glanced back up at Thayer while raising her eyebrows as if to say *are you on the bus or not?*, which led Thayer to take off without even the slightest remark to J. P. or Madison. She tried her best to maneuver through the crowd to the beat of the song while tracking Ruben's dreads as they bobbed up and down ahead of her. She wasn't exactly sure what Ruben was thinking by *going down to the bottom*, but much to her surprise, the security guards did nothing as they danced their way to a much-improved group of seats with plenty of space for each of them.

"I'm so glad we ditched them! Madison is maybe the most annoying person I've ever gone to a show with! She's so closed-minded, it's nauseating!" Cat yelled over to Thayer as they settled into their new seats.

"Yeah, she's an *Anti-Wookite!*" Thayer yelled, making Cat crack up. Cat relayed the message to Ruben, who laughed in between dance moves. "Ruben's band was awesome playing this song earlier. My bad for leaving you alone with them, that must've sucked!"

"He *loves* this song!" she said, laughing.

"Every Deadhead does!"

"Do you wanna come up to the Berkeley show with us? It's sold out, but I'm sure Ruben could get you a GA ticket!"

"Yeah, why not? I have nothing else to do!"

"Hell, yeah! Do you by chance know a good place up there where we could park the van after the show?"

"Yeah, I know the *perfect* spot!"

Lin was the guy who focused on his GPA instead of playing video games, practiced an assortment of instruments instead of partying, and had seconds and thirds of his mother's homemade dim sum instead of having second and third rounds of sex with the girls he grew up with. He was both ashamed and proud of his virginity, and his expectations of the *first girl* were comically preposterous. One of the main reasons why Lin studied instead of playing Xbox Live and practiced violin instead of going to house parties was because he intuitively *just knew* that it would all pay off in preparing him for that ensuing girl of his dreams. Inevitably, this hypothetical fantasy turned into more of an abstract expectation than an actual woman as the years kept ticking, but Lin unnecessarily kept the "big picture" in mind on a constant basis.

This illusion led to extravagant expectations of himself that controlled his decision-making on a daily basis toward what he thought were *smart moves.* When he stayed back in Chinatown instead of drinking warm beer on China Beach with his friends, he'd say to himself, *this is the smart move.* His infinite progression of smart moves created an all-encompassing box within which his life operated, and he generally had absolutely no problems with that. His comfort zone, after all, played a significant role in guiding him down the habitual path of becoming a virtuoso violinist with a growing YouTube audience and a scholarship to NYU, but he was just now beginning to understand the full scope of why marijuana was called a gateway drug. It might've gotten him more curious about other highs like the standard interpretation, but it also showed him the slightest exit portal leading outside his inner box.

"I just don't think it's a smart move for me right now," Lin said as he paced back and forth across his music room while looking at Sky, who wasn't listening as he focused on the cover of a home décor magazine featuring a small pile of weed and rolling papers on it. "Maybe you should just go without me. I'm sure one of your friends will want your extra ticket."

Sky subtly smiled to himself so Lin wouldn't recognize it, and he licked the adhesive of the newly formed joint with the tip of his tongue to finalize it. As he examined his latest creation, he continued scheming about how he'd convince Lin to come with him to see Furthur.

"Okay, dude. I get it, it's all good. If you don't wanna go to the Dead show, just don't go. I'm about to meet back up with O'Donnell, so it's not like I'll be by myself if you don't come. And let's be real, it's not for everyone, and everyone knows that. But before you decide not to go, can I ask you a few questions?"

"Umm, okay."

"So, do you have anything in particular you need to do tomorrow?"

"Tomorrow is Sunday, so my mom usually wants me to help her make dim sum in the afternoon."

Sky couldn't hold back his smile this time, which made Lin crack a smile too.

"That sounds *great*, we should definitely do that tomorrow afternoon," Sky continued. "I love dim sum, but I already talked to your mom, and even *she* wants you to come out and have a fun time tonight. She also said she might look for tickets and go to the show with your dad! I'm not sure if they're going to actually go, but the point I'm trying to make is that making dim sum tomorrow is a dumb excuse. It's not a smart move to prioritize lame excuses over a good time. So, let me ask you another, easier question: do you like playing violin in a philharmonic?"

"Yeah, of course I do. *Duh!*" Lin responded with a feigned tone.

"Well, then you're going to love this music! Furthur is kinda like the trippy philharmonic. They go off for what seems like forever on these instrumental tangents that suck you into a mind-bending time warp that no other music is quite capable of," he lectured as he lightly waved the joint in the air like a conductor's baton. "So, if you *actually* like music in general, then you should probably come tonight just to hear what this band sounds like. Now, my last question is the most important, and it's something I want you to *really* think about: how many of your friends are like me?"

Lin sighed as he compared and contrasted his friends and Sky, and he naturally resorted back to his comfort zone thought process within a matter of seconds. When it came down to it, if he didn't go to the concert, he'd simply do exactly what he always did, and he'd also risk losing Sky's respect. He also considered the fact that he was moving to Manhattan in less than two months and didn't know anyone there, so if anything, it was a smart move to practice introducing himself.

"You know, it might storm later," he warned as he rummaged through a closet and pulled out a raincoat, subsequently signaling his willingness to go.

"I hope it does. You could fry an egg on the hood of my Chevy right now!"

To put it simply, Thayer was *thirsty* later that evening as she mingled around Meryl's backyard from one guy to the next. She didn't fully understand why, but every conversation stirred up a snake within her that tingled its way from her belly to her throat, causing saliva to sporadically build up around her tongue. When Sky and Lin walked down the metal staircase and she got her very first glimpse of the Rose boys, that same tingling squirmed downwards to her waist. Sky conjured up a more fuckable memory of *Fast Times at Ridgemont High's* Jeff Spicoli, and his sarcastic aura as he yelled, *HEY EVERYBODY,* made her cheeks and chest feel as if they were on fire. By the time they left for the Greek Theatre, Thayer knew all about the Roses and how she was talking to the most talented musicians in the family. She also figured out that Sky didn't actually know anyone else at Meryl's pregame party except O'Donnell, who was the person she knew the least.

As the crew of about twenty people meandered up Telegraph Avenue, they naturally began to form their own sub-niches among each other. These harmless conversations did ultimately end up deciphering the entire night's sequence of events, especially for Lin. Meryl and her friends were intrigued by him and his Chinatown upbringing, and after a few minutes, he showed them the "Mary Jane's Last Dance" video that now had 40,182 views on YouTube. Everyone in that sub-niche told Lin how impressed they were with the Tom Petty cover, and Sky was over a block ahead, listening to Thayer describe what it was like to attend the LA Furthur show with Cat and Ruben, while he patiently waited to describe what it was like to attend the show at Red Rocks Amphitheatre earlier in the tour.

They all made it to the heart of campus about fifteen minutes later and found Cat and Ruben hustling their merch in the makeshift marketplace. It was the tour finale, and they were selling more in Berkeley than at any other show that entire summer. When Cat asked Thayer if she could help out while Ruben jammed with the sixties Ralph Lauren crew, it was a vague indication that she and Sky would temporarily split up.

Lin noticed how Sky was acting a bit strange, as he explained that he was going to stick around with Thayer for another couple minutes, but he realized why when he later saw them do a key bump of coke in Cat's van. He figured it'd be a smart move to give them privacy, so he meandered around the crowded parking lot by himself. That night's Deadhead type of preshow party was something brand new to Lin, and every vendor drew in his attention as he perused their inventories. He didn't know where he was going as he mazed his way past hundreds of Shakedown shoppers, but the mere fact that he was out of his comfort zone and around different people made him nod his head in approval. He eventually found O'Donnell, Meryl, and her friends by Ruben's impromptu show after five minutes of roaming the lot, and that was where Meryl offered him LSD. He quickly refused, but told her *maybe later* to keep his cool.

Sky showed up a few minutes later and told Lin that he'd been searching all over the marketplace for him, but he got sidetracked within a few seconds of hearing Ruben and his vintage-clad tour buddies. He homed in on Ruben's body language as his catchy drum repetitions drove the band's rhythm into a New Orleans funk jam. Sky had played with several drummers throughout his time in Boulder, so he had an attuned ear to recognize Ruben's embellishments, until he lost all bodily control as the jam transitioned into "Franklin's Tower."

Cat and Thayer rejoined the group on the GA floor right before the concert started, where Meryl was passing around weed cookies that she sneaked in through her purse's secret compartment. They all munched on the cookies featuring various amounts of THC as they waited for the show to start, and Lin was beginning to feel groovier than ever as Furthur took the stage. He had no idea what to expect from a live Grateful Dead performance, so he watched everyone else remaining in unison with the rhythm and followed suit. By the end of the first song, he was embracing the sweat accumulating around his ears in the middle of the hippest concert he'd ever been to. By the end of the second song, his curiosity toward all the uninhibited dancing around him began to itch, so he twisted his way over to Meryl and asked her a few questions about LSD. Meryl reassured him that if he took just one tab, he'd barely feel any effects. She also explained how he was in the right place at the right time to experience his first trip.

Things started to poke around within Lin's perspective by the time the band was coming back on stage for their second set. When he tried to explain to Sky how there was a tingling sensation in his fingers and throat, he was simply advised to *just enjoy where the music takes you.* That's when Ruben had the idea to go right in front of the stage, which put Lin in an awkward position due to his adamant need to not lose Sky in the crowd. As Ruben, Cat, Thayer, and Sky danced their way through the pit, Lin began to experience his very first hallucinations.

The lights started flickering just the slightest bit faster than they normally would, and their colorful refractions remained in the air just the slightest bit longer. Everyone's pulsating movements in the now-dark crowd became more complex to maneuver around, and the only appropriate way to do so was to catch the rhythm and try to slide by. It was becoming more and more obvious by the second that the LSD was kicking in, due to just how long it would take him to get from one tiny opening to another, but Lin *really knew* he was tripping when he glanced about twenty feet ahead and saw Thayer's face blinking back at him through the crowd. All the dancing in between them made it trickier to reach Thayer's face as it intermittently flashed every few seconds, and by the time he reached them near the front rail, it seemed as though he'd just finished an epic journey full of bends and turns through a potent abundance of humid humanity. Thayer and Sky laughed at Lin's exhaustion, and it started drizzling, right on cue. Lin looked up to the heavens as the raindrops fell on his face, and when he turned back to the stage to wipe his eyes, he noticed Thayer's hand reach out and hold Sky's.

Lin's mind started racing back to reality with thoughts like, *I should put on the raincoat, where did I put the raincoat,* and *maybe I should leave the pit and find shelter.* But he noticed how everyone else seemed to be thoroughly enjoying the rain, so he lifted his arms in the air and let out a loud scream that was then echoed by others behind him. He turned around and looked back into the sea of gyrating people, and he saw a blurry moonlight poking itself out from behind the clouds. He glanced back down at the crowd and made eye contact with a man over three times his age, and the sheer instance of locking eyes with one another for a couple of agonizingly long seconds made it seem as though their souls were reaching into a mystical nexus.

"Is the music in your bones yet?" the man asked, which took Lin a second to register as light sarcasm.

"It sure feels like it's in my bones!" he responded loudly, which made a few people around them start laughing.

The entire crowd rang out in unison: *Nothing left to do but SMILE, SMILE, SMILE,* and that's exactly what Lin did for the rest of the show.

☯

Meryl's crew dispersed to various munchie spots after the concert ended, which left Thayer, Sky, and Lin eating burritos by Cat's van. Cat and Ruben were still selling merch, while Thayer and Sky laughed hysterically at Lin's description of his conversation with the kindred Deadhead. They'd been hanging out by the van for over half an hour when a shirtless O'Donnell, who looked like he'd just gotten out of the shower due to his hair still glistening from the second set rain, seemingly popped up out of nowhere.

"Well, *that* got weird!" he yelled as everyone was happy to see him in one piece. "I gotta admit, those guys have this innate power to suck you in and *gazurk your gizzards*! Did you have a good show, young Padawan?" he asked Lin, who was stuffing his face with a burrito while sitting on the grass.

Lin nodded and tried to shuffle out a few words, but his mouth was way too full to be understood.

"Now *that* is what a satisfied Deadhead sounds like!" O'Donnell continued as Thayer and Sky laughed at how aggressively Lin was scarfing down his carne asada delicacy. This over-the-top laughter caught Ruben's attention, which drew him over.

"I still can't believe I have *a whole week* off till I go back to work. This is gonna be the best week of my life, unless my boss finds out I was tripping balls out here. You think my pupils will look normal again, Padawan, or are they stuck like this forever?" O'Donnell continued as he bent down and put his face near Lin's, causing him to nearly lose the food in his mouth from laughing. "Why don't you all come up north with us tomorrow, and we can all go see these big trees I've heard so much about. What else do you jokers have going on?" he asked the group as he stood back up.

"Well, this is the last show of the tour, so we don't have any plans right now," Ruben responded. "I know some pretty cool camp spots up in the Redwoods too."

"That's *pure* braw! I'm starting to like this one," he said, glancing over at Sky and Thayer. "Where else are you gonna take that hippie van of yours this summer? You might as well come check out the weird ole bird's nest when we head home next weekend, if you don't have plans, that is. The guy camps next to the most bonnie thermal pools I've seen in all my traveling years!"

"Is that *James Byrd's* nest you're talking about?" Lin asked from the ground, now finished with his burrito and glancing around the parking lot to find another.

Thayer's eyes widened. She could barely believe her ears.

"How do *you* know Byrd?" she asked Lin, demanding an answer.

"We grew up with him," Sky clarified. "How do *you* know Byrd?"

"He sometimes used to hang out at Meryl's house. He just so happens to be one of my favorite people on the whole gosh-darn planet! I can't believe you guys *grew up* with him! Let's take a pic and send it to him right now!"

7

yrd's motorcycle struggled to roll in the desert as its engine started to overheat. The immense pressure of the afternoon's rays caused all sorts of piercing sounds and jostling along the lifeless highway, and he had to find some way to get out of the sun. All he could think about was the sweat dripping down his face and the ceaseless noises coming from his run-down bike, but he found his stopping place: the same ole trusty gas station where he always filled up. He puttered off the road and parked next to a pump, and that's when he noticed the same van and girls he'd recently met at the next pump over from him. Jane looked exactly like she did the day they met, and just about everything resembled that same encounter besides the fact that she was having trouble getting any fuel out of her pump.

"Hey, I remember *you*," she said as she showed off her unforgettable smile. "You think you could give me a hand real quick? This thing seems jammed."

Byrd thought the pump looked fine and wasn't sure what to do, but standing in front of Jane once again had him in a trance about all the things he *wanted* to do. He didn't say anything as he walked over to her. They maintained the silence as he squeezed the pump, and as his hand clenched the pump's handle, he immediately noticed there wasn't anything wrong at all. Gasoline started rushing through the rubber tubing and her price/gallons began rapidly rolling up. The gas continued to flow out normally as they glanced at each other.

"It seems like you've got a pretty good pump on your hands, Miss Jane," Byrd assumed. "Everything is coming out just fine."

"Great, thanks! Do you wanna just pump it *all* in there for me till it's done?"

Before Byrd knew what was happening, they were making out. He let go of the pump. The pump fell to the ground and spilled out a bit of gas. She said *fuck the pump.* They continued squeezing and clawing at each other up against the van, and then he woke up.

As all his memories instantly rushed back, he felt an overwhelming feeling of regret. He regretted not getting more contact information from Jane, he regretted his choices that led him to waking up on the ground each morning, and he regretted not being a regular part of his mother's life anymore. It was 6:30 a.m., but it felt like noon by the way he was profusely sweating. He took a deep breath, got out of his sleeping bag, walked to his bike's panniers, and reached for his notebook.

He sat up against a tree and pressed the notebook against his knees as he wrote down the following list:

» *I'm thankful for my mom*
» *I'm thankful to live in this place*
» *I'm thankful for my job*
» *I'm thankful for my guitar*
» *I'm thankful for my friends*

Looking at the last bullet point made him shiver for a few seconds as he began reverting to more regretful decisions that had led to his lonerism. He wasn't just thinking of the actual decisions he'd made, but also the myriad of non-decisions that comprised an entire reality that he chose not to partake in. He still had plenty more questions than answers, but he also had a pretty good idea as to how to make everything seem worthwhile: more writing.

The real solar rays continued to beat down throughout the morning and into the afternoon, and by 2 p.m., there was nothing better to do than rest up against some shady rocks in the creek and forget about everything. As he slipped away from his thoughts and into a more transient state, the blurry image of the gas pump still lingered. He was surprised by the vividness of such a strange, sexual fantasy on the other side of the Unified Field, and as much as he tried to let the cold creek help him forget about her, the dreamy image of Jane exasperated any attempt at a tranquil afternoon. He reminded himself of how he was getting low on his food supply, which meant he'd more than likely have to go into town the next morning to greet the real world's obligations. But for right now, he was more than content with being lazy and not putting in any effort into planning for tomorrow.

"Saying *fuck it* just feels so great sometimes," he whispered.

That afternoon was progressing like any other day off he'd had that summer, except he didn't realize how his decision to say *fuck it* to going into town and possibly checking his emails at Surf Zone led him to not knowing about an entire group of road-tripping hooligans shopping in the same grocery store he would've gone to. Although he barely remembered how Sky mentioned that he and O'Donnell might be rolling through Utah around the twenty-third, he didn't realize just how many other people were currently thinking about what he'd enjoy that night for dinner.

He also didn't realize how this unexpected arrival of six guests would forever change his life's trajectory.

"Quit going so *fast*! I'm spilling my drink *all over* myself!" O'Donnell yelled from the back seat of Sky's van as they sped down the five-ish miles of dirt road in the direction of where they at least thought Byrd might be.

"I'm going as slow as I can. Ruben's right on my ass!" Sky replied as he looked over to Lin in the passenger seat and gave a brief wink, before purposely going over some large rocks.

"Jesus, Mary, and *the chain*, you're a harrowing maniac! There's only one solution for this mess you're putting me in, Sky!" he concluded as he chugged his whiskey ginger, to Lin's engrossed delight.

Sky glanced over at his howling cousin and smiled as he noticed how different Lin seemed, compared to a few nights earlier. He reminisced back to five years earlier, when he was eighteen and planning a move away from home with no collegiate enrollment and just an idea of Boulder being a new adventure, and as he listened to O'Donnell rambling nonsense with Lin, he was oddly confident how the next few months of Lin's life would play a significant role in reshaping his future. Those deep thoughts caused Sky not to notice a large pothole in the road.

"You gotta be *kidding me!*" O'Donnell yelled as the pothole's jolt made him spill onto his pants, which caused Lin to snort from laughing so hard.

A few minutes passed until they arrived at Byrd's campsite, which was mainly recognizable by the parked Honda in an opening near the creek. Byrd had just finished an afternoon dip and was hanging his clothes out to dry on a low-hanging branch, so he was naked when he initially heard the sounds of the first van pulling into his driveway. Luckily, his only towel was close by, so he was able to place it around his waist, but that lucky feeling sank down to his stomach and regurgitated itself into embarrassment when he noticed an unknown van following Sky's. As the vans parked, he hid behind a thin tree and succumbed to putting his wet clothes back on to meet his guests.

"Howdy!" he greeted, as he noticed some new faces like Cat and Ruben, as well as familiar ones like Lin and Thayer. "Oh, no way … are you city slickers lost? The hot springs are back *that way!*" he jokingly yelled, pointing in the opposite direction from which they'd come.

Thayer's pure joy in seeing Byrd's smile for the first time in over two years was a true sight to behold for the entire group. She ran up and hugged him with full force, which made them lose their balance as they hobbled in each other's arms for a few feet. She went off at a hundred miles an hour about how much she'd missed him, how awesome his campground seemed, how big his beard had gotten, how much fun she'd been having lately, and how much he was going to love Ruben and Cat. She introduced Byrd to the couple, and it was like seeing a grown-up puppy from the past when he was reintroduced to Lin. Sky explained how he'd recently sent a YouTube video that was likely still one of Byrd's unread emails, and from the moment Byrd high-fived O'Donnell to say *long time no see*, the festivities commenced.

Byrd and Ruben were clearly cut from the same cloth, and they all swapped stories for hours as they got buzzed around a fire and cooked up a dinner that Byrd would've never dreamed of eating earlier in the day. It didn't take long for them to figure out how Byrd didn't see their most recent messages and had no idea they'd planned out a two-day drive to come see him. For Byrd, that evening was already like a miracle water source that had randomly popped up in the middle of the desert, and it only became more magical when Sky suggested a hike to the hot springs.

It was about 10 p.m. when they'd finally returned to the campsite after a few hours of nonstop fun, and throughout the seven hours they'd been there, Thayer felt as though she was getting to know Byrd's lifestyle much better than through any of their recent email exchanges. It was a bit weird to be with him in the flesh and see his subtle idiosyncrasies firsthand, because the "rugged wilderness guy" she imagined while reading his messages was withdrawn, in reality. She'd always admired him for his determination to live out in the elements, but being in front of him helped her recognize his actual circumstances. As beautiful a place as they were in, Thayer couldn't help but sense how there was something significant she was missing about why Byrd enjoyed being out there by himself so much.

"*So*, what've you been writing lately?" she asked him.

"*Well*, I've got this," he responded as he handed over his notebook, which she immediately began flipping through.

Just as Thayer started reading, Sky recommended that they all whip out their instruments and build upon he and Lin's duet rendition of "Mary Jane's Last Dance." Byrd (on acoustic guitar), Ruben (on congas) and O'Donnell (playing Thayer's battery-powered keys) collaborated with the Roses as they improvised a couple of solos in between the verses of the Petty ballad; and while they teetered around with a cohesive sound, Thayer and Cat wore headlamps and sipped on plastic cups of wine while scanning through Byrd's journal.

There were well over a hundred pages filled to the brim with poetry, dream analyses, diary entries, and pencil sketches. It was all meticulously organized, and its intricate details helped solidify Thayer's belief that Byrd wasn't fully checking himself out in the middle of Utah. The boys kept jamming on as the night had developed into a special occasion for everyone, but *everything* was taken to a whole other level when Thayer flipped to the last written page and found a song titled "Waiting at Ethereal Station."

A few whispers were exchanged between Cat and Thayer, and eventually Byrd noticed them giggling on the other side of the fire. When his gaze went toward them, it left Ruben, who was telling one of his often-told stories from the road. As Byrd blatantly strayed his attention in the direction of the girls, Ruben stopped in the middle of a sentence. Everyone at the fire, which didn't include O'Donnell, who was taking *a leak,* glanced over at the girls to get in on the joke.

"This last one, uh, 'Waiting at Ethereal Station,' is pretty interesting," Thayer said with a smile. "What's the inspiration for this one?"

They all looked at Byrd, who remained silent for a few awkward seconds.

"This is a little embarrassing," he responded with a smile. "But I actually wrote that earlier today, because last night I had this kinda sexy dream that took place at a gas station."

Everyone laughed around the campfire. Thayer noticed Byrd looking down, just slightly laughing into his chest.

"What did I miss?" O'Donnell asked as he stumbled back to the campfire. Lin let him in on the conversation, which made the story sound even funnier.

"*Well,* let's hear you play the damn thing!" O'Donnell declared as he sat on the ground, picked a marshmallow out of a plastic bag, and attached it to a sugar-tipped twig.

"Yeah, let's hear it! Do you know how it sounds?" Thayer asked.

"I was tinkering a little bit earlier," Byrd replied with a smile. "But I just wrote it today, so I've barely played it."

"*Come on*, play us your gassy sex song, for Chrissake!"

"I don't know, let's just play something else," he responded.

"Come on, O'Donnell's *actually* right. We all know you're really good," Thayer said as she walked around the fire and sat next to him. "It'll be a real treat to hear you play a song you just wrote, *and* once we all hear it, we can help make it sound even better. *Right,* guys?"

They all expressed their interest in helping play the song, or at least wanted to be supportive of their host as they unanimously agreed to learn it.

"Yeah, I'm totally down! Let's do it," Sky said.

"Just give me a beat, and I'll give you a rhythm," Ruben confirmed.

"And I'll accommodate the rhythm section," Lin chimed in.

"And I'll play the keys!" O'Donnell exclaimed, which led to everyone looking around at each other as he played a few notes.

"I think the person that studied music in *Berkeley* should play piano!" Cat yelled out, which made everyone laugh.

"I could've gone to Berkeley. They *adore me* there," he responded as Thayer grabbed her keyboard.

"About time," Byrd said as Thayer settled into a comfortable position and handed over his notebook. "All right, here goes nothing," he sighed as they all listened to the first solo acoustic performance of "Waiting at Ethereal Station."

There's a place I like to go
It's in nowhere, nowhere you can roam
Facetious eyes, see me comin' through
Down the road, the way back to you

I like to go there, when I need some space
To get me the hell outta this place
You wait for questions but still got no answers
This place is rockin', it's all full of dancers!

Cuz I'm waiting, at an ethereal station
Just waiting, where no time is real
I'm still waiting, at the ethereal station
Just waiting, to see if you'll be here

When I feel down, you get my heart pumpin'
Astro van, my engines keep runnin'
You see me standing here all alone
So far away, so far away from home

And we'll keep going, going through the night
Don't be scared, baby, it's only twilight
Touching my skin, but I can't feel
Perpetual motion, an endless dream wheel

And I'm still waiting, at an ethereal station
Just waiting, where nothing here is real
I'm still waiting, at the ethereal station
Just waiting, to see if you'll be here

People ask me where I like to go
But I can't tell them, there's no way to show
You live in my mind, a memory I can't shake
A love that's forever, until I'm awake

And I'll keep waiting, at the ethereal station
I like waiting, waiting here for you
I'm still waiting, at an ethereal station
Until the next time you come passing through

Byrd gave the song a rhythm that sounded like a mixture of Bruce Springsteen and Paul McCartney, if they were both sailing together along the Creedence Clearwater. He utilized fast-paced chords during the verses and quickly rolled back the intensity for the choruses, where he held each note out to perfection. His raspy voice drew them into each stanza, the bridge showed off his range, and they were awestruck to the point of nearly forgetting where they were for a moment as they almost forgot to clap at the end.

"Now, *that's* what I call music!" O'Donnell yelled as the group whistled and cheered. "You'd never know it being out here in the middle of nowhere, but we're sitting with a lad that's got *it!*" Thayer took the reins by orchestrating how she'd incorporate piano, and she gave advice for Ruben's congas, Sky's mandolin, and Lin's violin. They decided on remaining in the G key to coincide with Byrd's solo, and they slowly but surely hashed out how they'd complement their instruments to the lyrics. It didn't take much longer to incorporate a few improvisational jams for Lin after each chorus, which made things really take off. After they'd rehearsed a handful of times, Cat recorded an audio file on her phone.

Their adrenaline was pumping as they recorded themselves playing a more comprehensive version of "Waiting at Ethereal Station," and afterward, Thayer was back to flipping through Byrd's notebook to see what else was in there. His poems were starting to seem like a treasure trove as she flipped through the pages, and she knew they could make them all sound good. When they realized it was a little after 3 a.m., it became clear that sleep was in order.

"*Well*, I'm about to pass out, but I'm guessing we're a band as of now," O'Donnell said as they awkwardly laughed.

"I'm not sure if our band has room for bagpipes," Byrd slyly remarked.

"I don't just play the pipes, you know. But I could be your manager," he said, extending the unified laughter. "*What*? I'm in the biz. Tell 'em, Sky!"

"He's a DJ for a community radio station in Boulder that no one listens to."

"*See,* told ya! Just a few calls and the whole town will know about this *Ethereal Station!*" he said as everyone ignored him and found their sleep spot.

Ruben and Cat walked back to their van while Lin and O'Donnell prepared to sleep together in a tent next to Byrd, who was on the ground in his sleeping bag. Byrd had trouble sleeping that night due to the heart-pumping validation of someone actually enjoying one of his original songs, but he also couldn't fall asleep, thanks to the sounds of Thayer and Sky having the coldest, yet hottest, sex of their lives in the nearby distance.

8

verything in life always comes back to equilibrium, which in its essence is the very rhythm of existence. When we're up above equilibrium on the *life-o-meter,* it seems as though some type of downer will find its way to drag us back. Fortune, thermodynamics, karma, dharma—call it whatever you want, but who we are as a species physically and mentally involves cyclical cell lifetimes that constantly revert us back to even the most microscopic of new beginnings. We tend to forget about the fleeting nature of our personal timelines because we tend to forget that life itself is fleeting, so we instead occupy ourselves within the instinctual need to stand on solid ground for as long as we can. But what exactly is this *solid ground* made of? Money? Love? Belonging? Stillness? It's of course natural to see where all this goes.

It goes to when we're down and out, and when nothing seems to be going our way. It's in those downbeat moments when a beautiful ingredient to life's balance presents itself: a tiny, barely recognizable spark. That spark is commonly referred to as *hope,* and it's all too common for hope to reveal itself in a flimsy manner when we're spiraling out of control and our better selves appear to be unattainable. Hope is many times flimsy, regardless of where we are in connection to equilibrium, and it's always a simultaneous saving grace and dagger for our psyches. Flimsy hope is often mocked by those who aren't brave enough to hold on to it long enough, but internally, we all hold on to our flimsy hopes—no matter how fleeting the upper side of the life-o-meter may seem to be.

Some Zen masters would say that we actually achieve peace of mind when we give up on our flimsy hopes and break equilibrium's cycle by letting it rest flat on the universe's floor, but isn't living supposed to be a thorough experience that gains its efforts in plainly embracing the fluctuations of life's ups and downs? What in this world is worth reaching for, with (or without) flimsy hopes?

For Ruben and Cat, there were many costs that needed to be better managed, about three days after that fateful night in Utah, and most of them had nothing to do with money. They ended up having their most successful tour from a bottom-line standpoint, primarily because Cat's social media sponsors were helping them cover their overhead expenses and remain financially afloat. She'd become confident in her ability to earn income via online modeling and promotional content, but she couldn't help shedding small tears as she scrolled through her profile and saw countless contrived smiles.

On the other hand, Ruben never had much of a clue in terms of what to do after each summer tour, which was why he typically retreated to his parents' house to lay low and spend as little as possible while working in their retail shop. They'd experienced this part of their yearly cycle before, but the high of making a significant profit while traveling across the country with Furthur seemed more fragile this time around. Neither of them realized it in the moment, but they were simultaneously at a crossroads in the middle of Arizona and their relationship together. Ironically, this desolate part of Arizona just so happened to be the perfect place for a showdown.

"What are we doing?" Cat asked from the driver's seat as she stared at the lonely intersection's random stop sign. She put the van in park and looked back at Ruben, who was petting Nikita on their bed. "For real, where are we even going right now?"

"I thought we were going to Havasu Falls," Ruben groaned while coming out of his relaxed posture. "Do you not wanna go anymore, babe?"

She watched him rub his eyes and essentially look like the human version of Nikita, and she cracked a smile and laughed in a way that cracked her voice. The lingering lump in her throat was like a massive weight holding both of them down, and the only way to relieve it was to actually address their ensuing return to reality.

"I do wanna go to the waterfall. I think it's a great spot for pictures, but we've already been there before. I mean, where are we going after tonight?"

"I dunno. I figured we'd go to my folks' place," he said as he crawled his way up to the front seat. "They said we're *always* invited to stay with them when we need a place to crash."

"Trust me, I know we're *always* invited there. But we lived with your parents pretty much all last winter. I guess I just wanna do something different. I kind of, honestly, I feel like it might be best if I go live at my parents' house for a little while."

Ruben pursed his lips and furrowed his eyebrows as he glanced back at her for a moment and waited for her to continue, until she didn't.

"Really? Are you saying you wanna split up? What are you actually gonna do in Brentwood? Go shopping at overcrowded malls and sit in traffic all day? C'mon, babe, we both know Brentwood sucks. Why would you wanna split up to go live with your parents?"

"Umm, I don't know, maybe because *I love them!*" she said, raising her voice, which took Ruben by surprise.

"Well, what about me? Don't you *love me*?" he responded. "You know your parents won't even let me sleep in the same bed as you, and I won't have a car, so I'll be pretty stuck on the east side of town. I don't even know what to tell you right now, but I'm *definitely* not working for my parents by myself for longer than, I don't know, a couple months. I mean, you know how boring it can be at their store. Why would you wanna make me go through all that alone?"

They silently meandered down the desert highway for a handful of minutes, until Cat started crying behind the wheel. She pulled over at an abandoned gas station, where she refound the courage to speak.

"I don't want *anything* bad for you!" she lamented. "I'll let you use the van if you really want it. I just wanna get my shit together!" she continued as she sucked in air through her mouth as best she could. "I just think if we both go home and *relax* for a little bit, then we can start to figure out what we wanna do. Like, not just keep following bands every summer, maybe go somewhere new, like Hawaii or someplace we've never been before. All I know right now is that I just wanna get the fuck out of this smelly-ass van and sleep in my bed at home. I'm really sorry, Ruben. I need us to take a break or something. I need some space."

A long silence ensued, and neither of them knew what to say next, but it mutually seemed like the roughly four hundred miles left till LA would be awkward.

"Hawaii sounds pretty cool. And *hey*, if you're back in Brentwood, then maybe we'll see Thayer more often," he said with an earnest smile.

In an enigmatic way she didn't quite grasp, Ruben's whimsical response provided a much-needed relief that subtly reminded her that their return to reality didn't need to be taken so seriously. As they quietly meandered through the desert with just music breaking their silence, she thought to herself that most guys would've simply assumed *I need some space* was a deal-breaker. But she knew after so many years that Ruben had a different way of seeing things than most guys, and to him, there was nothing that could break their deal.

She started thinking how maybe there was still a sliver of hope for them as a couple, although in the moment, it seemed flimsy.

Thayer never had to worry about her financial *solid ground,* and she was very well off, to the point of resenting the balance displayed on an ATM's screen outside the recent Furthur show in Berkeley. But after spontaneously extending her journey to Utah right after the concert, she realized how she could try to spitefully spend as little as possible on herself by being Byrd-like for the foreseeable future.

A few weeks after camping with Byrd in the desert, Thayer was living in a temporarily empty room of Sky's friend's house in North Boulder. Her new roomies couldn't care less how she was sleeping in the extra room for free, but she still ended up giving her thanks in the form of delivery orders and dispensary pitch-ins. Boulder was a brand-new place for her that seemed like a tamed-down Berkeley, and her face would always light up while hiking with Sky in the nearby Flatirons. She insisted on not sleeping at Sky's place, so she wasn't prying too much, but she ended up busing every day to the record store where he worked on The Hill, just to chat. The store was an unorganized mess from top to bottom, and she ended up convincing the shop owner to allow her to decorate and make the place seem at least somewhat desirable to browse through. It took over a week for her to complete that initial reorganizing, and afterward, things started getting a bit more awkward with Sky's boss when she kept hanging out while not doing some kind of volunteer project.

So she started exploring the town more, and she pretty quickly noticed how she wasn't the only one completely lost in Boulder as she drifted through the Pearl Street Mall. There were countless people just like her who managed to hitch a ride and stay put in Colorado, and she couldn't help but feel an obscure connection to the Pearl Street nomads (regardless of how lavish her circumstances actually were compared to those who slept in parks and nearby hiking trails). She knew her deep pockets could help at least some of them, so she'd give street performers and beggars sizable donations daily. This led to the street performers recognizing her, and she eventually became friends with a handful of them. She'd also give her new friends bumps of the blow that J. P. had mailed her, and that got the word out about her *really quickly*.

Her popularity along Pearl Street got to the point where people knew her name and would call out to her as she meandered through the touristy outdoor mall. She even started bringing her portable keyboard so she could sit in with musicians, which typically led to long instrumental jams that began and ended with someone asking her about free coke. Spending extended hours on Pearl led to more in-depth conversations that shed light on many heartbreaking journeys, and these tough talks would end up bringing Thayer's introspective capacity to a whole new level. As she learned the life stories of many helpless adventurers, she slowly drew connections toward her own helplessness and self-conscious frailties. Her external perspective was also taken to a whole new level on Pearl Street, because hanging out with down-on-their-luck performers made her better recognize how countless yuppie Boulderites would simultaneously look down on the street performers while also contriving admiration for them. She also found out that her friends had to do a ton of necessary walking when the cops would force them to leave certain places.

On one particularly gloomy July afternoon, her new friend named Eddie said something deeply resonating. "You wanna know something? I felt like I was special when I was your age, like there was something out there for me that I was *meant for*. I thought that something for me was making movie scripts, but when I was about your age, I realized I was tricked into thinking I could do anything if I *put my mind to it*. What someone should've told me was that you can do anything if you put your *wallet* to it!"

"I could maybe help you if you wanted to get back into movies," Thayer responded. "My dad's a producer in Hollywood, and you never know, he might like a script you've written," she responded.

"You're a doll, Thay, but I no longer believe in those types of pipe dreams. My best advice I could ever give ya is that if you don't wanna end up like me, you have to hold on to your dreams, no matter how far-fetched they are. There's nothing worse than living without dreams, let me tell ya," Eddie ended his rant as he displayed his decaying smile.

Thayer got up from the brick stoop by the county courthouse and began walking up to the Hill. Along the way, she got great views of the bronzed Flatiron peaks hovering in the clouds, but looking at such a beautiful sight oddly caused tears to run down her face. She cried as she concluded to herself that she didn't exactly know what her dreams were, which led to another conclusion, that she was just another lost soul in Boulder. As she glanced around at the all-encompassing mountain scenery, it made her feel like something was wrong with her. It seemed as though everyone was supposed to be happy in such a pretty place, and the fact that she wasn't only made matters much worse.

When she got to the record shop to talk things over with Sky, she overheard an angry O'Donnell from the sidewalk. She walked down the store's stairs to the basement level, and they instantly stopped their conversation when they noticed how Thayer's face clearly read, *I've been crying*, all over it.

"What's wrong?" Sky asked.

"Nothing, I just don't know what the fuck to do with my life. I feel like a useless sack of shit. But what else is new, ya know?" she replied with her eyes looking at the store's dirty carpet, unsuccessfully trying to make a joke.

"I feel ya. I'm making twelve-fifty an hour here, but I don't know where else to work. So, it is what it is," Sky dejectedly responded.

"Well, at least you have a job," she replied, trying to hold back tears. "I just got a dumbass music degree, and now I don't know what the fuck to do with it. I feel like college was such a waste of time, and I'm still wondering what it did to actually help me. I've always wanted to play piano, but it's just another unattainable dream. But if I don't have that dream, then I don't have *any* dreams. I don't wanna be dreamless, but all of a sudden, it sure as hell feels like I am."

"*All right*, I've heard enough!" O'Donnell cut her off. "You sound just like all the other snobby girls in this town: *Oh no, the entire galaxy doesn't understand me. I don't know what to do with myself! I guess I'll just have to ask my rich Paw to wire another year's supply!*" he mocked. "I mean, come on, we all know you don't need to worry about money, and quite frankly, I really don't wanna hear about your flailing dreams. I had a *really, really* bad day, so your unnecessary self-deprecation can wait at least until I go home."

"Wait, what happened to you?" she asked.

"I got *conned* by my job!"

"Conned? How did your job con you?"

"He means he got *canned*," Sky interrupted. "He just came in here a few minutes ago and has been going off on a tirade about how he got laid off today."

"Oh man, that sucks. I'm sorry to hear that," Thayer responded. "Did they tell you why they laid you off? Weren't you working at a community radio station?"

"Yeah, it's one big BS community, all right, and they sacked me as if all I am is a batch of Irish potatoes ready for market. The cheap bastards told me: *no one's listening. Sorry, dude,*" he said in an American imitation. "I'm thirty-one, and I just lost the best job I ever had, and you come in here hooting and hollering about just a bunch of rich-girl rubbish. You say you don't wanna be dreamless, well let me give you a lesson from the real world, where your daddy don't got an endless pocketbook: society *hates* dreamers, and dreams change. If you don't change with your dreams, society will take them from you."

Lin nodded goodbye as he shut off the lights and closed his bedroom door behind him, and he walked past the music room and glanced out at the large balcony's Chinatown view. He considered playing one last song on his favorite perch, so he walked back to the music room and picked up one of his old violins that he used during his middle school years. But when he looked through the sliding glass door toward the wicker chair he'd always sit in, tears uncontrollably ran down his face, as he couldn't maneuver his body enough to direct himself outside.

Growing up in San Francisco's youth orchestra scene had become a significant part of who Lin was as a thick-skinned musician, but he still wondered if he'd have the moxie to play solos in front of professors and world-class conductors day in and day out. He wondered if he even enjoyed playing violin with that kind of enormous pressure, which made him think back to the night in the desert that was now a handful of weeks in the past. There was absolutely no pressure while he played with Byrd, Sky, Thayer, and Ruben that night, and this was partly because none of them would've ever noticed if he made a subtle mistake. But everyone in New York sure as hell would know, and from what he'd heard, the professors at NYU were even more meticulous than the busybodies he'd performed for throughout San Francisco.

But even with all the bullshit of being a new student at a prestigious music school, the curious sparks of hope still slowly ignited within him like the origins of a fire built by Byrd's hand drill. There were no other options but to establish the solid ground to step forth and meet the challenges that awaited him in the City that Never Sleeps, where equilibrium was casually awaiting his arrival.

"Are you ready to go? We need to leave for the airport now!" Leanne said assertively, just before realizing her son was crying by the balcony window. "*Oh,* I'm so sorry, honey. Are you okay?"

"Yeah, just can't believe it's finally time to go. Even though I've imagined this day over and over again, now that it's here, it feels tough to leave. Will you come see me soon?"

"We're so proud of you," she responded, choking back tears. "I could have never realized that I'd have a son anywhere near as talented as you, and we saved up so much for college, only to find out that the *best of the best* wanted you to learn from them for free. We'll be sure to come visit at some point this fall. You're coming home for fall break, right?" she asked.

"Sure."

"Are you *excited?* College is the *best* four years of your life!"

"Yeah."

"What's wrong? You know I can tell when something's up."

"I'm sorry, I'm very excited … I just … I just can't help but think that maybe this isn't for me, and that I'm going to get lonely out there."

"*Oh,* I see. You know, even I've been lonely, *a lot* actually, and the one thing I can say about loneliness is that it's nothing to be afraid of. I guess we're both going to have to get used to being a little lonelier now that you're leaving, but being alone is just a part of growing up. It's not called *being on your own* for nothing, right?"

"Yeah. I get it, Mom."

"You just have to trust yourself like you always have, Lin. Your life's doors have swung themselves wide open for you, so you'd be crazy to think this isn't for you. This opportunity is a dream come true, and we can't wait to see you perform in New York! Everyone you'll be taking classes with will be so talented; I'm sure you'll love them. I'm sure you'll love *all* your college friends."

"I wonder who I'll meet."

"*Well*, there's only one way to find out! Let's go to college, mister!"

Byrd was always different in terms of how he embraced his reclusive habits, and he was also self-conscious about how others viewed his loneliness. Every now and again, he'd try to conceptualize what the people of his past would say if they could see him living in the middle of that Utah canyon, but these defeating judgments were typically warded off by the more pressing conceptualizations of where exactly tiny pieces of dirt might be scattered throughout his hair and face. Cosmetic concerns were often his way of returning from repressive obstacles, which was why he suddenly initiated a breakthrough between the fractal formations of the Unified Field while examining himself in his Honda's side mirror.

"*Wow*, now *that's* dirty!" he yelled out as he noticed how the right side of his face was a few shades darker than the left. He laughed at his blatant lack of symmetric aesthetics as he continued scrutinizing the rest of his appearance in the dusty mirror. "You're one filthy son of a bitch, and you know that!" he yelled again, while pointing at his oval-shaped reflection.

He grabbed his tiny towel out of a pannier, turned around, and began walking in the direction of the creek. By the time he'd taken three steps, the breakthrough had smacked him in the face as if the universe was swatting him like a fly. In that exact epiphanal moment, he busted out laughing while considering the idea of continuing the lonely conversation without the mirror. *It can't be that hard. All you gotta do is say exactly what you're thinking.*

"Well!" he yelled out, smiling as though he'd reached the nexus between the physical and mental partitions of humanity's conscious realm. "I damn well think it's about time to *hop induh crick!*" he yelled, imitating O'Donnell.

He stepped across a few stones, and created a big splash by plopping himself into the deepest spot of the creek. He stayed under water for a few seconds as he vigorously scrubbed all over, and he noticed the tranquility in not being able to speak. He resurfaced, baptized in the waters of the Church of Insanity's Disciples.

"*Whew!*" he yelled out, which echoed through the canyon. "Don't wanna disturb the other campers, now," he reminded himself.

"*Shit*, the odds of someone hearing that are pretty slim. I'm probably the only one out here right now."

"Well, what else is new, Big Byrd?" he asked himself as he watched the wind circulate a handful of dried-up, dead leaves.

"It's another drought year," he said, looking around at the gentle stream. "The creek seems fine, though," he retorted.

"The bigger heat waves will be coming soon."

"The nights will start to get colder soon too."

"Maybe it's time to leave *this damn desert*," he said, imitating a cowboy drawl.

"But late summer is the best time of year here. Why leave now?"

"This time of year brings in a bunch of hot springs tourists."

"Yeah, but only for a couple weeks. They won't take this spot."

"Maybe, but there will be more campers. Gil wouldn't even care if I quit; he's got plenty of guides better than me. It's time to get going."

"Go where, though?"

"Maybe south? Glen Canyon? Coyote Gulch?"

"No. No more desert."

"West, California?"

"Now we're talking."

"But," he sighed, "been there, done that."

"True."

"East, maybe Colorado?"

"Sky and O'Donnell are *thurr*," he said, chuckling at his contrived Scottish accent. "I wonder what those crazies are up to right now."

"That *surprise party* was the most fun ever out here."

"They're probably in Boulder, but Boulder's for rich people."

"They're not rich, though. Thayer might still be there too."

"*I like them*," he replied in a schoolgirl tone.

"Thayer's rich, though. They're all better off."

"How much is saved up from this summer? Five, maybe six grand? That's more than enough to move into an apartment in Boulder."

"Yeah, but then what? Sleep *without* the stars? Get a *real* job? What would I do in a place like Boulder? Be a barista? Work at REI?"

"*She'd* probably like that better than this," he said, referring to his mom.

"Maybe it's time to move back in with her."

"It wouldn't be so bad. Delaware isn't so bad."

"Camping isn't so bad there."

"It would probably be better to use a tent there."

"There are *a lot* of deer ticks in them woods."

"It could work out well there," he said as he proudly looked over at his campsite and motorcycle. He glanced down at his hands and noticed how they were beginning to prune.

"Let's get out of here, *right now*," he said as he got out of the creek, dried himself off with the towel, slipped his dirty underwear and shorts back on, and walked back to the Honda.

"It's time to check in with the rest of the world, ya fuckin' psycho!" he yelled into the mirror before heading out with all his belongings left behind, including his shirt.

As he rode to Surf Zone, he settled his vocalized thoughts down and replaced them with singing songs. He sang the lyrics to "Waiting at Ethereal Station" the whole way to the nearest gas station.

"I'm still waiting, at the ethereal station! Just waiting, to see if you'll be there!" he sang out as images of Jane flooded his mind.

By the time Byrd got to Surf Zone, he was practically floating on top of the scorching cement in one of the most liberated moods he'd ever experienced.

"*Billy Boy!*" he yelled out. "How's it going, buddy? Long time no see!" he said with a massive grin.

"I thought you were maybe gone for good," Billy said as he stood up from reading his newest copy of *National Geographic*. "Gosh, what's it been, a month since the last time you were here?"

"Yeah, I haven't been online in *a while*," Byrd said as they both laughed. "It's good to see you, man. I missed you out there in the brush!"

"I bet ya did!" Billy replied, now embracing Byrd's energy with his own smile. "I guess I missed ya too. I'm glad ya didn't skip town just yet!"

"Well, I got bad news then, Billy. I came to Surf Zone today to email Mama Byrd. I'm about to tell her I'm coming home."

"Oh, I see. So, you're going back to the nest! Where's home?"

"Delaware."

"Delaware, huh? You're a long ways from home out here. I guess it ain't too far if you're flying."

"I can't leave my baby," Byrd said, glancing outside at his parked bike.

"Oh, you're *riding* to Delaware? You really are crazy! Them Nebraska folks will eat your hippie ass alive before you get east of Omaha! You ever see *Easy Rider*?" he sarcastically asked while Byrd walked over to a desktop and logged on.

He didn't know that a life-changing opportunity had been waiting for him in his inbox for weeks.

9

The literal essence of our human being just so happens to be something that's easy to forget about: hydration. Nothing good ever comes from being dehydrated, and anything that makes you more dehydrated tends to not be good for you. Young people everywhere naturally like to party, and popular social drugs among party people, like alcohol and cocaine, are deceivingly dehydrating. Maybe the enrapturing effects of a night on the town make drinking water not a part of the party's *vibe*, but for whatever reasons, water will many times slip through the cracks during a night out. And this always leads to debilitating, throbbing headaches the next morning.

When Thayer fluttered her eyes open to see the remnants of a late night scattered across an unrecognizable coffee table and equally unrecognizable home, she couldn't think of anything else besides drinking water. The parched dryness in her mouth burned from the aftereffects of cigarettes, and her eyes throbbed with an unusual puffiness that she soon realized was from sleeping on a couch infested with cat hair. She slightly lifted her right cheek off a retro cushion that said *Relax* in bright-orange letters, but the rest of her body remained completely still. She started to drift back to sleep, but the morning light penetrating through the nearby window was enough to blind her to action. She wobbled herself to standing and examined the half-empty PBR cans and day-old pizza slices scattered around the living room. She rubbed the grit out of her eyes and pulled the string of the window's venetian blinds to block the sunlight, and that was when she noticed how she was hundreds of feet above ground in a Denver high-rise. Right on cue, she heard sex sounds coming from down the hallway, which took the form of repeated clapping that coincided with progressively louder *oh's*.

Now she remembered where she was. One of her new roommates, McKenzie (aka Mac), convinced her into seeing a *real band* play in Denver the previous afternoon. She'd been casually freeloading at Mac's house in North Boulder for two months, and the *real band* Mac wanted to see had a punk rock, party-on vibe that got the best of Thayer and the entire eight ball of coke she brought. She did have a lot of help and talked to a lot of new people she'd never see again, but the side effects of severe dehydration that morning were beyond unbearable. She practically crawled over to the kitchen sink and started filling her cupped hands with water in order to shovel liquids down her throat. This made her feel better for about a minute, until gulping an excessive amount of water caused her stomach to turn on her and discharge a viciously nasty liquid.

"*Maaac*," she groaned as she knocked on the closed bedroom door. "Mac, I need to get going. I'm feeling sick and need to leave now."

About ten minutes later, they were in Thayer's newly purchased Chevy Astro van that resembled Sky's, except hers was a little more maintained and a lot more vintage. She found it on Craigslist from a guy who only cared about an eight-thousand-dollar check and simple title signature, and she was an instant sucker for its retro, baby-blue exterior.

"You could've waited, like, five more minutes before knocking," Mac said during a radio commercial break. "I swear, every time I have sex, the guy just shoots off his load first thing *without even thinking* about making me come. Like, what the hell do I have to do, yell at the guy: *I wanna come too*? It's just so crazy how inept guys are, and it doesn't even matter how hot they are, they just, I don't know, aren't enough. You know what I mean?"

Thayer thought about Sky and how the sex they'd been having was the best of her entire life, although she didn't have much to compare him with. She started to think about coming and wasn't sure if she'd done it with him or not, which she realized meant she hadn't.

"I don't think Sky's ever made me come, but I still think the sex is good with him," she said unsurely, which made Mac laugh.

"That doesn't surprise me," she said, giggling. "Honestly, I know Sky is a really cool guy who's *awesome* at guitar, but I don't really get what you see in him. I mean, don't get me wrong, he's totally cool, but like, he works at that record shop on the Hill. He's kinda just a *huge wook.*"

"Yeah, well that guy you were with last night definitely isn't the most eligible bachelor in Denver either. There's no need to be such an *anti-wookite.*"

"He's in medical school, so at least there's some hope for him," Mac replied, laughing to herself. "With Sky, it's pretty much he's either going to be a successful musician or he's going to work in music stores his whole life. There's no plan B with a guy like that, so it's just a little sketchy to start falling for him."

"Who says I'm falling for him?"

"Look, I'm just saying something because a few of us are a little worried about you. We all know you're new here, and we don't want you being the one girl who actually takes Sky seriously as a legit boyfriend. I mean, the whole town pretty much knows he's broke, and there was even a rumor going around that he had chlamydia like a year ago. We just don't want you to get hurt, because *we love you,* Thay!" she said with an awkwardly big smile.

Mac's tone reminded her of Madison, and she slowly shook her head as she drove down the freeway in silence for a handful of minutes.

"Maybe it's about time for me to get a *housing* plan B," Thayer responded, finally breaking the silence.

"It *actually* is, Thay. That girl, Bridget, who's paying for the room you've been staying in, is coming back like next week to start classes, *so* you're gonna have to find a new place pretty soon."

"Great, thanks for the heads-up."

"Yeah, sorry!" she said cheerily yet insincerely. "You'll find something close by, though. Boulder is probably all booked up, but there's always like Nederland or Longmont or somewhere close by. You'll find something, and you'll find a job soon too. I just know it!"

Thayer rolled her eyes while her attention drifted to the panoramic view of the Flatirons as they approached Boulder from the southeast. She recognized how living there could be a good fit for at least a little while, so she started thinking about how much cash she'd have to put down to rent her own place. It seemed as though her attempt to live Byrd-like was becoming a sheer and utter failure, but at least her new friends on Pearl Street made it seem as though her spontaneous arrival had happened for a reason beyond following Sky across America. She couldn't help but consider Colorado as way more her speed than California, but she was still torn on whether Sky was worthy of a permanent move.

A few hours later, when she'd somewhat recovered from her hangover, she called Sky to tell him she was on her way to his apartment. She was coming all over his sheets a half hour later, and the sheer ecstasy of that orgasm convinced her that no one she'd ever known came close to *this*. As much as she'd try to tell herself that she wanted to explore a new town and see a new place, she realized right then that she'd lingered in Boulder that summer solely because of him.

It was turning into a lazy Saturday, which meant they both wanted to gorge themselves with greasy breakfast sandwiches stuffed to the brim with bacon, eggs, hash browns and sausage patties. They both laughed at each other as they devoured their food with whimsically ferocious bites and sounds, and it was in this light-hearted moment that Thayer decided to drop some truth bombs. She detailed her blackout night with Mac and how she woke up in a random high-rise apartment, and she gave a brief overview into what Mac told her. This predominantly entailed the fact that she wouldn't have a free place to stay much longer, and she also asked Sky if he'd ever had chlamydia in the past.

"What? Did Mac say that? No, of course not!" Sky said as he put his sandwich down and looked Thayer straight in the eyes. "Look, forget about all those other girls you've gotten to know here so far. You're *different* than all of them, and you're quite honestly the most talented pianist I've ever met. You don't need Mac's empty room to live here, because if you wanna stay in Boulder, you can stay with me until you figure things out."

So Thayer moved in with Sky, and the two of them were like best friends who also had sex with each other every night. Thayer would receive a vacuum-sealed package of coke from J. P. on an almost-weekly basis, primarily because the two of them would stay up late after sex and jam out until their fingers ached. After just a couple weeks of living together, it became clear that they were becoming a more serious couple. Although everyone knew Sky was completely broke and had no savings whatsoever from working at the record store, it was also subtly obvious that Thayer was rich and more than likely paying the bill at their regular happy hours. To Thayer, paying for some meals and groceries was the very least she could do to help Sky out, but it was an overboard extravagance when she surprised him with a new acoustic-electric guitar at the record store.

"Wow, this is seriously too good! I don't know if I can accept this," Sky said as he held the guitar up to closely examine it. "My buddies are already making fun of me because they think you're my sugar mama. This might just be the icing on the cake."

"It's the *least* I could do, Sky. You've really helped me out since I had to get out of Mac's place, and don't worry about what those douchey friends of yours are saying about us. We're better than all of *that*, baby," she said while nuzzling up for a hug. "You're gonna play the shit out of this guitar, I just know it, and I can't wait to hear what you come up with," she whispered into Sky's shoulder.

"You're right, I just won't hear the end of it from O'Donnell when I tell him you bought this for me."

This didn't sit well with Thayer, who instantly pulled back from the hug. "Who gives a *fuck* what *fucking* O'Donnell thinks?" she said, raising her voice. "Do you *seriously* care what other people are saying about us? Because if that's the case, then maybe I was *wrong* about you, and maybe it's about time I go home."

"C'mon, Thay. Don't be like that. You know I love the guitar. It's such a great gesture. Thank you." Silence filled the empty store. "And you can't go home now, you just can't. Ruben hit me up earlier today and told me he'll be here in the next day or so and wants to see us. It'll be fun. We'll jam out like we did with Byrd in the desert! I'm also sure your new song will sound a lot better with some drums!" he reassured her, which led to a hug, a kiss, and an *employee meeting* in the store's back room.

Thayer and Sky were doing the exact same thing the next evening, just tinkering around in the record shop after hours, when Sky got a text from Ruben saying: *Yo bro I'm here.*

They walked up the stairs to the street level and looked down the commercial district of the Hill toward a nearby parking lot, where they could see Ruben buying a parking slip for his dashboard. The California-plated van was completely covered in dust, mud, and dead bugs, and by the look on Ruben's face, you'd think the dirtiness was a first-place Road Tripper's Association of America trophy. It was his own testimony to the journey he'd made, and also the added recklessness he was willing to take on dirt roads without Cat and Nikita.

"What's up, guys!" Ruben yelled out as they approached the van. "Give me a hand with this and we'll get it all in the shop in one trip. It's just up the street, right?" he said, motioning to his drum kit.

"Not even half a block. I'm so glad you made it safe, bro," Sky said as they walked back to the trunk and started pulling out cymbals and floor toms.

Thayer watched them unload the equipment and began putting things together that she hadn't yet noticed. She was confused by how Sky now seemed to be the source of communication with Ruben, and she realized how she hadn't heard a peep from Cat about this impromptu trip. She figured something was up when she saw the pile of fast-food wrappers in the passenger seat.

"So, where's Cat? She's not with you?" she asked as Ruben handed her his snare.

"She didn't wanna come," he said, refocusing on unpacking before returning his attention back to Thayer. "To be honest, Cat and I are kinda taking a break."

"*Oh*," she responded. "But she's letting you drive her van around the country?"

"Yeah," Ruben said with a laugh. "I guess it's not *over*, over. We talked earlier today, and it seems like things are okay. She said she wishes you were home."

"I've been thinking about going back lately."

"Why would you go back? I'm thinking of moving here and making Cat come pick up her stupid van so she can see how awesome it is!" Ruben replied, giving Sky a fist bump that was met with a *hell yeah*.

"I don't know ... I'll just see you guys inside," she said as she started walking down the Hill in the opposite direction of the store.

She texted Cat a few times to say hello and tell her that Ruben had arrived, and she scrolled through her contacts and dialed *Mom*. They did their typical small-talk routine, after which the conversation got a little more medium sized.

"So, be honest. Did you run away to Boulder for a boy?" Isabella asked.

"What? No, of course not! C'mon, Mom. I already told you that I'm staying at an *all-girls* house."

"Yeah, well that doesn't make any difference at all, and I don't like it that you seem to think I'm so naïve to believe *for a second* that there isn't some boy involved with this disappearance of yours. Your father and I are worried about you, and we got your bank statement in the mail the other day. What did you write a check for eight thousand dollars for? And what did you get at Guitar Center for thirteen hundred dollars?"

"I got a van the other day so I could get around better. It's so cute, you'll love it. The other purchase was just for equipment I need. I'm in a band now," she lied.

"What about this *mystery boy*? Is he in this band?"

"Yeah, we started it together," Thayer admitted after a few seconds of silence. "We're about to play a new song I wrote recently. We've got a great setup to play at night in the record shop he works at."

"Now *that's* the daughter I remember. The music shop boy, huh? Sounds like a *real catch*. Well, keep us posted, honey. Your father and I have Dodgers tickets, so we need to leave before traffic makes us miss the first three innings. Feel free to drive that eight-thousand-dollar van back here whenever you want to come home. We love you, bye-bye now!"

Thayer rolled her eyes and turned back uphill, and she was surprised to see O'Donnell answer her when she knocked on the store's locked door.

"*Well, well,* if it isn't our fearless leader. What were you doing that was so important to skip all the heavy lifting? Did you have to talk to Daddy and explain that swanking guitar Sky's playing down there?"

"No, and *shut the fuck up* about the guitar! What're you even doing here?"

"Apparently, you've got a new smash hit about wooks?" he asked with a grin. "I'm here to hear it."

They walked down the stairs as they listened to Ruben and Sky lay out a jam, which featured Sky ripping up and down the neck of his new acoustic Gibson. As Thayer emerged from the bottom of the stairs, they both immediately stopped and motioned her to sit down next to them.

"So, you made a song called 'Anti-Wookite'?" Ruben asked her.

"Yeah, do you wanna hear it?" she responded, while sitting down and turning her keyboard on.

"I only drove a thousand miles just to hear it!"

Sky offered a plate of two lines to O'Donnell and Thayer. O'Donnell shook it away, referring to his need to stay clean while he job-searched, so Thayer did both.

"Anti-Wookite" was the first song Thayer had written in years that she actually liked. Her original interpretation featured a mellow, coffee-shop melody that ramped up with speed as it progressed into a fast-paced pub ballad. They initially listened to Thayer's solo performance, and then Sky brought in a melody to give Ruben a better idea of where to go with his rhythm. Ruben loved "Anti-Wookite" from the first moment he heard it, and he immediately sensed how it was set up for a big drum presence. When he brought in his louder-than-life percussions to invigorate Thayer's naturally soft-spoken voice, there was an interpretive collision of raw talent that blended together like a match made in music heaven.

Sure, a shower sounds great
Been a while since I felt clean
Sometimes, the wind whips my hair
It's so strong, and I don't care

Well we all gotta love a little bit better
Take the keys, it's your turn to drive
Where there's music, we got nothing to fear
Get to the next show, now we're in the clear

And we, we got a lot to learn
Cuz The Man wants to keep us in the same pattern
And well, well it's all I could do,
Singing these songs with a love that's true

So why, you such an anti-wookite?
Can't you see everyone's all right?
And when will you see the truth?
We don't got all day, we're running out of youth!

Our bond, is right here on this floor
It's a late night, what's life got in store?
Be here, for the friends you have
Cuz dreams change, The Man wants yours back

Hey man, why you high on that horse?
Can't you see your life's full of remorse?
Take this ticket, to be one of us
A wook lifestyle, jump on the bus!

And we'll dance, dance while we're still young
Cuz the world is better when our hearts aren't stung
Will I see you again another night?
I like your eyes, how they shine so bright!

So don't, don't be an anti-wookite
Just live your life, we're all upright
And why, you think you got none?
We're all just livin, spinnin 'round the sun

Let's ride, what're you waiting for?
This Stoner Express, it always wants more
More people, more friends
Now that's a dance floor!

So let's be, let's be fam tonight
We're all together, we're all wookites
Smell, who gives a shit about smell?
You anti-wookite, go straight to hell

So why, you such an anti-wookite?
Can't you see everyone's all right?
And when will you see the truth?
We don't got all day, we're running out of youth!

But in the meantime, we'll ring our Liberty Bell
And when we're gone, we'll have a story to tell

After a couple hours of hashing out minor details, they were satisfied with the song's happy-go-lucky, no-fucks-given sound.

"It's honestly not too shabby!" O'Donnell chimed in, raising his seltzer bottle toward Thayer. "I can tell you that Byrd would probably think it's amazing, that nutter."

"That's true, he would *really* like it," Sky agreed.

"I don't know who wouldn't, except maybe an anti-wookite!" Ruben joked.

"I'll email him and see what he's up to!" Thayer said with a validated smile.

10

As usual, it was difficult for Thayer to get in touch with Byrd, but it was now even harder for anyone to hear from him because his disdain for technology was at an all-time high. The main reason for Byrd's increased apathy in the real world was his newfound proximity to it, which kept him clinging to solitude. He immediately quit his job at Fundamental Roots and left Utah for good after his last login at Surf Zone, but he didn't go to Delaware like he'd planned. He actually ended up much closer to his friends in Boulder, and it was all due to one extraordinary opportunity that he felt obligated to carry out.

Byrd now woke up each morning in a run-down cabin with no electricity, outhouse plumbing, and a tiny fireplace just a handful of feet from his dingy mattress. It was far from being fancy by anyone's standards, but to him, it was like staying at the Ritz. He was still getting used to his accommodations, but waking up after sunrise with no loud cattle herds was rather easy to get used to. He also quickly got used to the rushing creek that was just a few dozen feet from his window, as well as the endless aspen grove that his new home rested within.

The fact that there were surrounding aspen trees made sense, because Byrd's new home was about fifteen miles outside the prim and proper boundaries of Aspen, Colorado. He had been in Aspen for about three weeks, and not once had he gone into the actual city. There was never any denying that he preferred to live his life tucked away from civilization, but the big difference now was that he didn't even have to go anywhere for supplies or food. And just like clockwork at 8 a.m., his new employer came knocking on his decrepit door.

"Good morning, James! Would you like some tea?" was how every day started with Byrd's new boss, Shankar Patel.

Shankar was almost sixty-five years old that morning, but between him and Byrd, they felt about the same age. He was a recently retired financial adviser, and he was the type of corporate colleague who did yoga stretches on speakerphone calls while closing deals from referral after referral that plopped into his lap out of nowhere. One of the reasons why Shankar was more popular than his coworkers was because he specialized in helping people plan retirement business ventures, which went a step further to help make golden years glimmer a little bit brighter.

Coming from humble roots in India, Shankar was barely able to afford his finance degree at a top-tier university (even with education loans), but he came out of college determined to help people make smart decisions, while making a ton of cash for himself in the process. His corporate ambitions led him to America, and climbing the USA's socioeconomic ladder was a dream come true for him and his entire family. He'd become living proof of just how far the American Dream can go when self-belief far outweighs any naysayer doubt, but all his success couldn't stop the tides of a twenty-five-year-old failing marriage.

His divorce hit him like a bag of bricks when he was sixty-one, which led him down a yearlong spiral of second-guessing everything else about the path he'd created. When he and his wife split up, he initially wasn't sure how to move on, and things only got worse as his loneliness became more established. He decided that the universe was speaking to him via the lemons of divorce, and it was his job to figure out how to make lemonade into his mid-sixties. As light bulbs started to flicker a few months into his single life, a reimagined version of himself began participating in yoga retreat after retreat for his own personal recalibration, which was why he showed up alone at a camping yoga retreat on Maryland's Assateague Island during the spring of 2008. Shankar was by far the oldest yogi at that beach retreat, so he figured it would be difficult to actually confide what he was going through to anyone who'd understand what a divorce at sixty-two felt like; however, Shankar wasn't aware of a teenaged retreat-goer named James Byrd when he signed up for that week of fun on the Assateague sand dunes.

Byrd and his mom, Janis, were doing the same retreat for their own form of family recalibration to make up for the many arguments associated with Byrd's adamancy to not attend college, and it only took a few minutes and a few smuggled beers from the communal coolers for both Byrd and Shankar to realize they could confide in one another. They met on the retreat's first day and ended up drinking together on top of a small dune for the next few nights, where Shankar was willing and ready to instill his three-quarters-of-a-lifetime of wisdom in Byrd. By night two of the retreat, Byrd knew all about Shankar's transition to a self-image that was rooted in his newfound dream to invest his life savings into his own yoga retreat center, which he envisioned himself running. But the most transformative portion of their conversations came on the last night of the retreat, when they were both buzzed on wine and yogi inspiration to the point of considering their goals to not be all that far-fetched, which allowed opportunity to knock on their doors.

"I've decided because of this retreat that I'm going to do it, James. I'm going to fulfill my new life's goals," Shankar said after a long silence of listening to the waves crash below the dunes.

"What exactly are your life's goals, again?" young Byrd slurred as he slurped on a Solo cup of Sangiovese.

"I'm going to be the guy that hosts retreats like this one, but I'm going to do it my way. Nothing too crazy like these past few days here on Assateague, just a real Zen experience in nature."

"Sounds pretty cool," Byrd agreed as he gulped his wine.

"I'm going to need some help, though. I'm not certified or anything like that; I only help people make good finance decisions. It all seems so trivial now, but at least I now know I want to help people make good choices about everything else besides money!" he continued, laughing at how far the universe had come to teach him an ironic lesson. "I now know that I have to work on myself, so I'll be ready one day to provide this type of experience, but there's absolutely no way I'll ever be able to do it alone, even if I do get certified and all that. If I ever do make this dream happen one day, I want someone like *you*—a young, hip, nature-loving guy, to help me make sure people would actually want to show up. Would you help me with something like that?" Shankar asked like a lost toddler trying to find his parents in a department store.

"I tell you what," Byrd said as he straightened himself up in the sand. "If you *really* put your whole life aside to build some Zen retreat in the woods, then you can count on me to be there when you need help getting it started."

"*Really*? You promise?" Shankar asked again, now crying about how pathetic it seemed for him to be drunkenly confiding his dreams to a teenager he barely knew.

"Call it a *Zen* promise," Byrd said as he lifted his cup.

When Byrd logged in at Surf Zone and was about to reach out to his mom about coming home, he read an email from Shankar explaining how he'd finally found the perfect location for his retreat center, and how it was finally time to fulfill their promises made on Assateague. They'd barely kept in touch over the five years after they'd met, mainly because email was Byrd's only means of communication, but the timing of that one particular email couldn't have been more momentous within Byrd's life.

Although Shankar considered the job offer to be a shot in the dark while he wrote that decisive message, Byrd didn't hesitate for a second as he immediately left Surf Zone to resign in person at

Fundamental Roots due to what he called a "private family emergency." At the end of the next day, his Honda was meandering through the potholes of Castle Creek's dirt road while he glanced at a piece of paper with directions to Shankar's new property.

When Byrd arrived at a decrepit wooden gate that was barely holding itself up by rusty hinges, he saw a shirtless Shankar wearing a tie-dye Speedo at the bottom of the driveway's gravel hill. He was casually standing in a clearing while waving him in.

"Welcome, James!" he shouted over the bike's engine as Byrd came to a stop next to him. "I'm so glad you could make it so quickly, at least after getting a response from your email!"

"Jeez, man! It's great to see you and all, but I didn't realize you were starting a *nudist* colony!" Byrd joked back with a wry smile.

"The clothesline is *very busy* at the moment. Park by my truck, and I'll show you around!"

As Byrd rolled into the woods, he began noticing a couple of dwellings over a story above him. Both tree houses had their own staircases, and one had a balcony, but all the woodwork had been beaten to shreds and was clearly unsafe to walk on. Shankar's new piece of land featured not only those two dilapidated treehouses, but also six equally shabby cabin dwellings that nestled up against Castle Creek in an L shape. Each building was made with an aged cedar that looked like it was beginning to rot, and the cabins seemed to be somewhat larger than the two treehouses. There was a centralized opening in between all the buildings, but all sorts of construction equipment took up this portion of the property. Byrd recognized a handful of coiled electrical lines and solar panel equipment, while Shankar walked into the cabin at the far end of the property, and when he reemerged, he was wearing beige harem pants and a light-blue tank top. He spread out his now-chiseled arms that he'd developed from years of strenuous yoga training as he walked toward Byrd, silently inquiring *so, what do you think?* Byrd's first thought was that the place was a dump of decaying huts, but at the same time, it had an innate, paradise-like setting that felt perfect.

"We have *a lot* of work to do," Shankar admitted. "Like we agreed upon, I'll pay for your food, your time, and your efforts, and I'll ensure that your cabin remains adequate and is what we work on first. I think you'll like what I've done so far with your quarters. It's that cabin over there," he said, pointing to one of the creekside cabins behind him. "We'll need to do plenty more renovations in there, but it's good to sleep in as of tonight."

"You're still gonna pay me a decent wage, right?" Byrd asked a bit skeptically.

"Yes, of course. Does $100 per day sound good to you? With food and lodging included, that's more like $200, you know?"

"I guess. Can I make my own hours?"

"I don't see why not. We just need to get a certain amount done each day. It's mostly going to be just the two of us, so we'll just do what we can."

"I'll do whatever ya need. I honestly don't even care about the money. I'm just thankful for the invite and excited that you're *actually* doing this!"

"I knew way back on Assateague Island that you were the right guy to help make this dream come true, because in some ways, you helped me realize that I truly needed to bring all this to fruition for my own good. It's such a blessing how you answered my request and that we'll undergo this journey like we planned back then, but for now, let's not worry about money or the past or anything, because for right now, we must focus on rebuilding this *wonderful* abode! Isn't it the most beautiful piece of mountain land you've ever seen? It used to be a Buddhist retreat center a couple decades ago, but it was then turned into rentals that the city recently condemned. Since then, it has been sitting here waiting for us!"

Byrd reexamined the rundown cabins and could even smell the mountain water of Castle Creek that was less than a hundred feet away, and he internally echoed the notion that this piece of land was *waiting for him.* Maybe everything had happened the way that it did because he'd subliminally always been waiting to fulfill this promise he'd made as a stubborn eighteen-year-old afraid of going to college. Maybe his diversion away from a traditional education and into a career in wilderness guiding, and all its subsequent loneliness on off weeks, was the path he was supposed to take, so he'd be at least a little more qualified for Shankar's obscure job. A hundred dollars a day with food and a livable shack was like a pinnacle achievement for someone who was used to working every other week, with winters mostly filled with side gigs. He'd never had a job that paid too well, but he sometimes helped handymen with random home-improvement projects during the winters, which directly coincided with the type of assistance Shankar needed. He predominately did that type of work while living out in the forests of Humboldt County, just before he had the slightest slivers of regret and temporarily returned to city life in Berkeley.

Maybe I should've stayed up in Humboldt longer and become a better handyman, he thought. *But what about the desert? What about those endless days of pure emptiness?*

There was no self-denial that could negate the loneliness of those empty days, but in retrospect, he now knew that leaving California for the Utah desert helped him stay the course to wherever his existential labyrinth was currently heading. But within those sporadic seconds of broad, overarching rumination, he found himself hung up on the decision to leave the Northern California forests for Berkeley. He was having trouble understanding how being a street drifter and sleeping on and off in Meryl's attic played any significance in how everything had led up to this precise point of him standing next to Shankar in the woods outside Aspen. *Maybe going to Berkeley was a complete waste of time?*

"But if I wasn't there, I would've never met Thayer," he mumbled out loud, which caused him to come back to the reality that was he and Shankar sharing a moment of silence while glancing around their new home.

"Huh? What's that?" Shankar asked as he slipped out of his own pensive state. "I didn't quite catch that."

"Nothing," Byrd responded as he shook his head. "So, what should I do first? Let's get the ball rolling."

Those first couple of weeks entailed one plumber and one

solar-panel specialist coming to the property for a few days each, but other than them, it was just Shankar and Byrd. Shankar had a large stockpile of building supplies and set Byrd up to help him redo the insulation and shingles on all the roofs, refinish and re-seal the exterior cedar walls, and completely rip out and replace the deteriorating hardwood floors in each of the cabins. The main reason Shankar insisted on doing nearly the entire renovation DIY style was because he wanted to *feel more* when the end product was rebuilt by his own hands. He insisted that this was the *right way* to begin their new chapter, and he also admitted that he needed to cut costs due to the prime real estate purchase depleting a massive portion of his savings.

Each day consisted of much more than just work, and Byrd was able to find time to play guitar by the creek while looking at small patches of yellow, purple, and white wildflowers just on the other side of the bank. He grew to like his new home, and living with Shankar was an easy adjustment from being alone in the desert. One thing that Byrd admired about Shankar was his attentiveness, because whether it was hammering shingles, building a chair, paint-ing, or reflooring, it was easy to tell that he focused on one thing at a time through calm, steady intention.

One morning, Byrd noticed how the water coming out of their grungy shower was completely brown, so he started rinsing himself off in the nearby creek like he would in Utah (even after a local plumber fixed the dirty water). But the Colorado High Country wa-ter was exponentially colder than the creek he was used to, and it was becoming more evident each night that fall was approaching. Their insulation tactics weren't working quite as well as they'd hoped, and as they woke up shivering each morning, it became clearer that they weren't working fast enough. They were both well aware of the first major winter storms typically rolling through Aspen near the mid-dle of October, so they set a due date to be finished with the renova-tion by Halloween, even though they weren't on pace to come close to that mark by doing things the *right way*.

"Good morning, James! Would you like some tea?" Shankar asked like clockwork at 8 a.m. on the day everything changed. "I have Earl Grey, Passionfruit Oolong, and Moroccan Mint. Which would you prefer?"

"Oolong sounds fantastic. Thanks!" Byrd responded with a big smile, which vanished as Shankar walked back in the direction of his cabin.

He sat up on his extra-springy mattress to get a better glance at the creek through an old, opaque window, and he got his first foggy glimpses of mountain frost forming on the aspen leaves that summer. As much as he tried to convince himself how serendipitously helping Shankar was a predetermined fork in the road that all made sense when adding up the recent past, things were still downright hazy when he acknowledged his near future. *What am I gonna do when this gig is over? Stay here during the winter, with barely any electricity?*

Winter always brought Byrd a lot of stress, particularly throughout his recent past while he'd been living in the wild. The California coast was his usual refuge spot when temperatures started to drop in the desert, and he realized that he'd never been living in a place *this cold* when fall foliage initially began. He put on his new long-sleeved shirt and walked across the crunchy grass to Shankar's cabin near the back end of the property, and he instantly felt how much warmer it was in there from a propane-powered stovetop heating a teakettle. Shankar's cabin was more established than Byrd's and even had adequate electrical outlets, but it was also roughing it for a retired financial advisor who was just beginning his transition into woods life.

"We'll need to start boiling the water from the pump just to be safe, but we should also refill those larger jugs from the creek and use the purifier as needed," Shankar explained as Byrd sat next to him in a homemade chair that seemed as though it would snap any day. Shankar turned his focus to the kettle and verified how the pouring moment had arrived. "This water is good, though. No brown."

"Shankar, I need to get something off my chest," Byrd responded before taking a deep breath.

"Okay. What's bothering you?" Shankar replied, while placing mugs of Passionfruit Oolong on an unstable coffee table.

They both sipped on their mugs in silence, except for the sighs of relief that the hot drinks provided.

"It's getting a little bit colder every night," Byrd said.

"It certainly is, but I don't think the cold nights are what's bothering you. Don't be afraid to express your thoughts freely. We're partners now, James."

"I don't think we're making good enough time to finish by Halloween."

"I believe you're correct with that assumption."

"So, what're we gonna do then?"

"Well, if the weather permits, we'll continue. If we don't finish before the snow falls, it won't be a concern. We'll do as much as we can and more than likely finish up the renovation next spring."

"You mean we'll live here the *whole winter*?"

"Of course, this is my home now. You're more than welcome to stay this winter, regardless of our progress. I have no intention of opening the retreat for business until next June anyways."

"Okay, maybe I'll stay, but we still need help. I know you wanna do this the *right way*, but we can't do all this alone anymore."

Shankar thought to himself for a minute, while sipping his tea and creaking back and forth in his rocking chair. "Maybe you're right. But I don't want too many more strangers coming here and doing the work for us. The plumbers and electricians have been enough. I have no problem with more help, but it just has to be the *right help*. I prefer help like you, James, and I know I say it a lot, but I know how lucky I am to have you here. I know you promised to help out a long time ago, but I would've never held you accountable for anything," he continued as he cracked a smile. "When I emailed you, it was a shot in the dark that fortunately came to a shimmer. But I honestly thought you weren't going to talk to me ever again after a couple of weeks went by without any response!" he joked as they started laughing, which led to another pause.

"I know some people in Boulder who might be interested in helping us out. I think they could maybe be the *right help*, but I don't know. They're all my age."

Another pause.

"I'm sure you've made friends with many wonderful people throughout your journeys. And if they live in Boulder, they're only a four-hour drive away, so even if they help for only a weekend, it would be good. Do you think I'm afraid of being *the old guy* around here or something?"

"No, not, of course not," Byrd spilled out. "I just didn't wanna assume I knew the *right help*. But to be honest, I sort of had second thoughts about my friends when I considered how young they all are."

Shankar laughed at Byrd's scrunched-up, I-didn't-mean-it facial expression. "You should *see* the look on your face! I'm just messing with you!" he said as he tried to hold it all in. "What, do you think I started a yoga retreat center in Aspen to only hang out with a bunch of old farts like me?"

Byrd couldn't help but chuckle. "I don't know, man. I'm just here to help you build this place up. I'm not the one to help you fill it with people. Your guests are *your business*."

"Maybe you and me are like *Dumb & Dumber* hiding out in the woods together when there are countless beautiful women right down the road in town!" he said, now wiping away a tear. "You're right. Getting some more young blood to help out around here sounds about *right*."

"How do you know who the *right help* is, though?"

Their laughter slowed down as they both returned to their morning teacups and contemplated the question.

"The *right help* ... they have to be willing to drop everything and really go for it like you did. I think this is an interesting opportunity, wouldn't you agree?"

"It's definitely not bad. I don't know too many people who'd be down for the cold nights, though."

"Right, that's the other part about doing things the *right way*. We need people who are willing to be out here facing the elements with us and won't take what's over *there*," he said, pointing in the direction of Aspen, "and bring it here."

Another pause.

"Yeah, I know what you mean. It's hard to tell with these guys. We camped together a couple months ago, and I grew up with one of them. He's cool, but the other guy … well … he's kind of *a lot*."

"Do you think they'd like to help us? I'll pay them, of course."

"Maybe? I'd have to go to town and ask them on my email, I suppose."

Shankar's stomach rapidly enlarged with laughter again. "Do you have a fear of going into town? You've barely left this valley since you got here, but I'm sure you know that."

About an hour later, Byrd was rolling into the downtown commercial district of Aspen, which seemed like the heart of Manhattan to him. He rolled past Gucci, Prada, Dolce & Gabbana, and every puffy-fur-jacket-wearing mannequin made him feel sick to his stomach. His routine morning was suddenly turning into chaos, and he checked his side mirrors for cops that he figured would pull him over for not wearing a helmet, or any other illegality to validate how out of place he was.

He parked the bike and began meandering around to figure out where he could get online, which he assumed would be the library that he had no idea how to find. He initially had his mind on asking a cop, but that was *asking for it*, so he walked along Hyman Avenue toward an expansive outdoor mall. As he turned a couple of random corners, he became more intrigued by the people who walked past him than by where he was going. He reeked from working every day with Shankar and not bathing enough in the cold creek, and he didn't know how long it had been since his clothes were washed. Everyone who walked by him seemed like they'd never gone more than a couple of days without a hot shower and a cozy bed, and *Wow, these Aspen women are hot!* He couldn't help himself from repeatedly whispering *holy shit* out loud, and he figured he might as well ask the next pretty girl he saw for directions.

"Hey, I'm lost. Do you by chance know where the library is?" he said out loud to himself, just to hear how pathetic the question sounded.

He was convinced that there was absolutely no way he could go through with striking up a conversation like that, but just as he was about to walk into a chic café to ask the hostess for directions, a stroke of déjà vu came flooding in from his peripheral vision. He saw two girls walking together from the corner of his eye, and the sight of them nearly caused him to lose his balance. It was *her*, the girl from the gas station, Jane, it *had to be*. The two girls continued approaching and noticed how Byrd had stopped in his tracks upon seeing them. One of the girls had blonde hair, and she glanced in his direction from behind her sunglasses.

"Hey!" Byrd yelled out as he walked up to them with uneasy enthusiasm. As he got closer, he realized that the blonde girl wasn't Jane. His smile dropped.

"Can I help you?" the blonde girl asked.

"Umm, yeah," Byrd said, trying to recover his composure. "I'm lost. Do you by chance know where the library is?"

The girls looked at each other and busted out laughing.

"That has got to be the *lamest* pickup line I've ever heard," the blonde girl replied.

"I know, right!" the other girl howled.

"I know it sounds dumb, but I actually need help finding the library. I don't have a phone that could give me directions, so I don't know where I am. I'm just trying to log in to my email and talk to some folks."

The two girls looked at each other and examined Byrd like they'd stumbled upon a time traveler visiting the future, almost as if they were getting a glimpse into a hippie ghost of Aspen's past.

"The library is three blocks behind you. *That way*, mountain man," the blonde explained, pointing down the street for clarification.

Byrd dejectedly walked down the street and trudged his way into the library, where he logged in to his email. He scrolled past a collection of spam before finding a message from Thayer that had arrived five nights earlier.

Hey Byrd!

What's up? How's the desert treating you? Is it dry out there? (only kidding)

I'm still in Boulder (I know) and I'm with Sky, O'Donnell and Ruben. We've been playing a song I just wrote and it made us think of you and that night we had earlier this summer. That place you live in is so special, it really is, and I think we're all down to come back out soon!

Between you and me, I don't really know what I'm doing anymore. It seems like there's this empty opening of some sort that I can't see, and I'm stuck looking around for it because I have no idea where the hell it is. It might actually be here in Boulder, but I don't know, it sure doesn't feel like it is. I do like it here. It's pretty, almost too pretty! I'm thinking of maybe going to real estate school now. It's just a thought, I guess.

It's definitely been really cool to hang out with Sky at the music store he works at, but mostly because no one ever comes down here and we mainly just hang out. They don't pay him much, but at least one of us has a job! O'Donnell just lost his job at the radio station, and Ruben randomly has Cat's van by himself and is saying he's moving to Colorado. I'm not sure yet if I'm officially moving here, but yeah, that's what's going on with us. We all miss you a ton, and we're down to come see you again soon.

Write back soon please!

Thay

He responded:

Thay,

I guess this late response isn't too unexpected given my track record, but I promise I've actually been really busy. I definitely should've reached out sooner, but I'm logged in right now to see if you guys would be interested in helping me out with my new job.

Believe it or not, I'm living in the woods outside Aspen and am actually sleeping in a cabin WITH WALLS. I'm glad you're still in Boulder and hanging out with those guys, and I know it sounds bad, but I'm a little bit excited that you and O'Donnell are currently un-employed. The reason is we're in need of some assistance up here, and it pays $100 per day plus lodging and food. It's a long story, but a few years ago I promised this guy named Shankar that I'd help him build a retreat center and he actually called me out recently, so here we are!

It's kind of nuts, but I told Fundamental Roots I was having a 'family emergency' when he offered me a job, and we've been remodeling a couple buildings since I got here. But we're clearly in way over our heads and need some help.

I think you'd like it here, and you're invited to come help. We REALLY need it. The best part is that we just rebuilt the fire pit and made it massive, so it's a great spot for playing music in the evenings (which I'm sure we'd do a lot of).

Let me know if you're interested and I'll send you directions.

One Love,

JB

I I

hange is inevitable. Reality is in a constant process of change, and we're constantly changing within that process. Our hair slowly grows, plaque expands in between our teeth, sustenance gurgles within our intestinal tracts, muscles sway between relaxation and contraction, and countless thoughts travel through our brains with each passing day.

Time is the only consistent element of humanity's standardized changing, but not every change consistently coincides with the passing of standardized time. The universe exudes itself through space-time at the speed of light, but metaphysically, it exudes itself through infinite variables we encounter on Earth. Life's variety becomes the hours and minutes associated with what's commonly known as *individual time,* which perceptually contrasts the hardwired concept of standardized time. Individual time is mostly subjective and open to an endless array of possibilities, which makes it predisposed to manipulation.

One ironic aspect of individual time is the clear behavioral tendency toward living as creatures of habit. Our habits often tend to become ingrained to the point that they develop priceless values for their own alterations. Habitual alterations are what end up becoming some of the most revolutionary time manipulations within our unique realities; because when we choose to change something about ourselves (no matter how big or small), we're essentially crinkling away the wrapper of the juicy, crunchy, full-of-flavor core that is our future selves. Stagnation can be one of the main obstacles that holds us back from our future selves, because it limits our potential to be ready for anything and everything that's out there patiently waiting, waiting, waiting for you to make a change.

When Thayer read Byrd's email, almost immediately after it was delivered, she felt a sense of stagnation holding her back. She considered her life story to be its own intriguing movie, but felt like she was in the audience and not directing. She could envision her future selves: a rock star of epic proportions, or a real-estate agent with an office rock star attitude. She could see herself with wrinkles, gray hair, and baggy clothes, sitting outside a Pearl Street bar with Sky and O'Donnell, having done nothing but the same thing they'd been doing, all of them frustrated at life and the unclaimed changes that time bestowed upon them. The urges of saying *fuck it, let the good times roll* were always strong, mainly because it was so easygoing. She didn't want to be a Realtor, but she was downright sick of not having anything to do all day. Byrd was right in that he'd found a temporary work opening, but was it the *right way* to go?

She started reminiscing about the recent events that got her to where she currently was. Earlier that summer, she'd left her parents' home with Cat and Ruben to go on a quick trip to see a Furthur show, and now she was alternating sleeping locations between a van and a new boyfriend's house in Boulder. This sequence of self-analytical notions made her start laughing on a Pearl Street bench while the nexus of the universe's absurdity remained on full display in every direction.

"I guess O'Donnell and I are gonna be roomies!" she said to herself as she laughed while scrolling through her recent calls. She clicked on Sky's name to tell him about the exciting, new change that may or may not put a monkey wrench on their budding relationship.

She officially was postponing real-estate school.

Eight days later, a trio caravan was clanking its way down the dirt road that followed Castle Creek: Sky's van leading the way, followed by Thayer's new van, and cabloosed by Cat's (driven by Ruben). The vans were loud enough on the gravel to alert Byrd and Shankar that their visitors were nearby, so they both walked out to the end of the long driveway and waved them in as they passed through the open gate. As the vans approached the parking area, the newcomers shared a sigh of relief while noticing the relatively good appearance of the cabins, which was partly induced by the fact that they'd just been making jokes at a pit stop in Eagle about the "dump" they were subjecting themselves to.

As Thayer parked and turned off the ignition, she noticed a couple of different wood stacks intended for construction and fires, dozens of mulch bags, a handful of power tools, large coils of electrical cords, the barely functional remnants of Byrd's latest DIY furniture project, and filled clotheslines that stretched between the aspens. She had offered to bring all sorts of household supplies like kitchenware, rags, and bedsheets, per Byrd's request, and both Byrd and Shankar noticed her awkwardly fumble out of her van with a massive smile on her face.

"Hey, guys," she said as she took her first steps on Shankar's land and glanced up at the treehouses and yellowish-green canopy.

"Welcome! You must be Thayer!" Shankar yelled as he approached her. "We're very excited to have you help us. Thank you for being here!"

"Yeah, thanks again for coming, and welcome to the empty opening," Byrd said as they hugged and helped facilitate the formal introductions for Shankar.

"As you can all see, we're *very far off* from being finished with construction before the winter storms start rolling in within the next month or so," Shankar explained around the fire pit to the whole group. "We're going to need to work rather long hours each day in order to be fully prepared for winter, but I don't want you to think that I think of you as my employees. I see all of you more as my very first guests, who just so happen to want to help out."

"Wait a second, Shankar," O'Donnell chirped in without any hesitation. "I was told there'd be pay. You're saying you want us to bust our asses for you out here in the middle of the woods, for what exactly?"

"I'll pay all of you, so there's no need to worry about anything like that. To make things fair, I think it would be best for you to be paid the same that I've been paying James. That rate has been $100 per day, plus food, and your own cabin. Does that sound like it'll work?"

They all looked over at Byrd while thinking he probably wasn't the best one to be doing their financial negotiations, and he just shrugged his shoulders before they collectively agreed. None of them had any better options, and even Sky (who'd recently quit his job) thought it was a decent deal. Thayer had persuaded him into thinking this was *the opening* for them to break habits and play more music with Byrd, and as for Ruben and O'Donnell, their lack of steady income was more than enough to keep them satisfied with Shankar's offer.

Shankar led a tour of the property that featured the unfinished cabins, the solar panels, the well, and the many views of Castle Creek and the surrounding wilderness. They were all jaw-dropped by the sheer beauty of the Aspen area, as well as the sheer amount of work that still needed to be done. So, they got right to work once the tour had ended.

Thayer organized the communal kitchen area of Shankar's cabin, Sky helped Byrd refinish a wooden dining table, and Ruben and O'Donnell helped Shankar with a hardwood floor installation in an extra cabin that was intended to entertain retreat guests during inclement weather. The learning curve was steep for the new group, who had never done any large-scale DIY remodeling, but any lack of experience didn't seem to matter at all. All that mattered was their willingness to learn, which was their only flimsy hope.

"I believe now is as good of a time as ever to make a toast," Shankar said later that evening around their newly finalized dining table, which creaked as he pressed down on it to stand up with his mug of wine in hand. "Welcome to the Castle Creek Ranch!" he yelled out as the whole group cheered and tapped their cups together.

"What we have all around us here is the foundation of a dream come true. This dream was something I thought would never, ever actually happen, but then I met our friend James, who was the first person to tell me that *this* was a dream worth dreaming!" he continued as a few cheers rang around the table. "It's true. *Everyone* I told this idea to thought I was a complete nut for wanting to leave my life behind and get certified as a yoga instructor. Now that I've gone through all sorts of training programs and am actually living in the woods, here's what I've learned so far: construction is *pretty damn hard*!

"But in all honesty, I'm beyond glad you're all here," he continued. "James and I realized not too long ago that we were completely screwed, just the two of us, so I'm grateful and forever indebted for this spontaneous act of generosity from all of you. This tiny sliver of land is truly remarkable. You could say it's an investment of mine, but quite honestly, I don't know who the hell is going to end up coming all the way out here just to *chillax* with me!" he joked.

"From now on, this land isn't an investment of any kind, except one toward perfecting our shared home. This is how I've always wanted this to happen: to build this place up with my own hands so I can truly say that I cared for it like a home was always meant to be cared for, just like how our ancestors built and cherished their homes. Tonight, I have finally found the *right help* to bring this dream to fruition, and so this dream is now *ours*, and our dreams will bring us together. So, to our dreams! May we all invest heavily in our dreams!" he yelled as he raised his mug for the last time, and they resumed their dinner of chicken masala, rice, and naan.

As they ate seconds and refilled their wine cups, Byrd felt déjà vu as he connected the resemblance between their group and his family. They were just eating dinner on their first night together at Shankar's ranch, but for Byrd, it was the biggest nonwork dinner crowd he'd had in recent memory. Any meal with over five people was like a holiday to him, but this dinner was unique and on a whole different level. He could sense there was something special about this moment, and he knew exactly what he needed to do.

"*Hey*, how about we take a picture of us around the table?" he chimed in as they all agreed.

Shankar took a picture with his retro film camera as the group sat around the janky, handmade table. There was nothing special about the picture itself, but it was one of those moments when everyone in the image thought something along the lines of *I wonder what that'll look like in five years.*

"What about the construction rules, Shankar?" Byrd chimed in after the photo moment had ended. "You didn't mention them in your toast like you said you would."

"You're right. I forgot," he responded with a smile. "But they're your friends that you've introduced to me, so maybe *you* should explain the work rules."

"All right, I guess I'll do it."

"You have to stand up, though. Make it official," Shankar directed, still smiling.

Byrd stood up and adjusted his newly cleaned shirt, which still looked dirty from the permanent stains that were now embedded in the cotton fibers.

"All right," he repeated himself. "Shankar and I decided on having two rules for while we're all here finishing the construction of the ranch. Rule #1: Consider each other first with *true altruism*. And Rule #2: If you're gonna play music, make it good."

The rules announcement got the whole group excited as they stood up and gathered their instruments. Within a few minutes, they had a steady, rhythmic jam going that was led by Ruben on the drums and Byrd on guitar. They added Thayer on her portable keyboard, and Sky on his new acoustic guitar. Byrd held down the rhythm, and they all followed his lead into a seemingly endless improvisation.

It was after midnight a few hours later, so they decided to disperse to their cabins and hunker down till morning. For Thayer, the cold

Aspen air was much different than Boulder. Although it was cold enough to put on a sweatshirt and pants, she found the brisk alpine air to be refreshing. She inhaled each breath as if she was finally breathing the right air in the right place, but it was still freezing along Castle Creek for an LA girl. She shivered as she brushed her teeth outside and became hypnotized at the closeness of the constellations, which were brighter than she'd ever seen them. The night sky didn't shine that bright even at Byrd's Utah campsite, and she realized that she'd never been literally this close to the stars.

She jogged back into her cabin, where she saw Sky in a sleeping bag on top of a grimy, floor-based mattress. She sat down on the mattress and nestled her body up against his.

"Get in here," he whispered as he showed her the extra space in the sleeping bag, which could easily fit both of them.

Her goose-bumped pores relaxed as Sky's body temperature raised her own, and she thought to herself, *I could do this every night.*

The changes that quickly presented themselves to Thayer at Shankar's ranch were like a reality TV show where a city slicker gets taken into the woods and forced into hard manual labor that exposes their sheltered lifestyle; but in Thayer's case, the city slicker was simultaneously making fun of herself and the audience each and every episode. She realized how every decision on the ranch would lead to some type of task she was inexperienced in doing, and this led to a whole new perspective on how she ended up managing her time. There were several important tasks that needed to be completed during that first week after the group's arrival, and she was often installing new siding on the cabins, nailing new floorboards, and even crawling underneath cabin foundations because she was the smallest and could maneuver the easiest. Each day flew by at a hundred miles per hour, especially because she was often the one who redid some of the work that the guys were doing in other parts of the ranch. She'd often find that Sky's flooring work didn't look quite right or that Ruben was sleeping by the creek, and no one else was willing to call them out except her.

Remodeling the treehouses was her main task, and one day while redoing the stairs, she personally concluded that her reality show would be called *Extreme Makeover: City Girl Wilderness Edition*. It seemed exactly like some of the sarcastic show ideas she'd heard from her dad's drunk friends at dinner parties, but now she was the show's star, and the script was developing with each of her passing decisions. She had the treehouse suites looking and functioning better within a couple weeks (minus some crucial plumbing and electrical work), and she would've finished much more if she weren't held back by helping with the other cabins. She was by far the busiest out of everyone, and no one denied her toughness to get each job done the *right way*, except sometimes herself.

As much as she loved every second of living in the forest and remodeling the ranch, the lack of clean running water and conventional electricity was quite the adjustment; however, compared to the other three newbies, she was adjusting to life in the woods the best. O'Donnell and Ruben become closer pals at the ranch due to being left out of the alone time between Thayer and Sky, and it wasn't all that uncommon to hear some kind of stomach complaint, hygiene issue, or minor work injury come out of either one of them. But at the end of each day, they'd still get a decent amount of work accomplished, which Thayer figured was thanks to Byrd's handyman directions.

All five of them looked to Byrd as the group's wilderness guru who knew how to properly build things, manually start fires, and cook meals the cowboy way. A lot of those cowboy-style meals were largely prepared by Shankar as part of his end, and even his delectable dishes were subject to complaints from O'Donnell and Ruben, due to a general lack of options. But when these types of grumblings would occur, Byrd would find his own weird way of flipping any type of negativity into a silver lining. His quirky advice would remind O'Donnell and Ruben to recognize how their lifestyle changes with Shankar were so much more than a temporary job, and he'd even say that their current situation was an opportunity to reach genuine joy. Everywhere Byrd went, he reeked of euphoria, which was all part of his attempt to follow their recently established number-one rule. For Byrd, *true altruism* was supposed to go far beyond any normal, societal scope and embody a relentless sense of inclusivity, and his altruistic relentlessness ended up making everyone feel as though goofy gifts and kind gestures were always on the horizon.

On several mornings, they'd all wake up to strong smells emanating from outside their cabins. When they'd slowly get their clothes on and emerge from their newly installed doors, they'd typically see a massive breakfast spread waiting for them that featured large baking trays positioned above the fire's embers. Almost every afternoon, each of them would be surprised by some kind of tasty snack when they walked past Byrd, and his blatant attempts to be a bit more conversational during the evening hours led to a little more fun and a lot more music. Byrd wanted to live by Rule #1 as extensively as possible, and this was mainly inspired by a deep discussion he'd had with Shankar a few days prior to Thayer, Sky, Ruben, and O'Donnell's arrival. In that discussion, Byrd argued that the true meaning of altruism had been manipulated by the growing tides of cultural time, in which vast regions of "civilized people" had stopped considering the full extent to which they'd actually like to be treated. He believed this "altruistic complacency" had modified our sense of what altruistic acts are meant to be, and his most obvious example of this was social media causing people to expect validation after acting altruistic. For hours they went over the fine details of answering the question, *Is it true altruism when you do something good for someone else, but with a social media post in mind?*

The first few weeks at the ranch were by far the toughest on the newbies physically, but they still enjoyed a tiny sliver of light throughout that same time: the evening fires. Every night they'd build a fire and gather around the flames to abide by Rule #2: *if you're gonna play music, make it good.*

Thayer noticed how Shankar was guiding Byrd through sitar

lessons around sunset each day, and she also recognized how Byrd wouldn't play sitar by the fire, out of respect for Rule #2. But the lack of sitar was ultimately trivial for those fireside jam sessions, partly because Uncle Tito would bring out the beach vibes when they wanted to mix things up. Byrd was always ready to plan a new song, and they'd often expand upon the songs in his notebook, but Thayer also mustered up the courage to share what she'd recently been writing. One of her songs from those first weeks at the ranch was called "Our Changing Dreams."

Have you ever realized how close you are to the stars?
Have you ever seen dreams come true in bars?
We can sail, away from here
Cross oceans, cross rivers, cross mountains, my dear

We can run, run all the way home
Across highways, state lines, under this big sky dome
And when you love, make it last forever
Cuz our dreams bring us together

Our dreams bring us together
Our stars ain't so far apart

So, let's dream and let's sail and let's run and let's go
All the way out there, let's make a new home
Where we're free, to be loved and be one
Make the most of our lives, all we need is fun

And our dreams bring us together
There's a change that we can feel
It's a-rumbling, just like a river
It's a-shining, like a star's new deal

Have you ever realized how close you are to the stars?
We can all see it now, you're gonna go far

Where you'll rise to who you're meant to be
A brand-new you, chasing our changing dreams

So, invest, my friend, invest in your life
Invest, my friend, invest in your dreams
Invest, my friend, invest in your love
Invest, my friend, invest in The One

Because our dreams bring us together
Your love is waiting on you
The stars don't have to be so far
Together our dreams will turn to memoirs

Have you ever realized how close you are to the stars?
Don't worry, my friend
Our changing dreams are not far

It was safe to say that Rule #2 was abided by.

12

hange is inevitable, so how we accept change ultimately helps define who we'll become. The famous Chinese philosopher Lao-Tzu once said, "Life is a series of natural and spontaneous changes. Don't resist them; that only creates sorrow. Let reality be reality. Let things flow naturally forward in whatever way they like." It seems easy enough to go with Lao-Tzu's flow, and yet accepting change is often one of the most convoluted mental processes we all experience to this day.

Resisting changes can be an all-too-sorrowful existence for many people, and these self-destructive habits become passageways toward the conventional veil of reality that waits for our reluctant arrivals. Accepting life's changes is something we all must face, no matter how reluctant we are, and the more we fight changes, the more we struggle to needlessly examine the inevitable. So, acceptance becomes a lifelong social experiment within our own cognitive laboratories, and these tests examine the apparent outcomes between our infinite perspectives and experiences. Loosely according to Lao-Tzu, we must encourage ourselves to accept spontaneity as our guide throughout the natural order of the Unified Field, and we must accept how spontaneity helps us see beyond reality's veil toward where its current flows.

What kind of spontaneous changes are you willing to accept, even when they subtly pop up out of nowhere? Have there ever been moments in your life when you've thought to yourself, *How much different would things be if I went out on a limb and did that one wild experience that didn't seem like the smartest move at the time?*

Lin had been living in a dorm room at NYU for just over two months, and his new life on the opposite side of America was not-so-spontaneously accepted. There were plenty of typical freshman opportunities that helped him meet his classmates and dorm neighbors, but each day he was haunted by a loud, internal voice that wouldn't stop asking, *what in the actual fuck am I doing here?*

Being a violinist with a full-ride scholarship to NYU's Steinhart Department of Music didn't come without its perks, and several of the faculty members Lin met within his first few weeks of classes already knew who he was and that he may be their next star student. Lin held himself together in New York similarly to how he carried himself in San Francisco: a stiff, rigid mannequin of a genius. Being a bit difficult to talk to also wasn't a solid prerequisite for living in a massive dorm in the heart of Greenwich Village, and after a couple months of trying to accept his changes and eventually reverting to old habits, Lin began to sink into a desperate isolation that had him wondering what at all he enjoyed about this new, less-recognizable version of himself.

Studying music in Manhattan was the core foundation of a dream come true that he'd had for years, but he was starting to realize there was something faulty about the way his longstanding dream was coming to fruition. Those first months brought nothing but self-explanatory perspective during each day of classes, and daily adventures throughout the city provided an endless supply of lonerism. He quickly realized that his habit of playing violin for entire afternoons was going to be held up by the fact that he had a roommate named Eric, so out of courtesy for Eric, he'd walk and take the subway to nearby parks, where he could play for as long as he wanted. However, the other reason he'd go to parks by himself was to avoid the social norms of dorm life.

When Lin wasn't rehearsing songs underneath one of his favorite trees, he was watching pedestrians going through their daily routines. He'd play the same type of game that he'd often play from his parents' balcony in Chinatown, but here in Greenwich Village, there was an entirely different energy to grasp onto. Here in New York City, people would walk with a sense of superiority with each stride, as if every step was laser-focused within a systematic strategy aiming in the direction of a well-deliberated future self. And at the exact same time on the exact same block, there would be people savoring each stride with no apparent purpose at all, as if they were loose stairs on a spiral staircase toward society's social gutters. Lin was keen to pick up on the similarities between San Francisco and New York, but their differences were what kept him wondering about what else was there in Manhattan's endlessly long alleyways, and who he could meet if he found the courage to explore them.

He gazed at a woman carrying multiple bags as she continued a shopping spree along a nearby sidewalk. She was wearing pink Dr. Martens boots and a beige trench coat, and as she passed by, he thought to himself, *What's in those bags? Where's she going with all those bags? Probably some loft in SoHo where she's been returning from shopping sprees for years. Her own private foxhole in the heart of a concrete jungle, which she knows like the back of her hand.*

He gazed over at several groups of children playing with their parents on a nearby jungle gym, and he recognized how those kids would grow up just like him in the middle of a city, and they too would learn rather quickly about how absurd humanity can be. But for right now, they were simply having fun within a refuge of prolonged innocence that sheltered them against the inevitable struggles of leaving home for the unknown.

He couldn't deny how he was attaching his own insecurities to these hypothetical people-watchees, but he knew he'd see the real changing leaves of New Yorkers as he picked up his instrument and began playing it for everyone to hear on that late-September afternoon. He'd inevitably draw some attention, sometimes just passersby, sometimes people who'd stop for a moment, and sometimes the children from the jungle gym would venture across the park to get an up-close look at the source of the musical sounds. These were the moments that produced a profound effect upon Lin during those first two months at NYU, because he'd frequently realize that he was playing violin for a child who'd never seen or heard one before.

It was his ninth Friday in New York, and he was finally about to find a reason to feel like he'd made a smart move by leaving home. That evening was when his personal purpose of venturing to NYU initially revealed itself, and this purpose had nothing to do with a conventional collegiate lifestyle. Although studying music in the heart of Manhattan was far from conventional, it still didn't change the fact that most freshmen wanted to drink in the dorms and go out to mainstream weekend spots with fake IDs. Lin was never that great at making friends or partying, so it wasn't uncommon for him to linger aimlessly inside art galleries, bodegas, and near-empty cafés on Friday and Saturday nights. Being alone was something that Lin was no longer troubled by, and this was partly the result of his mom's advice that she'd given him right before he left their home. That tiny kernel of wisdom was all he needed to realize just how accustomed he already was to living inside his own head, and how his intuition was the only guiding light he needed.

It was on that fateful ninth Friday evening when his entire perspective shifted and spontaneity grabbed the reins of his lonely stroll as he meandered around a bustling Greenwich Village.

He was walking back to his dorm from Washington Square Park, where he'd decided to play violin and people-watch after his classes had ended, but on that evening, he chose to go the long way home down MacDougal Street and onto the Village's famous Bleecker Street. Just like any other Friday, Bleecker Street was packed to the brim with people piling into restaurants and bars to begin their weekends. Lin looked through the glass windows into the dining rooms and saw socialites doing what they do best, and he wondered what he was missing out on with that type of New York experience. He thought to himself, *why can't I have some fun for a change?*

In that exact moment of extroverted contemplation, he

unknowingly found himself directly in front of the Blue Queen Lounge. He also unknowingly found himself directly in front of a born-and-raised New Yorker, who was eyeing him down at the top of the lounge's staircase.

"Hey, man!" he yelled over to Lin. "The show's about to start, so get on in there! I'll give you free a drink ticket."

"What type of show is it?" Lin asked, trying to look down the stairs and seeing nothing but cement steps.

"It's that *bona fide* jazz, of course! What do you got in the case, bro?"

"My violin," Lin said opening the box, subtly bragging about the luxuriousness of his backup instrument.

The doorman looked him up and down. "Wait a damn second ... do you play over in Washington Square Park?"

"Yeah, sometimes."

"And over by the school playground on Mercer?"

"Yeah, I've played there before."

"I knew it! I've seen you like a dozen times by now when I'm walking around here. You're always playing some way-outdated opera, and I mean, you're good and all, but I'm always thinking, *not every dumbass straggling around Greenwich Village wants to hear that sad, cry-me-a-river violin,* ya know?" he said as he cracked a smile. "But I see you getting little crowds and whatnot. You must make pretty good tips, right?"

"Some people insist on giving me a little cash, but I never keep it or anything. I just give it to a homeless guy on my way back to the dorms at NYU, where I live."

"Whoa, hold the phone a second," the doorman cut him off. "Let me get this straight. You're a *student* who's busking in the most expensive city in America, and you're giving away *all* your tips?

"Yeah, but I wouldn't say I'm *busking*. I just don't know where to practice yet. I moved down the street at the beginning of August, and my roommate doesn't like it when I play in our room, so I go outside when I've got nothing else to do."

"*Oh,* you're new around here? I *never* would've guessed!" the doorman replied. "I'm just messing with you, but you're as green as the grass. I ain't gonna lie—you might be evergreen, but you can really play, that's no joke. What's your name, bro?"

"Lin. Do you work here at Blue Queen Lounge?"

"What, do you think I'm standing out here for free like it's 1835?" he asked aggressively, making Lin's eyes widen. "Nah, I'm just playing, but you should've seen the look on your face. *Wow!*" he said as he laughed. "But yeah, I've worked here for a few years now, and I do more than just get schmucks like you to come inside. Here's my card," he touted, swiftly reaching in and out of his chest pocket and extending a business card that read:

Reginald E. Wallace
Assistant Co-Supervisor
Blue Queen Lounge

"Nice to meet you, Reginald," Lin said, extending his hand for a shake.

"Call me Reg," he replied, reciprocating the formal shake with an awkward fist bump.

"So, you're an *assistant co-supervisor*," Lin said, pointing at the card. "What exactly does that mean?"

"Yeah, I *assist* one of the Blue Queen's co-supervisors. It means I do all sorts of work around here. I mean, this place sometimes gets *wild* on the weekends, and we need all hands on deck! I do security. I do marketing stuff, like right now, and sometimes I get to hang out with the artists and make sure they've got everything they need. It's called show business, bro."

"That sounds pretty cool! It must be a dream come true to have a job like this!"

"Yeah, man, you know what they say. There ain't no business like show business," he said with a bright smile, which quickly changed back to a contemplative look. They glanced at each other in silence as Bleecker Street bustled around them.

Lin noticed Reg look him up and down, almost as if he was

examining the details of a New York strip that had possibly turned.

"You know, you're pretty good at violin. Are you at Steinhart?"

"Yeah, I actually got a full-ride to Steinhart," Lin responded with extra pride.

"*Oh*, that explains it then," Reg replied with a brief smirk. "They got you all locked down like those athletes not being paid shit and they're promising all sorts of *perks* and stuff like that, except they didn't even give you a place to *practice!* I mean, not even the scholarship students get a place to sit down and *practice!*" he continued, convinced Lin wouldn't catch on to his Allen Iverson reference. "Jeez, man. You don't need a school to teach you how to jam. I'll tell you what, I'm *genuinely* impressed by you, Lin. You're out here giving away your busking tips, and I think *you* deserve a free drink more than any of these other sheeplike tourists waddling around with their mouths open like they've never seen a real city before. So here, I'll give you a few drink tickets for this joint, and you just go down there and listen to some beats and have yourself a good time. I'll see you later," Reg directed as he handed Lin three drink tickets and wrapped a neon-green paper band around his left wrist.

"All right, I'm down. Thanks, Reg!" Lin agreed, now excited to be illegally admitted into his first Manhattan bar.

"Now I know it's like fifty-fifty that a kid can hold his drinks down, so this ain't gonna be any dram shop bullshit, Lin. I'll be watching you, college boy!" Reg yelled down the stairs as Lin walked into the Blue Queen Lounge.

It wasn't the first bar Lin had ever been in, but walking into Blue Queen with three drink tickets felt like the very first bar experience of his life. He walked straight up to the bartender in the front corner of the dimly lit basement and handed him one of Reg's tickets in exchange for a draft beer. *That was easy*, he thought as he walked over to a round table near the stage in the back of the room. He patiently waited and had enough time for two beers before the first band came to the stage. The band was called Retro Phat, which comprised three young women in their early twenties: one playing drums, one playing electric guitar, and the last on standup bass. It was only 5 p.m. when they started playing, so Lin was one of the only people in the lounge for their entire set.

It wasn't just the obvious facts of the standup bass player's stunning mocha complexion and sex appeal for miles that had Lin's jaw dropped for the entirety of the hourlong performance; it was also the bass player's nimble dexterity and quick fingers as she played each note to absolute perfection that kept Lin from looking away. Lin was well acquainted with standup bass and had played it several times, but never *like that*, and he'd never seen a bassist switch between standup and electric with each new song. He'd also never seen a bass player be so noticeable, and it was blatantly obvious how she was the basis for each song's rhythmic underpinning. He kept drinking beer, and when each song approached its chorus, he'd take a long swig and close his eyes as he concentrated on the bassist's sound.

"Oooh, I believe in *miracles!*" Retro Phat sang out in perfect unison. "Where you from? You *sexy thing!*" they continued as the bassist displayed her showmanship by maneuvering her instrument back and forth and grinding up against its maple back.

Lin considered how it certainly would be a miracle if he went out on a date with the bass player, especially considering that no girl had ever taken him seriously before. But the more he listened to her sing jazz and funk covers to the small crowd, the more enthralled he became by the idea of simply talking to her. The intensifying liquid courage from his fourth beer was only inflating his lackluster self-confidence, and it was enough to mentally allow him the general concept of having a conversation with a beautiful woman who was a few years older than him. It was one of those nothing-to-lose moments when harnessing an opportunity required a forced leap into action, and Lin could already feel the regret rumbling in his belly from the notion of leaving Blue Queen Lounge without having at least a word with the bassist. *You're gonna talk to her,* he whispered to himself, *but what're you gonna say?*

About twenty minutes later, the time came for him to take the initiative as he noticed the bassist putting her stuff away at the end of a backstage hallway. He spilled a few drops on his shirt as he chugged the rest of his beer, walked right past an *Employees Only* sign, and stood frozen in place right in front of her. He had no idea what to say, so a massive smile grew on his face as he recognized his drunken mistake.

"Are you lost? The bathroom is over *there*," she said, pointing back toward the entrance of the lounge.

Lin's face started to sink, but he knew now was the time to be as profound as possible while also not coming off as a complete creep. "It's all good. I just peed a few minutes ago," he said, drunkenly laughing to himself.

She laughed a little bit too. "*Okay*, so what're you doing back here then?"

"I, umm … I wanted to talk to you, if that's okay … I think you play the bass better than anyone else I've ever heard, and I'm in the music school at NYU and play with *a lot* of bassists."

"Oh, well thank you very much. That's sweet of you."

"I've literally never seen someone so easily switch from double to electric. Most of the bassists I've played with use a bow, and I just, I don't know … I just wanted to introduce myself. My name is Lin, Lin Rose."

"Maya Walker," she said with a smile as they shook hands. "Where are you from, Lin?"

"San Francisco, but I was born in China."

"So, what brought you to NYU?"

"Well, to be honest, the full ride they offered is what got me here. I don't know about you, but I'm pretty tipsy from all the drink tickets the doorman gave me, and I'm *starving*. Do you wanna get something to eat?"

Maya duly noted the subtle brag about his scholarship, which was clearly Lin's attempt to insinuate his talent. This was far from the first time that some drunk dude had tried to ask her out to dinner after a 5 p.m. set at Blue Queen, but through the typical apprehension she generally had toward flirtatious loungers, she recognized how Lin's direct approach to asking her out was thinly veiled in sheepishness. The fact that Lin appeared to be at least close to her age and not as old as her dad also helped him seem a little less creepy, and she also knew it would be at least a couple of hours until she'd be picked up by her mom in the Bleecker alleyway.

"I don't know. I don't even *know* you!" she responded with a haughty laugh. "I don't usually take chances like that from drunk guys around here."

"Well, how does *anyone* meet *anyone* without taking chances on each other?" he asked her with a goofy smile that won her over, at least for a free meal.

Maya knew exactly where they should eat: a nearby food truck, specializing in Chinese delights, named *Beijing Hutongs*. Lin was pleasantly surprised by its resemblance to the street food he was used to getting in San Francisco, and as they waited for dim sum, bao buns, sticky rice, and sesame balls, Lin explained how he was adopted and that it had been a few years since his parents had taken him on a vacation to China. Maya asked him if he ever thought about trying to meet his real parents, to which Lin quietly responded *sometimes* before quickly changing the subject and speaking fluent Mandarin to the food truck employees. He got them to laugh by poking fun at the menu's lack of frog legs, and Maya raised her eyebrows as she eavesdropped on the basic sounds of Lin's linguistics. They laughed later on when he explained the humorous details of the Mandarin conversation, and they continued walking along Leroy Street in the direction of the Hudson River Park, where Maya wanted to eat with a view.

"So, what are you, a junior or senior?" she asked as they ate bao buns while looking across the river at Newark's skyline.

"No, I'm a freshman," he replied. "Why? How old are you?"

"I'm *twenty-two* ... So, what, you got a fake ID or something?"

"No, the doorman was just cool with me. Do you know Reg?"

"Yeah, I know Reggie's crazy ass," she said, shaking her head. "Damn, that guy is *so stupid* sometimes! I can't believe he gave you a wristband without even seeing a fake."

"Oh c'mon, please don't say anything. He just wanted me to have a good time, I guess. He told me that he's seen me play my violin in the neighborhood, and I told him I was new here, that's all. Please, I don't want him to get in any trouble because of *me*."

"It's fine, I won't tell anybody."

There was an awkward silence between them as they watched a massive cargo ship crawl up the Hudson, and the same tingling nervousness Lin experienced during conversations with other girls started to crawl up his stomach. He didn't have all that much experience in maintaining conversations with women, but even his drunken self knew that *silence equals not suave.*

"What's that one song you played tonight called? The one that's like, *you sexy thang!*" Lin sang out, rebreaking the ice.

"Um, it's called 'You Sexy Thing.' It's by Hot Chocolate. They were big in the seventies. You've never heard that song before?"

"No, I definitely have, at least in like a movie or something. I just didn't know who it was by. I think it would be fun to learn," he responded, glancing down at his violin case with a smile.

"I actually think that song sounds *way better* with violin. It's really easy to find the sheets online," she said as she peered down at her phone and brought up the "You Sexy Thing" violin sheets within seconds. Lin scrolled through the song's violin details, but the screen was just blurry enough to make the alcohol churn in his stomach.

"I think it's better if I just listen to the song and play along," he said, followed by an immediate beer-and-bao burp.

"Okay. You sure you're good to play?" she asked, laughing at him.

He got out his violin, burped a couple more times, and gave her the nod to play the song on her phone via YouTube.

"All right, it's just a *complement,* ya know?"

"Yeah, yeah, yeah. Just play it already."

"Fine, I'm gonna play an instrumental version first so you can hear how it's supposed to sound," she explained before they quietly listened to a group of violins complement the soul classic's beat. While they both listened, Lin mimicked playing each note as he heard it.

"Fair enough. Play the real song now," Lin requested after the instrumental track ended.

"Okay. Are you trying to audition for Retro Phat or something?"

"I'll play music with you whenever you want."

She laughed. "All right. Let's see what you got, Lin Rose," Maya encouraged as she bit her lower lip and played the real Hot Chocolate via her phone.

Lin immediately found the perfect pitch and sounded exactly like the YouTube instrumental track. He complemented the melody exactly when he was supposed to, and what was so impressive to Maya was how easy he made it look, as well as his lightning-fast dexterity. She noticed just how precise he was with each bow movement, and by the time he was done with the song, she had a good idea of how Retro Phat would take itself to the next level.

A few days later, Lin was walking along the High Line by himself. He was looking for a scenic spot to sit down and play violin, and he eventually found a bench with a great view of the Empire State Building. He sat down and took his phone out of his pocket to snap a few shots of the iconic skyscraper, and just as the fourth image was taken, the screen automatically switched itself to an incoming call from an unknown New York number. He answered it.

"Hello? Who's this?"

"Yeah, is this *Lin*?" the voice on the other end asked.

"Yeah, this is Lin. Who is *this*?"

"It's *me*, Reg Wallace. I got some serious shit to talk to you about."

"What's up? How'd you get my number?"

"How do you *think* I got your number? Maya gave it to me, of course! So apparently a *little pigeon* told her I was letting underage college boys into Blue Queen the other day ..."

"*Oh*," Lin said, pausing for a moment. "Look, Reg, I'm sorry, man. I was a little drunk, and it slipped out. That's my bad, though. I'll make it up to you, I swear. I'm going to practice with Retro Phat later tonight. I'll ask Maya again not to tell anyone else."

"That's cold, bro. Seriously, like, what the hell? You know how hard it is to keep a job at a club in Greenwich Village? It's like … it's like a firefighter putting out a raging fire on the same house every damn day, but that house is a club, and the flames are crazy supervisors who don't know how to chill out! My point is this shit is *fucking hard*, so I don't need you telling Maya nothing about nothing. She knows everyone in that damn club, man! I would lose my assistant co-supervisorship if she wanted to tell on me! I don't need that type of drama in my life right now, Lin!"

"*Shit* … again, I'm really sorry, man. I don't think Maya will tell on you, but I really do feel bad about blabbing to her. If there's anything I can do to make it up to you, just let me know, and we'll figure something out."

"Okay … yeah, that's not bad. That's not bad at all … Actually, there is something you can do for me. Meet me at 132nd and Madison in an hour."

"Where's that?"

"It's Harlem, college boy. You think you can you make it?"

"Yeah, I guess. Why do you wanna meet all the way up in Harlem?"

"Just cuz."

"Well, *just cuz* what? I kinda wanna know before I head that way."

"Just cuz that's where I fucking live, bro!"

After three subways and a five-block walk, Lin was at the Harlem location that Reg had texted to him. When he eventually got into Reg's studio apartment, he noticed just how cluttered everything was. There were pizza boxes stacked up on the coffee table, dirty clothes hanging off all the furniture, dishes overflowing out of the sink, backpacks and shoes scattered across nearly every square foot of the hardwood floors, and half-finished soda cans jumbled across the windowsill and across the fire escape landing. Lin quickly caught on that the way Reg wanted to be paid back was by tidying up his place, which was mutually agreed upon as a fair reimbursement.

"You know what your problem is, bro?" Reg chimed in from the fire escape over an hour later, while he sipped on a soda and watched Lin scrub dishes. "You don't listen to enough soul music. You have to listen to soul, so you can *soothe yours* of all that sad violin you're always playing in the park. Us brothers know how to ease people's souls, you know what I'm saying? You just need to listen to more brothers and sisters, and you'll see what I mean."

"Is that so?" Lin loudly replied from the kitchen. "Who exactly of these *soul soothers* am I missing out on?"

"Go over to the TV and check out who I'm talking about."

Lin walked over clothes, chip bags, and soda cans until he came to Reg's disheveled TV stand. There were countless CDs in the surrounding drawers, which included artists like Curtis Mayfield, Gap Band, Otis Redding, Aretha Franklin, Miles Davis, Earth Wind & Fire, Sam Cooke, Tina Turner, Commodores, Prince, Kool & the Gang, Bill Withers, Albert King, Etta James, the Meters, Ray Charles, Stevie Wonder, Sly & the Family Stone, Al Green, Alicia Keys, Herbie Hancock, Marvin Gaye, Rick James, James Brown, and Parliament-Funkadelic.

"Now I know a bunch of yous young-young millennials just think brothers only like listening to that mumbling rap that everyone seems to be blasting at every corner. I don't mind getting down to *real rap,* but some of these mumbly lyrics coming out these days straight up suck!"

"I don't listen to much rap music, but yeah, from what I've heard, it's more about the beats than the actual rapping. It's not really that great of a vibe."

"I agree, but those CDs over there are the *best vibes.* Trust me, bro. You won't wanna keep playing all those sad symphony songs after you listen to some of those albums. You just need to be *enlightened,* or maybe *endarkened,* you know what I'm saying?"

"Yeah, I think so," Lin responded as he browsed through the classic CDs, and came across a saxophone that was buried underneath a pile of clothes. "*Oh,* look what we got here! You play the sax, Reg?"

Reg immediately got up from his lawn chair on the fire escape and poked his head through the open window. "Oh shit, I've been wondering where that was!"

"It looks pretty fancy. How long have you played for?"

"Since I was a kid. I used to wanna be a sax player when I was about your age, but I couldn't even get a gig in the neighborhood, and the gigs I did get didn't pay shit. So, a handful of years ago, I switched things up and started working for clubs, cuz they were the only ones actually getting a decent check every week. Since then, things have been really working out."

"That's cool, I guess. So, the club gigs pay better than the sax gigs?"

"Well, yeah. I try to keep things steady at Blue Queen, or at least I did until you showed up and started causing me trouble. But yeah, things are a lot more stable than when I was looking for sax gigs and living with my parents on Staten Island."

"All right. Let's see what you got, Reg Wallace," Lin encouraged as he held up the sax in Reg's direction.

Reg stepped through the windowsill and grabbed the sax out of Lin's hands. He fiddled with the keys for a few seconds, and played: *SHAO-WADA-BANG, SABADA-BOM-TAO-HAW-VEN-AYHAAAAY! HOOOW MOON-LOBBA-DA, SABA-DA, DOOBA-DA-DAAAAY!*

Lin was already sitting on the floor, but he was floored by the funky crunch that Reg put into each note. And just as quickly as the magic appeared, it disappeared when Reg placed the sax back down on a pile of clothes and resumed his seated position on the fire escape. They remained silent as Lin glanced at the back of Reg's head, while Reg listened to the loud sounds of Madison Avenue.

"That was *unreal*, Reg. Seriously, that sounded great!"

"Yeah, yeah, you're just saying that. But come tomorrow, you'll be chilling with some sax players that are half my age and twice as good."

"Well, I've definitely met some good sax players, but I know good sax when I hear it, man, and that really was good! I'll talk to Maya later today when I catch up with her. They don't have a sax player and might want one."

Reg couldn't help but crack a smile, but he was still shaking his head as he turned back toward the window.

"Trust me. I've asked Maya to be her backup sax before, but she's never been down. Blue Queen keeps an extra sax in the back, so I've sat in every now and again, but there ain't a chance in hell I'll ever play with Maya. She thinks she's such hot shit, which she is. But still, that ship sailed like a year ago."

"Do you think she's tough to work with or something?" Lin responded with a slight hint of skepticism.

"Honestly, I wouldn't know, bro. But right after she called me out for giving you drink tickets, she told me you're gonna maybe join her little trio. And If I were your sad, classical-playing ass, I'd start getting a funk tune-up before you make a fool out of yourself."

"*Shit*, you're right! I've only played one song for her so far, and I was drunk and totally less jittery than I normally am. How do I give myself a funk tune-up before their next gig at Blue Queen?"

"Take some CDs and that Walkman by the TV with you."

Lin looked at the top of the entertainment center and saw a round, portable CD player. He held it up and slowly rotated it like an ancient artifact.

"I bet you haven't listened to one of those in *a while!*"

"I've actually never listened to one of these before, *ever.*"

"*What?*" Reg yelled as he stood up on the fire escape and raised his arms in the air. "What happened to CDs, man? Damn, I'm getting old!"

For the next three weeks, Lin popped a CD into Reg's Walkman and listened to his collection at whatever chance he had. He even listened with headphones on during some of his most boring liberal arts lectures, and when it came to his studies at NYU, *everything* was starting to seem boring. The only thing that kept him excited during school hours was listening to disc after disc and deciphering how to add violin into the soul classics. The fact that he was quickly becoming a member of Retro Phat and subsequently spending more time with Maya and not studying also wasn't helping him concentrate on school.

By the third weekend after meeting Maya, he was backing up Retro Phat at Blue Queen and taking out all his boredom on the small, early-evening crowd. He dutifully maintained his role as a backup sound for Maya's vocals, but when given the opportunity to solo, he showcased his ability to improvise on the fly and take any song to new heights. In those brief moments just after his violin repertoire was on full display, he'd subtly glance over at Maya to see if she was offering her own subtle smile of approval. And in those magnetic moments, all the philharmonic conductors who had encouraged him his entire childhood seemed to vanish away, and now Maya was the sole person he cared to impress. Maya's harmless smiles were *it*: exactly what all those years of ceaseless practice had led up to, and that long-sought-after feeling of satisfaction was what naturally lowered his reality's veils during those fall nights in Greenwich Village.

In most ways, he was still the same guy who had arrived at the NYU dorms only a couple of months prior to his Blue Queen debut, but in other ways, he'd come to accept a new way of approaching himself as a musician and as a young man. After just a few weeks of performing with Maya and her friends, Lin felt a lot different from when he'd initially moved to New York. His newfound funkiness didn't help too much when it came to playing with his classically trained pupils, but it did boost his confidence enough to ask Maya if he could become a full-time member of Retro Phat. The fact that their gigs were a few blocks from campus and that he agreed to play for free helped persuade the band, but it was also easy to tell how he was a legitimate virtuoso who deserved a chance. He could perfect any song they asked him to learn within minutes, and he ended up becoming the type of complement that Maya didn't quite realize she was looking for.

The more he dedicated his time away from school, the more his grades started slipping. He wasn't doing so badly in any introductory music courses; however, he was barely getting by in his mandatory core classes. When his midterm grades were D-, D, and F for his core subjects, it was a gut check that had him second-guessing everything and reverting back to the mindset he'd always relied upon. *Maybe spending time with Maya isn't such a smart move, and maybe trying to impress her is just for nothing. How can I know if she likes me the way I like her?*

He ran his hands up his face and rubbed his eyes deeply. Holding his forehead up with both palms, he continued to glare down at the grades on his phone's screen. Self-deprecating thoughts sank in with each passing second, and as thoughts of quitting the band seeped in, his phone started ringing. It was Maya.

"Hey."

"Hey, Lin! I have some *awesome* news!"

"What's going on?"

"You're *not* going to believe this: the owner of Blue Queen called me yesterday and asked if he could share my number with a friend, so I was like *duh*, and today, I got a call from this guy who said he saw us play the other night and wants us to play at Bob's Place in Harlem next week. So, this is like a real dream come true! I went there a bunch as a kid with my parents, and I mean, I don't even know what to think right now. My mind is racing so fast, I feel like I'm going to start sweating!" she said as they both laughed. "The show at Bob's is in five days, so we have to start getting ready. Could you come over to my parents' place tonight? No one else can make it, so *I need you*."

"Wow! Yeah, of course. I'll be there."

"Great! I gotta go, but seriously can't wait for this show. And I just know you're a *big reason* why all this is happening. So, thank you again, Lin. I'm so glad you stumbled over to me all drunk at Blue Queen that night!"

"Yeah, me too," he said as they both laughed again.

"Okay then, I guess I'll see ya tonight. *Later!*" she replied before abruptly hanging up.

Lin sat at his dorm room's miniature desk, now looking at the midterm grades on his phone while smiling. Inside him was a rollercoaster of excitement and paranoia unlike anything even remotely close to what he'd experienced before, so he decided right then that he was going to need some help from someone much more suave than him. He didn't feel as though any of his NYU acquaintances were the type of people he could genuinely talk to about someone as important as Maya, and he also knew Reg would maybe relay their entire conversation directly to her at the first chance he got, so there was only one person he knew who could possibly offer some solid lady advice.

He picked up his phone and dialed his confidant, but the call went straight to voicemail. He tried again an hour later, but still not even a dial tone. So, he resorted to his email and began typing a message to Sky.

13

Hey Lin,

It looks like you're doing pretty well in NYC! I watched the video links you just sent, and you guys sound great. I'd love to see a video of your show at Bob's Place!

When it comes to classes, I don't really know what to say except school can be tough! I sure as hell didn't get the best grades when I was in school, and I just did a few semesters at community college before dropping out. But here's the real deal: if you wanna play music for your job, then just keep on keepin on. As long as you're working on your stuff, you're on the right track.

I'm just now realizing how long it's been since we hung out together this summer, and A LOT has changed for me too. I recently moved away from Boulder to the woods outside Aspen and am helping Byrd rebuild this retreat ranch by doing all sorts of remodeling work. Thayer, Ruben, O'Donnell and now Cat are all here doing the same thing helping this dude named Shankar get everything ready before next summer. I'm even getting paid more than at the record store!

I don't know if it's that we're way out in the middle of the woods or because this is all so new, but being out here has been really inspiring. We're playing together every night around the fire pit, and I'm mostly playing the mandolin you gave me these days. Thanks again for giving it to me. It's like a whole different world!

I'm even trying to write some songs, but my writing's not too great. It seems like every day either Thayer or Byrd will have some sentimental song they want to try out, but I don't know, it's a lot of fun to see what they keep pulling out of their sleeves. I'm trying to put together a song right now though, and maybe I just need that extra violin kick that only the Rose family can give ;)

But all I can say so far is that living on this little ranch has been one of the craziest, weirdest experiences of my life. I don't know how long it'll last, but you gotta come see us soon no matter what! We have a couple cabins that no one sleeps in, so if you and Maya wanna come out we'll accommodate you guys. Planning a quick trip out here could be the perfect way to impress her, although we might scare her off... Just kidding, but with what you got going on with her, just take it slow and see how things go as friends. Every crush is different, so when it comes down to it, only you will know if she's feeling the same way.

It's starting to get cold FAST, so if I were you, I'd come out sooner rather than later. I'd even skip going back home for fall break and come here!

Let me know if you can make it out, and don't sweat it about your grades. You're right where you're supposed to be.

Love you Cuz,

Sky

☯

The Battery was where Lin liked to sit and watch boats go up and down the Hudson as they made turns in and out of the East River, but what he also liked looking at while playing violin by himself in Battery Park was Lady Liberty herself raising her legendary beacon of hopeful light toward the Atlantic. Just looking at her from afar allowed him to sense how important her image felt to so many people whose first glimpse of America was her symbolic representation of a new beginning.

This notion of a *New York beginning* began to resonate as he glanced down at his old friend of an instrument and recognized how different it now looked. After over a month of listening to Reg's old CDs and playing with Retro Phat, his violin attuned to philharmonic classics seemed like a completely different entity that no longer resembled quite the same musical love partner he'd known for so long. He started comparing this new perspective to the relative changes occurring within his own new beginnings in twenty-first-century Manhattan, and that metaphorical comparison was what led to an uncontainable lightning bolt of creative satori.

He rifled through his backpack and pulled out a notepad and pen that he typically used for his quantitative reasoning class, and he flipped to an empty page. He wrote down the words *Lady Liberty* as he thought about Maya's voice, and he began conceptualizing a funky bass line only she could perfect.

All these boats keeping filing in
An assembly line, New York begins
How can you know what's in store today?
How can you know what hearts can't say?

I'm a lean, mean, workin' machine, she says
You better listen boy, when your Lady talks
You better believe it's true, cuz she's mad as hell
You better hear her too, when she rings her bell

Because I, I fell in love with Lady Liberty
An American girl, she's so right for me
And I'll love her till the day I die

Red and white, under a bright-blue sky

You better watch out, walkin' on these streets
Cuz in this place, it ain't just amber fields of wheat
She'll make you dance all night, until your legs feel weak
Our better union is here, it only needs one more tweak

Yeah, I'm headin down, down to the docks
Cuz it's the only place where I can't hear clocks
I need a break, but time can't get enough
She's a real fox, but on the edges she's rough

Because I, I fell in love with Lady Liberty
An American girl, she's so right for me
And I'll love her till the day I die
Red and white, under a bright-blue sky

She's a lady, we better love her true
Even if we ain't got a clue
Yeah she's a lady, and she'll show the way
What better day to learn what hearts can't say?

Because I, I fell in love with Lady Liberty
I see her waves of hair, her curls of history
She, she can always be mine
As long as we believe, she ages like fine wine

She's a lady, Lady Liberty
She's a lady, my reality
She's a lady, a Lady Liberty
An American girl, she's so right for me

He looked down at the written words and wasn't exactly sure how he'd incorporate violin with them, but he was more than sure that an unadulterated vent of funky, sexual frustration had just spilled onto the notepad's paper. "Lady Liberty" was unlike anything he'd ever written before, and he figured it was probably best not to show anyone, particularly Maya. Right when he started thinking of Maya on his favorite Battery Park bench, he noticed she was calling him.

"Hey, what's up? I'm in Battery Park right now. What're you up to?"

"Oh, that's a bummer! I'm just getting to the Village and was hoping you were around. I figured you'd be in class. Why are you all the way down there?"

"Oh, really? It's all good, I was just planning on heading home anyways!" he said as he quickly started putting his things together. "What's up, though? Do you wanna get some lunch?"

"Yeah, I was just about to ask if you wanted to grab a surprise lunch. I thought you had class this time on Tuesdays."

"I'm supposed to be in quantitative reasoning right now, but it was such a nice day! I don't know, to be honest, I'm feeling a little burnt out on math classes these days. I'm sorry I ruined the surprise by playing hooky, but I'll be back in about twenty minutes. Let's eat then; just wait for me somewhere. I got something important I want to talk with you about in person."

"Where should I go?"

"I don't know, I guess just go to Blue Queen. We'll meet there and then plan where to go from there."

"Sure, that works. Just don't keep me waiting too long. I don't got all day, ya know?"

"Well, yeah. Who does? See ya in twenty, gotta go!" he said as he hung up and started running across Battery Park in the direction of the South Ferry subway stop. When he got to Blue Queen a little over twenty minutes later, he noticed Maya and Reg chatting it up by the stairway entrance.

"What's up, bro!" Reg yelled out as Lin approached. "A *little pigeon* just came flying by a few minutes ago and told me you got something important on your mind!" he continued as Lin and Maya shared a glance.

"Yeah, I got something important on my mind to tell *Maya*. Don't worry about it, bro," he responded, causing Reg's eyebrows to rise before he handed over a paper wristband and gave Lin a quick wink.

They went down the stairs to the lounge, and Lin bought them drinks. Maya ordered a brunch-style bourbon cocktail called a Red Tartan, and Lin got a Dos Equis. They sat at a nearby table and discussed where they'd like to eat lunch, which was settled on with the Beijing Hutongs food truck that they went to on the night they met. After finalizing their lunch plans, Maya brought the small talk to medium talk.

"So, what's this *important thing* you wanted to tell me in person?"

"What are you doing this weekend? Do you have any plans?"

"No ... I kind of messed up and forgot to get a gig planned. I guess I got a little too preoccupied with that show at Bob's, but the guy that manages Bob's said he could maybe fit us in again sometime soon. I might hit him up to see what's good."

"Don't do that."

"What? Why the hell not?"

"Let's get out of the city this weekend. I have next Monday off for fall break, and I was maybe gonna go home, but I heard back from my cousin who's living in Colorado, and I think we should go there to meet up with him and his friends."

"Colorado?" she asked, confused. "How are we gonna get all the way out to Colorado *this weekend*? And why do you think I should come with you to see *your cousin*? I don't know him or his friends!" she said, laughing off Lin's serendipity.

"Look, I'll pay for your flights, and you won't have to worry about paying for anything. Sky told me they have a few empty cabins we can stay in," he explained as Maya took a long sip of her Red Tartan. "And I get it, *believe me*, I wouldn't ask you to come meet Sky and his friends if I thought you wouldn't like them. They're all great musicians who are now living together, and I had the *best time* with them earlier this summer. Here, check this out."

Lin pulled up a YouTube clip from Shankar's ranch showing Byrd, Sky, Thayer, and Ruben jamming out on handmade wooden benches in a fast-paced, folk rhythm. They maintained an ever-increasing crescendo, until the tempo shifted and Thayer slowly sang out, "Have you ever realized how close you are to the stars?" They listened as the song careened into verses and out of solos, and Lin looked over at Maya with a big smile by the end of "Our Changing Dreams." He waited for her to say something, but she didn't say anything.

"So, what do you think?" he finally asked. Maya sat silently and only glanced down at the ground as she shook her head. "What's wrong?"

"Look, they're good and all. I mean they're *really good* at what they're doing, but I have to be honest with you. That's some vanilla country music they're playing."

"She's right! I could hear the white noise from over here!" Reg yelled over to them from the bar. They both couldn't help but start cracking up.

"*Oh* ... yeah, I can kinda see what you guys are saying. It's definitely a little bit like country music!" Lin admitted with a chuckle. "But you gotta admit that it's more *folky* than anything else, and they got some serious skills! Right?"

"Yeah, they're not so bad! I like that girl's voice a lot!" Reg chimed in.

"Look, it's nothing against them. I love all music, and I do really like that song," Maya responded. "That girl-on-the-piano's voice is so *hypnotic*, but I just don't know if I fit in with that kind of group, ya know? I mean, look where we are, a *jazz bar* in the middle of the city. I've been playing jazz almost my whole life, so *this* is where I belong. I'm sure they might even go on and be a solid group one day. I mean, they *definitely* seem good enough for a record deal, even after just watching one clip of theirs. And there's a shit ton of people who'll love that song too."

They sat at the tiny round table in the middle of Blue Queen and sipped on their drinks in silence, until Lin broke down everything with a go-for-broke attempt to show Maya what all his spontaneity could offer.

"Well, look at it this way: we can all just go on with our lives and continue doing our thing here, and they can go on doing their thing in Colorado, and none of us are probably going anywhere. Sure, they might just end up being another cliché folk band playing barnyard concerts that only mountain hippies go to, but what do either of us have to lose in just going out to visit them? I mean, you never know how fun it could be for someone as talented as you to team up with someone like Thay!"

"Yeah, well so what if it's fun? It looks like they want to be a barnyard band, anyways. I got my own thing going on here, and it's *just now* starting to get some real momentum. Why would I wanna bitch out on maybe playing a show this weekend and go to Colorado? Where in Colorado do they live again?"

"Aspen."

"That's a *really* fancy town!" Reg yelled over from the bar.

They both shook their heads at each other, as they knew there was zero chance he'd stop eavesdropping on them and that they might as well invite him over to the table.

"Okay, let me get this straight," Reg continued when he sat down. "So, you're trying to get Maya to come with you to *Aspen* to play some music at a hippie ranch, and she's saying *fuck that* cuz she wants to maybe play a gig here in the city?"

"Yeah."

"It's more than that," Maya tried to explain. "I just don't know if I'd fit in with them, you know?"

"No, I *don't know* what you're talking about with all this *fitting in* bullshit!" Reg raised his voice. "Look here, Maya. I've known you for a while now, and you've been coming in here with your band on Wednesday afternoons or whatever, and y'all are good, but y'all got *way better* after Lin came bumbling in here the other day. And I don't know what it is about Lin, but this kid can play violin *for real.*"

"All right, *Reginald.* You're starting to remind me of all the old guys who come in here and won't stop babbling about literally *nothing*! Get to the fucking point already," Maya demanded.

"My point is, first of all, you need to chill. Lin is offering to pay for your *sassy ass* to go to Aspen right now. Like, let's just look at Aspen online," he said as he pulled up his phone and searched #ASPEN on social media. He flipped the phone around and showed Maya pictures of bright-yellow forests and panoramic views.

"It looks really pretty," she said. "What type of tree is that?"

"They're aspen trees," Lin chimed in.

"See what I mean? They named a *tree* after the place!"

"I still don't see where the hell this is all going," she said, sounding like she was about to leave.

"All right, all right. All I'm saying is, why not? You're all worked up about getting into different bars here in New York, but when was the last time you actually got out of here? Trust me when I tell you, I'm much older than you two, and I've been trying to get into *more clubs* my whole life! This shit right here, Blue Queen, it ain't going nowhere; but that smooth-sounding girl and those guys in that video, they're going *somewhere*. When I first heard Lin playing in the kiddie park, I thought to myself, *that kid is going places*, even though I figured it'd be like Carnegie Hall. Now look at Lin, all funked out and groovy, he's like a new man after I let him listen to some of my CDs! I mean *for real*, I know how both of yous can play, and if you two joined up with them, *who knows*. You could be something special."

"I totally agree," Lin responded after Reg's long rant ended. "He's right, Maya. They're all clearly good, but also clearly missing a certain sound that we'd be good at filling. So, it could just be fun to maybe make a video or two with them. It's not like anything *official*."

"And aren't you just going out there for a few days? In Aspen? *Wow*, Maya!"

"If she doesn't wanna come, would you be down? I'm sure they'd appreciate some good sax!"

"You know what? Hell yeah, I'm down! I've always wanted to go out to Colorado!"

"Nice, that's the spirit!" Lin exclaimed as they gave each other a high-five and looked over at Maya as if to say *you're seriously not coming?*

"Okay, Okay! Fuck it. Let's go out west this weekend!"

☯

Any flight beginning around 5 a.m. is a unique experience, especially if you've been delayed for hours on end and find yourself stuck in another city's airport *a lot* longer than you originally expected. But when you can look out your oval-shaped window at over thirty thousand feet and watch the day's first light creep up from behind you into the night ahead of you, you'll sense your own unique consolation. That type of optimistic feeling, combined with a general lack of sleep and slight lumbar restriction from the person-behind-him's knee, was what Lin's reality entailed as the sun rose during their connecting flight from Denver to Aspen.

They'd made it into Denver around 7 p.m. the previous evening, but the first snowstorm of the fall was quickly brewing up by the Continental Divide. So, they waited, and slowly watched each delay get pushed back further and further into the night until the flight finally boarded at 4:25 a.m. and departed over thirty minutes later. Maya unsuccessfully hid her reluctance of coming along for the trip while they were in airport limbo for ten hours, which was why Lin took a big risk in nudging her shoulder about forty minutes into the second flight so she could wake up and see the sunrise.

"*Fuck me,* those mountains are literally sparkling," she whispered as she looked out the window.

Lin scooted closer to her to get a better angle of the snow-crusted Elk Mountains, and saw what she meant by the glittering morning light refracting off the massive peaks like disco balls beckoning them closer. Maya looked back at him with a slight smile that suggested much more than any reluctance fading away, and for a second, he thought she deliberately used *fuck me* to express her initial reaction to seeing the early-morning mountaintops.

None of them had ever been to an airport as small as Aspen's, and they noticed just how convenient the end of the trip was as compared to their brutally long layover when they got their checked luggage only five minutes after landing. They glanced at dozens of parked cars outside the airport entrance with about six inches of fresh snow on the windshields, and they shivered in their warmest jackets as they waited for Sky's Chevy to arrive. About fifteen minutes later, they saw the hippie van come clanking up the passenger pickup lane.

"Sorry for being late, guys. I got stuck on the dirt road by the ranch," Sky explained as he helped them load instrument cases and luggage into the trunk. "Had to wake up Byrd, Ruben, and O'Donnell, which took them like *an hour* to get their asses up and help push me out of this spot where I couldn't get traction. I'm Skylar, by the way, but I suppose Lin's told you who I am, though. I know your names are Maya and Reg, and it's nice to meet both of you. Welcome to Aspen."

"It's nice to meet you too, and be here," Maya responded, smiling at Sky's blatant goofiness. "So, what's the plan? Where are we going from here?"

"Well, I figured y'all would be hungry, and I also figured it might be best to let a few more cars go down our road before we head back to the ranch. I don't think the plow guys work this early in the year, and it was *deep* on the way here. You guys ever had oatmeal pancakes?"

After eating at Poppycock's for breakfast, Sky decided they might as well see some sights while they were in town. This led the four of them into taking a scenic gondola ride to the top of the local ski hill, which had just received its first snowfall of the winter season. The panoramic view beyond the slopes showcased the epicenter of the Elk Mountains, including Pyramid Peak and the Maroon Bells massif still subtly glimmering in the morning light. Going from sea level to over eleven thousand feet in a little over seventeen hours had Lin feeling the thin air escaping him as they found a good photo spot along a ridgeline.

"Breathtaking," Lin whispered as he snapped a photo of Maya with her phone.

"Let me take a pic of you guys with *this*," Sky said, releasing Shankar's film camera from inside his backpack. "Now *that's* one heck of a backdrop!" he said as he snapped a couple shots of the trio awkwardly standing next to each other.

It was a little after nine thirty when Sky's beat-up, good-for-everything Chevy van entered the unpaved portion of Castle Creek Road. There had clearly been a few cars that had gone down the dirt road that morning, which helped make a clear enough mud path as they clunked their way through the snow-dusted valley. As they got closer to the ranch, it became clearer that Sky had been the only one to drive the more remote portion of the road; but like the true, intrepid traveler he always held himself to be, he hossed it through the slick spots and held a tight grip while keeping the van in its previous tracks. When they arrived at Shankar's gate, they saw a five-foot snowman with tiny aspen-limb arms, which was barely holding a cardboard sign that read:

WELCOME MAYA, REG, AND LIN !

Byrd and Thayer were shoveling snow around the driveway, and they each gave a wave as they watched the van come down the hill to the parking area.

"Welcome to our lil ole ranch!" Thayer yelled as they took their first steps outside. "Bring your luggage to those two cabins over yonder! That's where y'all are staying!" she continued in a contrived country accent.

Maya introduced herself and felt a sense of relief when she heard Thayer's actual speaking voice, and that was when O'Donnell woke up from his second slumber of the day.

"Holy hell, last night was freezing!" he yelled as he exited his cabin with several layers on. "*Ah*, you must be Maya and Reg. I'm Ryan, but I'm guessing you already know that everyone calls me O'Donnell," he said as he approached the newcomers.

"Yeah, Lin mentioned something about you playing bagpipes while hiking in the Redwoods, and Sky told us about how you helped him when his van got stuck earlier this morning," Maya responded.

"Now *that* was freezing, having to get my pants and boots on at the crack of dawn! Just look at all this snow! It came down like a motherfucking," he thought for a second on how to end his sentence. "Like a motherfucker!" he yelled out, making Maya crack an awkward smile and Reg showcase a loud laugh that insinuated *this is my kind of guy*.

Reg, Maya, and Lin walked around in jetlagged awe for the next half hour as Shankar guided them throughout the ranch. He showed them a few of the cabins and explained what they originally looked like, and how he and Byrd had no clue what they were doing as they tried to upgrade the foundation and fix the plumbing problems. Shankar had a lot to say about the property, as well as his newfound friends, who ended up saving the day before the weather started to turn. He explained how he'd been wondering that entire summer if everything would be ready by the first snow, and that they could've never come so far if it weren't for the help of Sky, Thayer, O'Donnell, Ruben, and Cat. He showed them the energy system he'd recently completed that redirected the creek water through a series of tiny turbines, which were connected to the property's generator. He explained how he'd be able to combine hydroelectric and solar power to the cabins during the summertime, and it was obvious that this sustainable electrical system was his pride and joy. They followed him through the snow as he pointed out the trajectory of an underground wire that led into his cabin, where he invited them inside, turned on a few lights, and looked back at them like he'd just done a magic trick.

"Does the shower water get warm here?" Lin asked.

"No, but it will! Follow me!"

Shankar then showed them the most tech-savvy part of the ranch: a miniature solar-power plant next to a wooden shack, which contained a generator and tanks for well water pressure and treatment. He explained how he was hoping to install a large water heater next to the other tanks in the near future, and how this tiny shack was the heart of the ranch's plumbing and electrical systems. He admitted how he always knew the run-down cabins could be remodeled but that he wasn't exactly sure what to do about electricity when he first bought the land. It was at this point in his long, elaborate tour when he confessed how his idea of doing everything the *right way* had led him to be blinded by his own stubbornness. He eventually came full circle as he lectured the three New Yorkers about the true camaraderie that came with asking for help.

"What can we do to help?" Maya asked.

"Yeah! We wanna help, too!" Lin agreed, noticing Shankar look behind them to see where everyone else was.

"I might be a city slicker, but I ain't afraid to get my hands dirty," Reg said.

"I tell you what, there is something you guys can do to help us out here," he said as he unnecessarily lowered his voice to a whisper. "I've seen you two play music in videos Skylar has shown me, and you guys are *dope!*" he encouraged to Lin and Maya, making them crack up at his blatant attempt to use slang. "Here's the thing: you three can help out by letting *them* know how good they are. I don't know if you know anyone in New York that could help them, but try to tell them they can *make it* without actually saying it. I keep trying to tell them they're good enough to play concerts, but they think I'm just a crazy old man who's only nice because I pay them to be here. It will be a lot different coming from *you,*" he said as he horizontally moved his index fingers in their direction.

They walked back into the woods and saw that the fire was just getting started while instruments were being brought outside, which also included a small battery-powered amp for Maya's electric bass. Although electric bass was her second-favorite instrument after its standup counterpart, she was still more than happy to jump in with the firepower of Byrd, Thayer, Sky, Ruben, Reg, and Lin as they all casually prepared their instruments. The first song they played together was "Mary Jane's Last Dance," mainly because Lin explained how he introduced Maya and Retro Phat to the idea of doing acoustic Petty covers like he and Sky did earlier that year. Maya's interpretation was more bluesy than the one the Rose Boys played in their formative moment, but she still had a good feeling why Lin suggested they initially play that particular classic. In the New York jazz bars like Blue Queen, no one gave Lin's background role in Retro Phat too much credit, until they let him loose on a song like "Mary Jane." So, she knew firsthand just how much Lin had worked on perfecting that song in recent weeks, and when she saw Sky's jaw drop as Lin's violin replaced the vocals he was about to sing and extended their intro jam, everything Maya believed when she first met Lin was once again reinforced. Sky sang the verses and the whole group harmonized during the choruses, and when they finished, everyone praised Lin by telling him how incredible he sounded.

They were all practically crushing over Lin, which caused him to deflect the praise and suggest another classic cover he knew they could all play: "You Sexy Thing." Lin didn't tell Maya, but Sky had told him that they'd started practicing the funk classic after watching a video that Reg shot of them at Blue Queen. Sky showed Byrd and Shankar the video when they were at the library going through their emails and checking out books, so they knew of Maya's voice, but Lin noticed Thayer's jaw drop as Maya dropped into the lyrics and led the tempo on bass. Ruben kept the rhythm steady on drums, and Reg brought his own pizzazz on saxophone. This sequence of suggesting songs continued for hours.

There was a true sense of a completed sound with the cornerstone additions of Lin and Maya making every song seem *just right*, and Reg's solos brought a new element that took their collective effort to a whole different level. The New Yorkers quickly learned some of Byrd and Thayer's original songs like "She Passed By," "Waiting at Ethereal Station," "Anti-Wookite," "Our Changing Dreams," and a few others. Lin and Maya both had incredibly fine-tuned ears that allowed them to listen to a song and instantly know how to provide their roles, and by dinnertime, they'd learned seven songs written by Byrd and Thayer. That night, they all shared a massive portion of chicken alfredo, and Cat and O'Donnell chipped in by baking homemade bread in their new wood-fired oven. The entire meal tasted amazing, and Lin started realizing just how different the ranch was to his NYU lifestyle when the wine broke out.

They kept the fire raging and continued jamming, until Byrd began playing sitar to peacefully wind down the evening in a way only he, with so much fireside experience, could do. As the group made their way to the treehouses and cabins, Lin and Maya walked over to the empty, two-bed cabin that they'd put their things in. They stepped through the wooden doorway and quickly realized how there wasn't any conventional electricity, as they searched for a light switch on the walls. Lin looked for the nonexistent switch as he stumbled across the DIY hardwood floor with his hands against a wall, and as he slowly teetered from foot to foot in the darkness, he felt Maya's hand on his shoulder. He turned around and could only see her face as her lips met his for the first time, and they continued kissing as they moved toward one of the two single beds. Maya zipped her jacket off, and her shirt and pants fell to the floor as they rolled around the bed in just their underwear. Lin could barely keep up as he tossed his outfit to the floor, but the feeling of her body up against his was greater than anything he'd imagined over and over again since the day they'd met. Maya took command as she rolled on top of him and mounted her groin up against his, and she initiated the very first sex of Lin's life.

After the second and third sexual encounters of Lin's life that next morning, he decided to aimlessly venture outside into the frigid air to boil some water. Maya was freezing in the thick blankets Shankar provided, so she requested a hot cup of tea to drink before even the tiniest fidget from bed. That was Lin's cue, and he began collecting his dispersed clothes with the promise that he'd return to his queen with whatever desirables she so requested.

When he stepped outside their cabin, he noticed Byrd sitting by himself at the fire pit. He was tending to the extinguished embers of the previous night by slowly rekindling a fire to life on top of them. By the time Lin had walked the fifty or so steps to the center of the ranch, smoke from small sticks was beginning to mingle with the morning frost. He noticed Byrd was already boiling a pot of water with a gas-powered camping stove, and that was when Byrd glanced up to him and placed his index finger over his lips to signal *be quiet*. Lin sat on a wooden stool and watched his intricate placements of tiny kindling, then larger kindling, and then small logs that transformed the smoke into flames. As the infant fire began to rise, Byrd sat back up on a stool to tend to the pot of water that was beginning to bubble.

"Could I have some water for a cup of tea?" Lin whispered, which Byrd responded with a nod that said *of course*. "It's for Maya. She's pretty cold and hung over … I guess we're both pretty cold and hung over. How are you feeling?" he asked, which was responded with a basic thumbs-up.

"I didn't drink last night, so I feel fine," Byrd whispered back. "That was just Coke in my cup. I don't really like to drink that much."

"I don't really drink that much either. Honestly, I feel like I've just started drinking recently. Reg works at the jazz club we usually play at, so he gives me free drink tickets. He just pretends to card me when I show up, so it's pretty much like the only bar in the entire city I actually can drink at."

"What's that like, playing at jazz clubs in New York? It sounds pretty fun."

"It's definitely a lot different than what I'm used to, but I think that's why I like it so much. Maya kind of just tells us what to do, and we go do it," he said, slightly raising his whisper, as he couldn't help himself from smiling. "But it's just us four, so it's a lot less people than when I'm rehearsing in my music classes. There's no anonymous blending in when I play with Retro Phat, but I like the extra attention. When we're in front of a small audience and everyone is looking straight at us, the pressure brings out this little extra *something* that I didn't know about till now."

"That's really cool. I'm glad you found a band to play with. I've kinda felt that way since everyone showed up here too. How much do you get paid to play one of those jazz club shows?"

"At first I'd play for free, but now Maya insists on paying me a little bit. So, I get fifty dollars for each show."

"That's awesome, man. You're like a *real pro* already. I need to find some new work pretty soon. I know things are gonna be a little different around here once the snow *really* starts coming in. We're about to finish everything Shankar needs help with, just a few more projects left," Byrd whispered as he turned his attention back to the fire and aimlessly poked the small logs with a stick.

"I'm sure you guys could find some gigs around here somewhere. Those songs we played yesterday were great, so someone will pay you guys to play them."

"O'Donnell and Thayer's been talking with the ski resorts down the road. They said they sometimes hire bands to come play at their lounge areas, but it's *background*. Kind of just entertainment to keep their guests buying drinks, ya know?"

"Sounds like a good place to *kind of* be heard."

"Yeah, I guess."

The water in the camping stove was now at a full-on boil, so Byrd ran back and forth from Shankar's cabin to fetch an extra mug. They sat in silence as Byrd divvied the hot water, and the silence continued for another minute as they both dropped and pulled their tea bags.

"Do you write?" Byrd asked, breaking the silence. "Like songs, I mean."

"Yeah, but not really. I wrote a song the other day, though. I named it "Lady Liberty" because I wrote it while looking at the Statue of Liberty. I haven't even told anyone about it till now."

"We'll learn it later. I'd love to hear how you think it should sound," Byrd encouraged as Lin nodded in agreement before turning around and heading back into the cabin to greet Maya with her long-awaited cup of English Breakfast. He noticed she was still sleeping, but just lightly, and she woke up when he nudged her on the shoulder and held out the mug.

"Oh my God, thank you so much!" she said as she sat up and rested her back against a handmade wooden headboard. She took a few sips and fluttered her eyes as the hot liquid worked its magic. "Damn, I'm hung over. I guess I drank one too many cups of wine last night, and they got some really good coke out here!" she said, regretfully shaking her head at a now-confused Lin.

He wanted to tell her how he and Byrd had just agreed to learn a song that he'd recently written, which was the song he wrote right before pulling the trigger on their vacation, and the only song he'd ever written about her. *Just say it's about the city if she asks,* he thought to himself as he nestled up against her and they slowly kissed to the rhythm of the creek.

The lyrics and proposed funky rhythm of "Lady Liberty" were a bit different from what Byrd had initially expected to come from Lin. The song itself made a lot more sense when Lin explained to the group how Reg had given him a Walkman and a bunch of old CDs so he could learn more soul music. And in that moment when Lin said the words *soul music,* it was like a tried-and-true headlamp turned itself on within the depths of Byrd's soul, which revealed a sliver of light toward the other side of the Unified Field. He looked around at each of the instruments they were all holding, and he could now *hear* them sound a little more funky, a little less folky, and a lot more groovy. This was especially the case when he glanced at Thayer's keyboard, Maya's electric bass, Reg's saxophone, Ruben's drums, and even Shankar's sitar. Playing sitar was something brand new for him, but in that moment, he had his first vision of playing an electric sitar as he wondered what would happen if he used digital modifications on such a traditional sound.

Within a few minutes, Byrd's lead helped the entire group calculate how to play "Lady Liberty." He started with Maya's bass line, had Ruben rap off that bass line, and gave Thayer and Reg the foundations of a funky repetition. The next part got a little harder, so he started by asking Lin how he thought his violin should sound within the song. Lin admitted that he considered his role to be more of background, and decided he'd play what he thought sounded best to complement everyone else. Easy enough, but Sky's mandolin was a bit of a mystery in terms of making it sound more funky. He knew he could figure out his own acoustic chords to go along with Lin's lyrics, but mandolin wasn't so simple. So, he asked Sky to walk back to his cabin and bring back a battery-powered amp and electric guitar, and just like that, "Lady Liberty" was born to be like an adopted baby between the Avett and Isley Brothers.

Shankar, Cat, and O'Donnell eventually interrupted the jam to tell the group that breakfast was ready, which was a large display of bacon, eggs, chopped fruit, and English muffins. While they ate at the cold picnic tables, Sky had a confession that he wanted to clear up. "I wrote a song a couple days ago," he said so randomly that it made the whole group start giggling with food in their mouths.

"What's your song about? Being a shy Jessie that's too scared to share his art?" O'Donnell mocked, getting one barely recognizable chuckle that came from Reg's direction.

"Actually, yeah. That *is* what it's about: being a shy Jessie," Sky replied, smiling at his own self-consciousness.

"Well, I guess I had a hunch then!" O'Donnell triumphantly responded.

"Let's hear it when we're done eating!" Thayer added.

"I agree. What're you calling it?" Byrd asked.

"Okay, I was gonna share it the other day because it's been taking me a while to finish and I'm just now feeling good about it, but then Lin told me he was coming this weekend, so I figured I'd wait till he got here to talk about it. The main reason I wanted to wait for Lin is because I'm calling it 'Your Second Fiddle,' so we obviously needed a fiddle player here!" Sky explained, wrapping his arm around his younger cousin like he scored the winning touchdown in a high school homecoming game.

"Your Second Fiddle" was not only the second song they learned to play together that day, but it also ended up being the group's twelfth video from Shankar's ranch that was recorded on Cat's phone. There was a much stronger bluegrass energy that emanated from Sky's lyrics, and it was clear he was embracing his love for mandolin.

I know I could fight it
I know I could walk away
 I could cause a fit right now
Oh, but baby you'll always hear me say

I'll be your second fiddle until the end

I see you standing there, braids woven tightly in your hair
You're playin on your phone, how would you feel here all alone?
Cuz I could go afar, hang with my friends at some lame bar
But I'm right here to play, I'd stay with you about any day

I'll be your second fiddle until the end
Down every road, and every bend

These mountains that surround us, they hover like a hurricane
Stressful winds be blowin', don't let it make you go insane
I'll watch you blossom until you're ready to bloom
I'll see you skyrocket right up to the moon

Oh, baby you're gonna make it, just you wait!

I'll be your second fiddle
I'll be your second moon
I'll follow your lead, just hope it comes round soon
I'll be your second fiddle
We'll rest by and by till we're in tombs
I'll be your second fiddle until the end

Well, I can hear you thinkin'
You're thinkin' about headin' out
You say there's a world out there, you say you want your clout
Well baby, just you listen, hear my thoughts come through
I don't wanna be with no one but you
I'll be your second fiddle until the end

Oh, I'll be your second fiddle
I'll be your second moon
I'll follow your lead, just hope it comes round soon
I'll be your second fiddle
We'll rest by and by till we're in tombs
I'll be your second fiddle until the end

Down every road, and every bend
I'll be your second fiddle, oh baby
This ain't the end

With a few improvised solos in between the lyrical stanzas, alternated by Sky on mandolin and Lin on fiddle, it was safe to say that the Rose boys were the stars of Cat's video. Each of them stepped up to the plate and hit home runs, and there was an authentic feeling among the whole group that they were beginning to develop a collective sound that transcended any categorized genre. Thayer in particular felt a tingling sensation go down her throat and arms toward her fingertips as she played "Your Second Fiddle," which was partly due to the pretty good hunch that Sky wrote it about her. A similar feeling came to Maya when the group learned "Lady Liberty," but neither of them verbally addressed these notions because neither of them wanted to slow down the group's brewing momentum.

Everyone was in high spirits, either from the joints Cat had rolled or the adrenaline rush of refining original songs. Those spirits kept rising for hours as they practiced more of Byrd, Thayer, and Maya's ideas, and while everyone was chatting around the fire about how great each song sounded and the social media videos that would later be posted, Shankar stepped up to the plate to say something he'd been thinking long and hard about.

"I have something I would like to say," he said as he stood up, and everyone suddenly stopped what they were doing. "I've been listening to you guys play music for months now, and it's always been very exciting, but now with the addition of Lin, Maya, and Reg, you *really rock!*" he continued, making the group laugh as he thanked the New Yorkers again for coming to visit them. "You all have the talent you need to succeed, and I'm not just some crazy old guy who doesn't know what he's saying. Each of you provides skilled instrumentals and wise writing abilities, and that genuinely applies to *all of you*. All you need is marketing, and then everyone will be blessed to hear this music like I have. I might only be a financial adviser, but I'll help you guys in whatever way I can. I would be more than happy to be your financial manager, or something like that, when the time comes."

"Whoa! Don't be trying to steal my meal ticket now, Shankar!" O'Donnell immediately interjected, making the group crack up. "Me and *only me* is gonna be their manager. I know a bunch of people in the radio biz, and they know I know people too. But hey, I guess I wanna say something," he continued as he stood up. "He's right, you know? Shankar can tell, and so can I. You all just need to get out there. You need to get *known*. The real question is, what do you wanna be known for? Do you wanna be just another alt-folk band struggling to get by, or do you wanna be *big* and actually get some cash in your pockets?"

"How do you suggest we get *known*?" Byrd responded.

"Well, first we have to make an album somehow. Then we have to get signed up with one of those big-wig labels at the tippy-top of the industry. There are a million bands out there trying to get *known* by doing it their own way, but in the end, almost all of them barely break even. The tough truth is you need to know *someone* who'll give us a shot. Do any of you big-city New Yorkers know anyone that sells records?" he asked, looking over at Maya, Lin, and Reg.

"I know a bunch of jazz artists that come into Blue Queen all the time, and labels are sending A&R scouts every now and again too," Reg chimed in. "It's tough to know who's A&R and who's another schmuck off the street, but I could start asking around to see who's who and who could help these kids. I guess I gotta say something too," he continued as he stood up and took the spotlight. "This has been one hell of a day out here in this valley full of big mountains, but I have to humbly back out when it comes to all this talk about *being in a band*. I mean, half of these songs we've been playing don't fit well with sax *at all*."

"But you definitely sounded great in some of the songs!" Byrd interjected. "I really liked your solo for 'Lady Liberty'," he said as the whole group reminded Reg how much they enjoyed hearing him play sax.

"Yeah, yeah, yeah. Calm down. I like playing sax more than I remembered, and I do wanna help out, cuz I got ears too and know this is for real. Maybe I could be a half-member or something like that, but I think I could help you guys like I helped Lin over here as a *creative manager* that does the little things that managers are usually too busy for," he concluded, glancing over at O'Donnell with a *let me get a piece of this* smile.

"I don't know about that," O'Donnell rejected.

"It's true, though!" Lin interrupted. "I feel like a totally different person after listening to Reg's CDs for a few weeks, and I think he'd be a great creative manager."

"Yeah, it's not like either of you actually have any real experience as managers anyways, so it's probably better for both of you to do the job of one *good* manager," Ruben chimed in, getting a laugh from the group.

Reg and O'Donnell glanced over at each other and simultaneously thought something along the lines of *doing half of a really tough job sounds about right*.

"Well, *actually*, that's not a bad idea!" O'Donnell admitted, which sparked a smile from Reg. "What about you other New Yorkers? You know anyone that works at a record label?"

Neither Lin nor Maya said anything as they lowered their heads and slowly shook them. Everyone's spirits began to drag down as they recognized the barriers to enter one of the world's most competitive industries, one in which the odds were around 100 percent against them. There was silence for a few seconds, until Thayer chimed in.

"I might know someone that could help us in LA," she said,

regaining the group's attention. "I mean, I don't know someone *personally*, but my dad does. He might be able to introduce us to someone who could help us."

"There we go!" O'Donnell yelled. "I knew Thay was the wildcard!"

Byrd and Sky shared a glance that admitted how they both had a hunch about Thayer's LA connections. This was the first time she mentioned anything about the city she grew up in since she'd moved to Aspen, and she'd remained quiet about her dad's Hollywood career since leaving Brentwood with Ruben and Cat, except when her buddy Eddie mentioned the screenplay he'd given up on.

"Maybe you guys should think about a name," Cat insisted. "All the people that saw the first few videos keep asking who you guys are," she said, waving her phone in the air.

"Yeah! Good point there, Cat!" O'Donnell jumped back in. "You gotta have a good name, cuz there's nothing that no one can do about marketing yourselves from this ranch without having a bloody brilliant name!"

"Maybe the name should be something about this place you guys have been living at lately?" Lin suggested.

"You two would know best about this place," Thayer said, looking at Byrd and Shankar. They all quietly waited for Byrd's response as they watched his eyes dart back and forth while staring directly at the fire's flames.

"Well ... when I first met Shankar, he told me about this dream he had to build a retreat center that was focused around yoga, meditation, and being out in nature. He said he wanted to create a real Zen experience for him and his guests, but if we're gonna make a name for ourselves then it has to be about *us*, not necessarily this place. I do like the idea of embracing this place, but what exactly are we doing here? Who are we at this ranch, ya know?"

"We're a bunch of wooks living in the woods!" Ruben yelled out. "We should be called *Zen Wooks!*" he said, causing everyone to laugh.

"We left our city lives behind us to come out here," Sky mentioned. "Maybe something like rebels? Maybe something like *Zen Rebellion!*"

"I like that better than *Zen Wooks*," Thayer commented, "but I don't think we're *rebelling* against our city lives out here more than just deserting them. I like the sound of something more like *renegade* better than *rebel*."

"How about *The Zen Renegades*?" Shankar recommended, thinking he had it.

Byrd, Thayer, Sky, Lin, Maya, Reg, and Ruben looked at each other at the same time, locking eye contact and smiling in a way that seemed to tell each other: *that's it.*

FIVE YEARS LATER

14

What classifies as a movement? Although the concept of physical movement is so ingrained within each of us, social movements tend to have a more abstract nature that's much less straightforward. But at the center of any social movement is one fundamental concept that wakes us up to believe there's a brighter side to life if we keep meandering a few more defiant turns: change.

So, when social movements are in their initial conception, change is the fundamental implication of every conversation, as well as how these implied cultural changes could and should be initiated. But every movement is unique and advocates for distinctive measures from an ever-changing group of individuals, which is why the actual changes from social movements generally aren't all that conclusive. Regardless of a social movement's success in implementing change, the shared collaboration built within them has, in many ways, been one of the most beautifully dangerous features of mankind. Because when we look back at the history of social movements, it clearly displays how many activists met violence and backlash when "King" didn't like them. But the world is different now, *right*?

It's sometimes hard to explain how so many modern movements fail to get mobile. Some movements fall flat due to scenarios like disorganization and a lack of political partnerships, but the main failure of any movement is a lack of people being actively involved. That diminishing, movement-killing inclination to keep to oneself and not offend "King" is alive and well. It has been chilling within the status quo for centuries like a smelly hippie who's overstayed their welcome and responded with *Nah'imastay* when asked to leave. Complacency looms over all modern movements, in yet we still so bravely find a way through our mazes toward the cheese of change. But what happens next after the cheese is eaten and the change is advanced? Several of our greatest accomplishments have been social movements, but what have we done to uphold the future plans that all these movements intended to implement? Setting out and achieving any grand accomplishment is a success story that's worthy of celebration, but how is success supposed to be managed once the celebration is over? This overlooked element that some movements fail to consider while their changes are still imaginary can cause those changes to run out of control in reality.

Five years had passed since Byrd, Thayer, Skylar, Lin, Maya, Reg, and Ruben first played music with each other on those fateful days at Shankar's ranch, and now this group of talented musicians was simply referred to as the Zenegades. Their artistic careers skyrocketed as their collective goals continuously came to fruition, and their relentless work ethic led them to releasing six full-length albums (two with more than twenty songs) within that handful of formative years.

They've since become known as a band that changes genres throughout their albums and live shows within a distinctive effort to differentiate themselves from any one taste, and their unpredictability became known for keeping audiences always guessing. Although many of their songs fell within alternative bluegrass and folk interpretations, there were also many others with jazz and funk influences that often featured Maya on lead vocals, Lin with pitch-perfect violin accents, and Reg with suave sax solos. Although Reg insisted on being a co-manager with O'Donnell, his presence as an on- and offstage band member became known as *saxy time*, which was a portion of each show's setlist in which several highly anticipated songs would feature his soul style. Sky held the reins in their efforts to introduce rock influences when he'd switch to an electric guitar, Thayer carried the sing-along piano and synthesized-rhythm torch, and Byrd could instantly turn everything on a dime during a concert when his ukulele, Uncle Tito, ushered in tropical themes. Their first five albums were called *Zenegades, Madre Naturaleza, The Unified Field, Castle Creek Concerto*, and *Humanity's Lifeboat*, each of which continued the general rise of their fame. They all kept writing as much as they could (particularly Byrd, Maya, Sky, and Thayer), and before they could even fathom just how popular they were becoming, they'd won a Grammy and had a dedicated following behind them that led pundits to refer to them as the *Millennial Beatles*.

Social media, as well as Thayer's familial connections, helped drive the band's snowballing success while they developed their first and second albums. And with the help of Cat and Lin's growing online pages, they were able to quickly get their sound out to a massive group of fans, who'd eventually jam-pack hipster venues all over America. The musicians also got a substantial amount of help from their supporting cast, including O'Donnell as their tour manager, Reg as their creative manager, Cat as their head of marketing, Shankar as their accountant, and even Ruben going above and beyond to design nearly all of their merchandise.

Up to this point in the band's history, the vast majority of their shows were at concert halls and amphitheaters, but all that was about to change on one particularly momentous evening in New York.

Talk-show host Andre Cavallo delicately held his eyes shut as a makeup artist examined him for his last looks before going live on air. Byrd and Thayer stared at him from the side of his set as he whispered to his facial assistant, while also getting waves from his cameramen. The studio audience was then instructed to get as loud as they could for the return from commercials, and the whole room was roaring as each camera's red light flashed.

"Welcome back! Tonight, we have a very special band playing for us, and our guests are two members of the Grammy Award-winning group: Zenegades. Jim Byrd and Thayer Feldman, everybody!"

The crowd roared as Thayer and Byrd walked over to the couch for yet another live TV interview. They both shook Andre's hand and sat down as the crowd was instructed to be quiet.

"*Wow,* I can't tell you how excited I am to finally get you guys on the show! I've been a huge fan for a few years, and I know everyone and their grandmas are listening to the Zenegades these days! But of course, there still may be some people out there living underneath rocks who haven't heard of you guys yet, so let's just start from the beginning. I know it's a fun story that everyone seems to be talking about since that *Rolling Stone* feature came out a couple years ago, when Jim said that really famous quote: *communal living is the fundamental basis of humanity that we've lost in the modern world, and it's the solution to our lack of peace and harmony,*" Cavallo continued as the show briefly cut to a screenshot of Byrd's quote, and then returned back to live action. "*So,* you guys first got started when you all lived together in the woods outside of Aspen? From what I've gathered, it sounds *a little bit different* than the hotels I'm used to staying at around there! I mean, the article said you guys barely had any plumbing or even electricity when you first moved in together, so my question is how on earth did a group of young Millennials get by without cell coverage or much of any modern world technology, *and then* somehow collide worlds together and build an audience on social media?" he asked as his hands comically intertwined with one another, getting a jeer from the audience.

Byrd and Thayer looked at each other and laughed, and Thayer motioned for Byrd to answer.

"Well, I've never actually owned a cell phone and still don't, so the lack of service never bothered me too much. But the two outhouses at the ranch definitely had a bit of an unpleasant smell when we first started living together!" Byrd said, trying to hold back from laughing. "But yeah, we first got started by helping a good friend of mine build a wilderness retreat out in the woods off of Castle

Creek. So before we were a band, we were a pretty crappy construction crew! But you know, we eventually started playing gigs at the resort villages and kept posting on YouTube, just small, one-song clips. Then eventually we got a record deal out in LA, and the rest is history, as they say."

"And you're like a Zen guru who lived all alone out in the desert for a long time, right?" Cavallo nudged, trying to get more of Byrd's backstory.

"Well, I'm definitely not a *Zen guru* by any stretch of the imagination, but before we all started playing together at the ranch, I was a wilderness guide for at-risk youth. And when I wasn't working, I lived out of my motorcycle in a canyon a little north of Price, Utah."

"That's *wild*! You must've had barely anything on you! I've heard of people living out of cars, but a motorcycle? That's Zen, all right! And I'm sure you guys have heard about all these young kids that are leaving cities to live on public lands in large groups, kind of like what you did. Some folks are saying this ongoing movement was inspired by you guys, so what advice do you have for all those people out there trying to make a communal living space out in the woods?"

Thayer and Byrd furrowed their eyebrows at each other. Byrd turned back to Cavallo and paused for a moment before responding.

"I actually haven't heard about this *movement*, but I don't keep up with the news that much. However, to anyone out there trying to live with their friends and families in the woods, I say: filter your water *and* your attitude," he said with a smile.

"I like that! So, do you guys still live together? How long did you stay out in the woods? You did leave, right?" he asked sarcastically, getting a laugh from the crowd as he motioned to Thayer for a response.

"We stayed at the ranch for, oh I don't know, almost a year? By the time we moved out, the first album was in the works, and things were going well, so we all rented this tiny, two-bedroom house outside Basalt for a little while."

"What was *that* like?" Cavallo interjected.

"That was even tougher than living in the woods! But we made it work for a little while and had a fun first tour, where we pretty much lived in our vans doing small shows at all sorts of random venues, and then the second tour was way bigger. After that second tour a few years ago, we decided as a group that it might be best to live separately."

"Well, it makes more sense to me now how you were able to make so many albums so quickly, because you were living together and had no escape from each other! It really is incredible how all of you take turns writing songs and each of them comes out with such different styles. What's the group's creative process like now that you're more separated?"

"It's definitely a little different now," Thayer said, keeping the reins on the talking. "We email each other a lot of lyrics and ideas, and we all practice a lot when we're not together, but we always try to do our best to get everything right before any studio recordings, so of course we have to practice in the same place. Today that place is usually Byrd's little farm in Hawaii. We rehearsed all of *Castle Creek Concerto* there before we actually did the recording at the ranch in Aspen, and we also were there when we created all the songs on our latest album that just came out last week!"

"So, even your latest album, *Unnecessary Walking*, which is out now on all digital platforms and vinyl, was rehearsed at Jim's house in Hawaii? This must be some place! The album is seriously wild, and it's so energetic. It must have driven the neighbors crazy hearing you guys practice this stuff!" Cavallo plugged, while holding up a vinyl copy of *Unnecessary Walking* toward the cameras.

"Well, there aren't any houses within earshot of where I live on this old farm on the Big Island, so you can all rest assured that we're not keeping anyone up at night!" Byrd chimed in.

"So, you guys are going back to your roots and getting dirty on a farm to bring out all these creative juices. Now, *that* makes *a lot* more sense, because this album really is an all-out, up-and-down ride of music that reminds me of some of your earlier work. All the changes in direction and how the songs move from one to another really is almost like a roller coaster, without the nausea of course!" Cavallo jokingly praised.

"Yeah, pretty much," Thayer responded with a smile. "The farm is a lot like the Colorado ranch, with these old, tiny cabins where the work-trade folks used to live, but it's a lot warmer at night than in the Rockies! But yeah, we'll all move in with Byrd and stay at his place for a month or even longer sometimes, and it's always such a stark difference from LA, where I currently live. I guess it's probably the same for Lin and Maya, who moved back here to New York a couple years ago."

"Wait, so you have *New Yorker* Zenegades too? And I thought I couldn't love this band more!" Cavallo egged on the crowd for another laugh.

"Yeah, their roots are being *big-city folks*," Byrd replied with a fake country accent. "Come on ... come up here!" he encouraged, waving off stage and getting a loud cheer from the crowd as they realized what he was doing. Lin and Maya stepped out from behind the stage curtains and into the TV spotlight as they sat down next to them on Cavallo's couch.

Maya was now twenty-seven and Lin twenty-three, and they were one of America's many adored celebrity couples (along with Thayer and Sky). Cavallo's crowd cheered as production assistants quickly tested two microphones and handed them over.

"So, you guys live here in New York? Are you both from here?" Andre Cavallo asked as his crowd settled back down.

"I'm a born *and raised* New Yorker!" Maya said proudly, getting a big response from the crowd.

"I'm actually from San Francisco," Lin admitted. "But we met just down the subway line from here in the Village."

"Oh, *wow!* We have to hear this story! How'd it go, *briefly?*"

"We met down at the Blue Queen Lounge, which for people who don't know, is a jazz bar on Bleecker where Maya played a lot with her band Retro Phat before we joined Zenegades," Lin explained. "But yeah, I made friends with a guy who worked at Blue Queen, Reg Wallace, who's of course now our co-manager and sax player, and I watched Maya play for the first time and knew right away that I'd found *someone.* Back then, it felt like a miracle when she gave me a shot to play in her band, and we played a handful of shows across the city before we took a vacation to meet everyone else in Colorado at the ranch. And when they asked us to play on the first album, it was like a no-brainer that we should go for it!"

"I *love it*! That's the type of love story that gives me hope for this crazy city we call home, *right*?" Cavallo replied, motioning to his audience for applause. "But I have to say that I was talking with Reg backstage, and he's *so freaking awesome.* We need to get him out here. C'mon out here, Reg! It's all good, it's my show. Let him through!"

Reg was sporting a swanky suit as he tried to give off a business-meeting aura for the talk show, so he ended up looking sharper than everyone else except Cavallo. He waved to the crowd and basked in the glory as a production assistant handed him a mic.

"So, Reg, let's quickly go back to when Lin and Maya met here in New York. How'd it make you feel back then that you helped set these two young lovebirds up?"

"Well, at first I was pissed!" Reg said with a smile, getting a huge laugh from the crowd and Cavallo, who asked why he was pissed for setting them up. "Well, you see, I was working as the assistant co-supervisor at Blue Queen, and Maya played there like at least once a week. So, when Lin told her that I gave him a few extra drink tickets on the night they met, she rightfully got pretty pissed, and I thought I might lose my job! So, I made Lin clean my apartment to pay me back for putting me in a tough spot at work."

"Wait, what?" Cavallo asked, cracking up. "You made him *clean your place* because he ratted you out? That's *too good*!" He continued laughing as the crowd joined in.

"Yeah. Back then, Lin was kinda like my protégé," Reg responded. "I used to see him playing all these sad violin songs in the park before we met, and when I got pissed about him ratting me out to Maya, he wasn't about to blow his shot at getting into Blue Queen to see her. So, I had him come clean my place, and that's when we started talking about music and became friends."

Cavallo sat at his desk with a bright smile as he noticed how squeezed together they all were on his famous couch. "Well, that definitely wasn't in the *Rolling Stone* article, and don't forget, you heard this part of their story here first, folks! I mean, we might as well get the rest of the band up here! C'mon guys, don't be shy! You can squeeze in with them!" he said as Sky and Ruben entered the spotlight to extensive applause as they too were handed microphones.

"*All right!* Now that you're all here and maxing out the couch's weight capacity, let's actually talk about this new album!" Cavallo wheeled back, keeping the crowd in stitches. "So, it's called *Unnecessary Walking*. What does this title mean to you, Sky?" he continued, motioning for an answer from Sky, who clearly wasn't prepared to answer any questions.

"Well, umm, I mean, it's definitely really great music to listen to while you're walking around," he responded, receiving a softer laugh from the crowd. There was another brief moment of awkward silence, which Byrd filled.

"I'd say the title track of *Unnecessary Walking* has a lot to do with actual *physical* movement, but it goes much further, in that it also refers to how we all manage our time. I think a lot of us sometimes need an escape from life's necessities, and this is generally because we tend to obsess over maintaining our own personal safety nets through just about all our decision-making. But when we start to do things because we *want to*, as opposed to *need to*, and we essentially break out of our comfort zones, we start to experience the exciting parts of life. In a way, this notion to *escape from necessity* is the modern-day division within the human experience," Byrd explained.

"Well, now *that* was the little piece of Zen advice we all needed tonight! We'll be right back after a few short messages from our sponsors!" Cavallo projected into the cameras.

When the show returned from commercial break, Cavallo was standing in front of a stage with the Zenegades behind him. "Let's give it up for our musical guests, Zenegades, as they play the title track off their latest album, *Unnecessary Walking!*"

They prepared their instruments for a moment before beginning "Unnecessary Walking," which started out slowly with only Byrd strumming his acoustic guitar and Ruben lightly tapping cymbals.

There's a package at my door, it's been sitting for days
It says it's from you, but my hallway's a maze
Green like jade on the ocean floor
There's always room for just one more

The rest of the band came in with all their glory, and Thayer took the reins vocally.

Oh Great Valley, I could see you grazing here
The winds breeze slowly, going straight into the clear
We can run down, down to the riverside
Get your fill, today we're more alive

All of them sang together.

Oh, escape from necessity!
Break free, so all your light may be
Free, free from society!
What's the wait?
Come with us, you'll see

Back to Byrd's vocals, now with the entire band in a full, rhythmic swing.

There's a new way of doing things out here
With no one near, no time for careers
There's a valley, of opportunity
Take the wheel, it's time to go and see
Just a trail, just some steps, till the dreams you seek
Let's walk it out, let's reach that peak

Sky stepped up to his microphone and belted out:

Take the train to the Great Valley
Where grass shines like jade and water tastes like wine
There's a spot for you here, it's waited all your life
Where the sun meets the shade underneath these pines

Leave now, these days of propriety
 Be free, free from society!

A bridge slowed down the band's pace and transitioned the rhythm to a jazzier style, where Maya came in soulfully singing.

Oh, sweet baby! How could you ever see us here?
In the great, great valley, tonight we're in the clear!
I see clouds, spinning to an eagle's face
There's something in the air, something about this place

Oh, sweet boy! Let's escape from necessity
I sent you the keys, to be here with me
Did you get my package? I'm waiting patiently

They all reunited in a massive crescendo of harmonic singing.

Oh, escape from necessity!
Break out, so all your light may be
Free, free from society!
What's the wait?
Come with us, you'll see

Lin's intricate solo maintained the song's climb, and it drew the rhythm back down to a crawl. They introduced an a capella harmony for one final stanza:

Oh, escape from necessity

Break free, let's see who we can be
Free, free from society
What's the wait?
Come with us, you'll see

The Zenegades faded into silence as a massive applause ensued, which capped off their live TV interview and performance. Going viral online was nothing new to them at this point, but wherever there was a massive amount of attention, there too came an imposing paranoia that perfection wasn't quite met and things could've gone better. For Byrd, it was just another workday, both on stage and during the interview. He was still coping with the pressures of his budding stardom, and he did so by not letting what ended up happening matter at all. The only thing that truly mattered to him was whether the faces in the crowd were smiling, and they were that night. So, when Byrd walked off the set and was greeted by a nervous O'Donnell, he was prepared for positive reactions.

Out of the entire crew, O'Donnell looked the most different after five more years of aging. But regardless of his subtle signs of hair loss and slight weight gain, he was as confident as ever being the co-manager of a successful, quickly becoming iconic band. Life had never been greater from his ambiguous perspective, and there was no denying how he literally wore his success on his sleeves. His gaudiness was on full, plaid-suit display for the New York TV producers, who he always considered to *run the media.* He was collecting over a dozen assorted cheese cubes on a craft services plate when Byrd arrived backstage, and he simultaneously swallowed a few cubes and waved him over for a talk as they made eye contact.

"What's up?" Byrd asked as he approached. "Are you all right?" he added after a few seconds of waiting for a response.

O'Donnell's mouth was full of cheese, so he had trouble clearing his throat without hacking up a lung. "I'm fine! But I got some bad news, Brother Byrd."

"What do you mean? What's going on?"

"Well, one of the producers told me they're mad at you for inviting

Lin and Maya on stage, because it completely changed the format and led to everyone else getting up there too. Did you forget about the show's guidelines they gave us earlier today? It was supposed to be just you and Thayer doing the interview this time."

"Oh, right. I forgot to read that," he lied.

O'Donnell's phone started ringing. He cussed loudly, getting glares from the backstage crew, and answered.

"Hey, Charlie! How's it going, mate? The Cavallo gig went swell. They killed it, I tell ya!" O'Donnell sounded out as he went quiet, listening to the voice on the other end. "*Oh ...* They already called ya, huh? Yeah ... He's here ... He's right next to me. Charlie wants to talk to you," he said, handing the phone to Byrd.

"Hello?" Byrd said as he put the phone up to his ear.

"Jim! It's Charlie Dyceman. Great show tonight, dude!"

"I know it's you, Charlie. I've been standing right next to O'Donnell listening to him talk to you."

"Right, *good one!*" Charlie responded, leading to a brief silence. "Well Jim, I got some tough news. You see, I just got a call from one of the producers that work with Andre Cavallo, and they told me they're pretty upset at you guys for getting *everyone* up on stage, and apparently you guys went against their show guidelines. Do you understand how hard it was for me to get you on that show?"

"No, not really."

"I didn't think so. You see, Jim, I have an agreement with that show to help my clients promote their work, and they're saying they might not want to keep that agreement going because of this little incident tonight. So, I don't know what to tell you, but ..."

Byrd took the phone away from his ear and sternly shook his head at O'Donnell, which was all the signaling O'Donnell needed as Byrd handed him the phone and walked away. O'Donnell quietly listened for a minute.

"Now you listen to *me*, Charlie! *No one*, and I mean *no one*, talks to *Jim fucking Byrd* like *that*! Not on *my* watch!" he yelled, getting the entire green room's attention as he hung up.

15

We all have the exact same human weakness deep within the hidden refuges of our personalities: ego.

Ego, by its very nature, is self-conscious, and it tends to keep us trapped within our obsessions toward reputation, safety, and life's purposed necessities. When ego entraps us within its indistinguishable confines, we inevitably develop an increased sentiment of separation that taints our interactions and worldview expectations. Fortunately, ego isn't impenetrable. It can often be manipulated, and with enough prescience, even overcome. It's obviously never an easy task, but one of the first things one must do to eliminate the clenching grip of ego is to initially eliminate any and all expectations.

Our expectations within any given scenario are completely syncopated with our projected ego; so, when we eliminate expectations, we at least temporarily push ego aside until it crawls its way back into the depths of our psyches and once again projects itself via the infinite cognitive data that stores our realities.

For someone like Byrd, who quickly went from a deadbeat hippie to a world-renowned musician, ego inflation became a daily struggle that ate away at self-care with validation for breakfast, fame for lunch, and popularity as every night's main entrée. An infinite supply of acclaim could inflate anyone's ego, and when Byrd was consistently acclaimed every time he was in public, the subsequent ego inflation he'd experience would initiate an internal war between self-satisfaction and modesty.

Fortunately, Byrd had someone to confide in when it came to these types of toxic thoughts: Shankar Patel. For advice on things as Zen as taming one's ego and forgetting oneself, Shankar was most certainly an astute instructor. Maybe it was simply because he was a successful financial adviser who reawakened later in life and fulfilled his dream of developing his own retreat center, or maybe it was the contentment he'd achieved in needing little to nothing from anything; but regardless of the validity of Shankar's general ethos as the person Byrd turned to for advice, there was plenty of validity in how he helped Byrd cope with his newfound fame. Although Byrd knew Shankar was far from perfect and could spot incongruencies between his advice and general way of living (particularly oriented around his retreat business), all that really mattered was that he was getting something tangible from those particular emails: a refilled altruism fuel tank.

According to Shankar, the key to taming ego was oriented around gratitude, and focusing on others while minimally thinking of oneself. These were the types of mind tricks that Byrd continuously played to keep himself focused throughout the early years of the Zenegades, but he still found difficulties in repressing ego when it came to how he'd spend his money (for example, buying a Hawaiian fruit farm, a couple of cars, a new motorcycle, and an old dive boat). So, in staying true to altruism, he made consistent donations to countless charities and crowdfunding campaigns, and he also gave plenty to Shankar to help him upgrade his ranch, which was now called *Zenegade Ranch*. Byrd also founded nonprofits based in Dover, Denver, and Kona that helped kids learn guitar, and when he wasn't thinking about donating his money, he was at least trying to solely think of his fans.

That paramount tenacity of putting fans first was partly what led him to write so many songs and collaborate with the rest of the

Zenegades in creating six albums in just five years. At first, they recorded at a small studio outside Aspen while several of them rented a house near Basalt, but once Byrd moved to the Big Island, they essentially moved their entire recording operation there. They would rehearse each new song over and over again at Byrd's place until they decided they were ready to record at a local studio in Kona, which was located a few blocks from Reg's new condo. Reg was the only one of the Zenegades crew who permanently relocated to Hawaii with Byrd, and his condo right in the heart of Kona was also located within walking distance of a jazz club that gave him stage time whenever he was in town.

There was no denying that having dedicated fans changed Byrd as an artist, which Shankar helped him realize was profoundly connected to his deepest desires to overcompensate for his old ways of solitary living in the desert. The old Byrd was mostly concerned with self-preservation, but that phase was long gone; however, he was still looking for a partner to help carry all his mental baggage, and loneliness still permeated at his small, decrepit fruit farm.

As for Sky's artistic transition, he no longer held any worries about seemingly needless concerns of being lonely, thanks to his long-term relationship with Thayer bearing so much rewarding fruit. They continued to collaborate throughout those six albums, and together they developed a songwriting capability that surpassed anything they could ever have accomplished individually. When they'd present song ideas to the rest of the group, they were often more fine-tuned and ready for recording, and it was easy to tell that they'd worked out all the kinks while perfecting their lyrics and knuckling down on proposed rhythms. Thayer was Sky's first real girlfriend, and it showed in a variety of ways, like when he'd drift off during conversations about the more mundane aspects of their life together; and although he was far from the best boyfriend a girl could ask for, he'd frequently make up for any inadequacies through a relentless sexual prowess that was *very altruistic*.

On this particular morning, Sky's altruism was expressing itself via his fingers underneath a blanket on a redeye from New York to

Burbank. As Thayer's eyes began to roll back and her lips began to quiver, they both realized how they were going to need a bit more privacy in the plane's bathroom. Flying in Charlie Dyceman's jet helped with the overall privacy within the cabin, but there were still several potentially prying ears on the private charter through O'Donnell, Ruben, Cat, Byrd, and Reg. There was only one bathroom on the sleepy plane, and the only obstacle between them and the mile-high club was Reg, who was awake and reading the latest copy of *Rolling Stone* right next to the bathroom door. They both knew all too well, like the rest of the band, that Reg couldn't keep a secret to save his life, but subtle foreplay simply wasn't going to cut it for Thayer. They quietly bickered for a minute as they contemplated their next move, and it was decided that Reg wouldn't be much of a creative manager if he cared about them having sex behind a nearby bathroom door.

They walked down the narrow aisle past the rest of the snoozing bandmates, and as they approached the bathroom and Reg's large recliner chair, Sky gave a slight wink. This subtle wink indicated all that was necessary as Thayer followed through the plastic, fold-up door and switched the cabin signal to *occupied*. Reg took a deep breath, marked his place in *Rolling Stone*, turned off his overhead light, and slid his earphones on as rattles that could've easily been mistaken for routine turbulence shuddered next to him.

They arrived at a Burbank hangar about four hours later, and as they walked down the private jet's staircase, they saw Thayer's van and a rental SUV that had been conveniently parked for them. There was also an equipment van parked in the hangar, so the first thing they did was load their instruments and sound equipment before deciding who would ride with who in the other two vehicles. O'Donnell and Reg volunteered to go in the rental, and Sky reluctantly rode with them as more of a short-end-of-the-stick kind of decision. Although there technically was room for Sky in Thayer's van, he knew it well enough to want to make sure Ruben, Cat, and Byrd would have the perfect amount of passenger space to ensure an optimal riding experience.

Thayer's run-down ride was now tricked out, and her countless renovations made the Chevy van look completely different from what she originally purchased in Colorado. Now there were only two standard seats in the front, and the back was completely remodeled with miniature lounge chairs, shag carpeting, colorful lights, and a built-in, tie-dye beanbag chair big enough for three. There was a detachable roundtable that you could insert into the floor as a centerpiece, which Ruben began using to cut up lines of coke as Thayer switched back and forth between southbound lanes on the 101 in rush-hour traffic.

Byrd sporadically looked back to see what Ruben and Cat were doing in the lounge area, and his relative ease became a bit edgier as Ruben held out the plastic roundtable in the direction of the front seats to offer each of them a line. The van was now barely moving within an endless maze of Hollywood-aiming cars, and although Thayer also invested in a lift that provided extra clearance and roadway stature, Byrd couldn't help but wonder if nearby drivers could see them. He immediately declined doing a line, which led to Thayer doing two quick lines as Byrd held the wheel.

"Where exactly are we going again? Should we just go back to my place and figure out what to do from there?" Thayer asked the group as her attention turned back to the freeway.

"I don't know. Isn't *this* what people do in the mornings around here?" Byrd asked sarcastically, motioning to the standstill traffic.

"You're all supposed to have a meeting at Charlie's office in like twenty minutes," Cat chimed in from the back. "How come *I'm the only one* who knows what you guys are supposed to do today?"

"No one knows what to do right now because we're being led by two famous wooks in the front seats who *never know* where the hell they're going!" Ruben yelled out as they all laughed, including a little chuckle from Byrd.

Byrd rolled down his window to feel some fresh California breeze, but there was no breeze and only not-so-fresh highway air as they continued crawling at three miles per hour on the 101. He held his head completely out the window to get the most out of the warm wind, and within a matter of seconds, someone in the next lane recognized him.

"Hey! You're Jimmy Byrd!" a twenty-something guy in a green Honda Civic yelled out. Byrd nodded. "Holy shit, dude! Why do you have your head out the window like a dog?"

"Just cuz!" Byrd said with a smile as he reached into his pocket.

"You're the man, dawg!"

"Catch, brother!" he responded as he Frisbee-tossed a guitar pick through the Civic's sunroof and reclined back into his seat. Thayer then careened ahead of the Civic and took the exit ramp for Franklin Avenue, and the heart of Hollywood.

As far as inflated Hollywood egos go, Charlie Dyceman truly took the cake from even the most prestigious label agency heads, in terms of his arrogant self-conception as a music industry mogul. Charlie was known throughout LA as being a success *just cuz* he inherited everything from his deceased father, who was, without a doubt, a much more respectable, lionlike figure in show business. When Charlie was introduced to Thayer via email through her movie-producing father a little over five years prior to that morning's meeting, he literally rolled his eyes at the seemingly comical suggestion that Thayer and her hippie friends were worth helping. That all changed when Thayer sent him Lin and Cat's popular videos of the group playing at Shankar's ranch. He quickly became hypnotized by the group's blend of styles from song to song, and when he noticed how each of the videos had over 250,000 views, he recognized something special within the newly formed Zenegades. He especially saw something within Byrd, and the more he learned about him, the more he felt an investment itch that urged him to follow up on one of the most fundamental pieces of advice his father ever gave him: *your gut, and not your heart, your mind, or your wallet, knows when to give an artist a chance.*

Intuitively rolling successful dice with artists was something that Charlie's father prided himself and his entire company upon, and it's partly why he decided to change his last name to Dyceman from Miller when he first gained traction in the recording industry back in the early fifties. He also thought Dyceman sounded more Jewish, which he nitwittedly assumed would score brownie points with Hollywood executives of the time (as well as Saul Feldman many years later). But when it came to Charlie Jr.'s successful roll of the dice with the Zenegades, there was nothing his father did that even remotely compared. Within two years, the band was an indie phenomenon with a dedicated fanbase, and by the time they'd arrived at his Hollywood office after their first live TV appearance with Andre Cavallo, they'd made going viral across the entire globe seem easy. Their success story had become the magnum opus of Charlie's career, which consequently inflated his ego far beyond even his deceased father's bleak predictions when he handed over the keys to the family business over two decades prior to the rise of the Zenegades.

As Byrd, Thayer, Sky, Ruben, Cat, Reg, and O'Donnell meandered through the glossy halls of Dyce Records, they were eyed down like a show-stopping entourage. Some agents were jaw-dropped as they gazed at the Zenegades requesting drink and snack orders on an assistant's iPad while not missing a beat through the office, but it was the sheer silence of the calamitous Hollywood record label that subtly said more than anything else. All the Dyce Records employees were used to seeing celebrities and artists of all types on a daily basis, but the aura of the Zenegades initiated a rare pause in the action that other artists didn't usually get. The group was then ushered into a conference room, where Charlie sat at the head of the table with a champagne flute in his hand. He chugged the rest of his mimosa as he waved them into the conference room, and he triumphantly stood up and spread his arms out wide in his royal-blue suit like Christ the Redeemer, before saying: "That … was… awesome!"

"What exactly are you talking about?" O'Donnell asked, breaking an awkward silence from the rest of the band.

"What do you mean, *what am I talkin' about*?" he responded, making fun of O'Donnell's accent. "I'm talking about *last night*! You guys *crushed it* like a steroided-baseball slugger! And to no one's surprise, the clip of everyone getting on the show went *viral*!"

"You didn't seem all that excited when I talked to you last night," Byrd said softly, juxtaposing Charlie's triumphant tone.

"Yeah, I agree. I wasn't joking around when I said *no one* talks to Byrd like that on *my* watch," O'Donnell chimed in, making the whole crew quietly crack smiles. "I'm starting to think that you should just mind your record sales and let us do what we do best," he continued as the awkward chuckling continued.

With his next remark already in mind, Charlie laughed louder and longer than anyone else, to the point of dominating the entire room, which subsequently created another awkward silence.

"I'm *so* glad you mentioned that, *Ryan*!" he remarked, emphasizing how no one called O'Donnell by his first name. "Because I did *mind me damn record sales*, and guess what? Somehow, this obviously mismanaged band *unnecessarily walked* its way all the way up to *number one on the Billboard charts*!" he yelled, turning on an iPad that showed the latest charts with *Unnecessary Walking* by Zenegades as the top Americana & Folk album in America.

"Holy shit," Thayer monotonely blurted out.

"Sick," Sky commented.

"No, fucking, way," Ruben said as he grabbed the iPad for clarification.

"Thanks again," Byrd said to Charlie's assistant, who had handed him a Coke.

"Mismanaged, my pale ass," O'Donnell huffed.

"For real?" Reg asked.

"For *fuckin'* real, Reg!" Charlie yelled out excitedly as he patted Reg on the shoulder. "Now, if all the co-managers and non–band members would please wait outside, I need a quick moment with the *talent*," he said with a fake smile that was directed at Reg, Cat, and O'Donnell.

Cat rolled her eyes, Reg looked Charlie up and down in true New

Yorker fashion, and O'Donnell muttered insults as they left the room.

"Okay, now let's get real for a minute," Charlie said as he sat back down at the end of the table and motioned for Byrd, Thayer, Sky, and Ruben to sit down. "Wait a second, where's Lin and Maya? I thought they were supposed to be here."

"They're still in New York," Thayer responded. "They fly in tomorrow."

"*Wow*, I told those idiot co-managers of yours to get everyone to LA today *for a reason*. It's the height of the spring monsoons this week, so their flight could get delayed because of the weather. You know, I know I've said this before, but we have a lot of great managers here that could be better for you than *Ryan and Reg*."

"O'Donnell and Reg are a lot more than just our managers. They're our best friends," Byrd blurted out. "They let us do what we want, and we wouldn't want to work with anyone else."

Another awkward silence ensued as Charlie anticipated more comments from Thayer, Sky, and Ruben, which never came.

"*Well*, let's just hope they make it on time, because tomorrow is *definitely* the biggest day of your careers," Charlie said, jumpstarting the conversation again. "This tour is going to be different than anything else you guys have done so far. It's *huge*. No more amphitheatres in Idaho and Maine, and it all comes down to one hell of a finale, with you guys headlining a two-night run at Red Rocks in a couple months. *Now*, the reason why I wanted to talk to you guys privately is because I want you to know that I've *always* believed that *Unnecessary Walking* would get to the top of this list. I want you to know that you *deserve* this current acclaim, even more than back when *The Unified Field* started bringing you guys a ton of attention. You've worked *hard* to get to this point, but the thing is that now everyone is going to buy tickets to your shows, knowing you're number one on *Billboard* and knowing you're generational talents, *which* means you're all going to need to dig that much deeper to back everything up that's gotten you to this point. From this day forward, your fans are expecting the *best of the best*, and I have to admit that I've been to a few of your shows and thought it was weird seeing people actually *sitting down*. I mean, tomorrow night is a *massive* tour opener. It's the fucking Hollywood Bowl, for Christ's sake, so with a big crowd like that comes a bit more of a ... how do I say this ... a sense of *urgency*."

The four Zenegades looked at each other for a moment, not knowing exactly what should be said in response, especially because Byrd seemed uninterested in the entire conversation. No one said anything, until Thayer nudged Byrd to get him to say *something*.

"Will you be at the show tomorrow night, Charlie?" Byrd asked.

"Hell, yeah! I'll be there, bro! Trust me, I'm pumped. I'm so *stoked*!"

Thayer started laughing underneath her breath, which created a chain reaction to Sky and Ruben. Byrd smiled as he stood up, subsequently leading the others to get out of their seats.

"Well then, see you tomorrow," Byrd replied as he stood up, which led the rest of the group to also stand up. "And by the way, *no one* talks about Ryan O'Donnell or Reg *fucking* Wallace like you just did. Not on *my* watch, and *no one* is going to repeat what Charlie just said here to *anyone*. I don't want them feeling any bit of discouragement right before this *gigantic tour*," he concluded as he prematurely ended the meeting and they left the industry mogul by himself.

Byrd, Ruben, Cat, Sky, and Thayer lounged together later that evening at Thayer and Sky's new house in the West Hollywood Hills, while their beloved co-managers fetched their dinners at a sushi restaurant in Sawtelle's Japantown. This new house of theirs was far from the largest in the neighborhood, but it carried an ultra-chic ambience and pool that Thayer simply couldn't resist as an ultra-rich, first-time luxury-home renter. A lot had certainly changed for Thayer over those five years since they lived together on Shankar's ranch, and one of those changes was an attitude shift toward the entire city of Los Angeles. Although Colorado always had a special place in her heart, becoming a well-known musician caused Angelenos of all illustrious shapes and sizes, including other famous musicians, to genuinely want to hang out with her. Suddenly, LA was the place where *everyone* was, including the Feldman Fam, so it seemed like the most logical place to settle down. She'd try to convince herself how LA made sense from a geographic standpoint because it was in between Shankar and Byrd's fun homes that she could visit whenever she wanted, but being a VIP in LA was like a childhood dream come true that was too thrilling to pass up in reality.

Her growing net worth helped fuel an egotistical determination to outdo her dad in terms of who had the cooler LA crib, which led her to the new party pad in West Hollywood that ever so voguishly resided a mile up the hill from Sunset Boulevard and the illustrious Chateau Marmont Hotel. Alas, when she'd look out at her night views of the glittering LA Basin, she'd acknowledge how those days of sleeping in her van were what it took to make living along the city's ridgeline possible. She'd gaze down at the myriad of miniature car lights meandering through the perpendicular intersections and she'd consider the possibility of some of those drivers being artists just like her, who would gaze up at the ridgeline's residential lighting while thinking to themselves, *Maybe, just maybe, I might catch that break and ride a wave all the way to a house up there.*

On that particular night before the band's sixth tour opener, Thayer's ego was in full force as she glanced at the city lights and recognized how *Unnecessary Walking* was the number-one Americana album in the country. Never had she felt more accomplished, not just within the music industry, but compared to the entire city itself.

"And then he was like: I'm pumped, I'm *so stoked*!" Sky told Cat for the second time, drunkenly mimicking Charlie with an obnoxious shoulder roll to make him look more rounded by a sport coat.

"*Hey*, I got an idea for the show tomorrow!" Thayer announced as the laughter started to subside. "I want to cover 'She's a Rainbow.'"

"We haven't played that one in a while. Why now?" Byrd asked, clearly being the only one sober enough to not be on board without any hesitation.

"It would just mean a lot to me to play it tomorrow, I guess. It reminds me of this beach house in Malibu where I played it in front of some people *a while ago*."

"What do you think, Sky? Should we cover the Stones tomorrow?" Byrd asked across the pool.

"You heard the lady! If it means a lot to her, then it means a lot to me too!"

"I agree with *that*. Give the lady what she wants!" Cat yelled.

"Do you think Lin and Maya will remember how to play it?" Thayer asked Byrd with a hint of skepticism. Byrd smiled back at her and sarcastically lifted his palms, as if to say, *Gee, I don't know, what do you think*?

"I'm not worried about them. I'm more worried about us," he responded. "If you wanna play it tomorrow, then we should go practice it right now."

"Right now?" Thayer asked in an exasperated tone, while looking down at the city lights and thinking about their ensuing sushi.

"You heard the Byrd! If we're playing it tomorrow, we're playing it tonight!" Sky declared as he slipped off his unicorn and swam to the edge of the pool.

After about ten minutes, everyone had changed their clothes and reconvened in the music room that Thayer and Sky created out of an extra third bedroom. As Byrd walked in with his acoustic guitar, he noticed several lines of cocaine lined up on a plate. The edges of Thayer's nostrils were also hosting a hint of white powder.

"Do you want a line?" she asked him.

"No, I'm good. I'm trying to get to sleep pretty soon. Tonight's not the night to stay up too late, ya know?"

"Oh, trust me, I know. This shit doesn't keep me up like that. It calms me down more than anything."

She did another line through a tiny straw, turned to her piano, and started playing the introduction to "She's a Rainbow," which sounded slightly faster than how Byrd, Sky, and Ruben remembered it.

16

here are loads of strategies that help people overcome ego, but all these strategies are oriented around one singular concept: balancing the mind. Ego will always inevitably bubble its way up toward mental surfaces, but it's the reaction to this bubbling that deviates the ebbs and flows of perspective. Balancing the mind by thinking something positive when something negative arises is ancient wisdom that's rooted in a variety of different religions, yet still today, it's so incredibly easy to struggle with mind balancing. Even with the limitless ancient wisdom that's readily available at our fingertips through a single click, our modern world is often incapable of making even the slightest adjustments when it comes to the rigid mental barriers that our egos set up as defense mechanisms. Maybe it's precisely the *click* that has held us back in our efforts of surrendering to a more grateful and forgiving collective consciousness, but when it really comes down to dropping ego, there will only be one mind that can be balanced for the better: your own.

But what a glorious nanosecond it is when you recognize your own cognitive dissonance and choose to positively engage with it, because these are the types of thought processes that confront ego and society's conditioning head-on. Where you go with your rebalancing is entirely up to you, but when you choose to reject your conditioned ego, you ultimately help yourself be more acquainted with something that's so much larger than yourself: the truth about self-awareness.

There's a lot to be recognized within the water molecule experiments of Dr. Masaru Emoto, which delved into the possibility of a connection between mental wavelengths and specific thoughts or spoken words. Fascinatingly enough, the orientation of nearby water molecules was microscopically impacted when someone looked at the water and spoke or thought a phrase or played music. Dr. Emoto would differentiate positive phrases like *thank you* and *peace* with negative phrases like *evil* and *you disgust me* by freezing small water trays after each phrase was thought or spoken, and later examining the molecular crystals. What his team found was that water molecules literally transform themselves into various shapes when exposed to our thoughts and sounds, with positivity being connected to intricate, snowflake-like shapes and negativity to obscure blobs.

Dr. Emoto's experiments have subsequently insinuated that our words and thoughts possess an ability to physically manifest themselves outside the realm of our relatively understood capacities, and these manifestations come in the form of unique energy waves that essentially make our thoughts and sounds so much more *real* than we'd previously imagined. So, maintaining positivity both internally and externally is absolutely paramount to so much more than just overcoming ego, because it also supports our well-being as we continuously trudge our ways ever closer to the truth about who we *really* are.

Byrd got out of Thayer's pull-out bed the next morning much earlier than he expected to, which ended up being the crack of dawn. His original expectation was to wake up around 8 a.m. and casually begin preparing for the biggest concert of his career, but a nightmare prematurely reverted him back from the other side of the Unified Field long before the sun rose over California. His mind raced as he struggled to return to sleep, and he couldn't control the insatiable suspicion that something was going to go wrong.

This delusion continued to fester as he put his clothes on in

Thayer's living room and barely made a sound as he slid a door open and entered the back yard to recalibrate for the day ahead. His thoughts were like a monkey incessantly banging cymbals, which reminded him of an endless array of hypothetical scenarios that could ruin *everything*. But when he looked out at the back yard's expansive view of the Los Angeles Basin, he noticed how a thick marine layer had stretched as far as the eye could see in all directions. Only the apexes of the downtown skyscrapers were visible that morning because the entire metro area had disappeared beneath the clouds.

"It's like a city in camouflage," he whispered as he examined the marine layer. "It's almost like there's nothing down there."

He began imagining the complete disappearance of LA and that he was in fact on a remote hillside far away from the endless hustle of Southern Cali's coastline. But as a helicopter flew overhead and descended into the abyss, his mind's monkey instantly reverted back to life's established rat race.

"I hope Lin and Maya's flight doesn't get delayed," he whispered to himself again.

This was the moment when he recognized just how different it felt while imagining that there were no planes, no freeway traffic jams, and no city below the blanket of early morning clouds. So, he decided to make a cognizant effort toward *believing* he was far away from where he literally was, and this changed his mindset to the point in which his creative juices were flowing at full speed. He took a notepad and pencil from the kitchen, picked up his guitar in the living room, and returned to the backyard view so he could begin writing a song he titled "Cloud Blanket."

There's a city so bare
But I prefer to think it's not there
Full of horns and bright glare
And the people like to stare

A city unreal
Let's get the hell outta here

A warm place to rest
It's time to manifest
We don't gotta go far
We can just listen to this guitar

In the clouds, we're in the clouds
There's no one here, let's scream aloud
Because right now, I, feel, like
We'll never get back again ...
Beyond what's here and there!
In the clouds we'll dare to stare!

You were a blanket so warm
Our love fell like a storm
A memory so worn
Without you my life is torn

But am I just another lonely castaway?
In a sea of sky
Are there still things you need to say?
Out loud
But for now, I, feel, like
We'd never get it back again ...
Beyond a city forlorn!
Half-full of life, we're reborn!

A future unreal
Let's get the hell outta here
I'd let you take the wheel
It's your touch that I can't feel

When will I know if, I'll, ever
See you gazing back at me again?
You're a dream so true!
We've been way overdue!

In the clouds, we're in the clouds
Imagine all our thoughts, spoken out loud
Because right now, I, feel, like
We'll never be here again ...

A savoring so sweet
Waking up in your bedsheets
A vision I still see
I just can't find the key

Because right now, I, feel, like
We're heading back there again ...

In the clouds, we'll stay!
Where life's meant to be gray

By the time he'd finished writing, the morning's fog was starting to dissipate across the basin from east to west, and the rest of the house had woken up after a long night of rehearsals. Their grogginess was apparent as he watched them go through their morning routines, and hearing the amount of coughing coming from Thayer and Sky regressed his thoughts back to what could possibly go wrong later that night. He started imagining Thayer choking on her own saliva in the middle of a solo, and he also imagined Sky missing note after note and completely screwing up the transitions in between songs like they'd practiced. But what scared him the most that morning were the thoughts that he wouldn't live up to his expectations, which he assumed would lead to a crappy performance by the entire group. On the pool's surface, Byrd seemed calm and collected with the help of Thayer's inflatable swan that silently glided him from end to end, but his heart rate was increasing, and his stress levels were spiraling out of control below the surface.

"Ease up, Byrd. Ease up and fly away *slooowly*," he whispered as he took in a deep breath and submerged himself toward the bottom of the deep end.

It was underneath more than ten feet of water where he found solace away from the sounds of the emerging city, and as he sat on the pool's floor, he recognized just how little time there ever was in these types of silent moments. Even holding his breath for as long as he possibly could wasn't anywhere close to enough time in this place, and his newfound passion for snorkeling allowed him to take in underwater silences for a couple of minutes at a time. Snorkeling and scuba diving were some of the driving forces that led him to the Big Island once he had enough savings to do so, but this underwater silence in LA was even more fleeting than usual. He couldn't help but wonder what exactly his mornings would look like as he began another large-scale concert tour across all of America, and considering just how many preshow mornings he'd come to have in the weeks ahead, he understood how far away he was from the cozy confides of Hawaii's peaceful coral reefs.

"I hope our hotels have pools," he thought out loud as his words made several large bubbles float back up to the surface and his impending reality.

It was almost show time a handful of hours later, at least for soundchecks. This meant it was time for Sky, Thayer, Ruben, Cat, and Byrd to pile into Thayer's van and cruise along Sunset Boulevard to the Hollywood Bowl. After about thirty minutes of driving through mid-afternoon traffic, they were rolling down Highland Avenue in the direction of the venue's entrance. Each of them had envisioned that initial arrival since they'd booked the show months earlier, but they could never have guessed how this momentous occasion of arriving at their career's largest venue would be tainted in such a strange way.

Byrd was the first one to notice what was going on, because when Thayer and Sky saw the group of about a dozen folks holding up signs in a form of protest, they initially dismissed it as just another LA protest about an off-kilter societal issue, like animal tourism rights or EV charging station shortages.

"Those signs are definitely about us. Look, that one says *Jim Bird is the worst I've heard.* Not the best spellers, I guess!" Byrd remarked, pointing at the sign holders.

"Slow down," Thayer commanded Sky as they approached the protestors. "Look, that one says *Zenegades hate God.*"

"*Need help finding my Zenegade son. Will pay for leads,*" Ruben repeated another.

"*Freedom doesn't mean no job,*" Sky read another.

"*Smoking pot is NOT Zen,*" Cat read out loud.

"What the fuck is going on here?" Thayer asked as they crept by the small group. "Should we go talk to them and see why they're so upset?"

"I don't know. They seem pretty pissed and literally insane," Sky responded, insinuating it may not be the best idea to give them validation. "They all look pretty old, so maybe they don't like it that their kids are fans. It seems like that one lady's son ran away from home or something like that. What do you think is going on?" he asked, glancing at Byrd.

"I'm not sure, but maybe this has something do with that *movement* Andre Cavallo asked us about the other night."

"I don't get that, though! What did we do? So fucking what if some kids want to copy what we did at Shankar's ranch? It's not our fault if they wanna live out in the woods!" Thayer yelled as Sky parked the van in the venue's VIP lot. "Should we say we don't condone people leaving their families to live in nature or something like that?" she continued, looking toward Cat.

"Yeah, maybe a social post wouldn't hurt," Cat responded with a shrug.

"No, we're not doing anything like that," Byrd responded firmly. "We have no right to tell our fans what they should do with their lives, including their living situations. And neither do the people with those signs!"

And with that rare forcefulness from Byrd, there was nothing left to say. Although the small crowd of protestors was easy to dismiss as having little to no semblance of reality, there was no denying how simply seeing people hold signs outside a venue on *their night* affected each of them during soundchecks. The early spring weather didn't delay Lin and Maya's airport pickup by Reg and O'Donnell, so they arrived shortly after the group in Thayer's van. Both groups got a good glimpse into how the protest pertained to them, which led to a surprisingly different mood as compared to what they expected to feel before such a momentous tour opener.

The whole crew was down in the dumps while they continued talking about what they thought might be going on, and the most deafening aspect of those talks was Byrd's silence, which lingered throughout the entire soundcheck. Most people would consider Byrd to be in a more artistically meditative state of mind when he's that quiet for that long, but the band knew him well enough to see the tenseness that permeated around his silence. They rehearsed a few songs on stage to get a good idea as to how they'd sound later that night, and it became abundantly clear that Byrd wasn't going to be satisfied.

"It's not good enough. We've have to be better than this *bullshit!*" he finally said, right before he marched off the stage by himself.

A little more than three hours after the condescending comment, Lin knocked on the door to a private room where he knew Byrd was. Byrd had kept to himself since denouncing the group's sound on stage, and he was quietly fiddling with different effects for an electric sitar when Lin barged in.

"They just told us thirty minutes till show time," Lin said as he entered the lonely cubicle of a room. "We need to talk," he added as Byrd stood up and gently placed the massive instrument on its respective stand.

"What's up?"

"You know what's up," Lin said as he shut the door behind him and locked it. "That dumbass remark of yours was uncalled for and made everyone feel like shit. I don't know what exactly is going on with you today. They're all saying you've been agitated since you saw those people with the signs, but I think there's something else going on here. So what's *actually* bothering you?"

Byrd took a deep breath before answering the loaded question, and said, "I don't know ... I just woke up this morning with this feeling that something was gonna go wrong today. Those people by the gates definitely made that feeling a lot worse, but you're right, I can't be taking it out on everyone else. I'm just scared, I guess. I keep seeing these images of, like, Thayer coughing during a solo, or Sky missing a bunch of notes, or my solo falling flat and putting the crowd to sleep. There's just a lot to be worried about right now, and I'm trying to keep it mellow and relax, but I can't stop being dragged back into worrying about dumb shit."

Lin nodded for a few seconds while soaking in Byrd's confiding rant, and answered, "Let me give you some advice that Maya gave me when we first started playing together in Greenwich Village, which helped me when I was freaking out that I'd ruin Retro Phat's sound and not be good enough. She said: *keep your shit together and don't worry about anything except* your *sound.* Now, obviously you're pretty different than me, so my advice beyond focusing on your sound is to do what you've always done and think about the fans. Those people out there protesting *clearly aren't* our fans, so you can't let them jostle your focus away from the people who're paying to hear us play tonight. We've got a big obligation to put on one of our best shows tonight, and we need you being *you* to do that."

There was a knock on the other side of the door that accompanied a voice that said, "Are you ready, Brother Byrd?"

"Okay, let's do this," he responded.

When Lin opened the door, they both immediately realized how the rest of the band, as well as O'Donnell and Cat, were standing in the narrow hallway. This took Byrd by surprise, which led to an awkward silence that O'Donnell broke.

"*Well,* is our noble leader back to flying like the little birdie we all know and love?"

"Yeah. I guess he is," Byrd replied. "And I wanna say I'm sorry about earlier. The stress of today got to me, and I should've never taken it out on you guys during soundcheck. That was wrong of me."

"You're damn right it was wrong of you," Reg said matter-of-factly. "We don't need any of that dramatic bullshit right now. I mean, right before the *Hollywood Bowl*, bro? C'mon, you gotta be kidding right now. You're acting like you've never seen hecklers before or something, and if there's one word that wraps up your little tantrum earlier, it's *unprofessional*."

Maya and Thayer tried to tell Reg he was being inappropriate and only making matters worse, but Byrd wasn't having it.

"Reg is 100 percent right," he said, cutting them off. "I was out of line, and I promise I won't have a temper tantrum like that before a show again. But do you guys hear *that*? *That* is the rustling and bustling of a packed Hollywood Bowl that's full of *our* fans. They deserve to experience one of the best shows of their life, and that's exactly what we're gonna give them."

"Hell yeah! Let's do this!" Thayer encouraged as they began forming a group huddle. "This tour is what we've been working up to since all the way back when we were at Shankar's ranch, so let's start it off with a banger!"

After a few more minutes of chatting and stretching, they walked down the hallway, stepped down a staircase, and took a sharp right turn onto the stage. The moment the packed crowd saw them approach their instruments, they were greeted with the loudest applause they'd ever experienced.

The Zenegades came firing straight out of the gate through a long jam led by Sky on mandolin and Lin on fiddle, but this was only just the beginning of what the band would showcase for their Los Angeles fans that evening. That tour opener's setlist was focused around displaying how multifaceted they were, which led to each song being piloted in an organized, alternating sequence. Although Byrd was the lead singer for many of the songs, there were just as many catchy songs led by Thayer, funky songs led by Maya, and songs of various genres led by Sky as they made sure to keep their

Angeleno fans on their toes by sporadically changing up the tempo and seamlessly sequencing the best of their seventy-plus original songs. The one thing that remained consistent with each song was that they all included solos, and these instrumental moments particularly took off when they unleashed one of their secret weapons: Lin's virtuoso talent. Although Lin wasn't a lead vocalist, he played an integral role in transitioning songs together as they flowed from bluegrass jams to slower folk melodies, and back to groovy funk rhythms without missing a beat.

They played several of their new songs from *Unnecessary Walking* that night, but they also stayed true to their roots by playing a few songs from their first album that was originally created at Shankar's ranch. And right when it seemed like the crowd could guess what they'd hear next, Reg stepped onto the stage for *saxy time*. The ambience quickly shifted as they played an improvised version of "Lady Liberty," which was followed up by a handful of songs headed by Maya on lead vocals and Sky on electric guitar. They seemed like an entirely different band as they weaved their way into a jazzy sequence, which was accented by Reg's sax solos that got the crowd swaying their hips from side to side.

They performed for around a hundred minutes straight, until they switched things up again and left Byrd alone on the stage for an electric sitar jam that acted as an intermission to divide another hour of full-band music. Externally he appeared to be composed and prepared to unleash his psychedelic potential, but internally he was shitting himself as he looked out at the increasingly quiet audience. He tried looking deeper into the crowd but could only see the first handful of rows, and he refocused his attention while glancing up and down at his massive, state-of-the-art sitar. That night in LA was the first time he played a sitar solo during a live Zenegades concert, and as his heart raced with angst, he tried to recapture the same kind of solace he'd found earlier that morning while gazing at the clouds. But now, instead of a massive metropolis engulfed in marine layer, it was a crowd of thousands of people hidden behind bright stage lights.

He started the solo by harnessing the sitar's natural sounds as he weaved his fingers up and down the instrument's long neck, but when he began utilizing delays, modulations, and looping to go along with the jam, the crowd quickly realized they were listening to a unique type of music that they'd largely never heard before. Those constantly evolving, synthesized rhythms suddenly became anything and everything that Byrd hoped they'd be, and these mind-bending syncopations led to the crowd lighting up bowls and joints throughout the entire venue. The more the crowd created their own blurry clouds, the more Byrd could envision no one being there at all. He hit trippy note after trippy note to perfection, and the marijuana smoke all throughout the Hollywood Bowl became more prevalent than patchouli scents at a Rainbow Family gathering.

Before he realized it, the rest of the band was back on stage preparing for the second half of the show. They tuned their instruments and patiently waited for him to finish his solo, and the crowd went wild as a crewmember helped Byrd exchange the sitar for his now-famous ukulele, Uncle Tito. They brought the show all the way back from the spacey depths of the sitar jam to some of their best Hawaiian reggae-style songs like "She Passed By," which got the crowd back to dancing after having their minds utterly blown by Byrd. Uncle Tito was then exchanged for an acoustic guitar after a couple of songs, and they returned to folk with "Your Second Fiddle" before once again switching up the energy with original funk songs, and even covering "You Sexy Thing." The set ended with rock songs featuring both Sky and Byrd on electric guitars, and it found its dreamy climax in a way that only "Waiting at Ethereal Station" could reach.

When they returned to the stage for the encore, it was Thayer's turn to take the reins with her cover of "She's a Rainbow." She went off on a long solo at the end of the song, which initiated a transition to one of the very first Zenegades hits, "Anti-Wookite." In the middle of it, Thayer went off script by giving a shout out to the counterculture side of the city she grew up in, and the entire band

viewed her double encore as the perfect way to end their performance. They all knew how one of her childhood dreams of playing
the Hollywood Bowl was finally being fulfilled, and by the look on
her face during those encore songs, there was no denying that this
dream had manifested itself in a monumental fashion.

About a half hour after the show had ended, everyone was hanging
out in the VIP garden bar near the back corner of the Hollywood
Bowl's property. Each of the band members celebrated their successful tour opener in their own unique way, and it became apparent
rather quickly who the most sociable Zenegades were, as everyone
scattered throughout the garden while Byrd and Lin sat together by
a bar, wondering what the hell they were even doing there. Both of
them aimlessly watched from afar as Maya mingled and took pictures with dozens of fans, which gave rise to some insecurities in Lin
as he noticed several attractive men talking to her. These insecurities
were obviously superficial and nothing to worry about, but it still led
him to drink just as much beer as Byrd was drinking Coke.

"*Yo, yo*! Aren't these the two young bucks I wanna see?" Charlie
exclaimed as he approached the bar. It was clear how Charlie was
drunk, given the fact that he had two half-full whiskey glasses in
his hands and his suit was disheveled. "Lemme tell you guys somethin'," he slurred. "No, seriously, I'm being serious now," he continued, trying to hold back from laughing. "That fuckin' show was the
best fuckin' show I've ever been to in my *entire fuckin' life*! And you
guys know me. I'm Charlie fuckin' Dyceman. I've been to literally
tonzuh shows! But *that*. That was somethin' *special*. You two. You two
are *special*! You're all special. We're all special!" he yelled with his
arms wide open.

"This is true, we're all definitely special," Byrd said with a slight
smile and a polite nod. "That's pretty profound of you, Charlie. How
many of those have you had tonight to get you speaking so deeply?"
he asked, motioning to his two glasses of Jack Daniel's.

"*Oh.* Don't even get me started, you sitar space cadet. Jimmy Byrd!" he randomly yelled out to the entire garden, getting a cheer from a few nearby VIPs. "All right, all right. I know I'm a bit fucked up, but I'll tell you why."

"I can't tell you how much we'd love to know why," Lin chirped.

"Yeah, we're on the edge of our stools," Byrd quipped.

"*All right.* Fuck the hell off, I'll tell ya." Another gulp of whiskey. "I'm all fucked up tonight cuz I was hanging out in the pit during the show, just minding my own business, just doin' my thing, just a couple *beers* in me. And then alluh sudden, this big-ass *sitar* comes out, and Jimmy Byrd here starts makin these sounds I've never *ever* heard before, and then these dudes next to me handed me this fuckin' *monster* joint, like it had to be thicker than my cock! And this *shizznik* was Snoop D-O-Double-G *chronic*! I got so high." Another gulp. "I got so high, I mean I went *out there*! I didn't know what to do. I thought someone who knew me would see me freakin' out, so I went backstage and had a drink with O'Donnell. And now here we are!"

Byrd waved over O'Donnell and Reg.

"Well, well. How the almighty have fallen! You look like you just got yourself gored by a bull and rolled down the Spanish Steps, Charlie!" O'Donnell joked, holding a near-empty glass. "I'll have what the old Hollywood hobo is having!" he requested the bartender.

"Me too!" Byrd yelled out, getting a quick eye from the group. "We played a great show, so *fuck it.* Let's celebrate! To tour we go!" he cheersed as they all held up their glasses and took a sip. "Now get this Hollywood hobo out of my face!" he requested, looking directly at Charlie.

"It looks like it's time for you to go back home to your wife. You need a cab?" Reg said as he put his arm around Charlie and began escorting him in the direction of the VIP parking lot.

O'Donnell's attention was instantly directed toward women at the thought of Charlie's wife, which led him far away from the rejects' corner where Byrd and Lin were once again alone. They laughed together for a couple of minutes without saying anything, but the laughter subsided, and an awkward silence ensued as they looked over at Maya still mingling with the same fans.

"So, what do you *actually* think of Charlie?" Lin asked, sipping his third beer.

"He's kinda crazy, but he can be a good guy sometimes, I suppose."

"Look, I didn't wanna say anything until after this tour, but after seeing just how much of an imbecile he really is, I have to tell you that I reexamined one of our new contracts with him, and he's 100 percent ripping us off. It's no wonder he's having such a good time. He knows he just made a killing tonight!"

Byrd sat silently for a moment, thinking about what he could remember from their contract with Charlie, which wasn't much. He downed his whiskey drink and ordered another one instead of thinking too hard.

"Don't worry about it," he dismissed as he grabbed his new glass and took a large sip. "Just enjoy the ride for now. We've got a *long* tour ahead."

17

So many of us strive day in and day out to differentiate ourselves as a unique individual through several all-encompassing aspects of our lives (school, career, family, friends, etc.), and this effort to develop our more intricate characteristics brings about a rather peculiar piece of the human experience's puzzle. There have always been culturally established prerequisites within professional industries that require an applicant to showcase what makes them *special*, and these professional and even social showcases tend to occur at young ages as we climb toward our destined glass ceilings. If any young person has an actual semblance of what makes them unique while applying for a college education or beginning their careers, they're subsequently falling into a societal paradox that often lingers well beyond their formative years.

Some esoteric folks may suggest that life's *true meaning* is to go about living in a way that helps one find the part of themselves that makes them unique, and act out upon these personal features within some sort of tangible effort to give back to everyone else. What tends to be amusing about this search for our unique selves is that it doesn't take any searching throughout the endless cornfield of reality at all, because just a quick glimpse in the mirror is all that's actually necessary in terms of identifying who you are and how there's absolutely no one in this universe that's close to being you.

Yet we consistently see our similarities, as well as our differences, in each other when it's entirely unnecessary. We can't help but compare ourselves, our relationships, our monetary successes and pitfalls, and our ubiquitous life stories against the life stories of others around us. As much as society will try to hammer it down our throats like mid-tier restaurant chains lined up along a commercialized highway, it doesn't always take countless hours and sleepless nights to perfect our crafts in order to distinguish ourselves among the masses. We are and have always been as unique as we'll ever be.

So, there's a universal sense of humor behind the general concept of telling someone *you're unique,* because this may just be the most redundant flattery anyone could ever receive. Nevertheless, something from a physiological standpoint can occur when someone is told they're unique. It's a validation for something we more than likely never needed validation for, but it still always, always, always hits the heaters on our hearts.

The Zenegades' tour buses left Los Angeles the next day and rolled up Cali to Santa Barbara, Santa Cruz, and Berkeley. It was in Berkeley where they had a grand reunion with their old pal Meryl Martinez, who informed the group that she was planning on leaving everything behind to bring her dreams to fruition by joining what she called a *Zenegade Commune* in a remote jungle on the Big Island of Hawaii. She of course knew that Byrd lived on the other side of the island and that the band had lived with him while they created their latest albums over the past few years. So, in her own way, she was confessing how she was one of their biggest fans and was beyond excited to leave the Bay Area behind and fully immerse herself in the lifestyle their origin story represented. Meryl was gifted a backstage pass to the concert at Berkeley's Greek Theatre, and she praised them when they reconvened in the green room at the end of the show by unabashedly expressing her love for the whole group. She also said their performance was truly unique, and she truly meant it.

Byrd had no idea what to think of the wilderness dwellings and counterculture ideologies that Meryl explained as she provided the details of the Zenegade Commune, but his main takeaway was that he evidently had a new neighbor and there were fans near his home. However, he also couldn't help but connect this new movement that Meryl was becoming a full-fledged member of with the sign holders outside all four of their California shows. There were never more than about ten to twenty protestors, but he considered even a small group like that to be a cause for concern. But whenever he mentioned it to anyone, he was told to not worry about *the crazies*, and when he decided to email Charlie after the Berkeley show to tell him there was a trend going on, he was told that it wasn't necessarily a bad thing and that *any press is good press*.

They all had a lot going on in their heads as they traveled to each show, and during their bus rides, they'd do their best to distract themselves by creating seamless set lists that even exceeded their own expectations in terms of how they'd continue to provide unexpected transitions. They wanted each show to be as unique as possible, and they took their time to craft one-of-a-kind performances that no one would ever forget. Switching genres from song to song was a major theme in several of their albums, especially *Unnecessary Walking*, so they made a herculean effort to keep their miscellaneous tonality fluctuating in a way that was cohesive, engaging, and always fun. Their catalog was now large enough for them to play a handful of shows without repeating a single song, but the one thing they continuously repeated for each concert was Byrd's sitar solo. Although it was originally only meant to be a brief break for the rest of the band while Byrd did about fifteen minutes of psychedelic sitar, it was quickly becoming the new thing making waves throughout their fanbase.

Every concert now had long rows of vendors selling random merchandise and food in the venue parking lots, and the people running these pop-up tent businesses were die-hard Zenegades fans who followed them no matter how far and wide they traveled. From Eugene to Portland and Seattle, the band blew hipster minds as the new *it show* to go see. From Seattle, they took the circus east to a music festival in Jackson, where they rested for a few days to bask in the elk-filled valleys of the Grand Tetons.

Getting out in nature felt like the right recharge they all needed, but when Thayer couldn't keep up with Byrd's pace during their group hike up Cascade Canyon, she and Sky decided to stay back and relax by Jenny Lake, where they were surrounded by sharp, jagged peaks. She positioned her nest up against a large tree with an unobstructed view of the nearby canyon, and she watched Sky slowly fall asleep on a boulder. She was essentially alone and had a few hours to kill before turning back to the trailhead, so she wrote a little number she called "Last Big Sky."

An endless road leads far away
An endless river where nothing stays
Present in the moment, flowing like a stream
Every single day feels like a perfect dream

People keep talkin', that's what they'll do
But we'll keep walkin', not stuck like glue
I can't imagine no one else but you

You're the last big sky on my horizon
You're the last big sky, you know it's true
You're the last big sky, I'm takin' what's mine
You're the last big sky, eyes shine so blue

I can't imagine no one else but you

There's a feeling out here no one will find us
So far away, away from it all
No cities, no buildings, no traffic, no trains
Fly north with the geese, can you hear their call?

We'll be here a while, even though we can't stop
A whole world is calling, and life can't be swapped

And I never realized the sky was so grand
Every single vista's in our clenched hands

You're the last big sky on my horizon
You're the last big sky, you know it's true
You're the last big sky, I'm takin' what's mine
You're the last big sky, eyes shine so blue

I can't imagine no one else but you

Can I make you believe? Can I change your mind?
It's all a big party, you took so long to find
Out here there's no difference, no ebbing waves, no tide
Just a grand big sky under the Great Divide

There's a fire still blazing, though it looks dim
It can take all your might, just to believe in him
Do you hear them flying, do you hear their call?
Do you feel the spinning of this space ball?

You're the last big sky on my horizon
You're the last big sky, you know it's true
You're the last big sky, I'm takin' what's mine
You're the last big sky, eyes shine so blue

I can't imagine no one else but you

From Jackson, they took the freeway to Omaha and headed north to Minneapolis. Milwaukee, Chicago, Indianapolis, and Ann Arbor all fell within a few days of each other, and their momentum kept rolling as they played Columbus, Pittsburgh, and Buffalo. They moved east to Ithaca and peaked in Burlington, where they let it all out with a four-hour show that blew the minds of Vermont's old-growth hippies, and from there they headed south to Lowell, Massachusetts. They played two consecutive nights in New York

City, one of which featured a jazz-themed set with the majority of songs sung by Maya. They kept going south for Byrd and Sky's homecoming show in Dover, and hit DC before settling down in the heart of the Blue Ridge Mountains: Asheville. It was in Asheville where they had their first three-night weekend run at a particularly accommodating venue that had teamed up with a local RV park to allow a surplus of Zenegades fans to camp along the French Broad River. It was no secret how people often camped in their cars or tents after their concerts, so a three-night run required a massive campground to accommodate the inevitable debauchery that would take place each night.

After the Saturday night show, which featured more electric rock songs than usual, Byrd decided he was going to do something *special*. Instead of checking in early at their downtown hotel, he decided to walk down to the river to check out what the campers were doing. Although he typically avoided subjecting himself to this level of drunken fan craze, the real adventure that night had everything to do with the matching wig and beard disguise he was wearing.

He looked like a crazy old man as he walked down the steep Asheville hills to the campground, and when he arrived, he noticed several fires burning with groups gathered around them. There was absolutely no telling who Byrd was because his disguise had him looking like the running version of Forrest Gump, so he was completely anonymous as he meandered around the campfires. His plan was evolving perfectly as he got a candid glimpse into what his biggest fans were like, and as he extrovertedly introduced himself as Robin, he got a glimpse into how inviting they were to an old dude who didn't quite fit in.

Byrd eventually asked a guy if he could borrow his guitar to play a song, and he put on a fake raspy voice to sing Neil Young's "Old Man." The campfire group was more than impressed by his acoustic dexterity and imperfect cadence, and they even gave him a genuine round of applause after he'd finished. They all wanted an encore as they sensed how something was off about *Robin* and all the nonsense he'd spewed about himself, so Byrd read the room and promised them more after he got to the bottom of where an overshadowing, savory aroma was emanating from. They pointed him toward an RV in the nearby parking lot, and they highly recommended the food, saying it was the best on tour. Although Byrd wanted to leave the fire pit because he figured he'd blow his cover at any moment, he was also starving. So, *Robin* ventured off to quench his munchies and come up with a few more believable ideas for his backstory.

"Were you at the show in Burlington?" the man with the RV asked as Byrd calmly shook his bearded head and scarfed down a Hawaiian-style pizza. "I swear you look familiar, man. It's like we've met before or something. I don't know what it is …"

Byrd examined the guy and noticed how he was maybe Native American, or possibly from somewhere in Polynesia. He guessed he was somewhere in his late fifties or early sixties, even though he came off much younger than his age. He was wearing a stained, sleeveless shirt to accommodate the heat coming from his pop-up kitchen, which was somehow connected to his swanky RV. He had long, black hair that was tied up in a bun underneath a sweaty bucket hat, which looked like it had been worn for dozens of days in a row. His scruffy beard with tiny gray spots was a clear indication of how he was considerably older than most of the riverside party, and Byrd got the impression that he was their godfather figure.

"What's your name?" Byrd asked.

"Ray," he said, handing a personal pepperoni pie to another hungry customer. "But everyone around here calls me Raymundo."

"Why's that?"

"Well, apparently it's got something to do with some kids show that guys *like us* are way too old to know," he responded, motioning to *Robin*. "Apparently, it's also got something to do with how Jim Byrd nicknamed his ukulele Uncle Tito. Were you at the Zenegades show tonight?" he asked as Byrd gave a subtle nod. "*That* was a good one, brah. A lot more electric stuff than even I expected, and I've been to every show this tour."

"You sell pizza at *every show*?"

"Hell, yeah I do! Pizza, grilled cheeses, Spam musubi, loco moco bowls, waffles, and sometimes poké bowls too," he explained, showing his cooking gear and depleted supplies. "A lot of these kids have gotten to know me over the past couple years, so I also hook my homies up with weed, and *others*. You know what I mean, champ?" he asked, giving a slight wink to *Robin*.

"Yeah ... that's pretty wild that you go to every show, but I'm sure you're having a great springtime. Is this RV your main dwelling?"

"Nah, I typically keep this RV at a buddy's house in California, and now I only use it during the band's tours. I actually retired from running a pretty big chain of Hawaiian restaurants about three years ago, and I started getting into the Zenegades around then and just loved everything they stood for. So, I sold my house and a bunch of my stuff and bought some land out in the jungle on the Big Island of Hawaii, which is where I grew up. A bunch of these kids camping here tonight live there with me, and we hang out and follow the band around when we're not at my *Zenegade Ranch*. I gotta admit that it's pretty wild living with a bunch of kids about thirty years younger than me, but we've been living the dream!"

"That sounds *radical*. So, what do you think about all these protestors with signs outside these Zenegades shows? I noticed a few of them holding signs that seemed to be against the type of communal living you started."

Raymundo revealed his bright smile as he tried to hold back from laughing. "I really try not to think too much about people who aren't worth an inch of my headspace, but I have to admit that it's getting harder and harder, seeing them at every show on tour," he responded as he took a beat to hand over a Hawaiian-style slice to another camper, and turned his attention back to *Robin*. "The truth is that all those people just don't *get us*, so there's no point in being upset with them for things they don't understand. Honestly, if anything, I feel bad for them. A lot of them are our age, and I can't help but think about how many years they've wasted on their myopic mindsets."

"It's sad, but true," Byrd replied as he took another bite out of his slice.

"It just may be the saddest truth about those *lolos*, and what's funny about all them is that I'm sure they'd love spending some time at my spot in Waipio if they *actually* wanted to see what it's like. We've had plenty of old braddahs come by and live with us temporarily, and they never once described our home as *radical*. They loved the vibes we've got going on, and I'm sure you'd enjoy yourself too. I'd be more than happy to host you one day, if you ever make it out to the Big Island."

"Maybe I will come check it out someday," Byrd said as he scratched his fake beard. "You must know my friend Meryl Martinez then. She said she was getting ready to move out to the Waipio commune," he responded, now seeming like he wanted to blow his cover.

"*Yeah*, I sure do! I finally met her at the Berkeley show at the beginning of the tour. She's a close friend of the band, so we're all really excited to have someone in the legit inner circle joining us pretty soon. How do *you* know Meryl?"

Byrd took his wig and beard off, shocking Raymundo as his eyes widened and his jaw fully surrendered to gravity. "I knew I recognized you!" he said, getting excited. "Look, Jim. I don't know why exactly we've crossed paths after all this time like *this*, but I just want you to know that I've been around the Zenegades scene for a while now and toured with the band the past few summers, and I can confidently say that you, my friend, are 100 percent unique."

"Thanks, I appreciate that. We're all unique in our own ways."

"Yeah, that's true. But I'm serious when I say *you're special*," he said with a big, psychedelic-induced grin.

After Byrd finished his conversation with Raymundo, he decided it was time to keep the disguise off and let the fans know the truth about the strange old guy who could rock out on guitar. Everyone by the fire who heard him play "Old Man" was thrilled to meet the famous Jim Byrd, and within minutes, the entire campground had gathered around him. Byrd asked them questions about where they were from and how they got into the music, and he learned how most of them had come from states far beyond North Carolina to attend the three-night run in Asheville. He took a ton of pictures with those who wanted one, and he eventually said it was time for him to walk back to the band's hotel. When he got there about an hour later, Reg and O'Donnell were waiting for him in the lobby.

"*Well*, it's about time! Are you happy now?" Reg asked O'Donnell as he stood up from his chair and prepared to head back to his room. He walked over to Byrd and pointed an index-finger gun at him. "Next time you want to disappear, you better tell me first, okay? Just say, *I'm disappearing, see ya later.* I honestly don't care what your crazy ass says, but tonight was some bullshit, bro."

"My bad, Reg. I didn't think you'd still be awake this late."

Reg pursed his lips and shook his head as he walked back to the elevator that would take him back to his suite. O'Donnell asked him to walk outside the hotel to the valet area so they could talk more privately. When they got there, O'Donnell walked around in a circle, clearly wondering what to say.

"Don't worry about Reg. He'll get over it," he said as he continued pacing back and forth. He then directed his attention right into Byrd's eyes and sternly said, "No disappearing until after Red Rocks. After that, I don't give a fuck what you do!"

After shows in Nashville, Atlanta, New Orleans, and Austin, the Zenegades were back in Colorado to play their tour finale at arguably the most iconic venue in America: Red Rocks Amphitheatre. It was their third time playing Red Rocks, but it was their very first time as a headliner of a two-night weekend run. Everyone knew the story of how they got started by living together in the woods outside Aspen, so they naturally had a big following in the Centennial State. They sold out the 9,500 seats for both evenings within a matter of minutes, and the entire weekend boasted a buzzing energy that set the group up for career-defining performances. Both Red Rocks set lists were different from the other sets they'd played all over the country, and the tour finale featured a couple of never-been-done switches that came at the very beginning of the show and halfway through the set: O'Donnell unexpectedly playing a bagpipe solo as the band entered the stage, and Reg taking the reins with the lead vocals.

Reg had recently voiced his concerns about his background role during the *Unnecessary Walking* tour, which led them to devise a plan that made him the frontman that no one saw coming. His singing voice had a unique rasp to it that worked well as a complement to the likes of Thayer and Maya's smoother tonalities, so they already knew he had the chops to take lead vocals. But Reg had always insisted on being a background singer due to his own insecurities, until they all insisted that Red Rocks was the perfect place for his first dose of the lead-singing spotlight. They decided to have him sing a couple of covers he knew well: Sam Cooke's "Good Times" and Lee Moses's "Got That Will." Reg brought the best times to Red Rocks as he epitomized a will to learn while just beginning to realize his singing potential, and he easily felt like he'd made it, given that his singing debut was at Red Rocks. O'Donnell also coordinated a local brass section for that portion of the show, and Reg roamed the stage while showing off his dance moves, which was by far the biggest crowd pleaser of the entire night.

When the band came back on stage for the show's encore, there was another coordinated moment in which all the lights shut off and a center-stage spotlight blasted on Byrd.

"Now, I know this is out of custom for some songwriters, but right now I'm going to tell y'all a story about how I came up with one of our songs. It's a pretty popular one of ours, so I'm sure you've heard of it. It's called 'Waiting at Ethereal Station,'" he quietly said into the microphone as all of Red Rocks cheered. "You see, this song is actually the very first song we ever played together *way back* when I was living out of a motorcycle in the Utah desert, and I'll never forget when these fine friends of mine paid me a visit that forever changed me." Another cheer from the crowd. "I remember all of them making fun of me for writing this song, and that was because I told them it was about this goofy dream I had one night. And in this dream, I met a girl at a gas station in the middle of nowhere, and that's a true story, but this *ethereal station* has stuck with me all these years. I want to dedicate this next one to that girl I met in Utah, who I assume I'll keep waiting to hear from again, and who ended up catalyzing all these dreams of ours that have now come to fruition. So, I want all of you to know that you must always, always, always believe in your dreams! You can do those things you've always wanted to do, you can go live in those places you've always wanted to live, and you can achieve anything you set your sights on, just as long as you keep trying! Those dreams of yours are a lot more real than you may think, so let your hearts, and not just your minds, do your thinking for you as you set sail with us for the rest of tonight! And let this moment stay with you, just like all our goofy dreams have stayed with us!" he belted out as the stage lights came back on and the Zenegades rocked out harder than ever to close out their most successful nationwide tour.

After the show ended, everyone was partying in the backstage caverns as they celebrated the culmination of yet another collective accomplishment. Shankar had come from Aspen to see the tour finale, and he made a toast, sharing how proud he was of them. He said he always knew, even back when they lived together on his ranch, that they had something to offer that was much bigger than themselves. It was a touching moment, and it generally made everyone emotional and want to party even more. Moments after Shankar's speech, Lin looked into Byrd's cup and asked him what was in it. Byrd responded saying it was only Coke, but also provided a tipsy smile in return. Thayer brought out the real coke in the dressing rooms about an hour later while they were preparing to leave, and that was when Byrd decided it was time to go outside for some fresh air.

As he walked through the Red Rocks hallways full of legendary pictures, he wondered if there would one day be a picture of the Zenegades on those walls. He headed up the stairs toward the ground-level parking lot and heard someone saying, "Hey, Byrd," over and over again.

"There you are," O'Donnell said as he walked up the stairs. "I just wanted to tell you that Cat forwarded this social media message to show you. Check this out. You're not gonna believe it," he said, handing him his phone.

Byrd looked at the phone and read the message, which had an original message that read, *Show this to Byrd.*

Below that message was a screenshot of a private message to the Zenegades Facebook page, which read:

Hey Zenegades!

My name is Jane Imberti, and I wanted to let you know that I was at your Red Rocks show tonight and that it was personally really incredible for me. The thing is that I'm almost 100% sure that I'm the girl Jim Byrd met at that gas station in Utah about five years ago. I remember him and that day pretty well, and I'm confident of this because he doesn't look all that different these days! I've also attached a picture of me that you can show him to see if he remembers me as well as he says he does!

I just want to say that I never knew "Waiting at Ethereal Station" was based off that encounter I had with him, but I'm absolutely flattered and love that song so much. I really love all the songs the Zenegades have come out with over the years. I'm a huge fan and have been to a bunch of shows here in Colorado.

But tonight really was unique, and I wanted to let you guys know somehow that I was there to hear Jim's story. And if you ever want MY side of the story, just let me know and I'll be happy to chat more.

Thanks again for a great show!

Jane aka 'the girl from the Utah gas station'

18

A glorious highway adventure was coming to a close, now that the *Unnecessary Walking* tour was over, so naturally, Ruben and Cat planned on dedicating the rest of the summer months to keeping the wheels rolling on their own road trip.

Throughout the band's touring years, Ruben had become a critical morale booster while they spent multiple weeks at a time never staying in one place. When they drove their own beat-up vans for their first and second tours, it was Ruben who helped keep the party going. As they got more popular and hired bus drivers to shuttle them from show to show, it was Ruben who wanted to jam out while rolling down the road. His bus performances never consisted of a full drum set, but simple congas were all he ever needed to rap off anyone. In an interview after the release of their second album, *Madre Naturaleza*, Byrd mentioned Ruben and Cat when a highbrow magazine asked him how he thought their music caught on and grabbed such a dedicated group of fans. Byrd explained how Cat's social media presence was the main reason their YouTube videos started getting viewed and shared at such a viral rate in the early days, and how he thought that Ruben's T-shirt designs got fans even more interested in representing themselves as Zenegades.

And it was true. If they didn't have Cat as their head of marketing, it would've been a lot less likely to have been found by other influencers who helped them reach countless young people, who ended up connecting with their music on an intricate level. And if

Ruben weren't around to put together a whole line of T-shirt de-signs, then all those fans wouldn't have found apparel that helped explain their newfound musical taste. Invaluable conversations simply wouldn't have happened if it weren't for Ruben and Cat, and the ripple could've effectively kept going on.

Cat's photography became the album of their lives, but at a certain point, she began realizing that her Zenegades photography had become the album of their *professional* lives. There was so much more she wanted to capture through her lens than rehearsals, studio recordings, and the coast-to-coast journey they were all experiencing together. That's why she came up with the plan for her and Ruben to go on their own Zenegade journey, and she wanted this particular journey to be like none other they'd ever experienced. In her mind, it was time to put their Hermosa Beach home on hold and jump across the pond to Europe, where they'd go explore a new land that neither of them knew much about.

At the exact moment Cat mentioned the words *Euro trip*, Ruben realized how that was their next move to keep the good times rolling after the Red Rocks tour finale. So, they made all the proper arrangements, including organizing the proper time to pick up Cat's now much-more-worked-in royal steed of a van. Organizing their paperwork and medical requirements to bring Nikita along for the summer vacation was also something of significant importance as they arrived in the Italian port city of Genoa.

"How much longer do you think it'll be?" Cat whispered into Ruben's ear as they peeked into a warehouse room with customs officers looking through the van.

"How much longer is this going to take?" Ruben asked a near-by officer. "We have somewhere important we need to be. We can't hang out here all day."

"Okay, here is the deal," an Italian customs officer responded. "I will let you come into Italia today, and you may take this vehicle throughout Europe wherever you choose, *but* this admission form means you must take your American-registered vehicle back to America within six months *or* properly register it here," he explained as he handed over a handful of forms and the key prize, their keys.

They walked over to the van and noticed how a few things had been moved around for the customs inspection, but they luckily didn't find the four ounces of weed that Ruben hid in a secret compartment. He slyly revealed the ganja to Cat as they packed their flight luggage into the van, and her jaw dropped at the sight of the vacuum-sealed bags.

"You crazy son of a stoner bitch," she whispered as they began laughing, which caused Nikita to begin barking with an excitement she didn't quite understand.

"So ... where to first?" Ruben asked as he turned the keys in the ignition and looked over at his beauty queen getting licked by their fluff child.

"I thought we were gonna drive up to the mountains today. Is that not the plan anymore?"

"Well, it *was* the plan, but what's the rush? The beaches looked nice around here from up in the plane."

"Then drive us to the most beautiful beach near here, my Zenegade prince. I've always wanted to see the French Riviera!" she decreed with a massive smile as their wheels began to roll.

New York City had an entirely new aura for both Maya and Lin, now that playing in the Zenegades had made them well-known musicians, and they were constantly being invited to chic parties and social gatherings that elicited obligations to make appearance after appearance within their growing concentric circles. But even though they were sometimes out and about, they had a home life that was rather distinctive as compared to the rest of the band members. Maya and Lin's apartment was quaintly luxurious, but it was still far from a large living space. Simply having a spare bedroom in Manhattan that they used for music was a bona fide convenience, and they made the most of this convenience daily. Maya would often invite the members of Retro Phat to come over and rehearse Zenegades songs when they were doing their *band homework* in between meetings at Byrd's farm, and they also worked on their own songs as they began the foundations of their first studio album. But more often than not, it was just the two of them playing together for fun; and when it came to their routines, Maya and Lin had become creatures of habit who had a hard time opening themselves up to other leisurely detours. For them, music was like a sex addiction that needed to be satiated. They'd build up to climaxes as their endorphins raged from one song to another, and in their minds, the only thing that felt better than playing music for several hours at a time was having sex immediately afterward. That home life routine was something they figured could last forever and never lose its charm.

Maya was now a rising star in New York's music scene, and people from all over the country were buying tickets in advance to cram into the Blue Queen Lounge and see her have full rein over her Retro Phat side project. She truly showed her loyalty, and jazz royalty, by deciding to have her summer residency at Blue Queen. She could have sold more tickets at larger venues, but in her eyes, her jazz sets were meant to be at the club that provided her first shot.

Lin was also still a member of the revived Retro Phat, and he'd still show up late for rehearsal sessions after playing alone in random places throughout the city. He'd gained access to several rooftops over the years, and he'd randomly go to a few different buildings and stare at skyscrapers as he tried to tune out city noises. But even though he had a few private places that would gladly open their doors for him, he still enjoyed going to the small, offbeat city parks to play the classical melodies that were now a nostalgic part of his childhood. A couple of viral videos came out of him playing to small crowds in random parks, and this one day led to the *Times* writing a story about him secretly performing in public throughout the city. He started playing at home more often after that article was published, but he'd still go and find remote places to play every now and again.

He'd even suggested to Maya numerous times that they leave the city behind, but she wouldn't have it. Her entire family lived in the

Bronx, the Zenegades had established solid ground rules to keep them all practicing when they weren't together, and she was just now beginning to live out her dreams as an A-list headliner in the Village. But her adamancy to stay put didn't stop Lin from looking into second homes, and one day when he was teetering around a tiny park on the Upper East Side, he got a few important emails all at once. The first one was from a Realtor on the Big Island who gave him information about a couple different condos in the Kona area, which he was considering so he and Maya could have a nicer place to stay than the off-grid bungalows on Byrd's farm when they reconvened with the rest of the gang to write their next album. He glanced over the message from the Realtor saying how excited she was to help them find a lovely new Hawaiian home.

The second email was from Charlie Dyceman, and it included attachments to revised contracts for him and Maya. Charlie explained how these new contracts were a *big step* for them, and Lin noticed that they featured representation clauses for the music they created outside the parameters of their Zenegades agreement (i.e., Retro Phat). He wasn't sure what to think of the massive PDF files, and he was upset with the fact that he wasn't kept in the loop about his and Maya's artistic rights. He tried to hold himself back from getting angry as he rubbed his eyes and dialed O'Donnell's cell number.

"Lin, my boy! How's it going, young Padawan?"

"Well, it's not going too good, actually. I just got an email from Charlie about new contracts for Maya and me. Why haven't you told us anything about this?"

"I honestly swear on my mum, who I'm sitting next to at the dinner table right now, that Charlie didn't say *anything* to me about any contract changes."

"*Oh* ... you're back home in Scotland?"

"Yep. My lease in LA ended, and I didn't want to renew, so I dumped all my stuff in Thayer and Sky's garage the other day and told them I'll be home for summer. You know, Ruben and Cat just got to Italy today. Why don't you and Maya come on over the pond for a little bit of fun? You don't need to be worrying about contracts right now. You just played the living hell out of Red Rocks, for Chrissake! You should get out and globetrot like Ruben and Cat are doing. It'll be good for both of you."

"Honestly, you might actually be right. That does sound like a lot of fun. We should play a show in your hometown someday."

"Now *that* is why you're the smart one in the band! I *love it*. My friends can help us out too. It would be a *blast!*" he replied. "*Now,* what is all this fuss about some bloody contract with Charlie? Why do you even *care* so damn much about all this corporate shit anyways?"

"All right. Well, you're clearly with your family, so it might not be the best time to talk about contracts, and it's my bad for not realizing you went back home and that it's dinnertime there. But the real point of me calling you is to once again remind you that we need to renegotiate our contracts with Charlie. We honestly don't need him anymore. We're at the point where we can start our own record label if we want to. It can really be so much better, man, but maybe we'll talk more about this another day. I'm gonna forward this email to you, and I want you to *actually* look through it and let me know what you think. Can you *please* do this for me soon?"

"Sure, in the morning! I'm a bit too tipsy to be reading legal jargon right now. *Oh,* by the way, I forgot to let you know that we got some *big* marketing news that's *way* more important than any of this contract crap with Charlie. Keep your eyes on CBS, because Byrd's gonna be on it! Gotta go, *ta ta!*" he said as he abruptly hung up.

Lin glanced down at his phone and shook his head, and he was particularly confused by what CBS show O'Donnell was referring to. He started breathing deeply as he let his mind wander to other things, and just when he thought he was coming back to a sense of normalcy, all sorts of uneasiness started to hurl itself outward as he looked at the third unread email on his phone. Just seeing it waiting for him in his inbox struck him like a bullet to the heart, and it was daunting to the point that he was too scared to open it.

It was from a man named David Fieldcrest, with a subject that read: *I Found Your Mom.*

Successfully surfing on Venice Beach's shoreline takes plenty of patience and perseverance, due to the inevitable hordes of surfers paddling out in the exact same spots while trying to catch the exact same waves, but there's nevertheless a rush that comes with riding any wave along the California coast. And in a city like Los Angeles that's largely enthralled in the entertainment industry, there are literally millions of people conglomerated together who are paddling out toward the same exact goal: *catching their break.*

Thayer and Sky caught their breaks through the band's success, and they'd gotten good at prolonging the smooth ride that came with industry acclaim. As they gained the means to do so, LA became more of a hub than a home as they traveled to rehearse with Byrd in Hawaii. And although Sky was never the biggest fan of LA, there wasn't much use in trying to talk Thayer out of leaving their home near the top of the West Hollywood Hills. He knew the symbolic feat their home meant to her more than anyone else, and being a celebrity musician in a city obsessed with famous people was easily more stimulating than the semi-off-grid living that Byrd would never give up. So, at a certain point nearly six years after the band's birth, the best thing either of them could do was keep catching waves and enjoying the ride in Cali.

Having her own panoramic view along LA's legendary ridgeline was a dream come true for Thayer, even though her younger self wouldn't have admitted it. She could still clearly remember the many moments she had as a young girl learning to play piano while imagining herself exactly where she ended up getting, and the disdain for her hometown began to dissipate as more people reached out to her for musical support and good times. They tried to keep their privacy, due to their increasing celebrity status, but that didn't stop them from inviting people over for parties on the weekends. Alternative musicians, indie-film actors, and artists of all types caught wind of the festivities happening at Thayer and Sky's place, and within a year of renting, their house became an exclusive sanctuary for dozens of famous people who wanted to listen to late-night sets by the likes of two Zenegades.

Not all the partygoers were celebrities, and two of their more ordinary guests who came by on a *very* regular basis were J. P. and Madison. Having a famous friend was just as much of a dream come true for Madison as becoming famous was for Thayer, and she loved every minute of talking with the people who clearly avoided all of LA's *Madisons*. Although hosting them at their parties didn't necessarily excite Thayer and Sky, they both knew J. P. had the best coke in the entire city. Their parties weren't always rowdy, but there was no denying that everyone was in for a wild night when they did turn things up. These lawless debaucheries were par for the course in terms of Thayer's idea of her dream house, but the increasing frequency of waking up by the pool with no recollection of the previous night was taking its toll. They'd made more money than ever by the time they'd returned home from the *Unnecessary Walking* tour, and it seemed like a good enough time to celebrate their latest triumphs via a weeklong binge of reckless abandon, until it wasn't.

The next morning after Lin's call to O'Donnell, Thayer woke up in a hammock with more than thirty mosquito bites and decided it was best to take a break from having guests. Her hangover throbbed as she rolled off the hammock and plopped into the pool with all her clothes on. She walked up to the house and slipped off her wet outfit, and she examined the living room wreckage from the previous night as she hobbled about the living room in her underwear. That's when the screeching sounds of a blender went off in the kitchen, letting her know she wasn't alone. She looked to her right and saw Madison creating a green-hued smoothie.

"Good morning, Thay! I'm making my famous hangover cure!" she yelled over the sounds of the blender, before pouring two glasses. "Oh, my, fucking, God. You're *not* going to believe what my online friend Stacey sent me this morning!" she continued as she handed Thayer a glass. Thayer gulped it down, until a crippling brain freeze ensued.

"I … can't … stand … up," she muttered as the brain freeze permeated throughout her mushy, hungover cerebellum. Madison grabbed the smoothie cup before Thayer inadvertently spilled it all over the floor. "No more parties," she whispered as she curled into the fetal position on her hardwood floors.

"It's okay, Thay," Madison whispered as she bent down toward the frail piano star and brushed hair out of her eyes. "Brain freeze is actually one of the best things you can do for a hangover. Just give it a second; you'll feel better in no time!"

The brain freeze eventually subsided, and Thayer felt almost as if she'd taken a shower or done some other home remedy. She was back to life for all intents and purposes, and now her intentions were set on drinking her green smoothie a little bit slower. Madison escorted her from the kitchen floor to the couch in the living room, where she mirrored her phone's screen onto the TV to project the trumpet sounds of *Sunday Morning*'s theme song.

"Did you know Byrd got interviewed for this story?" Madison asked as Thayer made no attempt to acknowledge her and instead curled into a few blankets with her smoothie and focused on its metal straw.

"The number-one Americana album in America right now is *Unnecessary Walking* by the Zenegades, a group that some are now calling The Millennial Beatles, and for good reason," the female journalist's voiceover rang. "With hit after hit since the band's beginnings over five years ago, it has become clear that the Zenegades have had a profound impact on the lives of young people across the nation and even the entire world, for better *or* worse."

The segment cut to a few seconds of their interview on Andre Cavallo's talk show, which displayed Byrd and Thayer being asked about a movement of people living in Zenegade communes, and Byrd saying he hadn't heard about it.

"Although even the Zenegades' frontman, Jim Byrd, hasn't heard much about this movement of people straying away from cities and into remote shantytowns, it's safe to say that young people everywhere are leaving their lives behind to live out their own renditions of a Zenegade lifestyle, and this lifestyle has proven to not always be so Zen."

The segment cut to an older mother in typical TV interview lighting, who was clearly on the verge of crying on camera.

"We knew she was always going to be a free spirit and that we didn't always see eye to eye, but now we don't even know when we'll see her again," the mother said.

"Do you know where your daughter is?" the reporter asked.

"No, not really. All we know is she's living somewhere in Hawaii on this guy's land, who's my age. It's all so screwed up and cultish, and I just hope she's safe and has a *real roof* over her head."

The segment cut to a montage of tents and commune footage as the journalist returned with her voiceover. "This is a common story for families all across America as their kids have left home to build communities made of tents and cabins in wilderness areas. The Bureau of Land Management has tirelessly removed many of these communities from public lands across several states, but there always seems to be another commune popping up every day in even more remote locations."

The segment cut to the journalist walking in a crop field with Raymundo, which led into another voiceover. "One of the reasons why these wild communes full of young Zenegades keep popping up is because of wealthy investors providing private properties for these communities to break ground. If there are any kinds of *cult leader* figures within this movement, this man, who wishes to simply be referred to as Raymundo, is one of them. He hosts over two dozen people at his property on the Big Island of Hawaii, and young people come and go on nearly a daily basis. But once you get to know Raymundo, you'll see that he wouldn't even harm a fly."

"So, why did you decide to buy this property here?" the journalist asked Raymundo while they walked through the farmland.

"Well, I grew up here and knew this would be the perfect place. But when I visited some of the other Zenegade communes out in places like Idaho, Colorado, Montana, and Oregon, I noticed how they sometimes struggled with large-scale water filtration. Some of the cleanest spring water money can buy comes straight to us, and I have to admit, doing all *this* near Jim Byrd was another big reason to invest here."

The segment cut to Byrd on his Big Island property. The quick montage of shots showed him picking fruits and doing other miscellaneous tasks.

"Just on the other side of the Big Island is the original Zenegade himself, Jim Byrd. He took his music earnings and created a home that he modeled off the now-famous Zenegade Ranch outside Aspen, where the group got started. Here on this old fruit farm is where the biggest band in America writes its new songs, and for an ex-wilderness guide who enjoys seclusion, it's the perfect place to call home. Even though both Jim and Raymundo admit that they've just recently met each other, they certainly know each other now."

"What do you want to say to all the people out there watching this who might be scared for their children and who don't quite understand what's going on with this movement toward a Zenegade lifestyle?" she asked him on his porch.

Thayer was now on the edge of her seat, wondering how no one told her that Byrd was interviewed by *Sunday Morning*.

"Well … I guess I'd tell them that I was just like them until recently, because I didn't understand what was going on either. But then I went out and got a glimpse for myself to make my own judgment, and now I realize how incredible it is for these people to have come together in search for their own harmony. As a musician who likes experimenting with different harmonies, I can say *this harmony* is a good one, and there's no need to be scared by it."

Byrd's interview cut to a montage of clips that showed him at Raymundo's property with the other Zenegades. All of them were wearing damp, muddy clothes in the jungle as Byrd provided tips on using wooden hand drills.

"Jim Byrd just so happens to know a lot about living in the wilderness, and he now is helping Raymundo's commune as they, in turn, provide a famous artist with a better understanding of his music's impact," the journalist voiced over.

"What would you say you've learned from your time on the other side of the island, with all those people who look up to you as much more than just a musician?" she asked, back on Byrd's porch in their interview setting.

"They're a family, and I'm just lucky enough to be a small part of the bond they share. For a while, I guess we bonded through music, but now it's becoming more than that. I guess I've learned that there has always been this true friendship between our music and our backstory. You, of course, don't have to pick up all your belongings and leave your life behind to be a Zenegades fan, but who are any of us to try to inhibit the real craving for adventure all those people at Ray's place have? A lot of them are people who are finally bringing their dreams to fruition, and that's an incredibly beautiful thing to see. Just hanging out there and seeing how they live is something I'm grateful for, and you're right that they make me feel like so much more than just a musician. I think that's how everyone wants to be treated, because we're all so much more than the boxes life likes to put us in."

Each morning started shady on the west side of the Mauna Loa volcano, and this shade helped provide an abundance of agricultural potential throughout the mountain's shadow. One reason why the Big Island of Hawaii was such a great place for farming was its unique volcanic soil, which had regenerated itself over many years to be perfect for vegetation like guavas, avocados, papayas, bananas, passionfruit, and endless coffee fields.

It was agricultural potential that attracted Byrd to the Big Island more than anything else, and he found the farm of his dreams on the very first day of house hunting along the hillsides above Captain Cook. Those five acres of land were perfect for a whole variety of reasons, the most prominent being the three cabins that were originally intended for young mainlanders (aka *haoles*) looking for a work-trade opportunity when the farm was still in business. The cabins were set up in a row that reminded him of the Zenegade Ranch, and just like Shankar's property, this place required extensive renovations. No work-trade haoles had worked there for nearly two decades, so the homestead's decaying nature ended up being a key selling point as he attempted to recreate the band's beginnings. His impulsive purchase led to the whole group renovating the buildings, but it more importantly led to an improved place for the gang to rehearse old songs and develop new ones. The music they created on the farm was well worth the initial investment in Byrd's eyes, but he more importantly saw his new home as a tiny safe haven in paradise where they all could relax together and be their pre-famous selves.

Owning a farm also entailed all kinds of manual labor, which Byrd found out about within the first two years of living in Hawaii. Although this farm was small as compared to the adjacent properties along the steep mountainside, it had dozens of dwarf papaya and guava trees, as well as a couple of open acres that were practically begging to once again grow coffee trees. The coffee field was immediately reseeded, and those trees were beginning to bear their very first cherries around the time the *Unnecessary Walking* tour had ended. Taking care of the fruit and baby coffee trees required a lot of attention that Byrd simply couldn't provide while he was too busy traveling with the band, so he needed a part-time assistant to be there when he couldn't. Those hands ended up being the big paws of a local guy named Hani, and Byrd paid Hani handsomely with an hourly wage of eighty dollars whenever he needed his services. Reg would also help out every now and again when Byrd needed someone, but their agreement was rooted in reciprocity, with Byrd helping him in return.

Reg fell in love with Hawaiian culture as he helped Byrd renovate his cabins with the rest of the gang, and he loved the Big Island so much that he bought a condo in nearby Kona before they'd even finished Byrd's project. One thing he loved about Kona was its small jazz scene, and he quickly got a side gig at a club that offered him stage time whenever he wanted. He later became a regular for tourists seeking saxophone jams during their vacations, and after about a year, Reg was a co-owner of the club. He helped transform it into a nightlife staple in the thriving beach town, and when Byrd needed Reg's help at the farm, he'd often exchange solo acoustic sets that would end up being the hottest ticket on the entire island.

The investments they'd made were going well. But there was also another time-worthy hobby that waited for them to break their new routines, below the ocean's surface. Both Byrd and Reg got hooked on snorkeling and scuba diving off the Kona coast, and on that Sunday morning when Thayer rolled out of her hammock and onto her kitchen floor with a hungover brain freeze, diving was the first thing on their to-do list.

They drove down the steep volcanic hills to a tiny marina, where they launched a small dive boat and headed out to a remote part of the coastline. As they reached a buoy marker indicating the nearby destination, the sun was just beginning to peak over Mauna Loa and cast its light on the reef. They lowered the anchor and started preparing their gear.

"You think we'll see any sharks today?" Reg asked as he adjusted his wetsuit.

"It's pretty early for sharks, so if they're down there, then they're probably sleeping. But that doesn't mean there aren't other things to be on the lookout for, like barracudas and eagle rays."

"All those rays scare the shit out of me, but *fuck it*. I want to use the good camera this time!" Reg replied as he double-checked his regulator and made sure everything was ready to rock.

They stayed below the surface for almost an hour as they soaked in the reef's early-morning underwater lighting. They also explored a seamount, which was the island itself quickly descending into the deep blue. Along the seamount's upper walls were eels, fish, turtles, and sponges, as well as an endless collection of vibrant corals. Reg snapped picture after picture as they swam down to depths of around a hundred feet, until their oxygen levels eventually decreased and they needed to ascend to the surface.

"O'Donnell texted me," Reg said as they settled back onto the boat.

"What did that *cheeky bastard* have to say?" Byrd imitated.

"He just says that he sent you the video link, which I'm guessing has the interview from the other day in it."

So, with that news, they decided to head back. About two hours later, when they'd returned to the farm, Byrd rushed over to his new laptop and logged into his email account. But instead of clicking on the email with the subject *Sunday Morning Link,* he clicked on the email with the subject *I have BIG news.*

This email wasn't from anyone associated with the Zenegades, but was actually the most recent message within a long thread of messages to Jane Imberti. The email read:

Hey!

I just wanna keep this short and sweet and let you know that I talked with Raymundo and he's officially letting me become a part of his Waipio family! I'm starting to pack my bags already and booked a flight for a week from today.

Hope to see you soon,

Jane

19

ust about everything in the world becomes commoditized, and this is partly because it's a significant part of our collective nature to take any particular product, service, or idea and throw money into a financial hole until that hole hopefully grows profit flowers. Even the most unmarketable ideas are taken advantage of by anyone with a keen eye for a business model, and one example of an unmarketable idea being commoditized is the incorporation of Zen into countless for-profit companies that degrade what this ancient philosophy stands for, in an attempt to portray themselves as a real-world example of *humble, inviting warmth.*

Even the ever-developing, ever-musically exceptional Zenegades were a part of this cultural phenomenon that takes renowned ideas and twists them in ways toward monetary success. Rarely was Byrd's background questioned as an individual who at least tried to embody Zen teachings, and this was especially the case in the early days as the group got to know one another better at Shankar's ranch. The entire crew would look to Byrd as a guiding trendsetter when they needed an extra push to continue their construction project, or when they needed an extra excuse to take the afternoon off and enjoy playing their instruments in the sun; but as their music suddenly became a popular commodity all throughout the world, inevitable changes implanted themselves within their daily routines and slowly but surely manipulated their artistic developments. These artistic changes were generally similar to changes that come with any successful commoditization within our culturally constructed economics, and questions of Byrd's background and Zen embodiment found their way into the group's perspective. But of course, the nature and practice of Zen helps remind us of our inconsequentially essential place in the universe, and this form of self-awareness is much older than modern culture and economics.

People didn't always scurry around in absurdity toward a sense of purpose that's validated by a monetized number on a computer screen. *Aye*, back in the days when every English speaker spoke similarly to O'Donnell, there was more self-reliance in making ends meet that came with all its hardships and peaceful surrenders. There's something about those old ways of the past that sparkles up to us today and stirs up the notion that we're the offspring of the most resilient people who ever lived, and that society itself was and can still be perfectly fine without the constant control imposed by commodities.

The idea of reclaiming self-reliance by isolating from the impacts of modern commoditization is the ironic effect that the commoditization of the Zenegades had on their young fans. Although the group's artistic roots were founded in a rebellious lifestyle that strayed far from monetary success, they ended up becoming financially successful through their rebellious art. As they created more albums, more people started looking up to them as trendsetters for their own lives, which subsequently inspired massive groups of teens and twenty-somethings to flee from their own ensuing commercializations. Instead of continuing education in a traditional fashion like attending classes at a university, many teenage Zenegades fans searched for communities that would accept their attempts to better understand their personal life meanings—without the potential of being misled by the status quo's suggestions. These seemingly illogical life choices led thousands of young people to the nonsensical conversations they didn't quite know they needed, and these talks were *deep, dude.*

The band's most obvious commoditized symbol was the stark difference between how Shankar's Zenegade Ranch looked during those early days and how it looked more than five years later. Although Shankar still lived on the ranch like he did five years earlier, his full-time residence was one of the only things that was the same as when Byrd and the gang lived with him. Most of their remodeling work was completely re-remodeled, and the rickety cabins that the band members lived in were now lavish bungalows that drew in rich Aspen tourists for over $500 per night. Everyone wanted to stay at the ranch where the Zenegades got started, and each guest was also able to experience guided hikes along Castle Creek, yoga, meditation sessions, well-cooked meals, and congregations around the same fire pit where many of the original Zenegades songs were created. There truly was so much more to the Zenegade Ranch than a place to sleep at night while visiting Aspen, and creating a special experience for every guest kept Shankar reeling in the rewards of a top hospitality commodity in the Rockies.

On this particular morning, Shankar was very busy as he helped one of his cleaning assistants prepare the larger treehouse for a very special guest. He knew this special guest would be arriving by plane at the local airport around 9 a.m., so he was racing across the property, making sure his other guests were taken care of while still maintaining his focus on getting things ready for his incoming VIP.

A black SUV rolled up the private dirt driveway around 9:45. Shankar knew it was the guest he'd been waiting for, so he walked to the parking area for a formal greeting. The car parked, turned off, and out stepped Charlie, who was unnecessarily wearing formal business attire.

"Mr. Dyceman, welcome *finally* to the Zenegade Ranch!" Shankar exclaimed as they shook hands and he helped him with his luggage.

"Nice to see you again, Shankar. Now, let's see what all the fuss is about with the humble beginnings of our friends!" Charlie responded with a witty smile.

"Well, Mr. Dyceman. I must admit that the Zenegade Ranch has undergone *many changes* since our friends started making a name for themselves, and this is due to the very generous donations they've provided us here that helped me upgrade the buildings, hire assistants, and maintain everything on a daily basis," Shankar explained as they kept walking. "But here we are in the communal area, where we still have the fire pit in the exact same place where the Zenegades started playing as a group. It's truly fascinating to think about just how far they've come, isn't it?"

Charlie didn't need much of a tour, as his mind hummed at a million miles per hour to the sounds of ATM machines, receipt printers, and cash registers.

"*Fascinating* is most definitely the correct word, Mr. Patel," he said as he twirled around in a circle, examining the treehouses and cabins. "There truly is *a ton* of potential here!"

Sometimes it feels good to embrace commoditization and go all out on a needless shopping spree while purchasing retail just for the hell of it, and that's exactly what Madison would talk Thayer into doing every now and again. Although if it were ever up to Madison, they'd be shopping in one of LA's ritzy districts like Beverly Hills or Brentwood, instead of Eagle Rock or Venice Beach, where Thayer felt like she was abiding by a nonexistent, shop local, hipster code.

They meandered around Abbot Kinney Boulevard looking for outfits that Thayer could wear on stage for the Zenegades' festival appearances and inevitable next tour, and although this type of shopping excursion would've seemed far too mundane for Thayer in the past, there was an added sense of excitement in knowing that Madison would dish out a bump inside every dressing room. The longer they shopped, the more extraneous their purchases became. After over two hours of searching for stage outfits, they weren't too sure about driving back to West Hollywood, especially because the afternoon gridlock was just beginning. So, they figured it'd be best to get a bite to eat and soak in another beautiful California afternoon like everyone else in Venice.

They ate (or at least tried to), but they realized the traffic had only gotten worse after their happy hour had ended. They'd essentially missed their chance at getting back to West Hollywood within any reasonable time, which meant they might as well hang out a little while longer. It was Madison's idea to rinse down their chic happy hour with homemade ice cream, and they kept strolling down Abbot Kinney with their coke-fueled shopping bags until they got to the local ice-cream shop, which was where they noticed a long line stretching out the door and up about half a block. They contemplated whether they should wait upwards of an hour for ice cream, but they figured they had nothing better to do than wait in line for sweet treats when they looked at all the cars at a standstill.

So they waited and slowly inched their way closer toward the door along the sidewalk, and it only took a matter of about two minutes for one of the young people in line to recognize Thayer and ask for a picture. Once one fan asked for a picture, the whole line started to realize who she was, which spread throughout the half block until everyone within the near proximity of the ice-cream store knew that Thayer Feldman from Zenegades was waiting for a snack. She was a sweetheart to her fans and would answer random questions about the band, and she never had a problem with taking pictures. This was simply part of the lifestyle of being a celebrity in Los Angeles, and there was no denying that she enjoyed fame much more than anonymity. Everything was swimmingly peachy as Thayer contemplated a fresh waffle cone of peach ice cream while attending to her adoring fans, but all that changed when a middle-aged woman approached her and Madison, guns blazing in her wild eyes.

"You're in that band Zenegades, right?" she asked as she approached them.

"Yeah."

"That's what I thought. You know, your music is one of the *worst things* that has happened to young people in this country. You should be *ashamed of yourself* for what you've started!" the angry pedestrian rattled back, now raising her voice and getting the queue's attention.

"Our music has nothing to do with all those kids living out in the woods ..."

"Like hell it doesn't!" she now yelled at full force.

Madison nudged Thayer, indicating it might be time to leave and forget about the ice cream; but Thayer shook her head, insinuating she was willing to give even this random heckler some of her time.

"All these young kids, just out of high school, just out of college. They listen to your shitty folk music and think they don't *need a job*. They think they can go live *la-dee-da* in the woods like money doesn't matter in this world, but let me tell you something, *sister*. Money does matter, and young people need to be prepared for what's ahead of them, instead of thinking they can be some kind of bullshit *Zenegade* like you've put in their naïve heads!" she yelled as a few ice cream enthusiasts told her to fuck off, until Thayer wanted to speak up.

"I'm truly sorry that you feel confused about some of our fans, ma'am. But with all due respect, everyone deserves to experience their own path, on their own terms. No one's idea of *what matters* is any better than anyone else's, because we're all one of a kind. Anyone that wants to live *la-dee-da* in the woods is just as on their own as anyone else, so I don't see anything wrong with the idea of straying away from social norms in the way some of our fans have done recently. They're finding their own way to do this thing we call life, and that's their prerogative."

About a dozen people in line cheered after Thayer's response, which made her expose the slightest bit of smile. The heckler's nostrils flared as she continued to glare directly at Thayer.

"Oh, so you're saying my daugther's *prerogative* led her to getting *H-I-fucking-V* at one of those communes upstate?" she yelled, waiting for Thayer to respond. "Yeah, that's what I thought!"

The heckler started storming down Abbot Kinney as everyone else began running her off in Thayer's defense. Thayer looked at Madison and nodded slightly, suggesting it was now time to head back to the van. As they searched for the van on Venice's side streets, Madison rambled on at a million miles per hour about the heckler's unnecessary offensiveness, until she glanced over at Thayer and saw the streams of tears running from her eyes. When they eventually found the fancy van, Thayer lifted her right leg and stomped the side mirror out of its hinges and into dozens of pieces. Their entire drive back to West Hollywood was completely silent, except for the sounds of the radio and sporadic thumbnail bumps.

As much as Maya enjoyed her increasingly popular reputation within the New York jazz scene, she couldn't deny just how exhausting the incessant, work-driven culture permeating throughout Manhattan was as she experimented in the extra-bedroom-turned-music-studio on a debut Retro Phat album. Sometimes it almost seemed to her like New Yorkers would get bent out of shape, or driven to insanity, if they weren't constantly focusing on their careers. She was absolutely sure they'd enjoy the freedom from themselves for a little while, and when she'd see rich Wall Street suits walking past packs of homeless beggars living in desperate hazes of isolation, she was also absolutely sure that there weren't many differences between anyone.

She'd play the people-watching game that Lin taught her while she sipped on her morning tea and stared down at Manhattan as it began to crank itself up for yet another day of big-city life. Together they'd see passers-by from all walks of life, but one woman in particular would typically stand out due to her lavish outfits that were often accompanied by several high-end retail shopping bags. Maya couldn't help but see a longstanding sense of quality over equality in that random woman, which she imagined was masked behind financial standing and contrived notions of status. As Maya struggled to come up with a Retro Phat single that would smack the New York jazz scene back to its senses, she found the inspiration for her latest song titled "New York (Fake) Times."

You'll see me on these streets
Making heavy, groovy beats

There you are standing tall
I'm just waiting for your call

Where are we going, why do we run?
Being ants ain't no fun
And with all certainty
We'll kill Lady Liberty

There's a reckoning a-comin'
Make sure your heart keeps drummin'

In New York, you'll see the edge
A precipice, a steep ledge
A lion pit, if you fall
An inescapable wall

Only the fake make it here
With time it makes itself clear
Good luck to call it home
It's a modern-day Rome

The city can't sleep
It's too loud, too many sheep

You got cash, you got style
But you ain't worth no one's while
A privileged life, a sad truth
I'll show you talent, in the booth

There's a train, goes all night
Are your blankets too tight?
Good chance, you'll never see
We share the same energy

You say you wanna be free

But you say you're different than me

See me along your way
No gray walls, a new day
Are our divisions lifelong?
Will we ever get along?

Cuz here in New York, there's endless possibility
So grab a pitchfork, we're at capacity
These streets reckon for a sinner
A hot shot, a chicken dinner

Get your ass back in line
We don't got time for swine

There's a reckoning, a-comin'
And yet we all just keep runnin'

Stepping aside from her accustomed role as the Zenegades' bassist was good for Maya in many creative ways, but she really just wanted to step aside from music altogether for an extended vacation away from city life. Both she and Lin had grown used to living in one of Byrd's cabins on the Big Island for weeks and even months at a time, and these work trips often did wonders for both their psyches. But they both wanted to do something different and see a part of the world they'd never been to, so after a few long conversations and an extensive amount of planning, Maya and Lin decided to meet up with Ruben and Cat in Europe.

Although their plans were a bit different from Ruben and Cat's van trip, they still successfully planned a meeting with them just as they arrived in London. This whole idea of meeting in England originally derived from O'Donnell, who put two and two together to organize a small, impromptu show outside his hometown of Glasgow. Ruben, Cat, Maya, and Lin saw the trio concert as more of an opportunity to get a free stay and rock-star treatment in Glasgow for a few nights, and it seemed like they could still easily put on a good show by playing the Zenegades songs that Maya typically sang. It seemed simple enough, or so they thought.

On the night Lin and Maya flew into London, they had a night out on the town with Ruben and Cat as they drank in pubs and saw the sights of yet another big metropolis, but all their city escape dreams came true the next morning when they were greeted by a friend of O'Donnells' who went by Roarkey. Roarkey explained how he had an equipment van that would transport them and their stuff up north to Glasgow, which was a two-day drive through the English countryside. None of them decided to bring their instruments to Europe, so Roarkey showed them what he'd bagged from one of the best rental shops in the UK and got their approval prior to departing.

Roarkey drove Lin and Maya in the equipment van while Ruben and Cat followed behind, and it couldn't have gone better as they meandered their way up Western England through Blackpool, Carlisle, and into Scotland. Seeing the lush green hills of the British countryside was exactly the right way to leave city life behind, and Roarkey was beyond an entertaining guide by keeping them relaxed and laughing throughout the whole ride, until they eventually arrived at the concert venue outside Glasgow three days later.

"Here we are. I hope you two are ready to rock out! Wait, what's *this*?" Roarkey remarked as they approached the venue.

It was in this moment that Maya felt as if a sharp needle punctured her skin and struck her directly in the heart. She felt fine a few seconds later as the pain subsided, but the initial shock was the most profound of her entire life. Just like in the States, there were dozens of people protesting outside the small Glasgow concert theater, and they were all holding signs indicating how they weren't too pleased with the Zenegades coming to their town.

"What the hell?" Lin asked rhetorically as they drove past the crowd and entered a gated alley that led to the venue's loading docks, where O'Donnell was waiting for them while smoking a cigarette on a stoop.

"What is all *this*?" Lin immediately asked O'Donnell after stepping out of the van. "Why are people so upset with us over here too?"

"Apparently, from my very brief understanding, there was a viddy on the news just the other day about a bunch of blokes up north that made themselves one of those Zenegade Communes, and these lads apparently are stealing from petrol stations and corner shops. I think a bunch of them are planning on coming tonight, so it's looking like there's some beef out there, but what else is new?" he asked sarcastically as he laughed and took a drag. "Don't worry about it, though. I told the owner not to let anyone with a sign into the show."

"We're not worried about that right now!" Maya chimed in loudly. "I can't believe this. I just can't. I can't do this. I have to go talk to them," she continued in a rambling-to-stay-sane tone.

"They're all just jealous they didn't get tickets cuz the show's sold out. Everyone and their cousins spent over a hundred pounds for tonight! People love you out here, although a bunch of them also seem a wee bit upset that Byrd, Reg, Sky and Thayer aren't coming. But don't let those pea brains get to you, and don't go out there, either. They're all clearly ticked the hell off right now!"

"We have to do something," she whispered to Lin, Ruben, and Cat, who just shrugged and shook their heads. "Call Byrd right now," she commanded Lin.

"Does he even have a phone at his house?" he responded, which none of them were sure of.

"Just email him then!" Maya directed as she went into the equipment van and started crying.

As Lin opened his email app on his phone, he noticed an unexpected message from David Fieldcrest with the subject: *Meeting With Your Mom.*

The most troubling part about commoditizing any kind of music is that the artists themselves subsequently become commoditized, which inevitably develops a double-edged sword effect oriented around being a creative-yet-commoditized individual. On one edge, the artists are able to express themselves to an audience and experience one of the greatest manifestations known to man; and on the other edge, they are defined by those expressions and ensnared within their branding. The desire to break away from conventional branding was a driving force throughout the early years of the Zenegades, and it led them to remain focused on their expansion to several different musical styles. But for a renowned musician like Byrd, the *Zen Guru* characterization he'd developed was something that followed him around, no matter how isolated he got from his fame.

Byrd's desire for a personal change when he was a lonely wilderness guide was what initially generated his journey up the artistic mountainside, but there was only so much professional development he could take until it eventually started to wear him down like a pair of sandals that had seen too many long-distance desert hikes. Even after a handful of incredible years as the leader of the Zenegades, he couldn't help but consider *what-ifs* and how things could've been different. As much as he wanted to put everything aside and simply focus on the present moment like he did back in the days when he lived by himself near the hot springs, there was a brand-new change that was literally drawing him back into his past: Jane Imberti. It was true that he needed time for himself to reignite his relationship with nature like back in the Utah days, but where he told Reg and Hani he was going to isolate himself wasn't true. Instead of backpacking across the depths of the Mauna Loa caldera, Byrd was deep in the Waipio Valley on Raymundo's property.

There was a mutual understanding between everyone living with Raymundo that they were to keep Byrd's presence, and budding love affair, completely secret. He'd have never truly gotten a glimpse of it without sleeping there, but Byrd quickly realized just how debasing their revival of the Zenegade Ranch was. In the exact same way his former life was oriented around a peaceful understanding of his meaning within nature, Raymundo's commune oriented their way of life around enjoying a meaningless party that never ended. It wasn't necessarily an all-out rager each and every night, but Byrd couldn't help thinking how they were mostly a group of entitled brats who merely thought they were VIPs of some kind by being accepted into their tiny village and taking part in a collective escape from society. In reality, they were actually bringing many of society's issues along with them into their new home, often without them even realizing it.

But even with all their blatant shortcomings, Byrd was still willing to do whatever he deemed appropriate to help Raymundo's tribe develop lifestyles that more closely resembled the ideals he cultivated while living alone in the desert; however, the majority of his willingness to bestow his convictions upon the group was rooted in his budding affection for Jane. After over five years of imagining what it would be like to make love with *the girl from the Utah gas station,* he'd never have been able to come close to understanding just how far she'd exceed his expectations. The way she forcefully pressed herself up against him and undulated her hips in all directions was something he'd never experienced before, and their conversations seemed to have no end in sight. She would hang on Byrd's every word when they weren't getting busy in her tent, which was far different than any other girl Byrd had ever dated. After all, no one knew who Byrd was just five years earlier, but everyone wanted to talk to him while he was initially getting to know Jane.

The strangest dimension of their budding relationship was just how open the entire commune was about keeping their secret completely shut and closed. Byrd understood that they looked up to him as a musician and the voice of their commune movement, but he didn't understand just how influential he was until they all started treating him like a god that could do no wrong. In many ways, they supported Byrd and Jane's fiery connection simply because they were utterly obsessed with the story of how they met and were later reunited, and they also couldn't help but want Byrd to spend as much time with them as possible. Most of them figured that the better Byrd got to know Jane at the Waipio Commune, the more likely he'd want to spend the night more frequently.

On the same day as the Glasgow fiasco, Byrd arrived back home to the fruit farm after spending a handful of nights with Jane in Waipio. As he got out of his truck and started walking toward the backyard, he noticed Hani walking in his direction while carrying a small basket of papayas.

"Hey, man! Reg came by earlier and told me some pretty bad news. He said you guys are supposed to be in Scotland or something."

"What? What's going on over there?"

"Apparently, O'Donnell billed a show wrong over there, and the whole crowd was expecting you to be there."

"Oh, jeez. That's not good. So, the show was today?"

"Yeah, it was *supposed to be* today. I think they canceled because the crowd was getting violent or something. I don't know exactly what happened, but I told Reg I'd give him a call when you got back, so I guess he can tell you more."

Byrd shook his head as he pulled his backpack out of the truck and started bringing it inside. Reg didn't answer Hani's call, so he wandered into the interior of the cabin and hid himself in his bedroom. He noticed his flashy new laptop sitting on a desk, so he opened it up and got online.

He then saw two emails of particular importance to him and his entire life's trajectory: one from Lin and another one from Charlie, which read:

Hey Jimmy!

I need you to come to LA and see me right away. I've got BIG news for you!

Here's the gist:

I heard what went down in Glasgow, and I have to admit, these protestors are simply getting out of hand. We're going to have to do something ASAP about the band's image, so I've come up with an idea I think we should discuss further in person, but I'm sure you're going to love this!

I call it 'The Campfire Concert Series', and it essentially is tiny concerts at Shankar's ranch where you play for a small group of people and live streamers online. We're even already setting up a website specifically for the residency, and it'll be heavily encrypted with a mandatory piracy protection software installation (so we can at least try to stop screen recorders).

By the way, I met with Shankar and he's down and thinks this is an awesome idea!

The thing I've realized is that all these people who got a problem with the Zenegades don't like the band for some reasons about how you guys got started. t's got little to nothing to do with your actual music. So, let's set the record straight about where the Zenegades came from and what you guys are all about on a more personal level.

These are going to be small shows, probably just you doing solo for now because the budget is tight; however, all the interested sponsors are willing to pitch in and pay you 10K for each show. I know... We're working on some more sponsors and other logistics right now, but we need to sit down together just you and me. Trust me, I'd come to Hawaii tomorrow if I weren't such a workaholic.

Get the next flight you can catch and I'll pay you back.

Charlie

20

Two days later, Reg slept through the whole flight like a baby while Byrd sat in his first-class chair and couldn't quite listen to his iPod's music. All his thoughts were drowning out every song that came through his headphones, and they continued to clamor like an orchestra of cymbal-smashing primates as they soared over the Pacific.

It was early evening when they arrived at LAX, and Sky was waiting in a nearby parking lot to pick them up in Thayer's tricked-out van. Byrd tossed his luggage in the trunk, which comprised of a small duffle bag, a guitar, and Uncle Tito, and he got a glimpse of a *different-looking* Sky as he stepped into the shotgun seat. He couldn't exactly pinpoint what it was, but the van reeked of weed, and he got the hunch there was more going on than just Le Ganja. Sky's skin looked bronzed beyond even LA's reasonable standards, his eyes were completely bloodshot, and the lumpy bags just above his sunglass tan line were a blatant indication that he hadn't gotten much sleep in at least a few days.

Sky zipped around 405 traffic like a nutcase looking for an adrenaline rush at the expense of some stranger's fears, and at one point, he nearly clipped a lane-splitting motorcyclist who had the same kind of mindset. No one got hurt, and the biker merely flipped them off as they continued speeding through tiny gaps, but Byrd and Reg were rightfully spooked.

"Damn, these bikers in LA are on some serious shit! They don't give a fuck!" Reg yelled out from the backseat lounge.

"One time I was driving down the 101 around North Hollywood and this biker was about to miss his exit or something, and he veered *all the way* across the highway right in front of me, like four lanes. I almost rear-ended him, and he completely spun out and slid into the barrier," Sky explained into the rearview mirror while barely glancing at the road.

"What'd you do?" Reg asked.

"Nothing. I just kept driving."

"Sounds like a casual occurrence around here," Byrd sarcastically responded as another lane-splitting bike sped past them.

"Yeah, man. These bikers out here are nuts."

They sat for a couple of minutes in silence.

"Reg, do me a solid and coordinate a bike rental for tomorrow. I wanna go for a ride up in the canyons," Byrd requested as they continued careening through traffic on their way up Sunset Boulevard toward West Hollywood.

Even though they were somewhat close by on eastbound Sunset, it still took them almost half an hour to get to Sky and Thayer's house, due to what Sky called *weekend warrior traffic*. It was just past sunset when they finally arrived at the swanky pad overlooking Sunset and the entire city, where Thayer and Madison were passed out with their sunglasses still on while floating on pool rafts. Byrd looked over at the lounge chairs and glass table next to the pool and noticed an empty bottle of champagne, two half-drunken glasses, a small stack of weed, and four lines of cocaine next to a tiny plastic bag. Sky, Byrd, and Reg looked at each other silently as they tried to hold back their laughter enough to keep them asleep, because Sky *had to* take a picture of them. By the time he was done with his photos, it was clear that Byrd had his own prank in mind as he stripped down to his underwear and quietly slipped into the pool. He swam underneath the surface until he was directly underneath Thayer's swan float, and he forcefully rose up and sent her flying into the air toward an immediate face flop. Sky had a video rolling, and in the background, you could hear him and Reg savagely laughing.

"What in the actual fuck!" Thayer yelled as she resurfaced, now jolted awake. She looked over to Sky and Reg laughing, realizing she was on camera. "What? Is this some kind of prank or something? Who flipped me?"

Byrd reemerged right in front of her.

"Hey, I'm here."

"Nice one, dick. I had a bag of fire coke on me that's wet now. So, *thanks*!"

"My bad."

"Hey, are these lines over here *fire*?" Reg sarcastically asked as he pointed to the glass table.

"Yeah, Thay, don't worry about it. I'll call J. P. and see if he can get us more. Should I tell him we're having people over tonight?" Madison lackadaisically chimed in from her float.

"*Oh*, we're having an LA party tonight? I don't know how long I'm in town, you know!" Byrd joked to Thayer, who ran her hand through the water to splash him in the face.

"Yeah, you know what? It's been a few days since we've had anyone over. Let's do a pregame over here tonight so Byrd and Reg can meet everybody!" she declared as she swam over to her champagne glass and commenced the evening.

As the night meandered on, it became clearer to Byrd that Thayer also seemed a little different as compared to the last time they hung out on tour. It didn't take long for them to catch up, but there were some pretty big topics they needed to talk about. Byrd told Thayer that he and Jane had been hooking up and that Charlie had requested a mano-a-mano meeting for the following morning, and when she pressed him to provide details, he simply replied: *we might become streamers.* Thayer confided that she was afraid to go anywhere in the city after an angry fan encounter, and her general fogginess made more sense as she explained how she and Sky decided to officially make their house *The Spot* so they didn't feel the need to go out in public. She detailed how they'd been hanging out with a whole bunch of hip celebrities who would frequently pop in and be a part of their scene whenever they sent out texts, and she tried to justify all their recent partying through her and Sky sometimes grouping up with a musician friend or two to play songs for their guests, which insinuated they were at least *kind of* rehearsing.

Byrd and Reg were still on Hawaii time, so it didn't seem late to them when J. P., Pierre and a few others showed up around ten with a whole array of goodies. Shortly after their arrival, multiple groups arrived at the pad, looking LA fabulous, and the once-quiet living room sounded like a loud bar. The music they were playing throughout the house was EDM and tropical space jazz mixed together, and Byrd noticed how none of the songs sounded anything like the Zenegades. He also noticed how none of the guests were musicians, and he found this out by asking every person who told him *I love your music* if they played themselves. There was a blatant sense of uniformity to Thayer and Sky's friends, and then it hit him. He walked outside to the pool, where Reg was solo-smoking a joint and drinking a glass of scotch while watching the city lights shimmer.

"You know what I just realized in there?" Byrd said as he sat down and took a quick hit of the joint. "Everyone in there is just like J. P. and Madison. Seriously, I can't tell you how many of them just showed me their social media profiles to try to impress me about who they are. It's like they care more about their online image than how they come off in real life, even when they're speaking directly to you!"

"That's why I came out here. There are only so many plain white tees, ripped jeans, and checkered Vans a man can take. Any one of those jabronis would probably get their ass whooped all the way down the block if they came to Harlem. That's the thing about Cali: all this chiccy, sunny weather and all these wannabes will make you feel like you need to be looking good *all the time* cuz that's what *everybody* is doing. Rain's the difference between New York and LA, cuz sometimes you just need a rainy day to kick back and forget about all this shallow bullshit."

"I'm clearly the only one sober around here, and I don't know, man, but it seems like the two of us need to start thinking about getting a hotel room instead of you crashing on their pull-out and me sleeping on a pad like we usually do."

"Now we're talking! What're you thinking? Bel-Air? Santa Monica?"

"I figured we could just leave our stuff here, sneak out the gate over there, and walk down the street to Chateau Marmont. Charlie said I could always go there and get a room on him while I'm in town."

"*Oh*, Charlie's got that French connection? Let's do this, then. *Au re-fuckin voir*, ya bozo, skater-shoed clowns!"

Both Byrd and Reg were essentially irrelevant at the pregame, so no one realized they were gone until long after they'd walked a half mile down a steep hill, checked in via Charlie's celeb account, and were lounging in two double beds in an obscure corner of Chateau Marmont. Although the sounds of Sunset Boulevard were loud compared to what they were used to in Hawaii, it felt like a serene silence in comparison to the over-the-top, chic party at Thayer and Sky's house.

Sky eventually wanted to know where they were, which was why Reg's phone randomly rang around 1:30, while they were winding down for sleep. After giving an explanation about their current situation and repeating a sequence of *no shit* and *that's crazy* responses, Reg put the phone to his chest and told Byrd that Thayer, Sky, and pretty much the whole pregame were hanging out in a VIP lounge just a handful of stories below them. They wanted to know which room they were in, so like a decent manager, Reg needed permission from Byrd to reveal that confidential information. Byrd gave the go-ahead to reveal the room number, but strictly said that only Thayer and Sky were allowed to come inside.

After about ten minutes, Thayer and Sky knocked on the door and stumbled inside the tiny room while blatantly slurring their speech. They made fun of how tiny their room was and how *this* was what Charlie's celeb access looked like. They both had glasses of champagne in their hands, and Thayer's glass ended up finding its way to the hardwood floor and shattering everywhere after an inadvertent loss of balance. This briefly alarmed everyone in the room except Thayer, who continued laughing as if she'd just earned her corporal rank in the Fail Army. That was when she asked if she could use a small mirror by the TV to do some coke, and that was also when Byrd had had enough.

"Fine, just don't break *that glass* all over our room and leave it there without picking it up," he snidely remarked, which caused Sky to bend down and start picking up the tiny shards.

"Why do *you* care? Isn't this a *free* hotel room?" Thayer snapped back. "Why don't you stop being such a loner that never has any fun and sneaks out of parties without saying goodbye? You're such a weirdo sometimes. No one likes it."

This put Byrd over the edge. "*Oh, okay.* Well, your friends seemed to tell me all the weirdo shit you two have been up to lately. It sounds like you're both just getting way too fucked up every single night and are always doing coke at every chance you get."

"*Yeah,* well you don't have the right to tell us what to do!" she barked. "*And,* for your information, cocaine is different for me than it is for most people. It actually calms me down, so it's a lot different than a normal reaction."

"That's because you're addicted to it!" Byrd yelled matter-of-factly as his eyes glared directly into Thayer's.

Thayer didn't know how to respond, so she looked at Sky in a way that said *back me the fuck up.* It was clearly obvious that he didn't want to start anything up with Byrd, but he at least tried.

"You just don't get it, man," Sky chimed into the argument. "This isn't Hawaii, where everything is paradise and *Jah Live* every second of every day. Coke is just a part of the culture here. Literally, every single one of our friends does at least a little bit to keep the party going on the weekends."

"I don't do it, though. And quite frankly, I'm starting to think maybe we're more coworkers than *friends*. It's time for both of you to go," he said as he stood up from his bed, subtly insinuating he was going to make them leave.

They quickly left the room in a huff, and neither of them could believe how rude Byrd was while they were just having a good time on a Friday night in West Hollywood like everyone else. From their perspective, they had worked their asses off to be able to party at a rock-star caliber, and even the leader of their band wasn't going to deter them from doing whatever the fuck they wanted to do, whenever the fuck they wanted to do it.

And that *fuck you, I won't do what you tell me* thought process was exactly what got them both thinking about fucking. Sky guided Thayer through the narrow, white halls of the Chateau Marmont, looking for an ice room, a narrow corridor, or any private place that would provide them with a few minutes of secluded thrusting. They stumbled up and down the old staircases, thinking about a sex spot here and there, and wondered what the odds of someone showing up out of nowhere after 2 a.m. would be. Even as a destination seemed bleak, there was undoubtedly nothing stopping them as their drunkenness propelled them to *hornt-up* levels.

After over fifteen minutes of meandering around the hotel's stairways and halls, there it was. It wasn't the most perfect spot in the hotel, but it had just enough privacy and offered an opportunity to hear if someone was coming. Neither Sky nor Thayer figured this sex session would last all that long, especially since it was going to have to be a stand-up doggie type of scenario next to a fire escape.

"Let's just be quiet and go quickly," Thayer whispered as she adjusted her panties underneath her dress and grabbed Sky by the back of the neck to draw his head in for a prolonged kiss.

Although saying they should be quiet and quickly have sex did initially make it seem like Thayer had her wits about her, the amount of drugs and alcohol they'd both consumed almost instantly took over and triggered an all-out raunchfest. They rolled along the obscure hallway's wall, sporadically pressing each other up against the retro French décor. A light switch flicked on and off, on and off, on and off for about a minute while Sky fingered her and forced her torso to fluctuate vertically.

Sky noticed how the best spot to lean Thayer over and get things really going was just by the fire escape, which was a door that opened up to a staircase facing a dark courtyard. He went in, or at least he tried as an awkward series of fidgeting ensued before ultimately ending in a loud sigh of relief from both of them. They then went at it, and they both couldn't stop laughing as they intermittently recognized where they were doing it.

As Sky was about to come, a rush of excitement burst through Thayer and caused her to shift her awkward positioning toward pushing the escape's handle. In some ways, it may have been a good thing that the alarm across the entire hotel went off, mainly because it drowned out their loud orgasm sounds; however, in most other ways, it was simply not a good thing that they set the fire alarm off while their underwear and pants were around their ankles. At the point of clearly no anonymous return, they both started hysterically laughing on the metal staircase, knowing how stupid, yet so fun, what they just did was.

"I love cocaine!" Thayer yelled out as far-off pedestrians on Sunset looked around and tried to figure out why the alarm was blaring throughout the Euro-style castle.

If it were only just the handful of pedestrians who heard Thayer yell *I love cocaine* who witnessed any semblance of this sex session, it clearly would've been no harm, no foul. But the two Zenegades musicians had an audience member they weren't aware of, and this particular audience member was someone any celebrity would fear when it comes to an embarrassing moment. He just so happened to be speaking with another Hollywood celebrity earlier that night in one of the hotel's bungalows, and he also just so happened to have a backpack containing a fancy camera and multiple lenses (one of which had a focal length that stretched to five hundred millimeters).

He was smoking a cigar in an outdoor courtyard by himself, simply thinking about how successful an evening he'd already had, until he realized he was the only person who had the direct vantage point to notice a light switching on and off, on and off, through a window two stories up in a random corner of the hotel. He recognized that a couple was hooking up with each other, which instinctively led his fingers to his backpack zippers. He attached the telephoto lens and instantly felt his egotism tingle as he zoomed in and recognized who he was filming.

"*That* is why you're the best," he said to himself as he ended his five-minute video and gathered his things to leave the alarm-blaring hotel.

21

yrd woke up early the next morning after an awful night's sleep in his chic bed at Chateau Marmont. He looked over to Reg and watched him snore a few times as he rubbed his scruffy beard and blinked back to consciousness. He continued to ineptly wait for a few hours as Reg's snores created a rhythm that diverted his thoughts far away from his body, and he remained awake yet completely motionless until a more appropriate time to make any loud movements. After a continental breakfast, it seemed as though he was going to have one hell of a day in LA, but his upcoming meeting with Charlie meant the fun was going to have to wait, at least until about 9:30. As he sipped the best coffee on the menu in order to compare it to his neighbor's homegrown crops, he imagined himself behind the bars of a Honda while gliding around each harrowing curve of Tuna Canyon.

Well, Tuna Canyon will have to wait here, he thought as he sat in the back seat of a town car that picked him and Reg up from the hotel's entrance at exactly 8:15. Of course 8:15 was way too late to avoid the hordes of cars crawling down Sunset, and for several minutes, he sat in silence while daydreaming about gripping handlebars, putting pressure on pedals, and revolving his palm around a vibrating thrust that would exhaust his forearms after hours in the California heat. The fact that Reg was still snoring for the entire ride to Charlie's office didn't hurt his imaginative gaze out the window either.

They walked through the obnoxiously clean floor plan of the office building, and everyone couldn't help but be once again jaw-dropped at the sight of Byrd and his disheveled sidekick, Reg. But it was also Byrd's disheveled look that gave him his Mystical Zenegade demeanor, and because everyone else in the office took about an hour to get themselves and their clothing ready for the day, Byrd's *I woke up like this in Chateau Marmont* appearance made him seem iconic. Showered with stares and smiles, they made their way to Charlie's office, where they found him with his head crouched behind his desktop computer and his tie loosened to a happy hour circumference.

"Charlie, Jim Byrd and Reg Wallace are here," his receptionist said as she opened his office door.

"Jimmy Byrd, my man! Come on in, brother," he invited as the receptionist closed the door directly behind him and began giving Reg a pseudo-polite rant about how Charlie only wanted to speak with Byrd. Within a moment of being alone together, Charlie's mannerisms shifted. "Close those blinds behind you. Are you two by yourselves?"

"It's just me and Reg, and we're both not quite adjusted to the time difference yet, so I'd appreciate it if this didn't take too long. Reg said he might go use one of those meditation pods on the first floor."

"Okay, good! I'm glad you didn't invite the whole gang, although I had a feeling it was time to have a group meeting, and I feel like a moron now that I didn't sound the alarm bells sooner. I got an email this morning, a really bad one. It's from *The Nooch*, Jim."

"Who's that?"

"Gilberto Tannuccio, aka The Nooch, is one of Hollywood's most notorious paparazzi. He's all over the place taking pictures of celebrities, but whenever he's spoken to me about a photograph or a video, it's usually involved embarrassing news about a client."

"What do you mean? Is he trying to embarrass *us*?"

"Yes and no," Charlie said as he stood up and poured himself a morning scotch that was absurdly early, even for his lavish life's absurdity. "You see Jim, The Nooch works in mysterious ways. What makes him so notorious in this part of town is that he knows how to make the most out of his line of work."

"Is that so?" Byrd sarcastically replied. "How exactly does he stay on the *cutting edge* of being a paparazzo?"

"Bidding wars." Charlie grimaced as he proceeded to take an abnormally large sip of scotch, which had Byrd wincing from several feet away. "What he does when he has something *good* is reach out to talent representatives, like me, and tell us to pay him what he wants or he's going to the tabloids with it, where he'll then tear them all to threads by giving the leak to the highest bidder. He's never had much of anything on my clients that I took seriously. An embarrassing neck fat angle here, a cleavage shot there. And the most I ever gave him was 50K for a video of an up-and-coming diva that drunkenly rolled out of a pool chair and cracked her head open against concrete, which in hindsight wouldn't have been so bad if it didn't lead her to jump into a pool and look like a fucking monster while scaring a bunch of little kids as she splashed and cussed like a complete idiot. Do you wanna know where that pool was, Jim?"

"*Sure.*"

"Just down the road at Chateau Marmont. Apparently, *now* I know *for sure*, it's one of his hangout spots to photograph celebrities. So, here's what I want to know right now from you: what *the fuck* happened last night?"

The hotel's fire alarm began to click in Byrd's head, and he felt a massive weight sink down from his throat toward his lungs and stomach.

"I don't know. What does The Nooch say happened last night?"

"Never mind him for right now; you'll see what he said in a second. I just want to hear what went down from you first."

"You know I'm the one paying *you*, right?"

"Yeah, I do, but you're stuck with me now, *bay-bee*. So just tell me really quickly. What went down last night?"

"We were planning on staying at Thayer and Sky's place, but then they had some people come over, and we wanted to leave, so Reg and I went down to Chateau Marmont because *you said* I could get a room there. Then we hung out in the room for the rest of the night until we fell asleep, and that's it. I was sober."

"That's *sort of* what I thought, and that's why I'm happy it's just you that's here this morning. So, you didn't see Thayer and Sky at the hotel, *at all?*"

"No, we saw them there too. They came up to our room for a few minutes, and yes, *they* were drunk. Now, can you explain what the fuck you're talking about before you piss me off?"

"Fine, fine, fine, fine, fine. Here, look at this," he said as he handed him his phone and showed him a five-minute video of Sky and Thayer having sex up against a window, which ended with the fire alarm going off and Thayer professing her love for her favorite stimulant. When the video ended, he was able to glance down at the email's text that simply read *250K*.

"So ... what should we do?"

"Well, I know he hasn't released the video and that he'll maybe sign an NDA with us if we pay him $250,000."

"How do you know he hasn't already brought it to someone or saved it a hundred times?"

"Because this is how The Nooch works. He's willing to protect secrets, but only for the right price."

"It's still *a lot*, though. Do you really think it's worth it to pay him? What's the worst that could happen? Everyone knows they're a couple, so who's really going to care that much, ya know?"

"I normally wouldn't think something like this would be deal-breaker bad, but to be perfectly honest, there's already too much heat on you guys right now because of all this hippie commune bullshit that people are pissed about. We don't need this type of noise coming out right now. What we need is the Campfire Concert Series to reestablish your brand, but that might not even be possible anymore as of this morning. Seriously, what in the *fucking ass* is going on with this band? I really thought you'd all make it big, but this might just be the nail in your coffin I didn't see coming."

They sat in silence while thinking about their futures, and how a gigantic anvil was bringing the soaring phoenixes of their careers to a flaming crash. Then, as if it were the clearest epiphany possible, Byrd had an idea. "Look, let's just keep this video between you and me and not tell anyone else about it. Here's what I'm willing to do: I'll be down to do those concert streams at the ranch, and I'll slowly pay you the $250K back with the $10k per show that you mentioned. It'll take I guess twenty-five shows before I can pay you back, but I don't know. I'm not sure what you're thinking about with that campfire series and all, and I guess ... I guess it depends on how much you can pay everybody else too."

Charlie thought behind his desk for a minute as he spun the tiny curls behind his ears like a bored schoolboy.

"Okay, let's do it!" he yelled out, as if they'd both come up with a brilliant solution. "But here's the thing, Jimbo." He started speaking like he was on top of the world again. "We can have the gang come play along too, but the bigger the shows, the longer it might take to pay the debt and keep everyone happy in the process. And the tough truth is that if someone like The Nooch is trying to pin us for an embarrassing video that he thinks is worth $250k to keep quiet about, then we've got some serious issues that aren't just going away if we don't tell anybody. We *have* to show Sky and Thayer the video, because they need to know just how much they've fucked up and how necessary it is for them to make some healthy changes."

Byrd slowly nodded, and for the first time in years, he began thinking that Charlie was making somewhat good sense. There was a contorted selflessness they sensed in each other, because each of them was confident that they were looking out for their struggling friends with an addiction, while pathologically being on the lookout for their own good. Charlie looked at Byrd and smiled as if the two of them could really make plans, not only for themselves and their friends, but maybe even the entire world.

"You know, Jimmy, I've been meaning to tell you for a while now that I think you should consider doing a solo album. I've actually been thinking that you should go solo for a really long time, but I think this video shows that it's now just time to move on."

"Maybe you're right," Byrd said as he pressed his elbows against the arms of his seat and lowered his forehead to his palms.

"Everyone I know says you're *way too good* for the rest of the band, and that you'd do great running your own show. And to be honest, man, I've heard about some of the solo shows you've been doing at Reg's little club in Kona, and from what I've heard, they've been *really* good. I just haven't wanted to say anything to you because I didn't want to disturb your whole ... *vibe*. But I can tell you need to start thinking about what's really best for *you*, before you turn into just another has-been in this town.

"And that brings me to another big reason why I'm glad you're here alone this morning," Charlie continued. "Because I have a new contract oriented around the Campfire Concert Series that I want you to sign," he said as he whipped a handful of papers onto the desk seemingly out of nowhere. "We can go through all the routine details later in Aspen, but if you just sign your Jim Byrd on the dotted line on the last page, we'll be good to at least get the ball rolling ASAP."

Byrd started reading the first page of the contract, and although he'd gone through a lot of contracts over the past five years, this one was full of legal jargon to the point of being incomprehensible.

"I think I should probably bring this to O'Donnell before I sign it."

"*What?* Of all the people to help—he's a complete moron! Look at how he fucked your billing up the other day in Glasgow. I mean, those people really thought *you* were gonna be there!" he yelled out with a sardonic smile. "C'mon, Jim. I wouldn't do you wrong like that, and plus, nothing is finalized. This is just to show that you're in, so we can start setting up Shankar's ranch for the shows."

So he signed it, and he then made the executive decision to end the meeting on that note. As he walked toward the door, Charlie held him back by telling him to wait.

"Do me a favor and tell our *Fantasy Island* couple to wake their asses up and get over here, because they're next to see the video. *And,* between you and me, Saul Feldman and I will be having a chat later today."

By one that afternoon, Byrd was talking to himself in Tuna Canyon and pretending that life as he knew it would remain relatively the same; whereas Thayer was bawling her eyes out onto a fluffy, white pillow with a picture of a kitten on it, which she typically enjoyed resting up against when she was high on ketamine.

There was no way of consoling her. Nothing was going to calm her down, even though Charlie reassured her that things were under control and that *hopefully*, no one was ever going to see the video. But none of that currently mattered, because she felt like her soul was being weighed down to the point of shattering.

She had a feeling that things were about to get worse too. She'd been waiting for it because Charlie had warned her earlier that day, and finally just after 1 p.m., her phone rang. The contact on the screen simply read *Dad*.

"Dad?" she said, sniffling through the tears. "I'm so *fucking* embarrassed!" she yelled out in agony as she dropped the phone and started bawling out massive tears. Eventually, she picked the phone back up and noticed how her dad was still waiting on the other end. "Are you still there?"

"I'm here, Thay. And look, I'm not going into details right now, and in fact I *never* want to go into details about this. If you want to know so badly, I didn't see the video; and I don't plan on seeing it either. I'm only going to say this once, so here's the deal: *rehab is mandatory!*"

"I know, Dad," she said as she heaved a few heavy breaths. "I know it is."

22

efore the 1940s, Aspen was a run-down mining relic and thought of as a ghost town nestled deep in a remote valley along the western slope of the Great Divide. It only took a revolutionary chairlift, a handful of real-estate developers, and a few trend-setting celebrities to catalyze its exorbitant prosperity into one of America's most affluent cities. Aspen, in many ways, is a prime example of what occurs all over the world in beautiful places, because we're all innately drawn to wanting to spend time in a location that's surrounded by natural allure. This desire, of course, doesn't just apply to lavish mountain towns, because there are countless destinations throughout the world that rested peacefully until the twentieth century, which was when the leisure lights turned on and these places became *Aspenized.*

When a small portion of the Earth becomes Aspenized, it gets flipped over and destroyed in the name of progress and development. It only takes a short time to realize that this once-isolated portion of earth was actually destroyed in the name of the One True King: money. Once wheels start turning and bank accounts start rolling up at slot machine speeds, there's no stopping until every relevant chunk of earth has been fully accounted for. This incessant *give me, give me, more, more* fiscal gluttony among elites then triggers an ultimatum for everyone else: pay up and see the beautiful portion of earth or miss out on the fun; and *oh baby,* how we ever so dumbly flock like the swallows of Capistrano in the process of choosing option number one. Whether you're there to ski, snowboard, hike, fish, or surf a wave of cocaine, there's something about Aspen that'll likely let loose a part of yourself that has been held back in daily routines. Maybe vacations to expensive places provide a tiny glimpse into all the fun a destination brings while we flex our egos, but the proclivity to release inhibitions in a beautiful place strikes true no matter which small patch of Aspenized earth you're browsing.

However, even in a small destination town that's as profiteered as Aspen, there are still hidden secrets that'll instantly transport you back to how that special spot of land was way before the Aspenizing process began. Sometimes these secretive areas will be known as a locals' spot, which is generally due to people's desperation to latch on to any last scraps of freakishly rare, pre-Aspenized solitude. In the Digital Age, when everyone and their grandma shares pictures online, the very last bits of authentic paradise are a lot easier to find. Fully pristine locations are now only for the most daring adventurers, who aren't afraid to go the extra mile (or nine) to see what the planet was like prior to our *progress.*

Sadly, the Earth's Aspenization has inevitably developed two opposing forces of human desire that coexist in unity: one force that draws us in toward beauty and adventure on a beautiful chunk of land, and another that hopes to draw others away once we're there.

The Zenegade Ranch was once a locals' spot about fifteen miles up dirt roads from downtown Aspen, but Shankar's dreams of owning a retreat center outside the renowned destination town were now seasoned and far beyond what he could've ever initially aspired to achieve. His home was now one of the most popular vacation destinations in the entire Roaring Fork Valley, and this led him to installing a state-of-the-art gate with a keypad, security cameras, and a massive wooden archway sign indicating to guests and passersby that they'd officially arrived at the location where the famous Zenegades first started creating their world-renowned music together.

Every fan of the band knew their origin story, which turned Shankar's retreat into a mecca that people from all over simply couldn't resist. It was a good thing Shankar was attuned with stress-relief techniques, because there truly was nothing he could do to stop the draw that kept people coming to his tiny patch of earth. The fancy new gate kept those without an invitation at bay, but he'd still see people almost every day taking pictures with the notable sign as their background. But with prices starting at $500 per night for one of his cabins, he found every bit of the attention to be worthwhile.

The layout of the Zenegade Ranch was set up perfectly for Charlie's dream, The Campfire Concert Series, to come to fruition. Although the ranch itself posed some organizational hurdles, he figured simply getting Byrd to Aspen would be one of the biggest challenges he'd need to overcome. Luckily enough, Byrd was more than willing to help boost (and save) the band's public image.

Byrd's emotions were mixing about as much as they could while he and Reg settled into a two-bedroom condo on Hyman Avenue that was fully comped by Dyce Records, and during their first few days in town, Byrd mostly stayed at the condo and rehearsed while Reg explored the commercial district in search of single women. There was no denying how their temporary presence was the talk of the town, and plenty of fans knew of Reg and could spot him from a mile away. After a couple of nights of going out to saloons on his own, Reg convinced Byrd to come along for a few beers. This outing helped Reg *really* impress his new friends, which subsequently led to more than one phone number being exchanged in his contacts. But by far the biggest highlight of that evening was when everyone at the saloon convinced Byrd to get on stage and play a few songs, which ended up being ten songs and the warm-up he needed to get prepped for his first solo show of the residency. The fact that this impromptu performance ended up turning into a viral video that perfectly marketed what was to come didn't hurt the streaming cause either.

The first performance was two days later, and Byrd's mini-concerts were what everyone was talking about literally everywhere.

The entire internet was prepped and ready for what was about to go down on Shankar's ranch, and for five dollars per night, anyone could tune in live and donate as much as they wanted to Byrd's charities. This mega-millions plot was predominately derived from the avaricious mindset of the band's record label executive, and in Charlie's eyes, the Campfire Concert Series was his greatest masterpiece, and the Zenegade Ranch was his Sistine Chapel.

The ranch had already been the magnum opus of Shankar's post-retirement life for several years, but when he and Charlie stood next to each other watching a few production assistants ignite the first fire of the project as about forty people slowly gathered toward wooden chairs in eager anticipation for the guy they both viewed as their sugar son, they were simultaneously hearing the exact same thing: *ATMs*.

The ranch itself looked spectacular, mainly because Shankar did his very best to make all the guests feel more than accommodated—dinner, drinks, clean facilities, rooms with comfy beds, tent camping near the solar panels, and the whole nine yards from a wilderness hospitality standpoint. One random thought that came through Shankar's mind during those exciting moments while they all waited on Byrd to arrive was his realization that he was the only one there who knew what the ranch looked like when he and Byrd broke the ground on what was a run-down group of decrepit shacks, and this drew a big smile. What consequently resulted after that humorous recognition was a less-beaming revelation in that Reg was the only other band member who was there that night, which he asked Charlie about and discovered that the first few shows were to be solo acts solely featuring Byrd, per contractual agreement.

No one saw Byrd coming when he first entered the ranch, and this was partly because there were so many artificial lights, sound boards, parked cars, and general sounds that thwarted the racket of his fully-comped motorcycle rolling all the way into the party. He drew in everyone's attention by intentionally revving his engine, to the cheering crowd's delight. He walked over to the stage without any hesitation, picked up a guitar, and gave a thumbs-up to the camera guys before starting a livestream across the world five minutes early. The opulence of the Zenegade Ranch was then brought into people's homes and phones instantaneously, and history unfolded itself right in front of the eyes of every Zenegades fan as Byrd encouraged a cultural revolution.

"I know a lot of people are getting upset that people are living in places kinda like this one," he said into the cameras as his first words of the show. "So, we're gonna play some songs and show y'all how life on the ranch ain't so bad."

And just like that, he began an acoustic jam that got everyone up on their feet in a rhythmic flow, and it progressed erratically from one riff to another for a few minutes until he transitioned into some of the band's most iconic songs like "She Passed By" and "Waiting at Ethereal Station." But the momentum started to slow down, and Byrd picked up Uncle Tito as he introduced a brand-new, Hawaiian reggae song he'd just written called "These Dirty Streets."

Cold cup of coffee in the early morn
Concrete steps, shoes all torn
Meet me on the corner, like every day
On these dirty streets, everything turns gray

There used to be a forest there
Now it's a big timeshare
Mother Nature can't help but stare
At these dirty, dirty streets

We're a-warmin up now, like a hot coffee cup
Open up shop, now wish us luck
This town ain't big enough for us all
One goes up, another must fall

And time just leads to more and more production
All they say is it's a natural corruption
It's about time we stand up and say what we believe

Before more dirty streets is all that we achieve

What can we do but walk around, round, round
Listen to our town's sound, sound, sound
The sun's a-scorchin' us now, now, now
So, let's be forest bound, bound, bound

Where we can meet hands and plant our future's seed
These dirty streets were made from one man's greed
Things could change if we wanted to just slow down
Embrace our love, give Nature back her crown

And time just leads to more and more production
All they say is it's a natural corruption
It's about time we stand up and say what we believe
Before more dirty streets is all that we achieve

Yeah, these dirty streets, they are our homes
Here we'll sit and rest our bones
Until the day we're meant to die
These dirty streets, can't say goodbye

An awkward, soft clap ensued throughout the crowd as everyone adjusted to the sudden, tropical shift in the acoustic rock show, until a voice from the back yelled, "Now *that's* what I'm talking about!"

O'Donnell had just flown into town and was ultimately late to the party, but his chant was right on cue as the small crowd came out of its ukulele stupor and back on its feet as Byrd shifted to a more upbeat portion of the Zenegades catalog.

The first few concerts featuring solo performances by Byrd far exceeded everyone's expectations, and by the time of the fourth show only a week after the Aspen residency began, the Campfire Concert

Series was a monstrous sensation across industry websites, social media, and pay-per-view streams. Byrd hadn't realized it yet, but the entire band was earning some serious cash through viewership revenue, and he also had no idea about the increasing fortune that was Charlie's cut. For all Byrd knew, he was essentially playing for free to pay back The Nooch and wasn't going to make anything from the streaming revenue due to agreeing to donate his slice of the pie; however, this type of financial altruism was to be expected from the rest of the gang.

The fourth concert featured Byrd, Reg, Lin, and Maya, who made one hell of a quartet that was capable of recapturing the intrigue among the band's most fanatic viewers, who'd already paid at least once to stream a show. Shankar put on a big feast for that fourth Campfire Concert in honor of the entire Walker family, who flew in from New York to attend the show and see firsthand where Maya ran off to those many years ago. During that festive dinner when spirits were as high as a kite flying over a Colorado dispensary, Lin explained the elaborate plans he'd made to meet his biological mother in Beijing with the help of a private investigator.

The fifth Campfire Concert added in Ruben on drums and Sky on mandolin and guitar, and after this show raked in nearly a hundred thousand views, Charlie felt secure enough with the financial prospects of the project to the point that he decided to scrap the idea of Shankar hosting overnight guests at the ranch and personally paid for the band to live together like old times. Things weren't quite the same, given that Thayer was getting treatment at a fancy rehab center in Mexico, but they did reach a sense of nostalgia as they privately rehearsed each day before the shows and even learned new songs like Lin's funk idea called "Bigger and Stronger." It was clearly a song about how he looked up to Maya as so much more than a creative and intimate partner, and its debut performance led to yet another night with six-figure streams.

There was no denying how the Campfire Concert Series had quickly become an unprecedented success, and this had nothing to do with streams and everything to do with the residency providing a once-in-a-lifetime opportunity for the band's biggest fans to see the Zenegades up close and personal at the famous ranch where their journey began. Celebrities like Andre Cavallo showed up for a show, and even Raymundo and his Waipio Family flew into Aspen to experience a handful of shows. One of those Waipio visitors was Jane, and her prolonged visit was an indirect way of Byrd showing the rest of the band that he'd officially found a girlfriend. Having Jane stay at the ranch with them was the pleasant distraction Byrd needed to keep his sanity in check, and although he enjoyed performing in front of a small crowd and particularly enjoyed sleeping at the ranch like old times, it was becoming clearer by the day that the frequency of the shows was starting to wear him down. Jane's visit only lasted a little over two weeks before she went back to the Big Island, and there were still several shows that the band had to play, per contractual agreements.

Byrd eventually needed to switch things up and get away from the concert preparation scene at the ranch, so he decided to sleep on a sleeping pad at night and wander in from a nearby off-trail path each morning. After the shows would end, he'd say goodbye and walk into the night with a headlamp guiding his path. Shankar was the only one who was concerned about those night hikes because he knew there were plenty of bears in the area, but he was also confident that Byrd would find his own way like he always did. What Shankar and no one else realized was that Byrd was drunk each night as he walked into the wilderness by himself.

Byrd always had a can of Coke on him during the concerts that he'd sip from on stage, so the fact that he was also drinking whiskey was difficult for anyone to recognize. Given his sober reputation, no one thought anything could go wrong when he decided to mix things up and take his rental bike downtown to attend an alt rock show at the Belly Up. Not a single soul at the ranch realized that the two Cokes he'd had that evening were heavily spiked and that he was far over the legal limit to operate any kind of motor vehicle, let alone a Honda.

So, the good news was that they only had nine out of twenty-five shows left on the schedule when they had to prematurely wrap things up, and it would only be just a few hundred ticketed fans who would end up receiving refunds. The bad news was that every Zenegades fan was soon to be disappointed when they found out that Byrd had been arrested for DUI on his way back to the ranch from the Belly Up. His arrest was sure to spread like wildfire across the Web and devastate thousands of fans who looked up to him as a role model for their own sobriety, and it was the exact type of negative publicity that the Campfire Concert Series had originally intended to dispel.

The DUI abruptly brought the residency to an end, due to the unanimous agreement that it would be too awkward to keep going after the whole world caught a glimpse of Byrd's disheveled mug shot. At least that was the gist of what Charlie and Shankar told Byrd when they met him outside Pitkin County's tiny jail the next morning after the arrest. They explained how it was probably best for him to stay in Aspen for the time being while they found an attorney and tried to figure out his legal situation. They also tried to convince him that Reg was having a *real good time* in the condo just down the street, and how this could be a good opportunity to write new songs and kick it with him while things cooled down. Byrd smiled at this idea, said okay, and handed Charlie the keys to his rental bike that were just returned to him through the bottom of a commissary window.

He explained how he wanted to be alone before he walked a few blocks down the street toward the condo, where he found Reg making a smoothie in a kimono and video-chatting a friend in New York.

"Hold up, I gotta go. He's here," he said as he closed out his conversation upon seeing Byrd. "You were in jail down the street, and you didn't think to call *me* with your one call?"

"I didn't call anyone because I can't remember people's numbers, but I gave them Charlie's email address, and apparently they contacted him."

"Now that is some bullshit! We're neighbors, I email you way more than him! Well, actually, now that I think about it, you're usually pretty close by, so I don't ever need to email you."

In that moment after Reg's flip-floppy rant, O'Donnell called Reg on his cell and explained how he was supposed to look after Byrd for the time being and make sure he chilled out and met up with a lawyer for a consultation appointment the next day. Reg left the conversation on speakerphone so Byrd could hear what was being said about him, and Byrd hung up the call right in the middle of an O'Donnell-style rant that was seemingly going nowhere.

"Fuck *all* of what he just said, and don't answer if he calls back. I'm sick of this bullshit. Pack up your stuff. We're leaving."

And just like that, the two of them were on the next private flight back to the Big Island.

23

We live in an enigma culture, and this is partly because we now sometimes learn more things about our friends through pictures and digital content than actual conversations. The idea of meeting up for a drink at a bar or dinner at a restaurant can sometimes feel like an increasingly obscure thing to do. Why do we have to go somewhere public to talk to each other? Why talk in person at all when it can be so convenient to text each other? The concept of the digital self has become an all-too-tangible reality, and should it really surprise anyone that people enjoy taking these fabricated identities to such great lengths? It's almost as if many of us want to prove to everyone that we're great people to be around, but that we're too busy being awesome to spend time with each other in the flesh. But you'll still see it online, so what difference does it make if you were there or not, *right*?

Many friendships that go long periods solely online become blurred by the stretches of time to the point that we don't actually know each other beyond the digital boxes we place ourselves in. The idea of your old friends becoming your online friends is a phenomenon that everyone is now just beginning to experience for the first time, and those individuals inherently become more mysterious as time goes by. Sure, you can get a good idea as to what they do on a regular basis, but *knowing* someone and *knowing of* someone has never been quite so comparable.

Do your friends really know who you are, or do they know a

depiction of yourself that you've voluntarily broadcasted through-out the Web? We're all enigmatic in our own unique ways, and that's not necessarily the worst thing in the world. After all, how many videos of your dog or cat can you showcase until your friends know a little too much about your weekday evenings? Sharing experiences with people we don't see often is something we should celebrate to a certain extent, but these types of self-published exposés become more problematic than cordial when the publisher's own introspection becomes befuddled. If people you know don't actually know you that well, then how well do you know yourself? Can anyone say they understand the full complexity of themselves?

The easy truth is that self-concept is, in it of itself, a concept. It's merely an idea we've developed on our own about who we are and how we fit within the broad landscape of the universe. It can present itself within a relaxing mental process while enjoying life's pleasantries, and it can be a disastrous existential crisis when one considers their meaninglessness within the grand scheme of the Unified Field.

So, maybe the purpose of friendship is to better understand each other and subsequently ourselves, and to provide each other with a sense of significance that makes life's meaninglessness just another bygone. Odds are, you take part in life's pleasantries when you're with your friends, and the number of friends who will be there for you when you're questioning the meaning of existence is limited. There's a general sense of pride we all have around our friends when it comes to appearing vulnerable, and this is probably because it's never cool to be the sad guy in the corner of the party while everyone else is having fun. Of course, there's nothing wrong with putting on a smile and trying your best to fit in, no matter how hard life hits you; and of course, it feels off-putting when we recognize how certain friend-ships function a lot better when left to be trivial. But no matter how trivial or fulfilling our friendships are, these relationships inevitably affect the very foundation of who we continuously become.

So, it's completely normal to maintain the front that *everything is how everyone is supposed to see it,* both online and in person, but these façades are never sustainable for anyone. The interior walls you put up against the world will eventually become brittle, and slowly but surely, they'll begin to crack. But funnily enough, it's the slight cracking of those walls that can unleash all the possibilities you're intended for.

Thayer had been in a rehab center for just over two months, a little longer than everyone expected her to be there. Her recovery was slow but still going well in her own drawn-out way, and several counselors helped her understand how her self-concept had played a role in careening her addictions out of control. What the rehab counselors came to realize was that her addiction directly connected to her unfettered craving for having as much fun as possible at all times, and that she'd impulsively considered drugs and alcohol to be her gateway to a good time after more than five years of extraordinary times. So when they caught her strolling back into the rehab premises after a five-mile hike to a nearby beach bar, they decided as a therapeutic group that she needed to stay much longer than they'd originally intended, regardless of her obligations to the band.

She was now beginning to feel abnormally comfortable in her small quarters at the swanky facility just south of Puerto Vallarta. There wasn't much to her room, but they allowed her to have a keyboard that served as her saving grace for all the lonely nights when scheduled meetings were over.

On this particular night, Thayer was sitting in front of her keyboard and reminiscing about all the experiences she'd had with her special instrument. This was the exact same keyboard she left LA with when Cat and Ruben picked her up in their van more than five years earlier. She remembered how uncertain she felt during those days, and how letting the universe guide her through that confusion to Shankar's ranch was the best thing she ever did. One tiny lack of faith here or fearful impulse there could've changed everything to the point where she wouldn't necessarily be in her current position of dealing with a drug addiction in rehab so she could get back to one of the world's most popular musical groups.

She couldn't help but wonder just how different she was in this moment, compared to who she was when she lived with her parents after graduating from community college. Even though it was only five years ago, she felt like a completely different person than she was back in those good ole days. Thinking about *Old Thay* made her question the fluctuation of herself, and it reminded her of how all the other patients were going through the exact same type of self-recollection. She picked up a pen and wrote the word *Enigman* down, followed by:

Roy could've been a big shot
Now he's workin' in a repo lot
Anna could've been on the big screen
Now she's cheering on her son's team

You can say, you can tell the future
But where are all the limousines?
There's a veil over all that's free
It's hiding who we're meant to be

Roy decided he'd play guitar
Anna said she'll still be a star
But their boy, he made things different
Their lives, there's no going back

Look back at yourself, who do you see?
Is it the same man you used to be?
An Enigman, is who you are to me
An Enigman, forever I'm he

Roy and Anna couldn't keep it straight
Their love faded, turned into hate
They used to say time's just a dial

But now sign here, it's time to file

There's a reason we're supposed to grow
It's something we'll never quite know
Am I an Enigman, because you can't see
Just how lonely my soul can be?

Look ahead of yourself, who do you see?
Is it the same man you intended to be?
An Enigman, is who I am to me
An Enigman, who the hell is he?

Roy never was a big shot
Anna never was a big star
But their boy, he made things different
Their lives keep going on and on and on
(On and on and on)

Every day's, a chance to be strange
Every day, an Enigman turns true
Every day's, a chance to change
Every day, you become anew

You can say, you can tell the future
But where are all the children's screams?
There's a light, so bright it could blind
It guides us to what we're meant to find

She looked down at the words scratched across a notepad sheet and examined several small scratches on the keyboard. She remembered the many moments from which each scratch originated, and the flood of memories—combined with the emotions of songwriting in a rehab center far away from home—made tears begin to well up in her eyes. Her breathing turned to panting as she thought about the regrets that had developed over the years. She looked back on all the memorable parties that seemingly brought about an endless supply of hilarity, and she now was beginning to understand how these moments fostered the habits that developed her addictions.

She looked back at the days when she first met Sky, Lin, O'Donnell, Maya, Reg, and Shankar, and she went even further back in time to when she met Byrd, Meryl, Ruben, Cat, J. P., and Madison. She couldn't help but instantaneously see everything that occurred over the course of many years, as if it had all happened within seconds. As she attempted to recognize how her memories were just as subjective as anyone else's, she tried her best to put that one night at Chateau Marmont into perspective. *What's happening with all that now? Is that video gonna go public and ruin the band? What does everyone think of Sky and me now? Are they gonna replace us? How long am I gonna be stuck here?*

The phone in her bedroom abruptly rang and unleashed her from a mental gaze. It also reminded her how she was still a part of the present moment, whether she liked it or not.

"Hello," she said into the transmitter.

"Hi, Thayer, it's Troy. I'm so sorry to disturb you so late in the evening. I need you to come into the main office as soon as you can. We're discharging you early."

Thayer didn't respond, but she immediately left the phone sitting on her bed without hanging up. She stepped outside her door and walked down a cobblestone path past a handful of fancy bungalows, around the edge of an even fancier pool, and into a large stucco building that was the only one with lights on. There she saw Troy, one of the rehab's lead counselors, sitting at a desk behind a computer.

"When can I go home?" she asked, breathing heavily from her brisk walk.

"*Well*, that was fast!" Troy said with an annoying laugh that calmed itself down as he noticed Thayer's silent death stare. "The truth is that I have some tough news, Thayer. Something has come up, and we now think it'd be better for you to finish your treatment somewhere else. I just need to go over a few things as to why we're okay with sending you home *right now*."

"Why am I going home early?"

"*Well*, it's kind of complicated, but I'll do my best to explain the situation," he said, smiling like a kindergarten teacher. "Let's just start with the good news first. *Now*, I know you know there have been some Zenegades shows at the Aspen ranch recently, but of course, you haven't been allowed to be on your phone or the internet down here, so I wanted to show you this."

He flipped the desktop screen around and clicked play on one of the band's official YouTube videos featuring Byrd playing "These Dirty Streets." The video was well edited and featured three different cameras cutting between one another, and it currently had just over a million views.

"That's a new song he recently wrote, but I'm sure you know that. Have you been writing any songs lately?"

"Yeah, I'm actually working on one right now. I think they might like it."

"That's *great*, Thay. I'm so proud of you! *Now*, what you should know is that things were going really great with the concert series, until recently. Jim seems to have a bit of a problem on his hands as well, and he got a DUI the other night on his motorcycle. He blew a .23, Thay. *No joke*, he could've died or even killed someone else, and apparently, he was swerving everywhere along a dirt road."

"That's not good."

"Yeah, it's definitely *not good*. And now it's definitely *not good* for you being here, either. We've recently gotten word that the media knows you're here, and now they want to speak with us. It's just not a good look all around, so we've agreed with your family and our buddy Charlie Dyceman that it's probably best for you to leave now and finish your treatment at a different facility. So, you're ready to go. I'm also supposed to tell you that you have a meeting with Charlie tomorrow afternoon, and that you're booked on a redeye that leaves in a few hours. I'll be giving you a ride to the airport once you've packed all your things."

Thayer looked down at the LA Basin from her window seat and watched the sun rise over the Mojave Desert's magenta skies, and it finally sank in that her episode at a rehab center in Mexico was officially over.

She had no access to a cell phone or computer for over eight weeks, and she decided not to call anyone when Troy offered his cell because she figured her parents and Sky already knew about her early release and were sleeping. Burbank never looked so majestic as it did that particular dawn with the sunrise's glow backlighting the Verdugo Mountains at a sharp angle, and it also never seemed so desolate. Barely anyone was on the highway at 5:30 a.m. that Sunday, and her veteran rideshare chauffeur got her to West Hollywood in less than fifteen minutes.

At long last, she'd arrived at her luxurious abode tucked away along the ridge, a moment that had been over two months in the mental making. Although she'd seen the early morning light at her house on plenty of occasions, she'd never seen magenta glowing across her pool while sober. The water's surface remained perfectly still, like a pane of backyard glass designed to help her reflect.

"There's no place like home," she whispered as she slid the screen door open and stepped inside.

The inside of the house looked a bit messier than the backyard, but nothing too cluttered. A couple of dirty plates rested on the coffee table next to a couple of near-empty whiskey glasses containing melted ice. There wasn't any coke nearby, but she recognized how a tiny mirror with a small plastic tube on top of it was an indication that it was somewhere nearby. She shook her head, knowing she and Sky were going to have a talk about doing coke in their home, because she *definitely* wasn't going back to doing it ever again—or at least she was going to try to quit.

She tiptoed across the hardwood floors past the kitchen and down the hallway toward the master, and that was the moment she

heard the whisper. Her stomach curled inward on itself like a retro taffy puller. She looked back at the two plates of food and two
whiskey glasses, and forced her step-by-step struggle to the bedroom door. Sure enough, a shirtless Sky was in their bed next to
a blatant body lump underneath the sheets, but to her surprise, it
wasn't some blonde LA bimbo she'd envisioned seconds earlier. At
first glance, she thought it may be a woman with short black hair,
but then she realized it was Pierre. They were both clearly awake as
Thayer stepped through the threshold, but no one said anything for
a moment. They just stared at each other.

"Look ... I can explain," Sky started as he got out of bed, while
Pierre quickly put his clothes on.

Thayer couldn't bring herself to say anything, so instead she
cried. She cried as she backed away from the bedroom, still looking at the carnage of her and Sky's relationship, and she turned
around and ran toward the garage. She took the keys to her van and
sped down the street to Sunset. There was barely anyone awake that
early, so she sped through stop signs and traffic lights with reckless abandon. She'd typically always listen to music while driving,
but now there was complete silence as she veered around dozens of
winding curves in the direction of Brentwood. Tears continued to
stream down her face as she whipped around her childhood streets,
and she didn't give a shit about anything except going to sleep. Her
parents' place was seemingly the only place to go, because the bed
she bought and shared with Sky no longer felt like hers.

She didn't want to make a scene, mainly because she didn't want
to speak to anyone. She parked on the street and quietly walked to
the backyard, where she again looked at another glamorous pool in
the morning glow. This pool view didn't hit so well, and her heart
pounded as she lay down on her favorite lounge chair. Now there
was no getting back up, and she cried herself to sleep much more
intensely than she ever did in rehab.

24

hree hours later, yet instantaneously in New York, Maya was beginning her morning routine on a scorching July day that was just about to start cooking. This was the best time of day to go out until the evening hours allowed for more comfy foot travel, and she made the decision right then at 9:17 to not do anything of any real-world importance for the whole day. Their open kitchen was connected to a spare bedroom that was essentially devoid of any seating area except one L-shaped couch, and this lack of furniture was in the best interests of utilizing the majority of the room for violins and stand-up basses. All she needed was right there, so there wasn't any need to go anywhere.

She was wearing a fancy kimono robe that Lin got for her during their trip to Japan with the whole gang a couple years earlier, and looking down at the bright flowers full of yellow and purple petals made her think about Asia. There was a moment right then when she second-guessed her plans and really considered doing *everything* of importance for the whole day, but this enthrallment toward thoughts of Asia subsided when she decided to maintain her routine by brewing some of the finest black tea in the entire city. There wasn't much to making this brew, just hot water poured into a cup; however, the tea itself was the type of intricate beauty that required close examination in order to be appreciated. It was a rare type of Black Dragon pearl that simply plopped into mugs at optimal temperatures, which caused the tightened tea leaves to moisten and unravel to caffeinated perfection.

Like many mornings, Maya decided to walk her teacup outside to the shaded balcony, where she'd sit and enjoy city views while scrolling through her phone as she waited for her morning pick-me-up to steep. She glanced at her few succulents floundering in the summer sun, and went straight to her social media feed while nestling into a plastic Adirondack chair. After just a couple minutes of scrolling through cat videos and other Web waste, she came across a magazine post featuring a mug shot of a wind-blown Byrd from Aspen's jail. The caption read *Is the 'Zenegade Movement' Just a Bunch of Bullshit?*

She clicked on the article and started reading the details of what happened with Byrd's DUI arrest, how much money the Campfire Concert Series made via pay-per-view streams, Thayer's rehab residency, and the countless communities of young people living in the woods who weren't necessarily the most Zen in certain scenarios. The article went on to conclude that the recent nonsense was just the icing on the cake when it came to proving how the band and their fans haven't practiced what they've preached.

A series of different emotions oozed through Maya as she guzzled down the Black Dragon tea a bit faster than usual. Her heart rate began to increase, and she felt the first beads of sweat drip down her temples much earlier than in recent days. She scowled at her phone's screen and whispered profanities as she reread the article, this time in an internal tonality that made the journalist come off as a complete snob. She laughed, but her laughter quickly turned to tears. She tried browsing other websites, but she couldn't go more than a few minutes without returning to the mug shot and the precise wording of the article's disparagements.

By the time Maya finished rereading the article for the fifth time, Lin was just beginning his day. She heard him rummaging through a hallway closet, until he pulled out a massive duffel bag. He had several outfits laid out on the L-shaped couch in the music room, and he was deciding how he'd start organizing. Maya discreetly watched him pack his underwear and shorts, and she realized how the reality of their situation was coming to fruition. Lin's flight to Beijing left later that day, and she wouldn't be joining him on his quest to find his mother. Apparently, the PI he found through Charlie gave him all the information he needed to arrange a meeting, but she still had her doubts. She looked down at her silky kimono and wondered again what it would be like to put it all aside and start packing her bags, but she knew she couldn't. She knew she had to practice what she'd preached and stick to her plans, which luckily enough were a different kind of dream come true.

She and Retro Phat (minus Lin) were preparing for a residency at Blue Queen in which they'd play three nights a week of Zenegades songs, covers, and some of Maya's latest originals to crowds that were sure to sell. She'd become a reputable figure throughout the New York jazz scene because she had plenty of pull for a completely different, younger crowd than most jazz bars were used to, and she chose to give back to her friends at Blue Queen when she had the option of which venue to sell out on a nightly basis. The rest of Retro Phat was depending on her, Blue Queen was depending on her, a lot of fans were depending on her, and even Ruben and Cat were depending on her for a solid gig to come back to as their Euro trip came to an end. Ruben was set up to be the band's new drummer, and she even helped them find a fully furnished apartment in Brooklyn they could rent month-to-month. All the residency contracts were signed, and they both knew this was an adventure that Lin needed to do on his own.

Lin walked out to the balcony with a cup of tea and sat down in the other Adirondack chair. Neither of them said anything as Lin rubbed his eyes from behind his sunglasses, and the silence continued as he looked out toward the city's endless maze and breathed a heavy sigh.

"So, what're you going to do when you get there?" Maya asked, breaking the silence.

"Go to my hotel and most likely sleep off the jet lag."

"Don't pretend like you don't know what I mean. What are you going to do *about your mom* when you get there?"

"Dave has helped me arrange a meeting with her at her house. She lives right in the middle of the city, about a mile from where I'll be staying. It should be pretty straightforward."

"Straightforward my fucking ass, Lin. How can you think about this moment as if it's some kind of *business meeting*? Have you even thought about what you're going to say to her?"

"Of course, I have. I've thought about that every single day for a long time now, but every time I start thinking about those things, it hits me that I have no idea who this woman even is. She may be my mom, but meeting her will in many ways be like meeting any other stranger."

"Well, you won't be a stranger to her. She'll remember when you were born. And you know, I'm just happy for you. She won't be a stranger for much longer."

"Yeah, I guess that's a good way to look at it, and *you know*, it's not too late to apply for a visa and maybe meet me out there. It was a lot faster than I expected to get mine at the consulate over by Pier 84, so it would probably only take you a few days to get one. *And I* was planning on going to the Silk Market at least once while I'm out there, *which means* we could get an outfit to match that kimono," Lin responded with a wry smile.

He could see the inner regrets on her face as she looked down at her cup of tea and sipped from it. She didn't have to respond because they both knew she was fully obligated in New York, and she never did respond, because at that moment, she received a call on her cell from Thayer. Maya kept the call off speaker while Lin watched, not knowing what was going on, but all the *what the fuck* and *that's so fucked up* comments were a dead giveaway that something had happened. Eventually she whispered, "Sky cheated on Thay," so he knew what they were talking about.

He initially experienced a numbing sensation throughout his head, arms, and legs as he slunk deeper into his chair and evaluated the ramifications of what he'd just heard. He considered the notion that Sky and Thayer breaking up may be the final straw to the Zenegades as they all knew it, which made his mouth begin to water as if he were going to vomit. He followed Maya inside to continue eavesdropping.

"Look, Thay, you need to get yourself a change of scenery. You can come here if you want. It'll just be you and me. Lin is leaving tonight for Beijing.... It's gonna be all good, we're here for you, and Cat will be here in just a few days, too.... Come as soon as you like, in fact, the sooner the better.... First class? Now *that's* my girl! I'll see you tomorrow, then.... Okay, call me if you need anything else."

Back on the Big Island, Byrd and Reg were taking it easy on the farm while drinking homegrown guava smoothies on the homestead's porch. It was several hours later that day, but it was only 9:17 a.m. when Reg's cell rang. It was O'Donnell.

"Yo, bro! How many times do I have to tell you about the time difference out here?" Reg answered. "Yeah, I'm with him right now.... No, he doesn't wanna talk.... Well, then you can tell me, and I'll tell him."

A couple of minutes later, Byrd glanced over at Reg as his mouth gaped open and his eyes widened. Out of nowhere, he said, "That's heavy," and went silent again. Byrd had never seen him so quiet on the phone, but he got the update about Thayer and Sky shortly after the call ended. The only reason why O'Donnell knew what was going on in the first place was because Sky had just told him everything, and now they were all worried that it was the end of the band.

Everything Byrd could see in a nearby puddle's reflection seemed to be rapidly deteriorating in every way, and he only knew one way to deal with these types of all-encompassing, intense scenarios: *fly away*. So, he stood up from his seat on his wooden steps and went inside. A few minutes later, he reemerged with a guitar case in his hands and started walking down the driveway.

"I'm disappearing. See ya later," Byrd said as he started marching down the gravel driveway without any hesitation.

Reg yelled out to him a few times, but after he didn't get a response, he realized how there was nothing and no one that was going to hold him back.

25

in's natural instincts were accustomed to cities. From growing up in San Francisco's Chinatown to becoming a violin sensation living in Greenwich Village, he got the gist of getting around city life. His parents took him on two trips to China as he grew up, but every time he stepped foot in a Chinese megacity, it was like stepping into a maze of urban mystery that could never be solved. And in a city like Beijing, where modern society and ancient history coexist in a harmonious set of concentric circles that make up the heartbeat of Mother China, Lin felt completely lost without any clue whatsoever.

He couldn't help but keep thinking *so ... many ... people* as he meandered around random touristy streets with a camera. The obvious truth was that he didn't go to Beijing to see the typical tourist destinations, but his nervousness in meeting his mom led him to multiple days of procrastinating at places like the Forbidden City, the Temple of Heaven, the Summer Palace, and the Great Wall. He stayed in a condo rental in the heart of Beijing's third of six highway rings, because this was where David Fieldcrest suggested would be conveniently located near his mother's house. She knew he was coming, thanks to Fieldcrest's fieldwork, but now there was no telling when they'd actually meet because of Lin's tardiness.

He was sweating profusely on a balmy July evening when he decided he'd go to a nearby park and think things through a bit more. City parks had provided him with a sense of solace for as long as he could remember, because with just a little bit of grass, a few trees, and a trusted instrument companion, he could escape all his surroundings. So, he found himself at the nearby Zizhuyuan Park, and he admired the intricate landscaping as he walked over arch bridges, through bamboo forests, and around ponds full of lotus blossoms. Tiny islands and temples dotted the pedestrian path as the adjacent Nanchang River slowly trudged its way in between surrounding high rises. He sat down on a bench and pulled out a tiny piece of paper he'd brought from New York, which noted his mother's address.

He plugged the pinyin words into his phone, reconfirming that she lived just on the northern edge of the park. He walked in accordance with his GPS through a courtyard, where a couple dozen women danced in unison to one of China's most traditional Plum Blossom Melodies. There was no chance he'd pass along his way before taking in such an alluring display of simultaneous steps, hand gestures, and rhythmic hip maneuvers being directed by a vintage boom box. This was the side of Beijing he couldn't see at places like the Forbidden City, and he soaked in the scene with his camera as he photographed the dancing women showcasing their genuine love for music's liberating power. Uninhibited, the large group continued to sway together with the type of imperfectly perfect synchronicity that could only be found in the most random parts of Beijing's streets.

Lin watched the group dance until they were done, which was more than half an hour later. This last procrastination was well-timed, because his mother was in that crowd of dancers and wouldn't have been home if he'd decided to pass them by. She lived right across the street from the park, about three hundred feet away from the courtyard, and her door was open when Lin finally arrived.

He couldn't believe how tiny her home was, a rectangular room that opened directly up to a bustling crosswalk. Everything she owned was in this tiny space of about 150 square feet, and yet nothing appeared to be cluttered. Her kitchen, consisting of a hot plate on top of a plastic shelf, was well-organized, her closet was tidy, her sink spotless, and her many artworks shone brightly around her centralized roundtable.

She had her back to the door as Lin approached, and she immediately knew it was her son who had come to find her as she turned around and saw a young man wearing fancy clothes in her doorway. She rarely had any visitors, partly because her space couldn't fit them, and she was relieved that her recent tidiness had paid off after awaiting this moment for a few days.

"Lin?" she asked.

"*Nǐ hǎo, Mǔqīn*" Lin responded in his Americanized, Mandarin dialect.

They continued speaking Mandarin with one another, only needing Lin's translator phone app a handful of times to better explain some ordinary personal information. She explained that her name was Shu Chen and that she initially wanted his name to be Lin after her father. She also explained that his American parents agreed to keep that name while she was pregnant, and that she always thought it was very honorable of them to commemorate his biological grandfather. This was something Lin never actually knew about his name, because his parents always told him his name's origin derived from them simply wanting a Chinese name and liking Lin as one of their preferred options. They never mentioned anything about his biological family, except that they met his mother in the hospital on the day he was born.

Shu was a professional street sweeper, and each morning, she woke up at the crack of dawn and started picking up trash around the perimeter of Zizhuyuan Park until it looked immaculate. She spent just about every day in the park across the street from her home, and she had lived alone in her small room for many years. She told Lin that she didn't know his father well and met him at a local bar for one night only, so there was no way of finding him and letting him know that he impregnated her. She had no money and couldn't even come close to affording a child, so she signed up for an adoption program when she first found out she was having a baby. She repetitively apologized to Lin saying she had no options and that she knew he'd have a better life in the United States.

Lin, blown away beyond any previous moment of his life, took his

mother out to a restaurant in her recommended part of the neighborhood. He began opening up more at their table by explaining
how he was a violinist, and that he was lucky to have established a
successful career as a musician. Shu responded by telling him that
she loved music more than anything in the world, but she never had
the time to learn an instrument. But what she did make time for was
interpretive dance, and she had many friends with the same interest.
She was beyond excited to hear how her son ended up having the
wonderful life in America she'd hoped for, and validating tears ran
down her face in confirmation that she did right by giving Lin a
different hand.

"I want to hear you play violin," Shu said during their dinner.

"How about I play you a few songs after we're done eating?"

"No, not tonight. I'm too tired and need to rest for tomorrow. I
finish work at five, and I can meet in the same part of the park where
I was earlier today around then."

Lin and Shu met up around 5 p.m. the following day in a stone
courtyard of Zizhuyuan Park. They small-talked for a few minutes
describing their days to one another, which couldn't have been more
of polar opposites. While Lin devoured street snacks and aimlessly explored the city's hutong alleyways, Shu had another routine
Wednesday cleaning up her neighborhood. Lin carried his violin the
entire day, and he even helped a couple of busking musicians bring
about a larger crowd. He figured he'd help them earn some extra tips
while getting some practice in before playing in front of his mom for
the first time, and later that evening in the courtyard, he immediately exceeded all of her lofty expectations.

The more he played, the more Shu realized that her son was truly
gifted. It filled her heart and brought her to tears as she listened to
him play one of the traditional songs she frequently danced to, and
it didn't take long for a few other women in the courtyard to begin
dancing to Lin's performance. Shu joined them, and a few minutes

later, there were more than a dozen women dancing to a song that Lin had played countless times as a child. He'd mastered just about every traditional Chinese song by the time he was sixteen, so playing them in Zizhuyuan Park for his mother and her neighbors really was like a walk in the park.

By the time he'd played for twenty minutes, there were nearly two dozen women dancing to his solo melody. Although he was used to playing in front of many dancing people at music halls and festivals throughout America, there was absolutely no comparison to the connection he felt with those women as they undulated their bodies and swayed in symmetry to each connected note. Out of all the times he'd played in public spaces in New York or San Francisco, the most engagement he ever got was a small, admiring crowd that stood still. *No one in America ever dances quite this freely in public,* he thought.

He could see Shu in the middle of the pack, fulfilling her role in the group's shaping, and he couldn't help but feel a similarly gratifying wave that he only reached when he saw his American parents in front-row seats at a Zenegades show. But this was unique as compared to any other musical moment he'd ever had, and his heart pounded with excitement in front of the intimate crowd like it would in any other of his career's most profound experiences.

He continued to play for the dancing women of Zizhuyuan Park for nearly an hour before taking a break, and afterward, several people walked up to him, wanting just a few minutes of conversation. They introduced themselves, and they didn't know who he was when he introduced himself. There was only one man at the park who knew who Lin Rose was, and he was eager to ask in English for a picture.

"Hello, Mr. Rose. My name is Le Qi. It's been a beautiful blessing to hear you play violin today in such a small setting. Would you please take a picture with me?"

"Of course, no problem," Lin replied as he adjusted his hair and stood next to Le Qi for a selfie.

"Thank you so much. My friends at the Beijing Philharmonic will now believe me when I tell them the story of this evening!"

"*Oh,* you're a philharmonic musician?"

"Yes, I play percussion. If you ever want to play music together, it would be a true honor, sir."

Later that evening, Lin logged on to his phone's email app and prepared to update Maya on everything that had been happening. He also wanted to let her know that he was making plans to renew his condo rental for another few weeks in order to help Shu relocate to a better home, which would give her an added opportunity to come visit. But when he first glanced at his inbox, he noticed an unread message from Reg that said:

Hey Lin,

I don't know what's up with calling you because you're in China and all, so I'm checking in here and letting you know what's going on.

Byrd disappeared with that girl Jane he's been hooking up with recently. We were just chilling out the other day, and then we got word about Sky and Thay and he bounced FOR REAL this time. That was a week ago now, and I haven't heard a peep from him. I even went out to that crazy dude Raymundo's place to see if he was out there, and they all said that they both left the island the other day and didn't say where they were going.

So far only a few people even know he bounced, so I'm just wondering if you've heard from him? I'm not sure what to do anymore, and I have to say something if he keeps ignoring me. There's some MIA clause in my contract that says I have to report to the cops when shit like this goes down.

Let me know if you've heard from him, and good luck meeting your momma out there in China.

Much Love,

Reg

26

ust like reading a book, our lives come in chapters, characterized in stages like growing up, moving homes, going to school, changing jobs, beginning or ending relationships, getting married, having children, retiring. We often inherently feel the magnitude of their presence, and sometimes we don't recognize them at all. But regardless of recognition, time tends to sweep us up when new chapters arise, and these moments are true embodiments of intuitive expansion. We're built to thoroughly analyze the past, but broad, overarching self-reviews can ironically keep us grounded toward the one thing we simultaneously can't let go of and yet can't maintain: the present moment.

Oddly enough, what's interesting about life's new chapters is that other people will often have less-than-optimistic views and may even try to dissuade a new chapter from forming. A new chapter can also be brought to fruition through the guidance of others, but in the long run, there's only one person who knows what your unique interests are. Maybe your confidante thinks you should apply for a new job in a new town that they know you'll love, or maybe they think you should heedlessly quit your current job and tell your asshole bosses to go fuck themselves without any plan B. As much as we all want to trust those who we think know us well enough to understand what's best for us, deciding how to go about decisions that drastically balance personal relationships with time is, in and of itself, personal.

Intuition ends up being the saving grace that counterbalances feelings of worry and caution with willpower and courage. It's almost like a needle graph with *GO* and *NO GO* axes that fluctuate thoughts on a constant basis. Back and forth and back and forth we'll sway, slowly but surely evaluating the pros and cons of each new chapter while wondering whether to *go* or *not go*. New chapters undoubtedly are the type of personal dilemmas that others enjoy putting their two cents into, and the input of close friends and family members should always be highly regarded when a change is on the horizon; however, the hardest of truths tend to be lonely, and the emergence of new chapters is a product of personal bonds with time.

So, the lessons of our past are essentially the prerequisites for new chapters, partly because looking back at what only you understand will ultimately point your intuitive needle graph in the right direction toward what lies ahead.

Maya's morning routine was always set in stone because it could fit into her schedule, no matter how busy she got: wake up, walk to the kitchen, boil water, and enjoy a cup of tea on the balcony. She'd then sit and enjoy her divine Chinese tea while listening to the city, which would meld into the perfect white noise for thinking of nothing at all. Now that Thayer had replaced Lin as her sleepy roommate, she'd think about nothing a bit longer than usual as she waited for her disillusioned friend to wake up around 9:30 each day.

This morning just so happened to be an appealing chance to stray away from typical habits, which resulted in her placing a delivery order to her favorite French bakery for a large quiche filled with spinach, ham, and mozzarella, as well as several sweet croissants. This was far beyond anything she was used to doing on a random weekday morning, and this extra bit of breakfast effort was her and Cat's idea to get Thayer in a good mood prior to a real-life conversation. It had been over two weeks since Thayer bought a first-class plane ticket to New York, and the majority of those days consisted of crying, sleeping, and aimlessly walking around Maya and Lin's apartment.

By 9:15, Cat had arrived with the aromatic treats and caused a rustling in the music room, which was now a temporary guest bedroom. After a minute of rolling around and massaging her eyes, Thayer appeared in the kitchen wearing a Stones shirt and pajama shorts. As they munched on quiche and croissants, Thayer realized how this morning was the first time in months that she'd woken up with an appetite. As she crunched through the flaky pastry toward the sweet almond cream, she began to see how her new life would now be lived: surrounded by friends and breakfast delicacies. She thought to herself, *what could ever go wrong with this dynamic duo?*

"So, Thay ... what's your plan now?" Cat asked, breaking away from an easy-like-Sunday-morning vibe to an obviously neglected forethought.

"I don't know. What's *your* plan now?" she responded, shrugging off the question.

"She means, what're you going to do about Sky?" Maya chimed in. "Are you guys breaking up?"

"Definitely, 100 percent. What, you think I should stay with him after *this*?"

"No, I guess not."

"I think you guys could talk things over and get through this," Cat replied. "It might not be as weird as you think. Ruben talked to him recently, and apparently Sky confided that he's bi. Ruben said that Sky only hooks up with guys every now and again, and it's strictly physical. Nothing *lovey-dovey* or anything."

Thayer sat silently for a moment as she imagined herself going back to Sky, and how that would more than likely entail an open relationship in which she knew about his affairs. Her thoughts started running wild as she saw them floating into separate bedrooms with other people for the night.

"No, I'm not into it, and that's the *last* I wanna hear about him!" she replied.

"Well, what about the band? You think we should kick him out or something like that?" Cat added on to Thayer's wounds.

"We don't need to worry about that just yet," Maya jumped in. "But to be frank, if it comes down to a vote, then my vote is to boot his cheating ass. But on the other hand, I think you guys should talk and see if you can still work together. It's tough for any group to lose their lead guitar, and we just so happen to have a great guitarist who'd be nearly impossible to replace."

"My vote is you guys try to work things out," Cat blurted out, receiving a scornful glance from Thayer. "For the band, not just as a couple."

All Thayer could do was shake her head. She continued to sit at the kitchen table in complete silence as the conversation took a sharp turn toward a different, meaningless subject: the ongoing, summer heatwave. Her heart rate started rising as nerve-wracking thoughts ran through her head at an increasing pace, and eventually a few tears ran down her cheeks. As Cat and Maya turned their attention back to her tears, there was no holding her back. She rushed back to the sofa, put on some clean clothes, packed up a tiny backpack, and returned to the kitchen to inform both of them that she'd be leaving for the day. She wanted to walk around and look at stuff, and she explicitly let them know that they didn't need to worry about her searching for drugs. Although this last presumption was a little bit hard to believe, as it seemed like she was on the verge of a relapse, they let her go on her own without any hesitations.

Thayer emerged onto the streets of Greenwich Village and went straight to the subway. She headed south through Tribeca and got off in the Financial District. Eventually she made her way to the Battery, where a small patch of trees bordered an endless sea of skyscrapers. And that's where she got a glimpse of the Statue of Liberty in the exact same spot where Lin frequented, and she couldn't help but stare out across the bay and see a strong, independent woman who existed free of mankind's restraints. She began thinking that the statue itself stood the test of time as a symbolic beacon of hope, and that she fulfilled her oath every day. No one could bring Lady

Liberty down, and no one could stop her from her destined path.

She felt a tingling sensation in her tongue, and her pupils dilated as profound thoughts began to emerge. She walked back to the trees and sat underneath their shade. She pulled out a notepad and wrote the word *Chapters* at the top of a page, followed by:

Do you see where you've come from?
Do you see that life just up above?
There's a trail up that path
It's a-winding away
It'll bring you where you're going
It'll show you the way

Oh, tell me now, friend, what time has done
Did the world come around and suck up all your fun?
Do you see that valley down below?
Can you tell the ways that your heart will grow?

Chapters, time for something new
Chapters, why's my heart so blue?
It's a rollercoaster ride, it's hurtling much too fast
It's a dangerous riptide, it's haunting all my past

I see a change on the horizon
It's a whirlwind, but it might work out
There's a new way to go, it's never been done before
It's a dangerous new land, just begging to be explored

Can you help me find where the lines are drawn?
Fog keeps flowing, it can't be undone
If you're in my boat, baby, I can't save you
The captain around here, she ain't got a clue

Oh, tell me now, ma'am, what time has done
Will the world come around and remind you how to have fun?

Do you see that peak, raised beyond the clouds?
Do you see that valley, full of lush green mounds?

Chapters, turn a new page
Chapters, set a new stage
It's about time to take yours, as sweetly as you like
It's about time to lay old dogs to rest

Chapters, will see you through
Chapters, it's your time too
Chapters, you've been due
Chapters, what's in store for you?

A couple of slow weeks went by before a lightning-fast buzz of support began galvanizing itself around Thayer and "Chapters." As much as the Dyce Records crew genuinely loved the lyrics Thayer had developed and wanted to quickly get the song out to the public, there was an extra sense of urgency to get the ball rolling toward a single, due to personal circumstances. Everyone wanted to help her move on, and releasing the song seemed like the most logical way to solidify her ongoing post-rehab/relationship transition. This collective impetus was exactly why Charlie got in touch with a producer in Manhattan to set up a few days for laying down the foundation tracks. The general plan was that if they busted their asses for a few days, they may get Thayer out of her slump within a matter of weeks.

Such a momentous occasion founded within such a myopic strategy called for O'Donnell to fly back to the States and cut his family time short. He was refreshed as if he'd enjoyed a frozen margarita in a pool while wearing a brand-new plaid suit that his mom had just given him. He looked and mainly felt fantastic, and he was beyond confident that "Chapters" would be one of Thayer's best songs yet.

He naturally had a few tricks up his plaid suit sleeve, because

"Chapters" was essentially Thayer's public announcement that she and Sky were no longer the rock-star couple everyone thought of them as. So, in many ways, he didn't want the song to be released at all; however, O'Donnell's mind always worked in complex ways. Even though it was far from true, he thought of himself as an objective band manager while weighing the pros and cons of the single's release during his overseas flight. He also took several hours to weigh the pros and cons associated with whether Thayer or Sky was the more valuable band member. In the end of his convoluted thought process that went back and forth for over twenty-four hours of travel, O'Donnell concluded that Sky was his best friend for life, no matter how disappointing his infidelity had become for the entire crew, and he also concluded that Thayer was the more talented musician who needed to stay in the band in order to keep the Zenegades gravy train chugging along.

So when Thayer, Maya, Cat, and Ruben arrived at the studio for the first "Chapters" recording session, they were all surprised to see O'Donnell waiting for them in the green room with Sky.

"What the fuck? Is this some kind of intervention?" Thayer asked in the exact moment she saw Sky.

"All right, *all right*! Don't go jumping off the Brooklyn Bridge just cuz you're in the same room as him!" O'Donnell blurted out, quickly trying to regain control of the room. "You two need to talk with each other. We'll set up the studio for you in the meantime."

The green room was empty except for Thayer and Sky as everyone else set up their equipment, and immediately Sky started apologizing. Thayer had blocked his cell number and wasn't taking any calls whatsoever, so this was their fist time speaking with one another since she walked in on him with Pierre. He came clean, admitting he was bi and didn't know how to tell her, and that his affair wasn't all that new. She explained how she needed a fresh start, and that it would be best if they made a clean break from each other and hit the reset button on their lives.

"But what about all *this*?" Sky asked, motioning to the studio walls. "What do you wanna do?"

She looked down at the carpeted floor, trying to think while not exactly knowing what to think about. The question was loaded, to the point that it wasn't possible to consider everything, even though she'd been going over everything for over a month while living with Maya.

"I don't know. I've been thinking a lot lately, and I still don't know what would be best for all of us. I don't even know what it's like to play music with you and not be in love with you at the same time. I mean, for fuck's sake, Sky, I even wrote a song called 'Last Big Sky' when you were asleep on that rock in Jackson. I wanted to keep it a surprise, but now when I look at those lyrics, I see a completely different me, and now I can't imagine recording or even playing that song. It seems like there will always be something missing from *this* from now on."

"I understand. It's never going to be quite the same," Sky responded, now showing tears welling up in his eyes. "I'm so sorry, Thay. It's all my fault, but I'm willing to keep doing *this* and strictly be business. But if you want me out, I get it."

Thayer could see the tears coming down his face, and she could also tell how he was petrified of what would happen to his celebrity status if he got kicked out of the band. Writing and preparing "Chapters" was her new therapy for getting through this unexpected part of her transition, and by the looks of his scraggly appearance, Sky had been going through a rough patch since her departure as well. She couldn't help but think that he looked pathetic as he cried in the green room while everyone talked about them behind their backs, but she also couldn't help but feel a little bit bad for him.

"We'll decide as a group on what *we* wanna do with you," she said, insinuating that he was on the outside of *we*. "We won't do that now, but for right now, I want you to leave. And I want you to talk to O'Donnell or Reg or Cat or Charlie or whoever about how you'd like to announce us breaking up. I'm not going to walk around LA or New York or any fucking place and have our fans thinking we're a couple when we're not. And the even tougher truth that you need to confront is that you have an addiction problem, Sky. I got the help I needed, and I can't tell you how great it feels to finally be clean and want nothing to do with coke anymore, so you honestly just need to get your shit together and get whatever addiction treatment you need, and then we can actually start talking again about all *this*. But you should just know that this rock-star couple image we've had for a while is over. I'll leave it to you in terms of how we *officially* end it."

She walked out of the green room without waiting for a response, and she immediately wanted to start the first tracks. Everyone stared blankly as she walked over to the piano in the corner of the room, and no one said anything. Ruben and Maya walked to their instruments and looked over toward Charlie's producer friend, who had no idea what the hell was going on.

"*Whoa,* hold your darn horses!" O'Donnell yelled, still trying to stop the recording session from happening. "Where's Lin? Isn't he supposed to be playing with you on this one?"

Maya explained that Lin was helping his mother in China, and that he'd extended his trip. This was not good news for O'Donnell, who had this whole elaborately envisioned sound for "Chapters" featuring Lin's brilliant violin. So in his self-absorbed view, the whole strategy of getting the song out quickly would now need to wait on Lin's return. He tried explaining his position to postpone everything, but Thayer wasn't having it.

"I don't give a fuck if Lin or Byrd or Reg or Sky aren't in this song!" she yelled over at him, interrupting his rant about hearing Lin in the song's lyrics. "In fact, new rule for this single: it's a *girls-only* song. Ruben is the only exception, because his hair is long enough!" she said, trying to lighten the mood for a split second. "I don't think we need you here anymore today. Maybe you and Sky can go play with each other's balls somewhere else," she said coldly.

Cat and Maya quickly glanced at each other with their eyes fully widened. Cat silently mouthed *ho-ly shit,* and Maya mouthed *what the fuck* in return. Ruben forcefully rubbed his cheeks and eyes, and he breathed out heavily as his stress-relief massage extended down his dreads. The energy in the studio fell completely flat.

"All right, if you *really* want to be that way, then we'll leave. But there's another reason why I wanted Lin to be here. I wanna know if any of you have talked to Byrd lately."

"I emailed him the other day when we planned this session, but I didn't hear back from him," Thayer responded. "Why?"

"He's gone missing."

"He's probably just being a loner out in the wilderness. He'll show up soon."

"No, you don't understand. Reg has been looking around for him for over a month now. We looked into his bank accounts, and there's no history at all since he left. We got cops and Charlie's PI investigating, and even *they* are saying he vanished without a trace. Apparently, he might have some cash on him, and I'm about to talk with Charlie about all that later today."

"So, what're *we* supposed to do?" Thayer asked, irritated. "*We* don't know where he is, but if he's been gone all this time, why wait till now to tell us?"

"*Well*, that's true, there isn't much any of us can do. The main reason I'm telling you about Byrd *now* is that we got word that the newsies on the Big Island know he's disappeared, so the news is about to spread online any day."

27

J ust a few weeks later, "Chapters" was released as a Zenegades single and listened to on radio stations, podcasts, YouTube channels, streaming apps, and in headphones throughout the world. Although it undoubtedly fell within the heartbreak niche, it was uplifting enough to help remind listeners that they too could bravely step into their life's next chapters. It was only a single, but it was also a huge success that made everyone's hearts fracture ever so slightly. The only letdown was that no one was able to get in touch with Byrd to let him know about it, but they figured he'd show up eventually and enjoy the surprise. However, the entire Zenegades family knew Byrd wouldn't be pleasantly surprised when he heard about how Thayer spoke to Sky during the first recording session in the Manhattan studio.

Like any time the band released new music, they had a party. Although things were now much different in that department for Thayer, Charlie was able to come up with the sober-safe idea of having a small breakfast party at his buddy's apartment off Central Park West. It would just be them and a couple caterers, so it felt low-key enough to get together while also knowing that inevitable tension between Sky and Thayer would more than likely materialize. It was no secret that the conversation they'd had in the studio green room didn't go too smoothly, so Maya at least had peace of mind knowing that nothing at *her house* would be broken if shit hit the fan during the celebration. As usual, her intuition was guiding her perfectly.

When the band arrived at the swanky apartment building, the doorman led them to the elevator and pushed the top button before waving goodbye. The elevator glided up to the top of the high rise, where they were immediately met by a hallway of glass windows looking over Central Park and tons of skyscrapers. The massive roof-top balcony was just next to the elevator, and an elaborate spread of food trays, drinks, and a long table indicated this was where the party would be. They meandered around the apartment, took pictures of the cityscape views, and ate fruits and pastries for about twenty minutes. During that time, it became abundantly clear that Thayer was going to avoid Sky as much as possible.

"I'd like to make a toast," Charlie said, raising a glass of orange juice. "You guys created one hell of a single. It's connective, emotional, and you should be proud of its release." The small group gave a soft clap. "Now, all *this* is fine and dandy, but we also need to talk more about the fact that no one knows where Jimmy is," Charlie continued, almost immediately shifting the party mood to more of a serious meeting. "I know you guys aren't too worried about him, and to be honest, I think he's fine somewhere with that new girl of his. *But* the disappearance of a famous musician for over two months is too much of a good story to be ignored. I've gotten word from a source of mine that the media has been holding off on running with it, thinking that he'd have shown up by now, but they're more than likely going to blow the whole thing out of proportion given that he's now a *real renegade*, running away from his legal trouble in Aspen. It's too engaging and clickbaity, they love it, and at this point there's nothing we can do except brace for yet another shit storm. Okay? Everyone on the same page about Jimmy? *Good*, because now I need to know what the fuck is going on with you two," he said, pointing at Thayer and Sky.

"We're breaking up," Thayer said matter-of-factly.

"That's what I've heard, but I didn't hear why."

Everyone's jaws dropped slightly. They glanced at each other and whispered a few nothings in disbelief that no one had told him.

"We're breaking up because he cheated on me, *with a guy!*" Thayer loudly responded. No one said anything, and Charlie was surprised to the point where he didn't quite know what to say either.

"It's true, I'm bisexual. Okay? Can everyone *please* be happy that I'm finally coming out? And can you all just *please* give me some time in terms of how I want to come out publicly? This has been a *pretty tough time* for me too, ya know?" Sky said as tears started to well up in his eyes. "I know it was shitty of me to keep it a secret for so long, but I didn't want to mess things up between me and Thay, and honestly all of us. But I feel like I'm finally ready to come out, and I'm going to try my best to do so with pride, not shame."

"You already know how Cat and I feel, bro. We love you," Ruben chimed in.

"I know we haven't talked lately, Sky, but you should know that I'm really happy for you," Maya joined in. "*We all* understand how tough it's been for you to come out, even just to us, and we're here for you," she concluded as she turned to Thayer, tilted her head slightly, and raised her eyebrows.

"She's right, Sky. We've all been talking a lot lately, and I owe you an apology for how things went at the studio the other day. So, I'm *really* sorry, but I just … I'm happy for you to be coming out, and I get how tough all this is, considering how much our relationship was tied up with our music, but I just … I just don't know if I can stand up on a stage next to you and pretend like we're still in love. I just … I can't see myself living a lie just to save face for our fans. They at least deserve to know that we're no longer together," Thayer more calmly divulged as tears ran down her cheeks.

"Whoa, what the—?" Charlie couldn't quite comprehend. "Let's all just calm down a little bit. We don't need to tell *anyone* that you guys are breaking up. If you really want to move on from each other, then everyone will eventually get the picture when they see you with other people."

"Honestly, I agree with Thay," Sky replied. "It's never been our style to hide things from our fans, at least *until now* with Byrd going MIA and all, and I think that's one reason why they like us so much. If you're okay with it, Thay, I'm willing to go on the record for a public statement, or something like that."

Charlie silently stood in front of them and looked out at the million-dollar view. Within seconds, the rosy tint of his cheeks got darker as a rush of blood flowed to his head. The group began whispering to one another as they continued watching an already-psychotic man begin to go over the edge.

"No one ... and I mean every last one of you *motherfucking* imbeciles, is talking to the press without my permission. We can't let them roast us anymore!" he echoed out to the entire neighborhood. "I'm not going to deal with this *dumbass bullshit* from this group anymore. If any of you *punks* screw with your public image again, I'll take *everything* from you!"

"*Oh,* is that right? You're gonna take *everything* from us?" O'Donnell blurted out. "Let's get something straight right now, Charlie. We don't need you like *you think* we need you. We've been talking about going our own way for a while now, and Lin and I know what'll go down when we do that. I'm starting to think this is *exactly* what we should do!"

Charlie cackled at O'Donnell and showcased a prolonged smirk.

"*Oh,* you think *Lin* wants to go independent? *Well,* then tell me exactly why *Lin* emailed me recently about putting out a solo EP. Why would he do that if he wanted to *go his own way*? I'll tell you why: it's because Lin knows he'll do *great* as a solo artist if he tries. He's literally the only one of you all who has his head in the right place, but I want to be *crystal fucking clear* when I say this: if the Zenegades want to still be a thing a few years from now, you guys better start thinking about moving on from Jimmy."

"Oh, c'mon, Charlie! That's some bullshit, and you know it!" Thayer yelled.

"You guys don't *need* him," Charlie continued, completely ignoring her. "Think about it, Jimmy is *clearly* deranged. I mean, just look at the guy! He probably is gonna be in a *real* nuthouse soon, not like the place I sent you to," he said, looking directly at Thayer. "You guys know him better than I do, and you can't tell me he doesn't show signs of schizophrenia? He's off his *fucking rocker*! He could even be dead right now. No one knows, including all of you!"

"I don't know if he's straight schizo, but the dude does talk to himself a lot," Ruben said.

The rest of the group looked at each other in relative agreement, as well as shock, by the turn of events from what they thought was going to be a celebration of their new single. Charlie recognized this deflation in spirits and looked to pounce in the way he always knew worked well.

"Look, I know you guys are going through a lot right now, but you should just know that I'm only looking out for your best interests. We all want to know Jimmy is doing fine, and I got Dave, my private investigator, on the Big Island right now. He recently told me that he doesn't think Jimmy has gone too far."

"How *the fuck* are we supposed to know that?" O'Donnell called out, throwing Charlie off guard. "We talked to the banks just the other day, and we know something's up with how you paid Byrd recently. So, tell us, how much bloody cash did you give him, Charlie? How long is Byrd gonna be able to live without a trace, cuz of *you*?" he asked, now inching closer to Charlie, who was backing away toward the edge of the balcony. "Tell us, ya sonofabitch. Ten thousand? Twenty thousand? How much *fucking money* did you give Byrd?" he yelled as he grabbed Charlie by his suit and dangled him above Central Park West.

Charlie's sunglasses slid out of his chest pocket as O'Donnell clenched his throat as hard as he could, and everyone else was seriously freaking out at this point. Ruben and Sky tried pulling O'Donnell off Charlie, to no avail, because the more they touched O'Donnell, the further he extended Charlie's body closer to a deadly fall. If O'Donnell were to let go, Charlie would've smacked the sidewalk just like any other New York jumper. So, jostling O'Donnell's grip would've only made matters worse.

"How much money did you give him, Charlie?" he whispered as he constricted his clenching hands further against his throat.

All Charlie could get out as his breath started to leave him was a subtle *thirty*. O'Donnell lifted him back onto the balcony, and the party ended. Everyone started walking to the elevator, until Charlie yelled out, "Shankar is worried about you guys!"

No one responded as they left him alone on the swanky balcony.

28

Finding an apartment in Beijing was a lot easier than Lin expected, especially because his budget was inflated due to the exchange rate. Within a couple of weeks, they were able to shop in Shu's preferred neighborhood, which was the one near Zizhuyuan Park she already lived in, and purchase a one-bedroom unit. She was now living on the opposite side of Zizhuyuan Park, about ten stories above it, instead of right next to the street. For years, she would glance at those apartments while working in the park, just wondering what the view looked like up there. When they had a showing in the building, she immediately walked out to the balcony and dissected every detail of the stunning new perspective.

She could see the entirety of Zizhuyuan Park, with each small island poking itself above the circulating perimeter trail. The bamboo forests, ponds, and courtyards were off in the distance, but it was beyond the park that really took the balcony view to a whole new level. Instead of looking up at the imposing buildings above the park, she was now seeing over and beyond them. The entire neighborhood seemed like a massive valley of skyscrapers with a small river flowing between them, and beyond the nearest buildings were even larger high-rises with garden rooftops that could only be seen at the right angle. But the greatest aspect of the balcony view was by far the Yanshan Mountain Range, peacefully resting far beyond the city's rings, featuring towering peaks and a portion of the Great Wall.

It was far beyond anything she could've hoped to see from her home, so they immediately arranged to buy the apartment. Lin reassured Shu he'd only invest in a reasonable down payment as a gift and leave the monthly payments to her, but the truth was that he paid in full for her new home. They swiftly moved all her belongings, mainly because she didn't have much, and started shopping.

Lin took her to the Silk Market and all throughout the city to find art to put on her walls, furniture to fill the living room, and just about everything beyond the bare necessities she already owned. She would look at prices and neglect them as too expensive, and Lin consistently reminded her that she didn't need to worry about money any longer. Those expensive household products were relatively affordable, especially considering the exchange rate, but it became clearer with each home décor store that Shu had deep-seated difficulties when it came to spending money.

They eventually came to the needed compromises and fully furnished her new apartment. She even got her very first TV, but kept the old radio she liked to listen to every night. Lin tried to convince her to get a cell phone that could store all her music, but a home phone was enough for her. They ended up compromising on an old iPod they found in a market full of knockoff retail, and Lin helped her store music on it that included the Zenegades catalog. One thing Lin thought was inspiring about Shu's personality was that she didn't miss one day of work as a street sweeper while they coordinated her new apartment, and he was also especially impressed by her love of music and dancing. There were several moments when Lin would look down at Zizhuyuan Park from the apartment's balcony and see Shu picking up garbage or doing some other type of cleaning, and every time he saw her working, he'd notice that she'd be dancing to her new iPod's library.

After Lin helped Shu settle into her new place, he ended up staying much busier than he thought he would. He did end up reaching out to Le Qi, and he rehearsed with the Beijing Philharmonic one evening. He also kept himself thinking of fast, urban rhythms and slower, traditional Chinese melodies, and he experimented on how to blend the two of them together. Growing up playing traditional Chinese songs and living as an adult playing Zenegades songs made this merger of sounds more feasible, and he reached out again to Le Qi and inquired about recording studios. This led to a stretch of a request to Charlie, who ended up being the one who coordinated his studio time.

Lin initially decided that he wanted to create a thirty-minute EP, which would be divided into four violin sonatas. There was one song idea he wanted to title "Streets of Beijing" that would work best with support, and with Le Qi's help, he was able to coordinate a few musicians to join a recording session. Things were moving very quickly for him within the first two months of renting a small condo in Beijing, but everything seemed to move quickly in China. He ended up getting so excited about so many different things that he'd forget to call Maya or catch up with anyone back in America.

So in the ninth week of living in Beijing, he coordinated expedited consulate appointments in San Francisco for his American parents, bought them plane tickets, and arranged to have them stay in his bedroom while he slept on a pullout sofa. When he mentioned this idea to them on the phone, they figured he meant taking a flight in a month or so, but Lin ended up booking flights for six days later.

On the first night after Jacob and Leanne Rose's arrival, they all went to a casual family-style restaurant just a handful of blocks from Zizhuyuan Park. Shu recommended it as the place she only went to on very special occasions, but it wasn't fancy and was reasonably priced. Immediately upon entering the locale, it became obvious how each dish on the menu featured unique aromas only found in authentic Chinese cuisine. Elaborate combinations of shallots, steamed fish, sesame oil, roast duck, and countless other ingredients filled the large room. They sat in a booth featuring a centralized spinning wheel that quickly held several appetizers, and as one dish was finished, another one replaced it. Lin and Shu told Jacob and

Leanne about their recent adventures, including how they got to know one another by hanging out in the nearby park. Although the Roses only knew basic Mandarin, Lin was able to translate what Shu was trying to tell them when it was needed.

Lin explained that he was able to come up with a few instrumental songs and quickly get them recorded, and that he was becoming pleasantly surprised with how his first solo album, *Streets of Beijing*, was coming together. It was unlike anything he'd ever recorded before, at least professionally with the Zenegades, and it was both figuratively and literally a return to his creative roots.

Jacob and Leanne felt noticeably a bit uncomfortable throughout that meal, mainly because it was becoming clearer to them how Lin had not only found his biological mother, but was now beginning to reclaim his identity. Although they were always incredibly proud to have raised a talented musician and all-around righteous guy, the actual manifestation of the reality they'd always known in the back of their heads that whispered, *we're not technically his parents*, was still pretty difficult to swallow. When Lin candidly told them in English that he was going to give Shu 80 percent of his personal profits from *Streets of Beijing*, it was almost like he was saying *it's time for me to take care of my real mother from now on*.

As they walked along the sidewalk after dinner, Lin received a phone call from Maya. She had just gotten home from Charlie's debacle of a breakfast party and was adamant about getting a few explanations from him, even though Lin insisted several times that it wasn't the best time to talk. After about a minute, he decided to have the group sit on a bench in Zizhuyuan Park as he succumbed to Maya's demands. He also recognized how this conversation was a good moment to indirectly provide a few explanations to the Roses, so he started spinning the propellers on a highly pent-up vent.

"Look, that sounds like a really shitty party, and I know this is a tough time for everyone, but you need to know that I have to help her right now. She was living in a closet when I first got here, and now I feel obligated to make sure she doesn't need to sweep the city streets any longer. It's just taking a little longer than I thought to finish mastering.... How's everything going with my understudy? ... *Oh*, he's not so bad.... Well, it sounds like it'll be more than fine until I get back.... Yeah, things are going well. Jacob and Leanne are here with us tonight.... Yeah, I'm still learning *a lot* about her, and I get it that all this is getting in the way, but like I said, I just need to get her feet on the ground.... No, I haven't heard from him in a long time now, but I've been in contact with Reg, who seems to be freaking out looking for him.... Okay, let's talk more soon. I love you."

It was clear that Lin intentionally made sure Jacob and Leanne heard his end of the call, and although it brought a tear or two to their eyes, they silently nodded to each other, knowing that their wonder child was doing what was best for him.

On the bench's other armrest, Shu had no idea what the phone conversation was about. She patiently waited for Lin to finish talking while making sure no one in the park was littering. Although she wouldn't have said anything even if she did see someone litter, she figured she'd at least dispose of the trash properly.

Lin gave Jacob and Leanne another subtle heartache when he decided to go home with Shu and said he'd meet up with them later. Shu always went to bed early so she could wake up at the crack of dawn, so Lin handed the condo keys to Leanne and plugged in walking directions on her phone.

Upon arriving at Shu's new apartment, she wanted to know more about the English phone conversation he'd just had in the park. At first, he tried convincing her it was nothing important, but she knew that wasn't the truth. She requested that Lin tell her *the whole truth*, and Lin knew by the concentrating look in her tired eyes that he wouldn't be capable of lying. So, he did what he thought was most honorable for their budding relationship: reignite his vent propellers.

He mentioned he didn't want her to worry about money any longer, and that he was going to help her as much as he could. He explained his plans to provide her with money from the music he was currently working on, and how he was more than confident it would help support her foreseeable future. He said he didn't want her to clean the streets anymore, and that it was much too difficult for her to do every day. Lin wanted her to consider going to the nearby university and learning something new that she was interested in, and that was when Shu cut him off with a swift wave of her hand.

"I enjoy my job," she responded in Mandarin. "Some days are harder than others, but they take it easy on me because I am an old lady. I love the new home you have given me, and I will always be grateful for your help. But you must know, I would not have stayed in my old home for so many years if I did not like it, and I would have quit my job a long time ago if I did not like it. It is a great blessing of my life to have met my son, but some things should stay the same as they were before we met."

She spoke slowly to make sure he understood as many words as possible, and her sheer honesty struck him unexpectedly. He hadn't thought of the possibility that Shu was genuinely happy with her life prior to his arrival, and he essentially assumed that everything he could provide her would be better than what she had.

"You're right," Lin softly responded. "I thought my fame and money could help make your life better, but I see now that I was wrong to think all these material things would make you *truly* happier," he continued as he brushed his hands against Shu's new sofa. "I feel like I've changed since we met, and now I remember why I love playing music so much. Maybe I've made too much money in recent years to see what this art *actually* gives me, because it's more than just a job, and I now see how you feel the same way about your work, too. But maybe it's about time for me to go back to America."

There was a moment of silence between them, and Shu decided it was time to prepare for bed and the next day's work ahead of her. She merely said, "my son is always welcome in my home," as she left the living room and went into her bathroom.

Lin figured he'd leave and meet up with Jacob and Leanne, but he needed a few minutes to think things over. He decided to step outside onto Shu's balcony and collect his thoughts while she got ready to sleep. He sat down on her new bamboo recliner and looked out at the expansive view of Beijing as he listened to the ceaseless chattering of the city. As he tuned into the clamoring of cars zooming along a nearby beltway, he couldn't help but realize just how long it had been since he'd left a major city for a significant amount of time. It had been several weeks since he and Maya left the urban glory of London for the English countryside, and he imagined those bright-green fields as they zoomed past his passenger window. Even then during that beautiful road trip with Roarkey, he was only back in Byrd Land for a few days at most. He began imagining himself on a remote hiking trail with Byrd leading the way, completely engulfed by a forest's canopy and the notion of *where to next?*

His mind raced away from the night-lit cityscape for a couple of minutes, until he received an alert on his phone. He opened it and saw an email from Reg that was logged in at 3 a.m. of that same day.

Hey Lin,

We need to talk. Some serious stuff is going down out here, and it looks like we need your help.

Dave finally got a lead on Byrd. He said he's somewhere on the island, and that those folks down in Waipio know exactly where he is but aren't saying nothing to no one.

What Dave said is that they actually will talk if more members of the band show up, so he asked me to ask you if you would come out here. He said he also asked Shankar to come out because apparently they're like in love with him or something. And check this out: the guy bought a plane ticket for TOMORROW and wants me to keep him company at the farm!

I know you're busy out there with your mom and all, but I don't want to be the only one from the crew here with just Shankar. Between you and me, those Speedos he sometimes likes to wear are way too skimpy! I also just talked to Maya and she seemed really pissed about some shit that went down with Charlie in NYC. She also said that Thayer and Ruben will be playing with her at Blue Queen for the next few weeks, Sky is checking into rehab to get some help with his coke problem, and O'Donnell is helping his friend's band on a small UK tour that won't end unt l next month.

I don't know who else can help us find him, and who knows if they'll even listen to Shankar and me. Who knows if Shankar and me will even be able get our old asses to wherever the hell Byrd's hiding!

Let me know if you can come out here.

Reg

29

few days after Reg's email, Lin patiently waited over twenty-two hours through two connections until landing at the Big Island's largest airport, the Ellison Onizuka Kona International Airport at Keahole. He glanced out his oval window at the lava-fielded coastline that surrounded the airport's only runway. It had been several months, but those massive lava rocks were his official sign that he was back in Byrd Land.

He always enjoyed landing in Kona because the passengers would step off the plane and onto the runway, but this time it was raining so hard that he was fully soaked by the time he got underneath the open-air terminal's roof. He retrieved his luggage and went to the entrance of the airport, where Reg was waiting for him in Byrd's vintage pickup truck. As they meandered toward Byrd's farm around highway 11's winding curves, Reg tried to keep the mood light by bragging about how sweet the living had been in paradise.

When they made it to Byrd's farm, they found Shankar sitting in a rocking chair, watching the rainfall. He quickly made his way over to greet Lin at the sight of the truck, and he was in much more somber spirits than Reg. He explained all his worries about Byrd's health and the potentially dangerous terrain that hid him from the outside world, but he was just as quick to explain how nice it was to meet up in Hawaii and maybe find Byrd with the help of Charlie's PI, Dave.

Dave exited the homestead after recognizing the outdoor

commotion as Lin's long-awaited arrival, and his cliché Hawaiian tourist ensemble made his presence immediately known: socks with sandals, tight khaki shorts, a technicolor Hawaiian button-down on top of a plain-white undershirt, and cheesy pink sunglasses above a strawberry-blond goatee and below a full-brim straw hat. The neon-pink fanny pack clicked onto the side of his waist was the icing on the cake to any and all of his first impressions, particularly those involving missing celebrities. As he walked out into the rain toward Lin, there was no stopping Lin from thinking, *This is the guy that helped me find Shu?*

"Lin, it's a pleasure to finally meet you. I'm Dave Fieldcrest," he said, firmly shaking Lin's hand. "How's everything going with your mom? I heard that you moved her into a new apartment, so good for both of you. From what I gathered, her old place was pretty tiny."

"Yeah, she seems to like her new home, mainly because it's really close to her old one! Thank you again for helping me find her, Mr. Fieldcrest. It means so much to me to have met her, and now be able to help her out."

"No problem. This is what I do, and call me Dave," he replied as they walked back to the porch's shelter. He pulled out an extra-long piece of gum from his fanny pack and began chewing it as he assumed his position in a wooden rocking chair. "*All right,* well now it's time for you to repay the favor, because I need *your help* finding James Byrd. Are you prepared to get caught up on the loop with the case's latest developments?"

"Sure."

"Great! Well, as you may know, James left this exact spot a little over three months ago, and there has been absolutely no activity within his bank accounts since then. However, we know because of Reg that he left with a guitar case, and we're *very* confident that this guitar case had over thirty thousand dollars in cash in it, which was given to him by my boss, Charlie Dyceman, just a handful of days before he got his DUI. That kind of dough would've made it possible to leave the island undetected, *but* we've now recently been informed that James is more than likely still here and healthy."

"We're not sure, though," Shankar chimed in.

"That's right. We aren't 100 percent sure if James is still on the island. What we *do know* is that there's another tip to be found over at that Zenegade Commune deep in the Waipio Valley."

"Do they know where Byrd is?" Lin asked.

"Yes. We believe they do, in fact, know where he's been this whole time. I went down there a while ago to get some information, and I tried playing nice and pretended like I was interested in joining their cute cult, but they saw straight through me once I started asking about James. So, I ended up going down there again and bluntly offered five thousand dollars to anyone who could give me information about his whereabouts. And sure enough, after waiting every night in a hotel bar in Honokaa for about two weeks, one of the hippies showed up and was willing to talk."

"And they told you they'd be real if more band members showed up," Lin gathered.

"Yes, that's right! So, that's why you're here now, and we also have Shankar here because apparently, the head of the commune, this local guy who goes by Raymundo, is pretty much obsessed with Shankar. They met each other in Aspen earlier this summer, so we think he'll behave himself a little better if Shankar is there. The tough part about this plan is that it's going to have to be just you three, due to a whole bunch of drama and busy schedules going on with everyone else. You guys are like our last hope in finding James anytime soon. And hey, it's like you can pay me back for finding your mom in China!" They relaxed at the farm for the rest of the rainy afternoon, as Dave explained how they needed to conserve as much energy as possible. The plan was to drive to the Waipio Valley the next morning.

Things didn't go quite as planned the next day, basically because everyone ended up sleeping in after binge drinking the previous night. Each of them had too many good stories to tell, so a late night was inevitable.

Reg had gotten used to hanging out with Dave, due to the agreement they made to let him sleep in one of the farm's empty cabins, where they'd both frequently spend the night and help Hani take care of the neglected farm during the day. After a few Hawaiian martinis, Dave was always more than willing to discuss the financial hole he'd dug himself into throughout the process of trying to find Byrd. Although there was a hefty reward from Charlie if he was able to safely bring him back to civilization, Dave's personal budget had now been stretched thin. So, Reg offering him free lodging helped keep costs from piling up, and it also formed the foundations of an unusual friendship.

Although Reg and Dave were polar opposites, they got along swimmingly. Whereas Reg would say anything and everything whenever he wanted, Dave was slightly more reserved; and whereas Dave would wear just about anything and everything as a part of his personal Hawaiian style, Reg was more reserved with his wardrobe. They started hanging out with each other all the time, initially because Reg thought Byrd might show up at one of their favorite scuba spots around the island. But being on Byrd's boat together would typically lead to copious amounts of drinking and mucking about, and it became crystal clear after the first month of the search that the only way to find Byrd was through a tip from the Waipio Commune. The entire group of about two dozen hippies had been unwilling to support the search for Byrd in any way, and they gave Dave the unilateral impression that they had no idea where in the world he and Jane could be. So things were starting to get real when they figured out how to get some real answers with the help of Lin and Shankar, and when Reg and Dave woke up hung over that morning, it felt like a quirky era in their adult lives was coming to an end.

It was a very slow morning, featuring a few visits to the communal bathroom from Shankar and Lin, who were flushing out their rum-filled bowels. Reg blended up some helpful smoothies for everyone, but their collective hangovers made actual cooking out of the question. They ended up eating breakfast underneath an outdoor roof at a nearby L&L while waiting out a torrential rainstorm, and the massive Hawaiian breakfast platters provided what they didn't realize would end up being much-needed calories.

They eventually made it to the Waipio Valley's cliffside entrance just before 2 p.m., but the rain had ended, and the sun was trying to peek itself out through a sea of breaking clouds. Showing up late worked out for them, because the steep road that led down to the valley floor had been flooding and was too dangerous to go down until the rain subsided. Byrd's pickup handled mud relatively well, but there were several moments, even at the very beginning of the valley's roads, when Reg thought he was definitely going to get stuck. Four guys in an old truck were a lot of weight for any road, but descending into Waipio that day was abnormally treacherous due to potential rockslides, flash floods, and slick, muddy roads. All of them had been to Waipio before, but it was Shankar and Lin's first time seeing this remote part of the Big Island during a storm cycle.

Mountainous cliffs and waterfalls butting up against a beautiful black-sand beach were what brought people to Waipio, but going into the actual neighborhood and seeing the many farming properties was an entirely different natural beauty to behold. Every farm in Waipio was full of fruits, taro, and all sorts of produce.

"The royal Hawaiians once lived in this area and originally developed all these farms," Dave said from the passenger seat. "Apparently, they also did the original construction of the path we're currently on as well."

The Waipio Valley Road was easy for the truck to handle, but things started to get messy when the pavement turned to dirt. Thick, volcanic mud smeared the windows with every touch of the accelerator, and Reg repeatedly said, "We're stuck," as he cranked it out of slippery holes and large pools of rainwater.

They continued puttering past farms separated by lush rainforest, and eventually came to a crossing over the Wailoa Stream that was faster than usual due to the recent rains. Reg handled the raging river just fine, but the flat road after the crossing was beyond drivable. The tires kept slipping out, so the only way to go forward was to swerve their momentum as they hugged themselves between a crop field and a drop-off above the stream. As the road veered away from the water, the mud only got worse, and it became apparent how the truck would get unbudgeable if it went any further. So, Dave told Reg, Shankar, and Lin to hike the rest of the way and let him know when they were heading back to the stream crossing they'd just passed. To make sure they could plan out the rendezvous accordingly, Dave gave them a walkie-talkie that could reach him several miles away at the beach. Dave figured he could chill out on the now-sunny black sand while waiting to hear back from them, and he was far too blinded by relaxation to realize how big of a mistake the intercom was.

The sounds of Byrd's truck faded away as Reg, Lin, and Shankar stepped along the muddy path with just the clothes on their backs and a tiny backpack that enclosed a three-liter bladder, six Spam musubis, and a walkie-talkie that looked like it came from the same era as Dave's fanny pack. The further they walked along the valley floor, the more it seemed as if they'd gone back in time due to the older, more dilapidated appearances of the farm buildings. The only directions Dave provided were to continue walking down the road past a handful of farms until coming up to another crossing, and to then cross the stream again and keep walking until seeing a path going uphill. Go up the steep hill, and you'll know when you're there.

Dave reassured them that they were only a couple more miles from the commune, but the muddy road made any distance seem much further than it actually was, which was 3.2 miles. Lin glanced at his wristwatch at 4:38 p.m. when they arrived at the next stream crossing, and they were now nearly ten miles into the depths of the valley. The best and worst thing the three of them did that day was wear sandals, which was Dave's specific advice due to the width and speed of the second crossing being too much for the truck to handle, and subsequently requiring them to wade across it. Lin led the way as he plunged each step below the current's surface to maintain balance, Reg successfully followed right behind him, and Shankar ended up slipping and finishing the stream crossing on all fours.

Only five more minutes of walking passed by before they saw a driveway that switch-backed up a steep hill for a few hundred feet. They trudged up the slippery switchbacks and admired the massive roots jutting out from the old-growth trees, which were boasting an extra shimmer following the morning's showers. When they reached the top of the hill, everything opened up and blatantly suggested that they were *there*.

A handful of shacklike buildings dotted the corners of a flat field that looked somewhat like a public park with a volleyball net, picnic tables, and a large fire pit surrounded by long, wooden benches. The distinctive proof that they'd made it to the commune and not some random park in the woods came in the dozens of tents in a corner of the field, which indicated how many people lived there. Each of the commune's actual buildings appeared to be handmade and barely holding their rusty tin roofs and peeling wooden sidings together, but it was easier to see just how well organized the entire property was at a closer glance. They had countless wild fruit trees beyond the open field, an elaborate veggie garden, three semi-private solar shower partitions, a sheltered common area with more picnic tables, seven ten-gallon jugs of water rested up against a shack, and a chicken coop. There were also a few makeshift bamboo huts scattered throughout the adjacent forest, and Shankar saw a little bit of his own mountain ranch out there in the Waipio Rainforest.

The largest of the structures was clearly a dining hall area where cooking and other communal activities took place underneath an open roof, and the surrounding structures were sleeping quarters and an outhouse. They even parked their vehicles in an organized fashion in the more obscure corner of the field, and Lin recognized how the number of cars didn't come close to matching the larger number of people.

There were well over two-dozen people scattered around the property doing some kind of activity, and all of them were teenagers or twenty-somethings. Some of them were carrying large baskets of wet clothes or collecting fruits into smaller bins, but most of them were lounging and beginning to stretch their legs after an afternoon nap. It had become a lazy day for the vast majority of the Waipio community, which was why no one cared to notice Reg, Lin and Shankar until they made their way to the dining hall. There were about a dozen people chatting while sitting on handmade picnic tables, and the entire room went silent when they entered through the beaded threshold. All of them knew exactly who they were, but the only person the three of them recognized was Meryl Martinez.

She still had the same hopeful glimmer behind her now-wilder eyes like she did those many years ago as a social butterfly in Berkeley, but now she appeared to be more content in disconnecting herself from the world's extroverted norms. She looked similar to the other kids in the dining hall in how she was boasting hair and skin that looked like it hadn't been washed in several days, and the not-so-subtle soil aesthetics all over her sleeveless shirt and khaki shorts were an indication as to just how much she embraced their simplistic lifestyle. Meryl wasn't just talking about free love and living life unconventionally from the safe confides of her Bay Area rental any longer, she was now living it deep within the Hawaiian jungle.

With a massive smile, she stood up and welcomed Reg, Lin, and Shankar to the community's humble home before needlessly introducing them to the small crowd. An awkward silence ensued as everyone in the dining hall understood the reasoning behind their unexpected visit, so Meryl was wise to catch the drift and escort them to a part of the property where they could be alone. She gave them a quick tour of the commune that lasted a few minutes and ended at a tiny bamboo cabin in the woods.

"Ray?" she asked like a mother checking in on a toddler. "We have some special guests here who just arrived."

Whispers and yawns came from the bamboo hut, and an incredibly beautiful young woman opened the handmade door about a minute later. Her dark-brown hair was tightly braided into cornrows as if she were Bo Derek in *10*, and her fine mocha complexion didn't hurt her resemblance to a eighties movie star either. She was far too young to even know about Bo Derek's acting career, and when she smiled at Lin, wearing a see-through shawl and a bikini, he guessed her age to be around twenty-two. She didn't say anything as she slipped her sandals on and sashayed through a cluster of guava trees while making her way toward a fast-flowing creek, which was making its way down to the Wailoa Stream.

Another few seconds passed until Ray, aka Raymundo, emerged from the hut. He was already a big guy to begin with, but he seemed massive when he first poked his head out of the bamboo building and stood up higher than the doorway. His long, black hair was dirty with countless specks of sand, and his barely-buttoned shirt exposed his broad chest. The moment he saw who his special guests were, his face lit up with enthusiasm. Seeing famous musicians like Lin and Reg show up at his door was beyond an exciting experience, but he was also excited to see Shankar in front of him at *his* dream ranch. He knew this was his chance to walk the talk and literally show Shankar how the Zenegade Ranch inspired him to set up shop in the Waipio Valley.

Without any hesitations, Ray continued the tour Meryl had previously started as he divulged his investment origin story that was largely inspired by the Zenegades. He bragged about how the Hawaiian aristocracy lived in those hills for centuries, and how Waipio farmland was some of the best in the entire world. He showed them a series of solar panels connected to a complex electrical system, which was used for basic household appliances and tech device charging. He also showed them a satellite dish and modem that provided a WiFi connection for many residents who remotely worked *real jobs*. The homemade smokehouse was one of Ray's favorite features of the property, and he explained how they'd often smoke wild boar meat that they bow hunted for in the deepest caverns of the valley.

He led them back to a fast-flowing creek and showed them an on-demand water filtration system that pushed creek water through resin beads, which effectively collected and dumped out any impurities. He showed them the pit latrine outhouses, and pointed out how his cleaning solutions and tablets would keep odors at bay. They walked through the open field to the tents and parking area, where he showed them four trucks full of trash bags that were prepped for a dump trip to Honokaa. He clearly wanted to display how he was modernizing wilderness living, and the whole tour seemed like an elaborate way to showcase his sustainability within an indirect attempt to justify the commune altogether. He then made a loud slapping sound by extended his arms out and releasing them to his hips as if to say *and that's it,* and Shankar was undoubtedly impressed by all of it.

Although Shankar's sex life had slightly improved since building the Zenegade Ranch, there were no women like the one who walked out of Ray's cabin who even looked in his direction. He was so thoroughly enamored by Ray's commune to the point that he'd temporarily forgotten why they'd hiked miles along the valley floor to be there, but Ray didn't lose sight of the obvious reason why they'd shown up to his wilderness property. It just made sense to show them around prior to getting down to business, which was why he ushered them into his hut after finishing the tour, so they could talk privately.

"Look, we all know why you guys are here," he said as they sat down on neon-orange flower-shaped cushions. "What you should know is that Byrd is perfectly fine and healthy and that you have no reason to worry about him."

"We want to know where he is so we can go talk to him," Lin said in an effort to interrupt Ray's rambling. Ray poured a cup of water for himself and took a prolonged gulp, until the cup was empty.

"I can't just tell you where he is and let you go off on your own."

"Why not?"

"Because it's too dangerous. If you don't know exactly what you're doing, you can get yourself killed."

"He must be way out there," Shankar chimed in.

"He *is* way out there, but I'll tell you what: I'll guide you to where he is, so everything is safe. I was planning on going out to see them within the next few days anyways, because we know they need supplies. The recent rains have been holding us back from doing a lot of stuff lately because the road has been too muddy to leave, and apparently the waves have been massive, but we'll head out tomorrow with all the gear we'll need."

"What kind of gear will we need?" Reg asked.

"Nothing too serious. *Oh*, that reminds me. Do you guys have any phones or communication devices on you?"

They explained how they had cell phones on them, and Ray politely asked to pull them out. When they reached toward the backpack, Ray less politely asked if he could look through it. That was when things started to get awkward, because it was becoming increasingly clear that it was Ray's way or the highway. So, Lin handed him the backpack, which he opened and found the walkie-talkie within. He nodded for a few seconds as he examined the walkie, now starting to realize the full parameters of the situation.

"Does this belong to the cops, or that *haole* who wears a pink fanny pack?" he asked them, which resulted in slight nods to the latter. "What's his name again?"

"Dave," Reg responded, now ready to spill the beans. "He made us bring that with us so we could tell him when we got back to the first river crossing on the road. Our truck couldn't make it much further than there, because of the mud."

Ray didn't acknowledge Reg's confession. He turned the walkie on and set it at a high volume.

"Hello, Dave. Do you copy?"

"Yes, I copy. I'm still on the beach. Are you guys at the river crossing?"

"No, Dave. This is Ray. Lin, Reg, and Shankar are here with me. I'm going to be brief and clear with you, Dave. They aren't going home with you tonight. They are staying here with us indefinitely until we get some of the answers you're looking for. If we see you or any police anywhere in the valley over the next few days, you'll have much bigger issues to deal with. Do you copy, Dave?"

There was silence for a moment, and then, "Copy that," from the walkie.

"Good. Now I want you to leave the valley and go wherever the fuck you've been staying lately. I will personally reach out to you via this channel when it's time for you to come back here and pick these guys up, but that'll be at least three days from now. Copy?"

"Copy ... but Ray, can I ask you a few questions really quickly?" Dave asked, which led Ray to turn the walkie off.

They looked at each other in silence for a moment, not knowing what to say, until Ray once again took the reins over the situation.

"I'll give your phones back once I get Byrd's permission. Let's go tell Meryl we're heading out tomorrow. She'll be coming with us, and she'll also get you guys set up in a tent so you can get some rest tonight. We've got a long ways to go, and it's probably going to rain a lot more."

30

hen the sun's first rays peeked over the Pacific and into the
east-facing Waipio Valley the next morning, Ray woke Lin,
Reg, and Shankar, asking them to be quiet so they didn't
wake up the roughly two dozen tents scattered throughout
the open field. They gently broke down their borrowed three-person
tent and ventured toward the dining hall to satiate their noticeably
loud, grumbling bellies.

The trio also happened to arrive at the commune at a particularly
inopportune time, because the community was on the last legs of its
food supply. Besides the boar jerky remnants that were hunted for
weeks earlier, the previous night's protein was in the form of dehydrated soups. Ray typically put out a much better spread, but the
rain over the past week had been relentless, to the point that they
couldn't risk getting a truck stuck in the road's thick mud, and the
unexpected *special guest* arrival elicited a collective understanding
that Byrd and Jane would be provided the last sets of dehydrated
meals. While everyone was put to bed early by a downpour, Ray and
Meryl had to come up with some real plans to prepare for a few
tough decisions. It was decided that they didn't have any choice but
to risk the road's conditions, and a morning caravan was in order.

So, any kind of quiet sunrise awakening was not going to happen,
as the other members of the caravan started waking up throughout
the field, which led to the entire campground waking up a lot earlier
than usual. Before Lin could even finish packing up the tent, he had

someone helping him get his stuff together for the big day ahead. By the time Shankar got out of the latrine, Meryl was preparing a breakfast of fresh fruit and fiber bars. As Reg meandered by the dining tables, the young woman from Ray's hut emerged from the pantry and gave him a new-day kiss on both cheeks. There hadn't been a sunny morning in several days, but Ray was still hammering it through the caravan's heads how they needed to get going before any morning rains added an extra-slippery layer to the waterlogged valley floor.

After they finished eating breakfast at one of the makeshift picnic tables, they were brought to a storage shed full of hunting supplies and hiking gear. There Meryl gave them extra backpacks, a water filter, dehydrated meal packages, trekking poles, fuel canisters, as well as other more obscure supplies like reef-safe sunscreen, a thin emergency rope, and hygienic products that included toothpaste, deodorant, topical skin creams, and antibiotic pills. Meryl began strapping a violin case to the outside of one of the backpacks, which surprised Lin and made him question why she was adding on unnecessary weight to an already-heavy load.

"He misses playing with you," she responded, and when Shankar asked why they needed to carry such heavy backpacks, she simply said, "They requested more supplies, and we haven't been able to get to them because of the storms, so you guys are actually doing us a big favor by bringing this stuff out to them."

The caravan left the property at 8 a.m., and the depths of their tire tracks made it immediately seem like the carpool lane was a big mistake. All four of the trucks were swerving back and forth as they trudged through the mud in an attempt to maintain momentum, and by the time they'd made it back to the area near the first stream crossing, Ray had winched two of the smaller trucks out of pesky holes. Within only a few miles of the commune, Ray scrapped the whole idea and made the executive decision that it was best for everyone to continue on foot to do whatever was needed of them. This meant that he, Meryl, Shankar, Reg, and Lin would split up from everyone else at the mouth of the valley and walk toward the beach, while the rest of the caravan hiked up the steep, paved road toward Honokaa.

After they passed by the many Waipio farms and made it to the junction in the road almost two hours later, Shankar, Reg, and Lin weren't so sure about this *big favor* they were doing. Each of them was carrying around twenty pounds on their backs, and their sandals weren't exactly the right footwear for walking along muddy roads. What they didn't realize was that those first few unexpected miles down the Waipio Valley Road were just the very beginning of their day.

Ray guided the way to the famous beach, which was starting to fill up with its daily influx of tourists, and they followed his massive boot prints in the wet sand to a raging river that butted up against the shore break. The tall waves were propagating into a swell, so the fast-flowing river mouth was fluctuating with the ebbs and flows of each Hawaiian roller. They decided they'd walk up the river about a couple hundred feet and cross in a spot where a long, flimsy rope hung in the air over a calmer section of the Wailoa Stream's grand finale. This crossing was usually dangerous enough to keep tourists away, so there was no one further down the beach once they got to the other side. Ray, Reg, Meryl, and Lin made it across just fine, but the thigh-high water made things more difficult for Shankar, who ended up soaking his backpack and sleeping bag.

Shankar's extra moisture weight quickly became a nuisance once they made it to the other valley wall, where they gained over a thousand feet of elevation within less than a mile of trail. Each of them gasped for breath as they tried to keep their balance along the slippery, fifty-degree single track that brushed up against deadly dropoffs, and it was obvious that any misstep would potentially be disastrous. Ray kept leading the way as views of several distant waterfalls became clearer, and when they finally got to the top of the cliff, they were officially turning into the depths of the Kohala Forest Reserve.

The group hiked through a series of lush canyons full of tropical foliage and rushing streams as they quietly listened to ceaseless bird sounds in the canopy. The conditions only got muddier and more treacherous as they got deeper into the trail, and Shankar's sandals weren't holding up. He periodically mentioned how he could feel blisters forming, and he was limping with each step by the fifth stream crossing. Lin and Reg held on to him as they came upon the next few crossings featuring nearly flooding rapids, and it seemed as though the more beautiful the forest became, the more dangerous it was to keep going. The combination of slippery conditions, heavy packs, and inadequate footwear made maintaining traction extremely demanding, and it only got worse around noon when it started to storm.

They each had a jacket and fly for their packs, so the afternoon rainfall initially felt more like a much-needed shower than anything else. But after another hour of struggling with each step, they all required a break. They had hiked over fourteen miles by the time they'd arrived at a random shelter, where they took off their packs and relaxed at a few picnic tables. Shankar crawled into his sleeping bag on top of a table and tried to catch his breath as his body heat fluctuated, and Meryl ventured back out into the forest as they wondered why she'd want more of the rain when being under a dry roof felt so relaxing. When she returned with her pockets full of fresh guavas, they snacked on the fruit and slowly closed their eyes as the rhythm of the rain put them all to sleep.

The storm came to an end around two hours later, and by then they were feeling much drier and more energized after napping on top of picnic tables in their sleeping bags. It was a blessing to take an extended break at that point in the trail, because they were approaching a more dangerous portion of the route: the Waimanu Valley wall. The mud seeping through Shankar's sandals worked like a natural bandage and alleviated some pain, but he still struggled with each step while maintaining the footwork he needed to get down the precipice. The clearing views off in the distance now featured a series of gargantuan waterfalls that seemingly began in the dissipating clouds atop a mountainside, and below the falls was untamed rainforest next to a wide-open marshland. To their right was the ocean rippling its way toward a black-sand beach well over a thousand feet below them, and a rainbow just off the coast was a hopeful beacon encouraging them closer to the end of an excruciatingly long day. Although there was no denying the Kohala Forest's utopian beauty, reaching the remote Waimanu Valley made them feel as if they were entering into a true paradise.

Actually arriving on the valley floor in Waimanu came with a physically demanding price. They had to wait multiple times to let Shankar catch his breath and rest his knees due to the slippery path, and they'd soak in the scenery for a moment while he regained his strength by watching the graceful cascades fall down the distant mountainside. Each step became a searing abrasion as Shankar's blisters opened further, and they weren't in the best place to be limping. Lin and Reg also lost their footing and slipped a few times in the mud, but the group eventually made it down the switchbacks and was on the valley floor after an hour of sidestepping. There was then one final entry fee in the form of a stream crossing that featured hip-high floodwaters. Although the rinse felt great after drenching their lower bodies in mud, the intensity of that final stretch had them ready for yet another necessary rest.

The five of them were now in a public campground that hosted about a dozen campsites along the beach, but they were completely alone. No one wanted to make the long journey out there in the storm, and they only passed one hiker going in the opposite direction at the beginning of the day. They decided to put their packs down at an opening where they could look out across the flat marsh that led to the closest waterfall doing its majestic thing. Even though it was a brute because of just how fast the water fell freely for hundreds of feet, it didn't appear all that daunting from about a mile away. They couldn't hear its beastly roar, so it merely looked like a small sliver of moving whitewater among the abundant foliage.

None of them needed to express it, but this beach was the most glorious place that Lin, Reg, and Shankar had ever been in their lives. Lin had a feeling Byrd was hiding out in a beautiful place, but he had no idea just how far this journey's manifestation of Byrd

Land would go. But if anywhere was Byrd Land on the Big Island, he now figured it was out there in Waimanu.

While they rested their legs and soaked in the hard-earned view, Ray was busy looking for tasty treats in a nearby coconut tree. He took his boots off for more traction and crawled his way up the skinny trunk, until he was within reach of over a dozen coconuts. He called for Meryl to be his catcher and severed the stems off with a collapsible serrated knife. Once he'd get one free, he'd toss it down about twenty feet to her, and she caught one after another until they had enough at their disposal for a five-person luau.

There was only one thing that could make the view of the valley floor better, and it was coconut water. Each of them slurped vigorously and replenished themselves with the tropical nutrients, and Ray decided to unfold their next moves once they'd each taken a handful of sips.

"We'll have to rest here for the night," he declared.

"Why? How much further is he?" Lin asked while looking into the valley.

"He's *very* close. Don't worry, we're almost there," Meryl responded. "The reason why we should stop here is, first of all, I think it's safe to say we're all beat to palm tree pulp."

"*Sure are!*" Shankar interjected.

"But the more important reason why we have to sleep here is because we can't get there while the tide is coming up," Ray clarified. "If we went to see them now, we'd *definitely* get swept out to sea."

The next morning, Ray woke them all up in time to walk out to the beach and watch the sunrise. The massive valley walls reflected a golden hue in the morning light, and the waves were much calmer than the previous day. Ray pointed out to the rocky north end of the beach that led to a point in the opposite direction from which they'd come. "That's where we're going."

They went back to their campsite and packed their things in

preparation for another weighted walk. They'd brought some topical cream to help Shankar's blisters, but he still winced as he put his sandals on and began reapplying pressure to his feet and knees.

Ray steered them across the Waimanu Bay's black sands until they were just underneath the north end's towering cliffs, where they began stepping over rocks covered in crabs, seaweed, and all sorts of bugs. The tide was as low as it was going to get, but the waves were still crashing up against the foreshore and spraying them with a morning mist. They used the vertical cliff to their left-hand side to maintain their balance as they crawled their way around the rugged shore's bend, until they entered a forested peninsula. There were now no more established hiking trails, just a slightly trodden footpath hidden within the thriving greenery. Lin, Reg, and Shankar were shocked by how Ray and Meryl were figuring the way through the trees once the path had disappeared, but they eventually noticed how every now and again there would be marked a tree with a tiny X cut into the bark. After more than thirty minutes of deciphering which of the countless trees delineated the makeshift path, they arrived at another rocky beach. This beach featured a towering waterfall that fell onto the shore from a stream-made crack, which emerged from a stretch of sea cliffs that extended as far as they could see.

"We're coming up to the gnarly part we couldn't do at high tide!" Ray yelled out over the cascading water and crashing waves. "We have to cross up there in between the breakers!" he continued, while pointing at a daunting area that separated them from the next peninsula.

Seeing the waves slam against the rocks every fifteen seconds or so made Lin, Reg, and Shankar wonder just how dangerous this place was during high tide, because crossing this stretch during low tide was also not an easy feat. The sea foam lingered on the scree as each wave temporarily receded, and Meryl warned them to watch their steps, as slipping could be problematic. It was the type of moment when there was no turning back, being so close yet so far, and the marked tree just beyond the wet rocks helped make the crossing seem a little more manageable. Safety was only about fifty feet from where they were standing, but the rocks were slick, and only a handful of seconds separated each wave that blasted the cliff and everything else in its path. There was no time to make any mistakes, and they naively decided to all go at the same time.

They watched several waves come and go, to get one last idea as to how long they had to get across the rocks, until Ray said he was ready as the last preliminary wave collided with the cliff. He swiftly stepped into the last inches of receding water and began the passage across the slippery rocks, and they followed behind him with Shankar as the caboose. Ray, Meryl, Lin and Reg were nimble enough to recognize which rocks were best to avoid, but Shankar was considerably slower. He could barely get any grip with his now-tattered sandals, so he crouched down onto his hands and began cat crawling across the rocks as fast as he could. The rest of the group was now safe on the other side, and they glanced out and noticed a large wave curling about sixty feet away.

"Hurry! The next wave is coming in!" Ray yelled to Shankar, who still had about halfway to go.

Shankar looked out at the wave barreling toward him and remained still like a mussel attached to its substrate, and Lin raced back out onto the rocks without any hesitation and reached his arm out. Still on all fours, Shankar grabbed onto Lin's forearm, and Lin pulled him as fast as he could. But what Lin forgot to keep in mind was his own footing as he backed himself up while facing Shankar, and just as he was about to slip, he felt a force from behind him that lifted him completely off his feet. It was Reg's arms wrapped around his shoulders, and as Reg pulled Lin, Lin pulled Shankar. They fell onto dry rocks in unison as the wave hurtled into the cliff, and it took them a couple minutes to catch their breath and soak in the close call's gravity.

Another tree-marked path guided the group into an overgrown forest full of bulky koa and twisting banyan trees, as well as an endless number of vines. The unfrequented path became more difficult to move through as they ventured further into the woods, until they arrived at an incredibly beautiful location: a slightly shaded opening that featured dwarf fruit trees lined in perfect rows. Avocados, guavas, mangoes, and bananas basked in the tops of the small trees, and garden beds lined along the outskirts of the opening displayed tomatoes and arugula. They walked in between the fruit trees and saw another smaller opening with a few beach chairs and two hammocks. Ray unclipped the chest strap on his backpack and pulled a whistle to his mouth. He loudly blew into the whistle three times, and a few seconds later, they heard a voice coming through the trees. It was difficult to distinguish due to nearby waterfall sounds, but Lin, Reg, and Shankar could tell it wasn't Byrd's.

She appeared out of the forest like a gazing siren as she realized Ray and Meryl had brought unexpected visitors to the hideaway. Her skin and hair were relatively clean, given her circumstances of being a missing person on one of the most obscure places in Hawaii, and she wore a long, beige shawl over a teal, one-piece bathing suit. It came as no surprise to Reg, Shankar, and Lin that Byrd was hiding with Jane, but her beauty was still jarring for the three members of the Zenegades who had only briefly spent time with her during the Campfire Concert Series. Her tan legs gracefully glided as she walked barefoot in between the fruit trees, and she smiled as she recognized who her unexpected visitors were.

"Hey, guys!" she said, waving a hand at the group. "It's nice to see you three again," she continued, getting slight nods in return.

She turned to Ray and Meryl and gave them prolonged hugs. Ray said they'd brought food and supplies, and he apologized for the delay due to the recent rains.

She told them the weather had been *wild* in recent days, and that they'd arrived just in time for another beautiful day in paradise. "Follow me," she said as she guided them beyond the fruit trees.

When Lin read Reg's email detailing how his assistance was needed to find Byrd, he figured they'd be roughing it somewhere deep in the jungle at a primitive campsite with little to no shelter. The reality of their hideaway turned out to be far beyond his expectations, as Jane showed them their cabin made of large logs and driftwood. A natural, dark plaster connected the seals between each log, clay shingles made up the roof, and the cabin's interior was even more remarkable. They had a large bed with a foam mattress, a kitchen table and chairs, kitchenware, a wood-burning stove, and a sturdy bamboo floor. Behind the cabin were two smaller buildings: one being a food locker hosting large slabs of salted boar meat, and the other an outhouse that included a twenty-foot hole and decomposing powders. In their back yard was a camouflage tarp protecting a fire pit that still looked warm.

"Where is he?" Meryl asked after Jane's tour wound down and they were giving her supplies from their bags.

"He should be back any minute. He's spearfishing right now, but he left almost half an hour ago. He's gotten really picky about which fish he'll kill, and the recent swell has made it *really hard* to catch anything. Let's get this stuff organized later and go find him!"

Jane guided them further into the forest as they listened to birds and walked next to a shaded creek that rippled its way in the direction of the nearby ocean. After ten minutes of following her along a barely visible path, they came to an opening that led to a black-sand beach. This beach was much smaller and rockier than the Waipio and Waimanu bays, but it still had plenty of space to relax and glance down the shore at even more cliffside waterfalls. Only tiny sets of waves came to this spot, and the water just so happened to be a crystal-clear patch within an endless, bright blue.

Ray reached into one of his cargo pockets and whipped out a long, plastic tube containing a half-ounce of ganja, and they smoked in the shade per Jane's request to not venture onto the sand. As the THC established its effects, the group got quiet, not knowing what to expect next. Jane understood how it would only be a matter of minutes before Byrd showed up, because she knew he only had a limited amount of oxygen and tried to avoid wasting it. Sure enough, a dark blur appeared inside a whitecap and glided toward the shore like a boogie boarder. As the wave arrived at the rocky beach, the blur momentarily disappeared before catapulting itself above the surface at a shallow depth.

Byrd ran his hands back and forth through his shaggy hair in an effort to shake out the salt water, and his bushy beard rounded out his hippie pirate appearance. He was wearing a camouflage wetsuit, scuba tank, mask, and flippers as he emerged from the water, and his extended spear cradled a relatively small, sixty-pound shibi tuna. He immediately recognized his visitors underneath the nearby coconut trees and took his flippers off in excitement as he began jogging toward them.

"Aloha, Aikane! Welcome to Hua Huna!" he yelled.

Although he looked somewhat different with his longer facial hair, the same sparkle in his green eyes displayed itself as he got within arm's reach. He gave Reg, Lin, and Shankar wet hugs and explained how excited he was to have finally been found by them. But he wasted very little time saying hello because things still needed to be done, so he invited them on a tour of the peninsula that started at a wooden table where he'd gut his catches. They followed him back into the forest, where he pointed out things like a small motorboat and wild fridge, which essentially was a ceramic cooler that was securely sealed below the ground in a muddy hole full of leaves. He also showed them a natural spring that formed next to the waterfall by the cabin.

When they got closer to the cabin, Lin asked Byrd about the large slabs of meat hanging in their pantry. Byrd explained how he'd been bowhunting wild boar in the nearby, completely wild Honopue Valley. He bragged about how he was getting better at bowhunting, but that the many inherent risks forced him to prefer spearfishing. He showed them his vast supply of twenty scuba tanks and fifteen ten-gallon fuel cans that rested up against the back of the pantry, and he explained how he was running low on both oxygen and gas.

Ray chimed in about the recent weather making it too dangerous to take a boat out to help him with those types of supplies, and Byrd understood, but he also had a few other concerns on his mind. He began rambling on about how scuba diving was his only safe form of hunting due to helicopter tours sporadically flying down the coast on clear days, and right on cue, the group turned to the north as a helicopter revealed itself through the canopy's gaps. He described a few close calls they'd had with the helicopters when they first arrived to Hua Huna, but they were yet to be clearly seen by one due to their many low-profile rules. Some of these rules included things like only having fires and traveling by boat in the early morning or evening hours, spearfishing only in short increments, and never relaxing in the middle of the beach, where it could take too long to find coverage when the chopper sounds materialized. He also voiced his concerns over seeing some coast guard boats in recent weeks and how he was worried they'd try to come ashore.

"I wouldn't worry about the coast guard if I were you," Ray responded. "If they haven't come here yet, then they probably think you're Koa."

Lin, Reg, and Shankar needed an explanation, and Byrd reiterated that the remote peninsula they were on was nicknamed *Hua Huna*, or *hidden fruit*. Byrd wasn't exactly sure who planted the fruit trees and cleared the land underneath the canopy, because no one knew who did all that work. The original tilling likely happened a long time ago, but a hermit named Koa had been taking care of the land for the past thirty years or so. Koa constructed all three buildings by himself, and a select few authorities knew of him and covertly allowed him to live in peaceful seclusion.

Barely anyone knew about Koa, but Ray grew up with him down the coastline in Hilo and had agreed many years earlier to help him by periodically providing him with supplies via his parents' boat. Although Koa initially didn't want any of Ray's Waipio commune residents to know about his secret paradise, he'd come to enjoy their company, and two of the trustworthy people Ray had revealed Koa's secret to in recent months were Meryl and Jane. Both of them were more than impressed by Koa's reclusive lifestyle, so Jane immediately thought of him when a flustered Byrd showed up in Waipio with a guitar case full of cash and said *let's get out of here*. She, Meryl, and Ray guided him to Koa and introduced them to one another, and Byrd offered thirty thousand dollars up front to temporarily rent Hua Huna. Money didn't mean much to a guy like Koa, but 30K for a few months of seeing family and traveling was something even he couldn't resist.

It had now been over three months since Koa's departure, and Byrd and Jane had become accustomed to being the Kahunas of Hua Huna. They learned how to be patient while spearfishing and how to camouflage themselves to avoid being seen by overhead tourists. What ended up becoming their daily routine was Byrd writing a song and Jane helping him fine-tune it for her voice. They'd work on new songs each day, mainly because it was one of the most fun, heli-safe things to do on the forested peninsula. They also enjoyed exploring the remote valleys where they were guaranteed seclusion, but nothing felt quite as fulfilling as sitting in their neck of the woods creating music. They provided for each other in just as many intrinsic ways as the land provided for both of them, and when Byrd noticed the violin case strapped to Lin's backpack, he decided it was the right moment to showcase what they'd been working on.

Byrd and Jane escorted their guests to a shady spot by the fruit trees where they'd often play music, and it quickly became obvious how they were sometimes writing under the influence of hallucinogens. They didn't explicitly admit to doing any drugs, but introducing a song called "Mushroom Flower Shower" was self-explanatory. They also played them another tune more oriented around their unique connection between nature and reclusiveness called "Mountains Between Us," as well as a more traditional Hawaiian-themed song they named "Fortunes of Koa." Byrd explained how "Fortunes of Koa" was based upon many different hitchhikers across the Big Island, and how he imagined Koa hitchhiking back to Hilo after leaving Hua Huna to them. Byrd played a soft melody on guitar while Jane sang the song.

The road keeps winding, where do they all come from?
The gentle sounds of waves crash on and on
We keep learning about the island way
On just another timeless sunny day

Warm air and rain, wash all your troubles gone
Where do your troubles come from, I don't know
Try now to see me, because I can see you now
I'm a bird of paradise without wings

Aloha, good sir, where are you off to now?
Would you mind a little company?
I'm just a little down the road, I won't take much of your time
We can talk story about the island way

Mountains of mine, they stop feelings too kind
I'll walk in the rain if I want to
Go where you can't, see what you won't
Lessons of the land live in each blade of grass

You don't know me, but I think we could be friends
Even if just to make you feel good about you
Life can be simple and sometimes a bit too tough
This thumb feels like it's full of luck on my side

Aloha, good sir, where are you off to now?
Would you mind a little company?
I'm just a little down the road, I won't take much of your time
But we can talk story about the island way

What can a man be worth if he don't know love?
I couldn't make it home without you
Is there another way to say it's all relative?
Or could you show me the world still knows how to love?

Big Man on the land says it all belongs to me
Big Man can't learn to love as he should
There's a way we can go, it's gonna be a bumpy ride
It ebbs and flows, just like the tide

Aloha, good sir, where are you off to now?
Would you mind a little company?
I'm just a little down the road, I won't take much of your time
But we can talk story about the island way

We can talk story along the island's way

After a couple hours of embracing a hypnotically light mood, it was time to start planning lunch. Jane offered to cut the fileted tuna into sashimi, and Shankar and Meryl decided to wander through the fruit trees and arugula beds to make a salad. Ray and Reg figured it was a decent time to set up the tents before a potential afternoon shower, and their departure to the cabin put Lin and Byrd alone near the two shady hammocks that beckoned them closer.

They relaxed on the nylon and listened to the ocean's rhythm swaying back and forth in its eternal balance. The tide was now coming up, so the waves were loud enough to suspend any lingering awkwardness. But there was a tremendous amount of awkwardness between them, and Lin seized the opportunity to address it.

"So, why exactly did you disappear like this?" Lin asked, breaking the silence. "You know, pretty much the whole world is worried about you right now."

Byrd perked up from his cozy position in the hammock and started laughing, which made Lin furrow his eyebrows and stare back more intently.

"That whole media frenzy is so bizarre. Ray told me he saw an article saying my body was found in Indonesia!" he responded, while trying to hold back chokes of laughter. "It's not like I *actually* disappeared. I just couldn't tell anyone about this place."

"But all those people in Waipio know you're here, or at least they know how you're doing okay. Why didn't you let Reg, or me, or anyone know what's been going on lately?"

Byrd took a deep sigh and spun his legs around, now facing Lin while sitting horizontally in the hammock. "Look, I don't know how else to say this, but I just needed a break from being in a band for a little while. I missed the life I had before the Zenegades, when I was completely anonymous and could literally go anywhere and do whatever the hell I wanted, when I wanted to do it. I know I probably should've given the Waipio clan permission to get the word out to Reg, but so much shit kept going down, and I couldn't help but think that the moment one of y'all showed up, you'd start dragging me back to reality. Out here, I can be much more than just a professional musician. Out here, I can write songs with absolutely no strings attached."

"But what about all our fans? Don't you miss playing in front of an audience, and not just for yourself?"

"Yeah, I get that," Byrd responded, taking a moment to rub his beard and nod his head. "But I really just missed the life I had when I was a guide in Utah, or when we were all living together on the ranch. We sounded great back then, and it didn't matter if it was just us. We played *just to play*, so to me, the point of being a musician is just to have fun with instruments. When it comes down to it, it doesn't actually matter who's listening. And to be perfectly honest, I'm not sure if I want to stay in the band any longer. I feel like that period of getting up on stages is over for me now."

"But we've built something *so much bigger* than what any of us could've ever imagined back then, and it's because we found an audience that enjoys our sound. I understand how you've gotten burned out on the band lately. I think all of us are feeling the same way, to a certain extent, and you're right that *so much shit* has been happening, to the point that it seems unclear if we'll even keep the show going. But when it comes down to it for me, I know we'll be all right and we'll all keep playing whatever seems right for each of us. And to be perfectly honest, from how I see stuff, playing music will never be quite the same without you."

"I know what you mean, and I really am sorry for all the BS I've piled on top of Shit Mountain. I just needed a clean break from it all, but I can tell my fortunes are starting to turn, now that you're here. As high as I've been for so long out here, at a certain point, things must equalize themselves."

Neither of them knew what to say next, so it was a good thing Shankar and Reg interrupted them by carrying salad bowls and a sashimi platter. Byrd glanced into the forest to find Jane, Meryl, and Ray, and he saw them walking in the opposite direction of the hammocks, toward the cabin. Neither Byrd nor Lin realized it, but Shankar requested they be left alone. Reg held out the fish so they could grab a few pieces, and he placed the wooden tray on a nearby stump.

"Okay, we now need to talk about things that need to be said," Shankar initiated as Byrd and Lin chewed on mouthfuls of raw tuna. "First of all, I want all three of you to know that I'm no longer hosting guests at the ranch. I've decided to close it off to the public indefinitely; it's too much for me to handle and too far off from my original intentions, but I'd still always love to have your company whenever you want to visit."

"I'm not gonna be out here forever; this is just a *rental*. I'm sure we'll all come see you at the ranch soon," Byrd dismissively chimed in.

"I understand that now, and it's good to know that. The truth is, James, you've lately not been a good friend to the people who care about you the most. We have all been worried about you, and for a long time, we thought you might be gone for good. I want to know right now: why did you think it was okay to not tell any of *us* where you were?"

"I don't know how many times I'm gonna have to say this, but *I needed a break,* and that means I needed a break from *us,* too. I knew if any single one of *us* knew where I was, I'd be back in the studio, recording radio songs by now. It doesn't seem like any of us really gets me anymore, except maybe you, Shankar. I can't help but see everyone in the band come to my house from New York or LA and pretend they're like me, when the truth is none of them have the slightest clue as to what life is even like outside a city. Sure, I think everyone was more of a Zenegade back in the day when we lived together on the ranch, but things are different now. These days, I can't help but wonder what it would've been like if I hadn't made a band

and just kept writing for myself, and then I realized that I needed to free myself from this prison in order to actually start living. I needed to *let go* and return to the simple life I had when I lived out of my bike in Utah. So, that's why I'm here, and that's why I was okay with not letting you guys know what I was doing."

"*Oh*, so I'm guessing you think that completely freeing yourself from life's attachments is getting you closer to a more meaningful existence?" Shankar asked, getting a slight nod from Byrd. "Well, I hate to break it to you, but *Zen* doesn't always provide such easy solutions. In fact, the Zen way to face the struggles you just described would have nothing to do with this purely renegade life you lead now. Do you honestly think you're solving your problems out here?" he asked rhetorically. "I doubt it, and I doubt you're finding more meaning while neglecting all the people like Lin and Reg and Maya and Thayer and Skylar and Ruben and Cat, who you should be most grateful for. It seems like you've forgotten what it means to accept the perfect imperfections that make life worth living, and instead you've gone down the rabbit hole toward the illusion of perfection with this *perfect paradise*. Let me ask you this, Jim Byrd, King of the Zenegades: how much more of this perfect isolation could you possibly need when all the fulfillment in this great big world is not here, but with your friends?"

"I think about another month or so until Koa returns sounds about right!" Byrd snarkily responded, which didn't land well.

"*Well*, I think you should come back to Colorado now so you can clear your name. You missed court dates, you have unpaid fines, and now a warrant is out for your arrest. You cannot ignore your problems, James. You have to face them in order to be truly freed from them."

"I'm not going anywhere," Byrd responded softly, yet ice cold. "I knew you guys would try to come here and bring up all this BS right away, as if it actually matters what happens with me and those dumbass Aspen cops! It's all just a load of nothingness, and I'm *sick* of people knowing details about my personal life and saying things about me that they've got no idea about, and I'm *sick* of creepy motherfuckers taking videos of us in bad taste. It's like we all worked relentlessly to make names for ourselves, and the end result is a relentless validation of that public image again and again and again until we now are spitting, walking *images* of human beings! The only time I can actually feel like myself anymore is in places like this *perfect paradise,* because I'm not being encouraged to impress people that I don't even know every waking hour of every fucking day. You're damned if you do and you're damned if you don't give everyone what they want when they want it, so I started thinking to myself during the campfire series: *what do I want?* And I realized pretty quickly that I wanted to spend more time with Jane, and when she introduced me to Koa and this beautiful secret of Hua Huna, I knew I wanted to live here in the way I did before people viewed me as a Zenegade. I sure as hell don't feel like going anywhere anytime soon, but you guys should know that I will go back to my house soon. But I paid *good money* to be here on this patch of earth, and I intend to take care of it until Koa comes back."

Lin, Reg, and Shankar looked at each other and silently confirmed there was no chance they'd convince Byrd to leave with them. There was an unspoken agreement among the three of them that they wouldn't know what they were doing throughout the entire time of traveling to Hawaii just to talk to their friend, who clearly wanted to be left alone. It was the right time to get everything off each other's chests when Ray, Meryl, and Jane left them alone by the hammocks, and there was a sense that a serious tension had been eased now that everything had been said. The three of them smiled at each other, but Byrd wasn't quite on the same level of contentment.

"I wonder what else I could do besides be a musician?" Byrd thought out loud.

None of them knew how to respond, mainly because they each regarded him as the type of person who was meant to play music, but they also were speechless due to Byrd clearly not having everything moving correctly upstairs. They weren't prepared to indulge him, but luckily, they didn't need to, as Byrd kept venting on.

"I *do* wanna be there for everyone and make the world a better place, and I *do* wanna give back in my own way. I just feel like I'd rather give back in a more private way these days."

"Well, what about your old job in Utah that you had before you moved in with Shankar?" Reg responded in an attempt to be equally encouraging and coddling. "I bet if you went back to the desert again, it would be better than it was before."

"I *love* that idea!" he yelled out. "I tell you what, let's get all this real talk over with and just have some fun while you guys are out here. You're welcome to stay as long you'd like. We have everything you'd need. You don't need to worry about me. This sabbatical isn't permanent, just like anything else, so let's move on instead of sulking about what's brought us to this point. I'm going to leave when Koa said he'd be back in about a month, so let's plan a band meeting at the ranch for around then."

"Perfect, I love *that* idea!" Lin responded.

"But here's the deal you guys need to remember," Byrd shot right back. "Hua Huna is a secret that only a few people know about. You can't tell *anyone* about this place, even that weird Fanny Pack Dave guy who's apparently been looking for me. I'll let you know when I'm back home, but until then, my whereabouts have to be kept a mystery."

31

spen is one of those places that obtained its name for an obvious reason, like any ubiquitous Cascade Falls or Deer Creek, because the Roaring Fork Valley's millions of aspen trees were a true inspiration to Silver Boom prospectors. Although every season is a good time to walk in an aspen grove, arguably the best time is in the early fall, when a forest's foliage transforms from a green hue into pulsating, effervescent shades of yellow and orange. This natural phenomenon only occurs for a few weeks each year, but it's always one hell of a reminder in terms of just how majestic *Madre Naturaleza* undoubtedly remains.

The aspen leaves along Castle Creek were at the peak of their transformation when the Zenegades flew from all over to converge upon Shankar's property on an October evening. They hadn't all been in the same location since their tour finale in early May, and they still weren't quite fully reunited when the bonfire's initial spark commenced the band meeting. Thayer, Sky, Ruben, Cat, Lin, Maya, O'Donnell, Reg, and Shankar sat around the fire and enjoyed each other's company with stories of China, Europe, Mexico, Hua Huna, and other recent happenings. It had now been a few months since Thayer caught Sky cheating on her, and it seemed as though their tension had become more subdued. Each of the bandmates also had their instruments on them and figured there wasn't any point in postponing a jam session for Byrd's arrival, especially because Reg relayed a message detailing how he'd be late to the gathering due to some legal troubles that needed clearing up.

A couple of hours passed as they rehearsed their catalog, and they even worked on a few of Maya and Thayer's new songs until Shankar announced it was time to reconvene by the kitchen cabin for supper. They slowly but surely rested their instruments down and walked over to a massive spread of burgers, hot dogs, and side dishes that steamed from their trays. They sat down at the long communal table, just like they did when they helped Shankar build the original foundation of the ranch, and they sat in the exact same seats they always would. This subsequently meant that one end of the table remained unseated.

Just as they sat down to eat, they heard a loud rumbling off in the distance near the dirt road. Although Reg mentioned he had a ride, none of them was exactly sure how Byrd was planning on getting to the ranch. But the unmistakable loud exhaust sounds were clearly Byrd on a motorcycle, and sure enough, the rowdy engine noises got closer and closer until Byrd rolled up near the fire pit on the same pannier-filled Honda he used to live out of. He quickly glanced at the group eating dinner without him, waved, and proceeded to ride the bike through the property until finally kicking the peg stand out just behind his empty wooden chair. The group clapped and cheered like he'd just stepped onto a stage as he got off the bike, and it was abundantly clear they were excited to see him. Although he looked more cleaned up than he did at Hua Huna, his hair and beard were still longer than most of them had ever seen before. He took off his full-brim hat and side-shield sunglasses and bowed to his adoring fans. As questions started flying out all at once, Byrd hushed them with a wave of his palms and an announcement that he'd prepared a speech. He pushed the chair aside and stood before everyone against the end of the table.

"First of all, I just want to say I'm sorry to all of you. I'm sorry I disappeared. I'm sorry I neglected all the hard work we've put in together, and I'm sorry I let things get out of hand in terms of where I was mentally. I can't tell you *exactly* where I've been, but I can say that I was living off the land on the Big Island and was safe the whole time I was away."

"We missed your crazy ass!" O'Donnell yelled, getting a group laugh.

"I missed all of you too," Byrd responded. "I had *a lot* of time to think while I was gone, and before we get back to dinner, I just want to tell you guys what I've been thinking about. The first thing I want to tell you guys is that I'm planning on turning myself in to the cops within the next few days. I just met with my lawyer, and he's assured me that everything will eventually be okay, but I'll likely have to serve a short sentence because I ran away, and I'll be on probation for a little while. I guess I thought I was *letting go* and releasing all sorts of built-up tension by hiding out in Hawaii, and I guess I've always thought I could run away from my problems by immersing myself in nature. But what I've come to realize about who I am and who we are as a band is that I've had things all wrong for far too long. I started thinking you guys didn't get me anymore because you live in cities, but I now know that was just a load of conceited bullshit. I now know how being a Zenegade starts *and ends* here, and it has nothing to do with where exactly you spend your time," he continued, pointing at his head. "The next thing I want to mention is that Jane and I have decided to take a break for the time being because we realized we were moving a bit too quickly, but we wrote some songs together over the last few months. I've been going back and forth in terms of whether or not we should do something with these ideas, and I now think we should record at least a few new songs. But before we get into anything like that, we first need to clear the air about some other stuff that's been going on lately. So, that's all I really needed to say, but I want to open it up to you guys now. If you have anything you think needs to be said, now is the time."

They sat in silence for a moment, while some of them returned their attention to their dinner plates.

"I need to say something," Sky announced as he mustered up the courage to stand up. "I'm sure you guys know that Thayer and I are no longer together, and that it's because I wasn't faithful to her. I know it may be surprising for you guys to find out that I'm bi after all these years, but you have to understand how I was scared that coming out would screw up this wild ride we've all been on. The truth is ... this is just who I *really am*, and I'm actually feeling a lot better recently because I no longer feel like I'm putting on a façade every single day. I've just returned from an addiction center, and I've stopped doing coke, and I feel like I'm finally finding out who I am beyond Sky Rose from Zenegades. And when it really comes down to it, I get it if you guys think this will be too weird, and I understand if you want to kick me out of the band."

Another awkward silence ensued, as no one knew what to say. Instead of vocalizing words, everyone just looked toward Thayer as if to ask, *do you want him here or not?*

"Everyone here knows how Sky broke my heart a few months ago," Thayer announced as she stood up from her chair. "And since then, I've been learning how I'm going to move on and pretty much *relive* my life going forward. I learned *a lot* during my time at an addiction center as well, and I've come to terms with the basic fact that I can't control everything that happens to me. Plenty of our songs will be a little bit awkward for me from now on, but that doesn't mean they'll be any different for our fans. Just because I don't plan on being in a relationship with Sky anymore, it doesn't mean those old feelings should no longer be felt through our music, and us breaking up doesn't mean I can't be on stage with him. I think we're both in better places now, so I'm willing to keep Sky as our guitarist going forward."

"Well, ain't *that* a relief!" O'Donnell blurted out, saying what everyone was thinking. "I have something to say too," he continued as he stood up. "A lot of craziness has happened of late, but I think it's safe to say that it's all water under the bridge. This group is *special*, so we'll get through any muddy waters, no matter how thick it gets," he said, getting a group clap. "I do have some serious things to say, though, and it's that I want to move on from Charlie. I think Dyce is a half-decent label, but we can make it work without them now. Like Lin has said in the past, we can go independent and do our own thing."

The group nodded and agreed to O'Donnell's risky suggestion, and they also looked over at Lin for validation.

"I do think we could go independent and be just fine, but I also think Charlie can continue to be valuable for us," Lin chimed in. "I'm not sure if all of you heard, but I met my biological mother in China a little over a month ago. I've also been working on an instrumental album out there, thanks to Charlie's help. It's so weird to be spending time with her after not knowing her till now, but I have this feeling that giving her a real shot at being my mom could make up for lost time. I'm thinking of buying an apartment in Beijing soon, so I'll be spending more time there."

"And I just heard about this apartment purchase a couple days ago!" Maya quickly responded. "I hope you guys see how this is a small sample of what I've been going through with him lately. Literally, I've felt as if I was left in a dark hole for the entire summer," she continued, giving a slight eye roll. "I guess I should update *everyone* on what I've been doing lately too," she said, motioning to Byrd. "I've been doing a residency gig at The Blue Queen in New York with my friends in Retro Phat a few days a week. Ruben has been killing it on drums, Thay has been playing keys, and Cat has been like a saving grace keeping me sane during a pretty stressful time. But it really has been fun to play jazz on a consistent basis again, and I'm hoping we can start playing some of the songs I've been working on lately!"

"That *does* sound badass. I miss that hole in the ground!" Reg jumped in. "I'm pretty sure I've called all of you at some point recently, but I went through some *muddy waters*, to say the least, while looking for this crazy knucklehead! But yeah, now that I'm back from the island, I'm going home to see my little nieces and nephews and my mom and dad, and I'll definitely be swinging by to see all those cats down at Blue Queen. I'd even be down to be the assistant co-supervisor again! You think you could hook me up?" he asked Maya, who just laughed and shrugged.

"I also have some news," Shankar said as he stood up from his chair. "I'm not sure how else to say this, but ... I'm thinking of selling the ranch."

This led to a chorus of *what, huh,* and *no* from the group, which Shankar quickly hushed back to a silence.

"It's just not the same anymore, and I don't think this is what I intended this place to be. Even with all its success, I can't help but think I'm sometimes driving myself crazy by constantly worrying about this business. I have officially stopped having guests for over a month now, and it has been such a relief to live here in peace without any hassles. I now think it might be time for me to *really* retire."

They sat silently at the large table and looked down at the sweet and savory delicacies that Shankar's generosity provided.

"Shankar is right that it isn't quite the same as it was, but we all know how this ranch is the best thing that ever happened to all of us," Byrd responded. "I miss how this place used to be when were out here building it. Those were some of the best nights of my entire life, when we were just beginning to play together, so I'm thinking we should do the exact same thing we used to do back then and have one hell of a night tonight! How does that sound?" Byrd proposed to the group, which got a chorus response of *hell yeah, all right,* and *let's do it.*

Leaving the dinner table and their venting conversation behind them was exactly what they needed to brighten up the meeting's mood. Within a matter of minutes, their instruments were properly tuned, and a stout joint was being passed around the fire. Although it had been months since they'd played together, their typical preparations made it seem like no time had passed at all. The THC swirled through their minds like ripples in a pond as past dilemmas disappeared into the subconscious repositories in which they belonged. Trivial grins and giggles were the coherent suggestion that they were ready to begin, and they started out with a newgrass jam that quickly led to Zenegades songs. After finishing improvisational renditions of "Unnecessary Walking", "She Passed By", and "Lady Liberty", Lin mentioned how they were playing the same opening sequence from Red Rocks earlier in the year. That particular show was one of their all-time favorites and worthy of a tour finale, so rolling with the entire setlist was a nostalgic déjà vu.

They dug just as deeply into the cores of their creative juices as they did on Colorado's biggest stage, which led to an effortless myriad of notes that cohesively blended into each melody. They'd let Ruben, Byrd, and Sky introduce a rhythm and unleash Maya's bass notes to ever-so-wholesomely fill in the sound. Thayer's portable keyboard complements provided that extra touch of pizzazz, Reg's sax and singing helped them remember just how unique their last tour finale was, and Lin's violin solos raised the fire's flames just as much as the drought-ridden logs. They alternated lead vocals just like they would within their live routines, and their pitch-perfect harmonies made their small audience of Shankar, Cat, and O'Donnell feel real butterflies. The fire continued to rage at the Zenegade Ranch as the night darkened, and the later it got, the more intricate the music became. They oddly sounded more refined and played with more swagger than they did during that May evening at Red Rocks, but no one needed to mention it. No one needed to say all that much of anything, because every space between each note was understood to hold a purpose: *maintain the magic.*

Slight cues were whispered as they transitioned from one song to another, but each Zenegade's focus primarily homed in on the relentless flickering of the flames as they simultaneously perfected each lyric and instrumental note to their renowned songs. Byrd fixated on how his acoustic chords syncopated with Ruben's drums, Maya's bass, Reg's sax, and Thayer's keys, and the Rose boys remained focused on providing the extra tempo progression that brought each tune to a new level. The fire began to embody the band's energy as they played more passionately with the climbing heights of the blaze. The bonfire raised the nearby temperature without posing any serious threats, but the internal campfire within each of them was inextinguishable. Sweat seeped out of their foreheads and fingertips as they put everything into themselves and radiated their collective, unfeigned power that no hiatus could ever erase. Only their intuition could validate it, but they played the exact same sequence of songs better by themselves than they did in front of that tour finale crowd of over nine thousand people.

Three and a half hours of post-supper music went by until they decided it was time to call it a night. They laughed with each other while recounting some of the inaudible mistakes they'd made, and it was finally beginning to feel as though things were normalizing after several tumultuous months. Although it got a bit awkward between Sky and Thayer when they started splitting up toward their respective cabins, Shankar was ready for this scenario and ushered Sky to his cabin's futon. They hadn't had a night at the ranch quite like that one in years, and they were already beginning to coordinate studio time for a new album as they prepared to sleep. The insatiable itch to create more music was fully back in each of them, including Byrd. But Byrd had other plans that he didn't yet get a chance to reveal, so he made another announcement just after midnight.

"Hey, I need to say something before we go to bed," he declared, getting the whole group's attention. "Tonight *rocked*, and I promise with all my heart that we'll get the ball rolling again on a new album soon enough. I'm not sure what's going to happen to me when I go to the police station, but there's just one more thing I need to do before I turn myself in."

32

The old parable of *The Hawaiian Fisherman and The Mainland Business Executive* is one that resonates within our innate desires to live a fulfilling life.

One day, a business executive was vacationing in a small Hawaiian fishing village far away from the fancy beach resorts, and he sat on a secluded beach next to a small dock. As he sat there, he saw a fisherman coming back to the reef in a small rowboat. The man had caught several large fish.

The business executive walked over to the dock and yelled out to the man, "Those are some good-looking fish! How long did it take you out there to catch all of those?"

The fisherman shrugged and gave a small smile. "Oh, only just a little while," he responded. The business executive scratched his holiday-developed facial scruff in astonishment and asked, "So, why don't you want to be out there longer so you could catch even more for yourself?"

"I have enough in here to be able to feed my entire family, and even a few friends," the fisherman responded.

"So, what exactly are you going to do for the rest of the day?"

The fisherman took no hesitation in responding, "Well, most days I'll wake up very early so I can be out on the water at the right time to catch fish, and once I've caught some, I'll go back home and play with my children. In the afternoons, I take a nap with my wife, and in the evening hours, we'll take a walk down to the village and meet friends for a couple of drinks. I'll bring my fish and a guitar, they'll bring their instruments, and we'll play songs and dance into the night till it's time for bed. My life is very busy, and my schedule is always full every day, sir."

The business executive listened to the fisherman and took pity on him. He felt like it was his need to help this man and give back to the community he was visiting.

"I'm a successful business executive from the mainland. I have an MBA and a Fortune 500 company, and I think I could help you become a success. What you should do instead of going home this early in the day is stay out in the water as long as you can, so you can end up catching as much fish as you possibly can. Once you've saved up from all the extra money you'd be making, you could then buy a better boat and be able to catch even more fish. Eventually, you'll be able to catch enough fish to necessitate an entire fleet of fishing boats, and that's when you'll establish your own enterprise. You can then start investing in other portions of the means of production for your fish, like developing a canned-food facility and establishing your own distribution network. At that point, you'd probably want to leave this village and move to Honolulu, where you can create a reputable headquarters for you and your staff to manage your many fishing branches."

"What would I do after all of that?" the fisherman inquired.

The business executive laughed at the fisherman's naïvety, and said, "Once you've done all of that, you'll start living like a king in a fancy mansion. Within twenty years or so, you'll be able to take your business public and manage your shares of the company. You'll be a multi-millionaire."

"What would I do after I become a multi-millionaire?" the fisherman asked.

"After you're rich, you'll be able to move from Honolulu and back to a remote fishing village of your choosing, and wake up early every morning and catch your own fish for fun. You'll have more time to enjoy yourself with your wife and kids. You'll also have enough money to have a lot of fun and hang out with your buddies worry-free."

The fisherman looked confused at the business executive and said, "But isn't that exactly what I'm already doing?"

Byrd simultaneously felt like the Hawaiian fisherman and the mainland business executive, which was why he decided to recommit himself to the present moment in a way that was familiar to his past. From the moment Koa returned to his home, Byrd was convinced that he'd reemerge into society like a phoenix rising from the ashes of the hidden paradise's fire pit. It took a different kind of introspection he was used to during his daily routine of playing Tarzan with Jane in the Hawaiian forest, but he was beginning to recognize the types of moments that genuinely made him feel fulfilled. This epiphany was initiated by Reg, Shankar, and Lin's visit to Hua Huna, which was exactly why he found himself in familiar territory more than a week after the meeting at the Zenegade Ranch.

He couldn't help but feel a nostalgic sensation as he walked through the doors of the Surf Zone Internet Café in the middle of the northern Utah desert. Although he looked a little different compared to a handful of years ago, the shopkeeper Billy immediately recognized him. For Billy, seeing Jim Byrd in the flesh again was like a dream come true. He had always told his friends how a famous musician used to come into Surf Zone when he was unknown, and several of Billy's buddies broke out of their cliché country music routines after he introduced them to the Zenegades. Even though more than five years had passed since they last met, it was like no time at all, and they essentially did the exact same routine they always did. Byrd was by himself, like he always was, and still looked like he'd gone at least a few days without showering, and he of course needed an internet café to check his emails, since he still didn't own a phone. Their conversation led to a few selfies with Billy's phone, and it concluded in the same old way, as Billy provided privacy for Byrd to log on.

There were a few other people in Surf Zone, mainly young field hands catching up with family far away. Byrd got a Coke out of the vending machine and walked over to one of the vacant monitors, which looked old enough to be powered by Windows 95. He logged in with the same username he made when he first started frequenting Surf Zone: *@SurfByrd*. He clicked his way to his emails, opened up a new draft, and wrote:

Hey Thay,

I'm just checking in to let you know that everything is all right. I'm not suffering from severe thirst in the middle of the desert or anything, and I promise I'll be out of here pretty soon. I think it's time to start planning some jam sessions at my place for whenever I can make it back to Hawaii, and I hope you're taking care of things and not just lounging all day while I'm gone (Just Kidding!) In fact, I think it sounds like a good time for all of us to plan a grand vacation that we can do once I'm off probation. Lin's got me thinking a lot about China, so how does Tibet sound?

There really has been a lot on my mind lately that I still can't quite seem to shake, like Jane, you and the guys, my mom, and of course the impending legal troubles that I'm still scared to face. You name it and it's going on up in this here noggin! But it feels good to be back in Utah. I missed this place a lot more than I thought, and the weather has even been cooling off lately.

Let me know what's going on with you and if you need any extra help taking care of the farm, and I (or my lawyer) will be sure to get back to you once there's more info about what'll happen to me. I'm not gonna lie, I'm pretty scared right now. I'm planning on spending one more day here, and then packing my stuff up and riding to Aspen to turn myself in.

One Love,

JB

Byrd flew from Surf Zone on his old Honda, once again sporting panniers. As he careened through the desert air, he audibly reflected upon just how much he missed Utah's dust storms. His entire outfit and facial hair were completely covered within a matter of minutes, and it took him well over an hour to finally arrive at his favorite campsite.

There was no rush getting there, especially because he could barely see through the endless billows of dust that flowed beyond his goggles, but reaching the wind-protected canyon provided an ingrained relief that only homecomings tend to have. There weren't any campers along the way to his preferred spot, but he still felt a stroke of luck when there weren't any RVs or tents near his campsite as he came around the ride's final bend. He took the panniers off the bike and meandered around the area to collect dead wood. The entire canyon seemed much drier than it used to be, but the nearby creek still gurgled along in the exact same way it always did. It didn't take long for him to strip down and rest his legs in the shallow pool, and he relaxed as the water's rhythm helped every trepidation dissolve into oblivion.

Once he'd dried off, it was Uncle Tito time. He sat by his fire underneath a barren cottonwood tree and improvised rhythm after rhythm as leaves fell all around him. He strummed a handful of songs he wrote in Hua Huna, and he played tropical Zenegades songs he'd written over the past five years. He also attempted ukulele interpretations of some of his favorite classic rock songs he always enjoyed playing when that same site was his seasonal home, including Steve Miller Band's "Take the Money and Run" and Stealers Wheel's "Stuck in the Middle With You." He sang each song as loudly as he wanted, and he maintained a conversation with himself for hours until dinnertime. After eating a dehydrated dinner out of a plastic bag, the sky was starting to darken. He didn't feel like staying up late, so he unrolled a sleeping pad and bag on open dirt and looked up at the stars as he drifted toward dreams.

One of the things Byrd loved the most about his favorite BLM campsite was the way he'd wake up every morning. As a painstakingly thorough life review steered him to consciousness within milliseconds, the sounds of free-range cattle acted as a tangible reminder that the new day had arrived. The angled refraction of the early morning light against the canyon cliffs was at its best when the cows came around, and the temperature still offered a cool feeling that never lasted past eight.

He made a friction fire in less than a minute by spinning a hand drill against a fireboard and tinder nest. He was now much better at this technique, thanks to his recent getaway to Hua Huna, and he audibly acknowledged how he could make fire faster than any REI-loving dude using lighter fluid. He followed up his primal triumph over nature by taking the easy way out and lighting his new, cutting-edge, propane-powered water-boiling system. He recognized the blatant hypocrisy of his naturally made fire building itself up next to a cup of rapidly warming creek water, and he said, "*Fuck it. Time's a-wasting, and I'm even hungrier than yesterday.*"

Within two minutes, he had three cups of boiling water ready to go. He grabbed the boiling system's built-in pot and poured part of it into a plastic bag of dehydrated eggs and bacon, and the remaining water was poured into a collapsible rubber cup. The hot water mixed itself with coffee grounds at the bottom of the cup, and he watched closely as the coarse grounds floated for a few minutes before settling down. Just like the cowboys who still monitored the valley's herds, Byrd had finished a filling breakfast and was jacked up on caffeine by seven sharp. He knew it was best to get an early start, because it was a Saturday and hordes of hikers would inevitably want to go exactly where he was planning on going next.

He warmed up his bike for a few minutes and headed to the mouth of the canyon, where a trail led to a series of hot spring pools. It was rare to not see any cars at the parking lot, but he was apparently the earliest of the early birds. He got out on the trail and eventually crossed a large bridge that went over a much larger river than the stream near his campsite. Even though it was the driest part of fall, rapids continued to rush as if the river itself was adamant about proclaiming it was here to stay. He applauded the river as he watched it do its thing from its bank, and he recognized the convergence of harsh desert elements and life finding its own way yet again in the shaded watersheds. He felt as though he was at the nexus of two distinctly different climates, and he recognized how the river was a bona fide lifeline for countless creatures and plants further downstream. Although he didn't have any immediate need for it, he scooped the river water with his palms and replenished his chapped lips. This place was a lifeline for him as well, but it supported him beyond the dependency for life's essentials.

"The city folks will be showing up soon," he said. "Good day for a hike above the falls."

Over an hour went by, and he'd already started to soak in the best hot spring pool, which was the exact same one where he, Sky, and O'Donnell spent an evening with the gay Mormon couple more than five years earlier. He sat silently in the picturesque pool next to a series of cascading waterfalls and contemplated deeply about the future of the Zenegades, especially in terms of how things might transpire between Sky and Thayer. There didn't seem to be any doubt that Thayer was momentarily on good terms with Sky, and it would essentially be her call in terms of whether or not the band would retain its original core. He relaxed longer as his fingers began to wrinkle, and he came to realize how certain parts of his future weren't in his hands, as well as why that was exactly how it was always supposed to be.

He caught himself drifting back toward a rat-race mindset that solely focused on the future, so he realigned his mental imagery to the present moment. He understood that other hikers would be arriving for their morning soaks within a matter of minutes, so he figured it was a good time to make his way further up stream. This was a lot easier said than done, especially because a series of waterfalls were just above him. But it wasn't his first time scaling these falls, and he'd recently become adept at reaching areas above waterfalls while exploring the adjacent valleys near Hua Huna. So, without hesitation, he began grabbing on to exposed tree roots and branches as he made his way up to the top of the first falls.

There was a freezing-cold swimming hole between the two cascading falls, and he decided to jump in to cool his body off after the prolonged hot spring soak. He walked along the submerged rocks in his sandals and continued across the pool to the other side of the creek, where a dinghy towrope hung down the steep hill. He grabbed on to the rope and pulled tightly to check its strength, which revealed how nothing had changed since the last time he was there. The sturdy rope made scaling the second falls much easier than the first, and he knew he was entering an area where most hikers didn't venture when he reached the top. Another pool floated just beneath the third falls, and he decided to rest for a couple minutes behind the falls' veil like he always used to. Not many people knew about this secluded swimming area just above the hot springs attraction, but it wasn't a complete secret either. So, he crossed the stream again and scaled more steep rocks to reach the very top of the cascade.

The creek may have flattened out just above the third falls, but the rapids were raging much faster than anywhere else on the trail. He saw a log bridge that made the mandatory crossing easier, and he was surprised to see how it was now covered in moss. The bridge was composed of a handful of tree branches that hovered just over the rapids at the slimmest portion of the creek, where the highest falls began, and Byrd glanced at the mossy logs in disbelief that he'd finally made it back to this place that had been relegated to his dreams. More than five years had gone by since he'd been beyond the log bridge to the more manageable part of the off-trail excursion, and his eyes widened as he glanced at the shaded forest that awaited him on the other side of the twelve-foot bridge.

He took a few small steps on the logs to test the bridge's stability, and the moss was much drier than he'd anticipated. One foot in front of the other, he made his way a few more feet toward the middle of the bridge, where the rapids were at their highest. He took a second of his attention away from his feet and extended his left foot outward in front of him while glancing at the water, and without seeing his precise placement, his foot slipped in between the logs and submerged into the water. His left ankle rolled and instantly sprained, and the rapid's forces were strong enough to push the rest of his body off balance. He began floating feet first, belly down toward the top of the falls, which was just a few feet away. As he was about to slip off, he was able to grab on to a rock underneath the surface and stop his momentum. His entire body hung over the falls' ledge, but he was able to hold himself up with both hands on the submerged rock. He looked down at the free-falling water racing around him toward the shallow pool he was just swimming in, and he laughed. It wasn't the worst height to fall from, but it was also high enough to do some damage. As he flexed his biceps to pull his torso up, the rock jiggled, and without another moment's notice, it gave way.

He desperately grasped the air, trying to reach the slick rocks behind the fall's veil, which caused him to squarely smack the shallow pool's surface on his upper back. Although he was able to crouch in the pool a few moments earlier, it was far too shallow to support his fall. His upper vertebrae collided with jagged rocks just a few feet below the surface at the precise angle to instantaneously puncture his skin and sever his spinal cord. At the exact same moment, the rock that had previously held him up smacked the water's surface and his forehead.

A surreal sensation swept throughout every nerve connection and muscle fascia in his body. He yelled, but no sounds came out. His arm shifted, but it didn't actually move. He looked upward at the top of the falls, but he was quickly losing awareness. It took him more than forty seconds to realize he was under water and that he wasn't going to be able to breathe. He tried to force himself above the surface, but nothing budged. Luckily, the creek's natural flow pushed his body out of the pool and in the direction of a shallower area, where his head could emerge. He inhaled, and oxygen went into his lungs as if it were the very first time at birth.

After a few breaths, he opened his eyes and came to the understanding that he was still alive. He tried to readjust himself against the rocks in the shallow water, but neither his arms nor his legs would move. He tried moving only his eyes, which allowed him to see what was emerging from the nearby rocks. Three Mojave rattlesnakes hissed at him with their tails chattering loudly. He wasn't able to distinguish the sounds of the snakes until that very moment, which was when they collectively lunged at him. The first snake bit him on the shoulder, easily sinking its teeth through his wet T-shirt and into his skin. The second snake slithered around him and bit him on his right forearm. The third snake took its time and examined Byrd's bloody head before striking his neck. The remnants of the murky, brown venom lingered on him as the snakes slithered away toward nearby bushes. He continued to motionlessly rest up against the edge of the pool as sharp and dull sensations intertwined with one another for several minutes, and he was completely unable to adjust himself as he went into neurogenic shock and found it more difficult to breathe. His heart rate began to rapidly decrease as he lost nearly all the color in his face and turned clammy. His lips and fingernails became blue as he began to slip out of consciousness.

"Help!" he yelled as loud as he could, which wasn't louder than a whisper. He repeated himself several times, until a cold, chilling sensation overtook him. His vision was now terrible as blood continued to trickle down his face, so he closed his eyes and did his best to breathe. All he could do was focus on his breath as his heart rate continued to decrease, and his eyes remained closed as the strength within him began to subside.

His heart stopped beating, then continued to beat, then stopped again, then picked back up again. Blood was all over his forehead, nose and mouth, and the breaths he could manage weren't enough to maintain the essential biomechanical intensity he so easily took for granted. It required every part of his being to open his eyes through the encrusted blood and see the waterfall continuing to flow as it always did, and he blankly stared at the fall as he floated like an endless river into the unknown division of the Unified Field.

33

For comedians like Andre Cavallo, talking about any type of bad news was more than challenging. Even though he always managed to get through negative news and drift his way through his talk show on a regular basis, it was a lot easier said than done. Preparing for a bit that wasn't meant to be funny was like poking thorns in his Puck-like charm, and staring down at notes about Jim Byrd's death was like seeing an eviction letter declaring that tonight was the last night in his TV home. Although sporadic thoughts drifted in and out of his mind, the one phrase that kept creeping in was *why did this have to happen right now?*

In the woods along Castle Creek, the band members, Shankar, Cat, Jane, O'Donnell, and Byrd's mom, Janis Byrd, sat quietly around a tiny TV that had been recently installed in Shankar's cabin. The entire Zenegade Ranch was full of trash bags and other remnants from the funeral that took place earlier in the day, but now all the guests had left, and it was time to return to their seemingly rejected reality. No one wanted to leave each other alone that night, because everyone knew the intense emotions that were waiting to pour out once they'd had more time to think. Still, the soft whimpering sounds of tears dropping down their faces were what broke their silence as they watched a medication advertisement fade out and Cavallo fade onto the screen. Instead of embracing the applause like he usually would, he did his best to hush the crowd down.

"Hello, and welcome back," he said into the camera withz his million-dollar smile, which quickly faded. "Before we go further into the show, we'd like to take a minute and let you all know about the tragic death of Jim Byrd that you may have already heard about. Now, you guys know I've always been a Zenegade at heart and have been a huge fan for years. We've even had Jim and the band on the show before," he continued as the crowd came to complete silence. "I don't really know how else to say it, but I'm devastated, and I know a lot of you at home are probably devastated as well. We also have heard about some of the online rumors that Jim committed suicide, and we want to be one of the first to clear that up. Jim Byrd *did not* commit suicide, and after an autopsy and thorough investigation, it was discovered that what happened to him was completely accidental. It was also discovered that he had no alcohol or drugs in his system, so these rumors simply need to stop as well."

Andre took a deep breath and paused for a moment. "Jim Byrd was so different than all the musicians I've met throughout my years of being in show business, and I've definitely met *a lot* of really talented artists. He and the Zenegades possess this incredible family bond that's impossible to miss, and whenever you were in a room with them, it felt like you were with friends that you've known forever. I know their live performances were the exact same way, and I feel so grateful to have gone to one of the Campfire Concerts earlier this summer, where Jim and a few other Zenegades played an intimate show by a campfire. And this is really what the Zenegades have always been about: making it seem like the outside world has drifted far away and that you're dancing to music in a campground, except they made it clear that *we're the fire* that keeps them warm. The fans are the ones that helped inspire so much great music over the past few years, and you could tell how they stayed true to all of us and never made a song with the sole intentions of just being popular," he said, pausing again as he wiped a tear welling up in his eye. "I know there's so much more a guy like Jim Byrd could have done for us and the entire world, and I'm so happy that his perspective will live on through his music. So, rest easy in Zenegade heaven, Jim. You surely will be missed by us all."

The show continued as it always did, and Shankar's tiny cabin stayed silent. What Cavallo was now saying didn't matter as much, but none of them felt sociable enough for conversation. They continued crying in their own unique ways, and a few of them went outside into the chilly night for privacy.

"That was a nice speech he did," a teary-eyed Reg finally said, breaking the silence. "I like that guy, Andre. He's a good dude."

O'Donnell's cell rang obnoxiously loud, startling the rest of the cabin. He answered with a loud *hello* and went quiet for a couple minutes. None of them were used to seeing him listen so intently, and they watched him without saying a word.

"Make it ten instead of nine," he finally replied. "Okay, see you then," he said as he hung up.

The rest of the group looked at him, and he looked back at them as he breathed heavily in an attempt to regain his composure.

"We all have to go into town in the morning to talk to Byrd's attorney."

The next morning at 10:15, the entire group was outside the Law Offices of Chadwick Eckelberg III on Hopkins Avenue, which was directly across the street from Lululemon and Gucci. They were all a bit confused by the fact that Byrd would hire a lawyer who worked in the gaudiest part of town, but they understood how Chadwick Eckelberg III got the job when they first laid eyes on him.

Chad was a little over fifty when Byrd reached out to him, but he was more like a twenty-three-year-old college kid who never stopped partying on the inside. Pretty much every other attorney in Aspen would wear sharp suits or highbrow business apparel to work, but Chad chose his office near Lululemon and Gucci because it was also close to a gondola—allowing him to meet his clients wearing ski gear in the winter and mountain-biking clothes in the summer. The first thing you noticed when you met Chad was his distinct sunglass tan, which indicated his proclivity to wear frames that were obnoxiously too big on him. During the winter months, these tan lines were in the shape of goggles. The next thing that was instantly recognizable about Chad was his hair, which was long and bleached blonde, even though he'd always insist it was natural. The last instantly recognizable personal trait about Chad was his voice, which sounded like he smoked ganja on a daily basis in between Trestles surf sessions outside San Clemente. Although he was far from the California coast to have his classic surfer drawl, he'd surfed enough pow pow on his snowboard to be Aspen's most hip lawyer for local delinquents, for sure.

Chad ran his firm on his own, so he met the group outside and escorted them through the brick building's entrance and up the stairs to his office. As they walked into his unit, they realized they might not all fit. It was just a single room with a large desk and three comfy office chairs, with snowboarding pictures and images of the Maroon Bells-Snowmass Wilderness designing the walls. He only had three chairs for eleven guests, so he offered his chair as they crammed together in the small space with barely enough room to stand.

"Well, first of all, I just want to tell you guys that I'm really sorry for your loss. I'm a *huge* Zenegade myself, and your music has been truly inspiring over the past few years," he said from behind the desk. "I know you guys just did the whole memorial service in the park the other day, which was awesome, by the way, and I know you had the more formal funeral at the ranch yesterday too. I also know none of you guys except Ryan even knew about me before yesterday, but it's really crucial that you came to see me today while you're all still in town. The thing is, Byrd hired me about a month ago to help him settle his arrest warrant after he skipped out on his DUI charges and court appearances. That most likely seems pretty irrelevant to you guys, but what you may not know is that he also asked me to certify a whole bunch of other legal documents. He apparently was thinking a lot about his will and estate when he was on the run, and all you guys in this room right now are his beneficiaries."

They murmured to each other while wondering what Byrd had in mind for them, but they quickly came to realize how his will was considerably different than any conventional bequeathal.

"So, I would usually just explain all the terms of Byrd's will out loud, but I don't think that's what he wanted. So, what I did was print out some copies of what he wrote to let you guys read it for yourselves."

He pulled out a manila folder and held it out toward Janis with both palms underneath it, and he bowed his head as if he was handing over a religious artifact. They pulled out the sheets of paper and passed them around the room, and they remained quiet for the next few minutes as they read.

Friends & Family,

If you're reading this, then you outlived me. If you're reading this, then I considered you to be one of the most important people in my life. I understand how it may be hard to come to terms with the fact that this will be the last time I directly communicate with you, but you should find consolation in knowing that I'll always indirectly speak to you in your memories.

I've decided to begin writing my will at an early age, partly because I've had a lot of time to think things through, and partly because I now have a much more thorough understanding as to just how fragile life can be. It's a funny feeling to be seemingly self-fulfilled and yet wondering what else is out there for you, but I would be remiss to not admit first and foremost that my life was surely a stunning ride of peaceful solitude, days and nights filled with friends and fans, and endless emotions that helped me enjoy creative expression. My intention is to come back to this document time and time again for refinements, but if you're reading this, then you've come across my final draft. No matter how I end up going out, I'm hoping we were able to have a moment to say goodbye. If not, I hope you'll consider this document as my final farewell.

I know these types of legal documents are meant to be about material things and who gets what of my personal possessions, but you should know that my intentions for you are far greater than anything my stuff could provide. However, I do have some things that should probably be accounted for. So, here's the "who gets what" part.

I want all of the money in my bank accounts to be donated to several different nonprofit charities throughout the United States and abroad. These nonprofits will include my guitar programs in Dover, Denver, and Kona, and these charities are oriented around supporting at-risk youth with wilderness survival training. My attorney, Chadwick Eckelberg III, can provide more information about the allocation of these funds upon request.

It's likely that there will be continued royalties that flow into my estate in the years after I'm gone. I turn the entirety of my future royalties to the remaining living members of the Zenegades, to be divided evenly among each member of the band. You've earned every penny our music will provide, and supporting you with this tiny gesture is the very least I can do.

As for my farm on Hawaii, I turn the property rights over to my manager, bandmate, scuba partner, and close friend, Reginald E. Wallace. I can never truly repay you for all the laughs and good times we've had, Reg. We're all truly blessed to have you be a part of our family, and I want you to make sure that the farm remains a fun place for our friends to gather together in paradise. And yes, you can have the boat and truck as well.

I have many different guitars throughout my home, and I want all of them (and my motorcycle) to go to Skylar Rose. Sky, you have always been the most talented guitarist I've ever known. May the force of my strings be with you, and may the roads treat you kindly.

I have two sitars in my home, and these should go to Shankar Patel. Shankar, thank you for introducing me to this unbelievable instrument and being my mentor throughout my entire adult life. I could never have realized just how special you'd be when we first met, but you being extroverted that one night on the Maryland coast changed our lives forever. That life-changing moment happened because of your genuine desire to live life with curiosity and treat every person as a chance for spontaneity, and this fundamental idea is what helped shape the Zenegades. I know I played my sitars untraditionally, but from now on, they'll be yours to get weird with.

I also have a keyboard that I tinkered around with from time to time. This will go to Thayer Feldman, the most talented singer-pianist on the planet. It has been one of my life's greatest honors to create songs and share the stage with you, Thayer. From the time we met in Berkeley, to the time I lived alone in Utah, and to the times when we traveled the country together, you were always there for me when I needed someone to talk to. You may have just thought you were being nice by staying in touch with me via email when we weren't together, but you'll never truly know just how much your messages have meant. When I think of what a friend should be, I think of you, and I want you to always remember that our friends need you as well.

Lin Rose, continue to experiment with your sound and yourself as a violinist. You could have done anything you wanted to as a musician, and the fact that you chose to play in our band will always be the celestial blessing that helped the Zenegades truly tick. I remember when I first met you, even if you don't. You were about five or so, and you came over to Sky's house with your mom when I was there. I showed you my guitar, and I'll never forget your face as you tinkered around with it, and that's partly because it's the exact same face you still make when you're performing on stage. This childlike wonder for music is what I love most about you, and I'm sure it'll still be within you as you read this. My message to you is to continue to spread this wonder to more people, because you have the power to inspire us all.

Maya Walker, you are the secret ingredient that took the Zenegades from good to great. Your jazz experience gave all of us an entirely new outlook on how we should approach each song, and I can confidently say that I became a better musician because of you. And it wasn't just because you helped me get in touch with that beautiful, funky feeling. What I think I've learned most from you is work ethic and putting the audience first. There's absolutely no denying how your beats and rhythms will live on forever within our souls, and I ask you to keep carrying the torch of being an incredible role model for all of us, as well as countless artists everywhere.

Ruben Bazan and Catalina Carvajal, your love for one another is the purest I've ever seen in my lifetime. The moments that I'd see you laughing and enjoying each other's company helped me better understand what companionship truly means, and one of my goals in life is to feel a love like you two have. I'm hoping that I've finally found my partner in crime in Jane, and my message to you two is that we've always shared the same zest for adventure. I want you to hold on to that curiosity to keep seeing more and always going that little bit further down the road.

Ryan O'Donnell, I know we haven't always seen eye to eye in terms of a bunch of silly stuff, but you should know that you've always been an incredible leader to me. I've never forgotten that one night in Utah when you suggested that we should be a band, because it was the first time that someone truly believed in our potential. Whenever we were in an awkward or stressful situation, we could always count on your sense of humor to get us through to the other side. This is something you should be most proud of, because most people have difficulty seeing silver linings that are presented right in front of them. From the very first night I met you, I knew you were the type of person that anyone would be lucky to know. Each laugh I've shared with you is like a brick of gold, because the values of those good times only increase as we get older. Continue to be you and bring that extra bit of enthusiasm into every conversation you have, and please, continue to look after the rest of the band. They need you around a lot more than you may think!

And of course, the girl from the gas station, Jane Imberti. Laying eyes on you for the first time was the most profound experience of my life, because I immediately knew that I was looking at the most beautiful woman in the world. You were always the girl of my dreams that I thought would slip away into ethereal obscurity, and I can't describe how thankful I am to have met you again. As I write this, we're tucked away in our little piece of paradise along the Hua Huna coast. Each day is like a dream, and I know we can make an incredible life together, no matter where we live. I know our relationship is just getting started, which is why I want to reiterate that this document is subject to change. But for right now, I want you to have something special to me. There's a gold ring on my nightstand that my mother passed down to me, and if for whatever reason I haven't already given this to you, I want you to have it. I want you to know that I planned to give it to you when I proposed, but hopefully this will all be done in due time!

Last but certainly not least, my mother, Janis Byrd. If you're reading this, then you've outlived me for some reason. I first want to apologize for putting you through such a terrible situation that you didn't deserve. Secondly, I want to say that I was incredibly lucky to be guided by you throughout my childhood. I owe my love of music to you, so thank you for helping me learn what music truly is. You helped me realize how guitar could help me cope with Dad leaving, and your strength to keep fighting for us helped me know what it takes to make it in this often-cruel world. I love you, Mom, and I want you to be in charge of my nonprofits, so you can help more children fall in love with music.

The last piece of advice my sentient self will provide goes to the remaining living members of the Zenegades, and this message is clear: NEVER, EVER STOP PLAYING. Before anyone knew us, we played just because we enjoyed each other's company. Those moments of blissful creativity were the catalyst for us to end up making a lot of music together, so it goes to show how we're living proof that one camping trip can change the world. Don't forget that playing music is first and foremost for fun, no matter how big of a check you're getting. That electric feeling you get when you're playing is your food, so don't go hungry, and don't forget that the world always needs more of your art. It's through our art that we'll all live on forever, so if you're reading this, don't worry about me being gone. You too will be immortalized when your time comes, so make the most of your legacy while you still can.

I love you all and want to thank you once more for making my life extraordinary!

One Love,

JB

FIVE YEARS LATER

34

Nearly five years after Byrd's untimely death, Shankar sat near the fire pit in the middle of the Zenegade Ranch. His hair and beard were now noticeably whiter, and his often-used hiking stick that helped him meander around the property rested against a nearby tree. The aspen grove was once again in its electric yellow hue, and the autumn winds caused countless leaves to trickle through the air in one final commemorative dance. And just like the dancing aspen leaves, Shankar's mind was dancing around limitless trajectories.

There were no guest arrivals planned at his renowned retreat center, because no one had been able to book a trip for years. Although tourists from around the world were still dying to see the place where the Zenegades originally formed, the ranch was off-limits to the public. He gracefully accepted the decline of his business venture's prominence, and he always enjoyed speaking with curious passersby at the ranch's gate about what it was like to bring Byrd and the whole gang together over a decade earlier. Part of him still wanted to host guests on a nightly basis, but he was getting too old to run the property in the way he thought was rewarding for paying customers. He tried to fill the empty treehouses and cabins with friends and family at least a couple of times each summer, but his two five-year-old dogs were his main companions.

He had an Irish setter he named Indra (nicknamed Indie), and a big black Labrador he named Bali. Indie and Bali were well trained, and they loved running around in the nearby wilderness until they heard Shankar's dinner bell ring each afternoon. He'd typically rest his legs while sitting in a handmade chair as he watched Indie and Bali munch the pebbly food in their bowls, but today was different. He was too preoccupied to recognize Indie's voracious bowl licking, and he wasn't looking upward as the cold Colorado wind blustered through the trees and triggered the foliage to descend. He wasn't listening to the sounds of Castle Creek gurgling in the near distance, and he wasn't thinking about what he wanted to eat for dinner in the ensuing hours. He was completely silent as his attention solely rested upon a handful of real-estate contracts.

He was deep into the process of selling everything and moving on for good. He'd hired a Realtor, he'd helped host showings, and he'd even witnessed an Aspen-like bidding war that ended up creating a too-good-to-be-true final offer that was over ten times what he originally paid when it was just him and Byrd cleaning up a group of dusty, decrepit shacks. Although he personally invested a lot into the ranch, it was the land's cultural value that created such a skyrocketing increase in value. The main reason why he was holding a handful of paperwork by the fire pit was because the buyer and Realtor had just come by to check things out and plan a few inspections that were to be conducted in the coming days. Everything was underway for a quick and easy transition, and the contracts were now under review.

He glanced around at the remodeled cabins and thought back to when a group of down-on-their-luck Millennials helped him make something out of nothing. Back then, it was the kids who were going out of their way to help him achieve *his* dreams, but he now fully understood how mistaken he was to assume that developing the ranch was a part of his own self-fulfillment. In the end, the purpose of his journey to the woods was directly tied to the dreams of the Zenegades, and it was always destined to be that way since the day he met Byrd on Assateague Island. Without their help, he likely wouldn't have been able to make much of the property from the get-go, and without their help, he surely wouldn't have developed a retreat center that people were eager to experience.

He rubbed his stringy, white beardand scratched Bali's head while continuing to examine the precise terms of the contract, but he couldn't help himself from drawing his attention far away from the words on the pages. Memories of each tiny spot on the property would pop up as he looked around in between sentences, like the time when he and Byrd almost fell through the dingy flooring in one of the treehouses; the time when Thayer, Sky, and Ruben first parked their vans by the treehouses and walked around with facial expressions that said *what the hell did we just get ourselves into*; the time when Lin and Maya showed up as friends and ended up sleeping together for the first time in a cabin by the creek; the many meals they shared together as a family by the main cabin; and the over-the-top Campfire Concert Series that featured a small stage in between the aspens. The more he thought about the many more memories associated with the guests who came from far and wide to meet him over the years, the more he realized how he'd accomplished what he'd originally set out to do when he put his financial adviser life behind him.

He rubbed his eyes in an attempt to regain his concentration on the contract, but there was no chance he'd get through it. He inserted the papers into a folder, set it down on the ground next to the fire, placed a few logs on top of the embers, and looked at the golden fall foliage above him. The leaves were just as yellow as they were when Byrd and the whole gang reunited after the long hiatus caused by Byrd's disappearance to Hua Huna, which was the last time the original core played together. The continued thoughts of *those days* sparked the catalyst for moisture to build in his eyes, and he wiped a small tear that fell down his cheek a moment later.

He reached for his hiking stick and began meandering around the property with Indie and Bali at his heels. He needed a distraction, and he knew exactly what type of distraction would do the trick. The advice from Byrd's will to *never stop playing* was pretty easy for the professional musicians, but for someone like him, it took a little more effort to muster the courage to pick up an instrument. Byrd's old sitar was in his cabin, and within minutes, he had it resting on his lap by the fire pit. He looked up and down at the intricate, one-of-a-kind design, and he examined the tiny bird etchings along its neck that were made specifically for Byrd.

While he gazed at the etchings, he heard a bird up in an aspen tree whistling its midmorning tunes. He glanced up at it and saw another bird land on the same branch. Several more birds flew into the same tree and the surrounding trees, and he could see more gliding in circles overhead in preparation for a temporary landing. By the time he'd finished tuning the sitar, there were dozens of birds in the canopy right above him. He started to realize how his fans were arriving just in time, and each of the birds reminded him of someone from his past who was now gone, whether it was James Byrd, his parents, family members, or old friends. In that moment, he could feel a strong tingling sensation in his belly that crept up his torso and into his cerebral cortex. His white hair began to rise with electromagnetic energy, and he could hear the wind whispering its reassurances that nature itself was what we reverted to and that nature itself was what kept us all alive forever.

He tossed the contract folders into the fire and started playing a dreamy sitar rhythm that he and Byrd had invented, and although he was only with his pets at the Zenegade Ranch and no people were in earshot, he was fully convinced that his audience was immeasurable.

ACKNOWLEDGEMENTS

Thank you so very much to everyone who helped encourage this project.

To all of my Beta readers, thank you for providing your perspectives and advice. To Joe Pierson, thank you for being my editor and helping me fine-tune every last detail. To Stewart Williams, thank you for providing an incredible cover design and interior layout. To Sony Music, thank you for permission to use lyrical excerpts. To all the referenced artists, thank you for inspiring this fictional band of musicians.

And a special thank you to everyone who asked me about this project while it was still a work in progress. You may not have realized it in the moment, but you helped keep a flimsy hope alive.

ABOUT THE AUTHOR

JOE WIRTH was born and raised in the Plaza Midwood neigh-borhood of Charlotte, North Carolina. He studied journalism in Boulder, Colorado and published articles via *Boulder Weekly, Skiing Business, Next Gen Journal, About Boulder* and *CU Independent*. He later transitioned to fiction and freelanced on independent film sets throughout California as a behind-the-scenes photographer and videographer.

He then started a company called Wirthwhile Writing, ltd. that supports businesses with content marketing strategies, and he now lives in Breckenridge, Colorado.

Zenegades is his first novel.